"A dynamite read . . . Golden gives himself a big sandbox to play in here, using the cultural melting pot of the Veil to bring in creatures from many mythologies and religions. . . . a journey that many readers may wish to share. . . . Recommended."
—*SFRevu*

"Most excellent . . . Golden's got a knack for taking familiar themes and twisting and sculpting them into something a little different. . . . Literary enough to keep the mind interested, yet written with an easy reading style pretty much anyone can understand and enjoy." —Three-Media.blogsplot.com

"Golden [has a] blistering ability to enchant and entertain. . . . Golden conjures up new ideas and characters into moments of high drama with a flawless sleight of hand. . . . Reading *The Myth Hunters* is a journey that surges with energy, vibrancy and a glowing affection that Golden has poured into his new universe and the characters that inhabit it." —*SF Crowsnest*

PRAISE FOR *WILDWOOD ROAD*

"*Wildwood Road* is a brilliant novel of supernatural suspense that reminded me of the early classics by Ira Levin—think *Rosemary's Baby* and you won't be disappointed. There's no baby, but oh baby, there is one creepy little lost girl that kept me turning the pages *long* after I should have gone to bed. This one's a keeper." —Stephen King

"I love a good scary story, but scares alone are not enough to carry a book; a good horror novel needs to be a good novel first, with a strong plot, interesting characters, and vivid and evocative writing. Golden delivers all of that in spades in *Wildwood Road,* the best ghost story I have read since . . . well, since the last time Stephen King wrote one. Wonderfully atmospheric and creepy." —George R. R. Martin

"Anxieties over marriage, home and work amplify the eeriness of Golden's engrossing suburban horror novel. . . . This above-average stab at Stephen King–style horror draws the reader irresistibly into its mystery." —*Publishers Weekly*

"Golden delivers another spooky thriller." —*Booklist*

"His style with the pen is just spot on. His characters are real and palpable. Even his reflections of life within marriage hit the nail on the proverbial head. This kind of horror has a fusion of normalcy and suspense that cannot be quantified by most writers in the horror genre. . . . It all makes for the best horror I have read in some time. A truly great, fast-paced read that hits all the buttons and gate-crashes the reader's composure with wild abandon. Just brilliant." —*SF Crowsnest*

"Golden latches onto a very intimate situation that's thoroughly understandable, and makes the fear all the more chilling because of it. . . . The novel's internal logic is, perhaps, its greatest strength. . . . Golden is becoming more assured in his plotting and pacing . . . and it has only made him a more effective, readable author." —*Fangoria*

"The most important thing that Christopher Golden does with his horror is to always go for the truth of the moment. . . . It is in these truths that Golden excels—the fears of the real world. Never mind the fact that his pure horror knocks the wind out of you as well. *Wildwood Road*, like every other Christopher Golden novel I've read, will knock your socks off with its brilliant dialogue, truthful characters, and its plot—which always leads you exactly where you would never think you were headed. A new horror classic!" —G-Pop.net

PRAISE FOR
THE BOYS ARE BACK IN TOWN

One of **Booklist**'s Top Ten SF/Fantasy

"Christopher Golden collides the ordinary and the supernatural with wonderfully unsettling results. *The Boys Are Back in Town* is a wicked little thriller. Rod Serling would have loved it."
—Max Allan Collins, author of *Road to Perdition*

"Christopher Golden is one of the most hard-working, smartest, and talented writers of his generation, and his books are so good and so involving that they really ought to sell in huge numbers. Everything he writes glows with imagination."
—Peter Straub

THE MYTH HUNTERS

BOOK ONE OF THE VEIL

CHRISTOPHER GOLDEN

BANTAM BOOKS

THE MYTH HUNTERS: BOOK ONE OF THE VEIL
A Bantam Spectra Book

PUBLISHING HISTORY
Bantam trade paperback edition published February 2006
Bantam mass market edition / February 2007

Published by Bantam Dell
A Division of Random House, Inc.
New York, New York

This is a work of fiction. Names, characters, places, and incidents either
are the product of the author's imagination or are used fictitiously.
Any resemblance to actual persons, living or dead, events,
or locales is entirely coincidental.

Book design by Lynn Newmark

Library of Congress Catalog Card Number: 2005053629

Bantam Books, the rooster colophon, Spectra, and the portrayal of a
boxed "s" are trademarks of Random House, Inc.

ISBN 978-0-553-58778-4

Printed in the United States of America
Published simultaneously in Canada

www.bantamdell.com
OPM   10 9 8 7 6 5 4 3 2 1

For my sister, Erin Golden, another journey.

ACKNOWLEDGMENTS

First and foremost, thanks to Anne Groell, for setting off on this adventure with me and always being open to finding out where the road would take us. Thanks also to the entire team at Bantam, especially Josh Pasternak and Loren Noveck. As always, thanks and love to Connie and our children, Nicholas, Daniel, and Lily Grace. Thanks also to Mom and Peter, to Jamie, and to the usual suspects, Tom & LeeAnne, Jose & Lisa, Bob T., Ashleigh, Allie, Amber, and Rick. For the camaraderie and support, thanks to the cabal and the Vicious Circle. You know who you are.

THE MYTH HUNTERS

CHAPTER 1

The promise of winter's first snowfall whispered across the low-slung evening sky. Oliver Bascombe shivered, not from the December wind but with the same anticipation he had felt at his seventh birthday party, just before the magician performed his act. Oliver did not believe in magicians anymore, but he did still believe in magic. He was stubborn that way.

The green cable-knit sweater was insufficient to protect him from the cold, but Oliver did not mind. At the edge of a rocky cliff a hundred and twenty feet above the crashing surf, he hugged himself and closed his eyes; felt the north wind prodding him and smiled. His cheeks were numb but he cared not at all. There was a delicious taste to the air and the scent of it was wonderful, exhilarating.

Oliver loved being by the ocean, relished the air, but this scent was different. This was the storm coming on. Not the metallic tang of the imminent thunderstorm, but the pure, moist air of winter, when the sky was thick and each misting breath almost crystalline.

It was bliss.

Oliver inhaled again and, eyes still closed, took a step closer to the edge of the bluff. All the magic in the world existed right here, right now. In the air, the portentous gray sky, the mischievous auguring of winter. A solemn oath from nature that soon it would bring beauty and stillness to the land, at least for a while.

A few more inches, a single step, and he would fly from the bluff down into the breakers and serenity would be his. One final enormous disappointment for his father to bear, and then he would not burden the old man any further.

One step.

A flutter against his cheek. A rustling in his hair. A gust swept off the water and struck him with enough force that he stumbled back a step. One step. Back instead of forward. The wind blew damp, icy stings against his cheeks.

Oliver opened his eyes.

Snow fell in a silent white cascade that stretched from the stone bluff and out across the ocean. For the longest of moments he stood and simply stared, his heart beating faster, his throat dry, holding his breath. Oliver Bascombe believed in magic. Whatever else life brought him, as long as he could hold on to such moments, he could endure.

He would endure.

Oliver chuckled softly to himself and shook his head in resignation. For another long moment he stared out at the ocean, his view obscured by this new veil of snow, then turned and strode across the frozen grounds of his father's estate. The rigid grass crunched beneath his shoes.

The enormous Victorian mansion was an antique red with trim the pink of birthday-cake frosting, though Oliver's mother had always insisted upon referring to it as rose so as not to impugn the masculinity of the household. Her husband wanted his home to be finely appointed, but drew the line at decoration that would be inarguably feminine.

Thus, *rose*.

The house was warmly lit from within. The broad bay windows of the formal living room on the south wing revealed the twinkling multicolored lights on the Bascombes' Christmas tree. Oliver strode up to the French doors, melting snow slipping down the back of his neck and into his shirt, and rattled the handles, sighing when he realized the doors were locked. He rapped softly on a glass pane, peering into the rear entryway of the house at dark wood and antique furniture, tapestries and sconces on the walls. When his mother was alive, his parents had done everything in their power to give the interior of their home a European flair, such that it looked more like an English manor than a place in which people actually lived.

Oliver rapped again. The wind whipped up anew and rattled the French doors in their frame. After another moment he raised his fist again, but then a figure appeared in the corridor. The house was lit so brightly within that at first it was only a silhouette of a person, but from the hurried, precise gait of the figure he knew immediately that it must be Friedle. He was more than simply a caretaker, but that was how the man himself referred to his job, so the Bascombes did not argue the point.

The slim, bespectacled man smiled broadly and waved as he hurried to unlock the doors.

"Oh, goodness, come in, come in!" Friedle urged in his curt Swiss accent, then clucked his tongue. "I am sorry, Oliver. I locked the door without even considering that you might be outside on such a chilly night."

A genuine smile blossomed on Oliver's face. "It's all right. All the preparations were becoming a bit overwhelming, so I thought I'd take a walk. And now it's snowing."

Friedle's eyebrows went up and he glanced out the door. "So it is," he noted appreciatively. But then his eyes narrowed and a mischievous sort of grin played at the edges of his lips. "We're not getting cold feet, are we?"

"I was out for a stroll in the first snow of winter. Of course my feet are cold."

"You know that isn't what I meant."

Oliver nodded amiably. "Yep."

Friedle handled all the day-to-day business of running the household, from the largest details to the smallest, leaving Max Bascombe to focus on his work. Friedle paid the bills, answered the mail, and attended to small repairs and general upkeep, while at the same time overseeing the employment of the twice-weekly cleaning service, the landscaping crew, and the hiring of a snowplow man in winter.

When Oliver's mother had died, it was Friedle who realized that someone was going to have to be hired to cook for father and son—the two men living in that silent old house. Mrs. Gray arrived promptly at seven o'clock every morning and remained until seven o'clock every night. Oliver hoped that she was paid well to spend so much time in someone else's home. Friedle was another story entirely. He lived in the carriage house on the south end of the property. This was his home.

Oliver smiled warmly at the man, wished him good night, then strode down the corridor. The paintings on the walls reflected his father's interest in the ocean—lighthouses and schooners and weathered lobstermen—and his mother's passion for odd antiques, in this case crude portraits most visitors mistook for Bascombe family ancestors.

His damp shoes had squeaked from the moment he entered the house and Oliver wiped them on the Oriental rug before striding through the formal living room and the vast dining room. Though it was still early in December, the entire house was decorated for the holidays, red ribbon bows and gold candles and wreaths throughout the house. And from the other end of the vast place came the scent of a fire blazing in the hearth.

His path took him past the grand staircase and to a room his mother had always insisted upon referring to as the parlor. Despite or perhaps because of the fact that it drove his father crazy, Oliver had for years preferred to cozy up with a book or a movie in his mother's parlor rather than the so-called family room. Katherine Bascombe had always kept her parlor filled with sweet-smelling flowers and warm blankets. The furniture was delicate, like his mother; the one room in the house where Max Bascombe hadn't trammeled his wife's decorative instincts.

Now Oliver paused a moment just at the door to the darkened room. The parlor was small by the standards of the Bascombe home, but it ran all the way to the rear of the house. The far end of the parlor was an array of tall windows that looked out upon the back of the property, at the gardens and the ocean beyond.

But tonight the view was obscured. Oliver could see nothing outside those windows but the snow that whipped icily against the glass. He looked at the small rolltop desk where his mother had liked to sit and write letters. Bookshelves revealed a combination of paperback Agatha Christie mysteries and antique leather-bound hardcovers. From time to time Oliver would take one of those older books down and read it, not minding the way the binding cracked and the yellowed paper crumbled. Books, he had always thought, were for reading. Writers put their heart and soul in between those covers, and it seemed to Oliver that if the books were never opened, the ghosts of their passion might be trapped there forever.

He inhaled the lemon scent of wood polish in the room, noticeable even over the powerful smell of flowers, and felt his mother's absence keenly. In the wake of her death, Oliver had done as his father asked. He had gone on to law school and become an attorney, passed the bar not only in Maine but in Massachusetts, New York, and California as well. You had to be versatile if you wanted to be a partner in the firm of Bascombe & Cox. The problem was, this particular junior partner had no interest in being a lawyer. He had spent all four years at Yale in the Drama Club, doing Chekhov and Eugene O'Neill.

Oliver Bascombe was an actor. He wanted to live on the stage, to travel the world not in a private jet but by car and train. As an attorney it was his job to erase the trials and tribulations of others, yet he barely understood what his clients were experiencing.

He was a fly trapped in amber.

"What are you doing?"

Oliver started. He turned abruptly away from the parlor to find his sister, Collette, standing in the hall gazing at him. She had an odd smile on her face and he wondered how long she had been there, waiting for him to notice her arrival.

"Way to go," he said, a hand over his chest. "Give the groom a heart attack the night before his wedding."

"My, my, little brother. You're not *nervous*, are you?"

Collette laughed and a ripple of warmth went through Oliver. So often he felt that the only warmth in this house came out of the heating ducts, but having Collette back in town, even if only for a few days, had been wonderful. Oliver, to his regret, was the image of his father, though somehow at once both thinner and more robust. But Collette was petite and her features fine and angular, so that she revealed in every glance the Irish heritage that had come down to them from their mother. A light of mischief gleamed in her eyes and, though she was his elder by six years, Collette was often mistaken for a girl half her age.

"Why would I be nervous?" Oliver replied. "It's just my whole life changing forever tomorrow."

Collette smiled again, the skin around her eyes crinkling. "You make it sound like a death sentence."

A shudder went through Oliver and he caught his breath. His good humor faltered a moment and though he tried to summon it again, he saw in his sister's gaze that she had noticed this lapse.

"Oliver?" she ventured. "Oh, Oliver, don't."

Collette shook her head as though she could deny what she had seen in his face. He had no idea what *don't* meant, exactly. Don't say it? Don't feel this way? Don't get married? Don't fuck it up? But he could imagine some of what Collette was feeling just then. Her own marriage—to Bradley Kenton, a television news producer out of New York City—had failed spectacularly. They had no children, but Collette had friends in the city, a job she loved as an editor at *Billboard* magazine, and no desire to live with or even near her family again.

"I'm fine," he assured her. "Really," he lied.

His sister responded with a long sigh, then glanced around the hall before taking him by the elbow and ushering him into their mother's parlor. She turned on a tall floor lamp whose glass enclosure had been designed by Gaudí. It threw strange, almost grotesque arrays of colored light across the room and upon Collette's face. Oliver never used that lamp when he came here to hide away.

"Is it terror or dread?" Collette demanded, as though the question needed no more explanation than that.

Oliver was unnerved to discover that it didn't. He turned away from her searching gaze and went to sit upon a sofa rich with deep crimson and blue. The tasseled pillow he placed on his lap as though it might protect him. Collette sat on the edge of the coffee table, arms crossed, one hand over her mouth. *Speak no evil,* Oliver thought as he turned to look at her again.

"I'm not afraid to be married. I guess I ought to be; I'm not sure I know anyone whose marriage I can honestly say I admire. But the idea of it is pretty appealing. The way a marriage is supposed to be, who wouldn't want that?"

Collette frowned. "You don't think you can have that with Julianna?"

Oliver swallowed hard and found his throat dry. Slowly, he shook his head.

"I thought you loved her."

Images of Julianna crashed through Oliver's mind like the ocean against the rocks. She was laughing and dancing on the hardwood floor in nothing but white socks and Oliver's flannel pajama top, her raven-black hair spilling around her face. She was playing the piano and singing so sweetly at her parents' fortieth anniversary party. What was that song? He could hear the melody in his head but was unable to put a name to it.

"I think I do," he replied at last. "But how can you ever be sure? Honestly. Still, the idea of being married is nice."

Collette leaned forward, her blonde hair draped across the left side of her face. She did not bother to push it away, but instead laid a comforting hand on his knee.

"So it's not terror. Where's the dread coming from?"

"I don't know."

His sister sat up straight, surveying him carefully.

"You lie."

A soft laugh escaped Oliver's lips. "Yes, I lie." The words were barely a whisper. "It isn't fair, is it? Not to me or to Julianna. It isn't fair that my cowardice has brought us to this."

Collette shook her head and threw up her hands. "You lost me, Ollie. Stop playing Riddler and elaborate, if you please. How are you a coward? The only person in this world you won't stand up to is . . ."

Her words trailed off and Collette stared at him. She tilted her head slightly to one side as though seeing him from a new angle might shed further light upon their conversation.

"*Dad?*" she ventured. "You're dreading getting married because of Dad? In what world does that make any sense at all?"

Oliver held the pillow more tightly and slid down into the sofa cushions. He turned to gaze across the long parlor at the darkness outside, the snow almost phosphorescent where it fell near enough to be illuminated by the lights of the house.

"It doesn't. Doesn't make a bit of sense. But it's been

haunting me. Julianna's family are wealthy and they're local and they're very tightly knit. We both work for the firm
. . . the firm Dad helped found. Her father and Dad are
both on the board of directors at the bank. They've golfed
together at the club. She's entrenched in that whole scene,
same as me. If I marry Julianna, it's the final concession. It's
not even defeat, but surrender. I'm giving up whatever
chance still existed that I might someday do what I want
instead of what he wants. Just like . . . just like Mom."

"Ollie, Mom never surrendered. She never stopped lov-
ing the things she had a passion for."

He laughed bitterly. "Maybe she never surrendered, but
she was captured, sis. Think about it. Look at this house.
One little room where she could do exactly what she
wanted, where she could have it look like she pictured it,
instead of how Mr. Imagination thought other people
would expect it to look."

Collette put one comforting hand on his shoulder.
"Oliver, I know he can be awful, but you're being unfair. All
couples compromise. That's what marriage is. Yes, he could
be bullying—"

Oliver cut off her words with a curt glance. "If she was
forced to compromise her passions to mix with his, that I
could understand. But he doesn't have any. His only passion is work. He had an image of how things should look
that had nothing to do with what he liked or disliked, and
everything to do with what he thought was appropriate.
Mom used to tell me he wasn't always like that. She said
when she met him he had stars in his eyes. 'Just like you,'
that's what she said. But at some point, that part of him
went away. But not for her. She was filled with passion,
and . . . look, never mind." He brushed at the air. "I'm sorry

I started. It's just . . . with her gone, I see it all around me, all through the house, and it's just so fucking tragic."

Collette hesitated a moment, gnawing her lower lip, then forged on. "And so, what? You think your life with Julianna's going to be the same thing, only in reverse? Is that it?"

Slowly, he nodded. "The really twisted part is, I'm going to end up resenting Julianna just as much as I already resent *him*. How is that fair?"

Collette shook her head. "It's not." For several seconds she only stared at him, then she ran her hands through her hair and laughed, not in amusement but in obvious disbelief. "Jesus, Oliver. Now what? It's two weeks before Christmas. You've got three hundred people coming to a wedding tomorrow. Flying in from LA and London and New York, some of them. I'm not telling you not to do it. I know as well as anyone what a mistake it is to get married if it just isn't right. But if you're going to call it off, you'd better be damned sure."

A chill ran through Oliver. He stroked his chin, taking some odd physical comfort in the rasp of the stubble he found there. Something burned in his gut, but he had no idea if it was that dread he and Collette had discussed or simple guilt. His throat was still dry and his chest felt hollow, too quiet, as though his heart had paused to let him think. He lifted his eyes to gaze balefully at his sister.

"I guess running away isn't an option?"

Collette smiled tenderly. "I think you're a little too old for that."

"Pity."

He fell into contemplation once again and his sister rose and began to drift about the room as if she were seeing it for the first time. She caressed certain knickknacks that she recognized from their childhood, ran her fingers along the spines of several books, then slid one of the Agatha Christies off the shelf. Oliver took all this in peripherally and only glanced over at her when she grunted softly in appreciation of the book and then continued to peruse the shelves, paperback clutched against her chest like a talisman.

Oliver lay back on the sofa, his head against the wall. It would not be a bad life with Julianna. She came from a similar background, but she still understood his dreams. Yet that was the worst of it, in a way, for though she understood what he dreamed of, she had never once considered it more than a dream.

He closed his eyes and imagined his future in this house or one much like it; his future with this bright, funny, beautiful girl who wanted to marry and raise a family with him. Perhaps it was the time of year, but images of Christmas mornings came into his head, of his children opening gifts beneath the boughs of a tree Oliver himself would decorate. If they were wealthy, so much the better. He would never have to fear for his children's well-being. That was a worthy pursuit, wasn't it?

"Shit," he whispered, one hand on his forehead.

Collette turned quickly to regard him once more. "What?"

Before Oliver could reply, a familiar voice boomed out in the hall, shouting his name. Brother and sister turned to stare at the open doorway of the parlor, then Collette glanced at him.

Oliver took a breath then shouted, "In here!"

Heavy footfalls came nearer and a moment later the doorway was filled with the figure of their father, his face etched with the usual impatience. He was Maximilian

Bascombe, after all, and it was not now nor had it ever been his place to go chasing about his own home for his children.

"I should have thought to look for you here first," the old man said.

Old man, Oliver thought. *What a quaint expression.* It seemed almost insultingly ironic when applied to Max, who at sixty-six was in better shape than Oliver had ever been, salt-and-pepper hair the only hint at his age. But the phrase had never been associated with age in Oliver's mind. Max had always been *the old man* in his mind. It was a crass term, reminiscent of bad sixties television. But as formal as they were in the Bascombe home, *Father* seemed too generous an appellation.

"What's wrong?" Oliver asked.

"Nothing. I couldn't find Friedle," the old man replied dismissively. Then he held up a portable telephone Oliver had not noticed at first. "Julianna's on the phone."

For a moment Oliver froze. He stared at his father, his mouth slightly open, aware that he must look foolish, as though he had gone catatonic. His gaze shifted toward the phone and only when he reached out his hand to receive it did he understand what had happened within him.

"Thank you," he offered, more from practice than purpose.

"Ollie?" Collette ventured, her concern and wonder clear in her tone.

Oliver cast her a resigned glance, then took the phone from his father. The old man muttered something about wanting to talk to him later about a case that needed to be dealt with before he and Julianna left for their honeymoon in South America. Oliver barely heard him.

He put the phone to his ear. "Hello?"

"Hey," Julianna said, her voice soft and near, as though she spoke to him from a pillow beside his own. "What's shakin'?"

A melancholy smile spread across his face and Oliver turned his back on his father and his sister.

"Oh, just celebrating my last night as a bachelor with a bit of perverse revelry."

"As is to be expected," Julianna replied. "I'm just getting rid of the gigolos and the mule myself."

Oliver could not help himself. He laughed. Julianna was a wonderful person, kind and beautiful and intelligent. And he had made a promise to her. Wasn't it up to him to keep his own passions alive? His mother had surrendered. And where his father was concerned, Oliver had always done so as well. But that did not mean that his marriage had to be a cage. It was up to him.

"It's good to hear your voice," he said.

As he did, his father retreated into the hallway. Collette came over to kiss her brother on the cheek; she stroked his hair a moment and he saw the regret in her eyes and knew it was for him. He nodded to her. *It's going to be okay,* he thought, and hoped she would read his mind or at least his expression.

"So, what are you doing tomorrow?" he asked Julianna as Collette left the room, disappearing into the massive house with their father.

"Why?" Julianna asked. "Did you have something in mind?"

"As a matter of fact, I did."

Hours later, Oliver was still in the parlor. It was late enough that Mrs. Gray was long gone, so he had made a trip to the kitchen for some hot cocoa. Somehow, in the short time he was gone, Friedle had come into the parlor and laid a fire in the stone fireplace. When he returned with a large steaming mug, a dollop of whipped cream bobbing on top of the cocoa, the blaze was roaring. Oliver was more than happy to feed new logs into the flames from time to time. Friedle had put a large stack of wood aside for him, and now it was nearly gone. Across the room, one window was open several inches and there was something delicious about the combination of the heat of the fire and the chilly winter wind that swirled in. Snow had begun to build up on the windowpane and some landed on the wood floor, slowly melting there.

This was magic; right here in this room with his cocoa and a worn leather-bound copy of Jack London's *The Sea Wolf* in his hands. He had rescued the book from its lonely place amongst the other abandoned volumes on these shelves, but it was not the first time. *The Sea Wolf* was an adventure he had returned to many times over the years. Always in this room, in this chair, beneath this light.

With the snowstorm raging outside and the house gone quiet now, time slipped away. Oliver might have been twelve again. The fire crackled, casting ghostly orange flickers upon the walls.

He was lost in the book, adrift upon the sea aboard the *Ghost* with Wolf Larsen at the helm. All the world had been pushed aside so that Oliver existed now within the pages of *The Sea Wolf,* far from his concerns about the future and the delicate irony of his love for a woman destined to become, for better or for worse, his anchor.

Oliver had shivered several times before he really noticed how cold it had grown in the parlor. The fire was down to one charred log licked by weak flames. Reluctantly he slipped a finger into his book, dry paper rasping against his skin, and went to kneel before the fireplace. He used a poker to push back the black iron-mesh curtain in front of the burning log—the metal would long since have grown too hot to touch—and then carefully arranged two thin logs within.

The fire began to spread and Oliver picked up another log, this one fat with a thick layer of bark, and placed it diagonally atop the others. For a moment after he had closed the mesh curtain again he remained there, watching the blaze. Then, finger still holding his place in the book, he stood again and started back toward his chair.

Cold wind raced through the room, trailing chill fingers along the back of his neck. Again Oliver shivered, though this time he noticed it.

"Brrr," he said, mostly to himself, a smile creeping across his face.

The open window rattled hard in its frame. He glanced over to see that the snow had built up much more than he had realized. One corner of the gap between window and sash was packed with pure white and enough of it had powdered the floor that it was no longer melting.

"Damn."

Oliver started toward the window. The edge of the Oriental rug was easily six feet from the wall but some of the snow had reached it. He paused to try to brush it away with his shoe but managed only to melt it into the carpet. The window rattled harder, buffeted by the storm. The sound was so loud and abrupt that Oliver jumped a bit and turned to squint in amazement at the snow outside his windows. The night seemed darker than before. The air whipped so hard against the panes of glass now that where it rushed through the opening it howled softly. More snow blew in with every gust.

"Wow," he whispered to himself as he stood peering out through the glass. Even in the dark, he could see that what had begun as a light snowfall had become nothing short of a full-fledged blizzard. The snow was thick and plentiful, the ground already completely blanketed, and the wind drove it in twisting swirls and waves.

Oliver held the book up against his chest with his left hand, keeping it away from the open window. For a moment he simply enjoyed the storm. Then the glass rattled again, the window seemed to bow inward as though the storm was trying to get in. He reached out to close the window, but enough snow had built up on the sill that it slid only a fraction of an inch before jamming. He brushed as much of it out as he could. Even then, it seemed frozen in place. Awkwardly, finger still holding his place in *The Sea Wolf*, he set both hands upon the top of the window and put his weight into it. The window began to slide down.

A powerful gust slammed against the house, shaking all of the parlor windows, as though in defiance. The open window seized again and he worked hard to force it closed. The storm raged outside, buffeting the walls. The wind that passed through the narrow gap remaining between window and sash fairly shrieked.

The wooden frame shook and a long crack appeared in the glass, stretching a tendril from one side of the window to the other. Oliver cursed under his breath and let the book fall from his hand. *The Sea Wolf* struck the damp floor on its spine and something in its binding tore. Oliver barely noticed that he had dropped it, never mind that he had lost his page.

Swearing again, he struggled to close the window, worried that at any moment the glass might splinter further, even shatter. It would not close that final inch, however, and his fingers were numb with the frigid air, the whipping snow. It seemed impossible that it could be so cold.

Oliver paused, suddenly certain that he was not alone in the room. Friedle or Collette, perhaps . . . someone had heard the banging and come to investigate. But no . . . the presence he felt was not within the room, but without.

He narrowed his gaze and for just that moment, twisting with the currents and eddies of the wind, he saw a figure dancing in the storm, eyes like diamonds staring in at him, from a face with features carved of ice. All the air went out of Oliver then, as though his lungs expelled his final breath.

The wind drove in through that narrow opening with the force of a sliver of hurricane. The crack in the glass spread no farther, but the storm blew in so hard that it knocked Oliver backward. He stumbled, slipped upon the melting snow, and fell sprawling onto the Oriental rug.

Snow poured through the opening in the window and swirled and eddied about the parlor as though there were no difference between outside and inside. The storm had knocked, and now it had come in, uninvited. In a steady stream the blizzard slid through the inch-high gap between window and sash and raced around the room. Cold and damp, it slapped against his reading lamp and the bulb exploded, casting the room in darkness save for the light from the fire, which guttered weakly, only the iron mesh curtain keeping it from being doused completely.

Oliver gasped, sucked icy air into his lungs. His eyes were wide as he gazed about the room. He was too cold for this to be a dream, and his stomach hurt from the gust of solid air that had knocked him down. Splayed there on the carpet, he felt a sense of wonder but it was tainted by a primal fear that welled up from somewhere deep within him.

The storm began to churn and then to spin more tightly at the center of the parlor. The fire surrendered and went out, smoke sifting from dead embers and being sucked into the white ice whirlwind that knocked knickknacks off the coffee table and twisted up the rug beneath its feet.

Oh, Oliver thought. *Oh, shit. What the fuck am I still doing here?*

It was as though the frozen wind had numbed his mind as well as his body. No longer. He scrambled to his feet and ran across the parlor, bent to one side to fight the wind. His cocoa mug slid off a side table and shattered on the floor.

As he ran for the door, a gust of wind rushed past him, nearly knocking him over again, and blew it shut.

Oliver stood unmoving in the middle of the parlor, staring at the door. There had been purpose behind that wind. He was not alone. The storm was here, but it was more than just a storm.

He turned slowly. The vortex in front of the dark fireplace was changing, taking shape. Through the snow churning within that whirlwind, Oliver could see a figure, the same as he thought he had seen outside moments ago. A man, or so it seemed, made from ice, his body all perilously sharp edges, dagger fingers, and hair that swung and tinkled musically like a crystal chandelier.

Its eyes gleamed pale blue and with every twist of the vortex, every swing of its arms, it stared directly at him. At first Oliver had thought it was dancing but now he saw that it was carried by the snow, the storm.

"God, please, no," Oliver whispered, shaking his head. "What the hell *are* you?"

The vortex slowed and then stopped.

The snow fell to the floor, blanketing the wood and carpet and furniture.

The winter man stood, chin proudly lifted, and cast a cold, cruel eye upon Oliver. Then he staggered, icy tread heavy upon the floor, and his sharp features changed. Pale blue eyes narrowed with pain and exhaustion, and Oliver saw that there was a chink taken out of his left side, like someone had chipped away a large sliver of ice.

"Help me," the winter man whispered, in a voice like the gusting wind.

Then he fell hard, jagged features scoring the wooden floor. He lay half on the wood and half on the carpet. Where his wound was, water dripped onto the Oriental rug. Mind in a frantic tumult, Oliver stared at that spot and wondered if the winter man was melting.

Or bleeding.

CHAPTER 2

Y ou have got to be fucking kidding me."

Oliver took a step closer to the figure that had collapsed on the parlor floor. Fragments of shattered lightbulb crunched beneath his shoes. The wind had died, the windows no longer rattled, but he could not tear his gaze from the still form of the winter man to spare a glance out the window. Snow or not, it seemed clear that the real storm had not been driven by nature but by the being who lay at Oliver's feet. A wet spot spread on the rug around the winter man as though he were bleeding out, dying right there.

But it was melting ice, not blood. And this thing could not die, for it could not possibly be alive. Things like this did not exist. They did not whisk through barely open windows, dancing on snowflakes. This kind of shit just did not happen in real life.

The winter man twitched.

Oliver held his breath, afraid to move for fear that he would draw its attention. *Help me,* it had said. Even if Oliver knew how to do that, he doubted he would have the courage to try. After several moments, when the intruder had not moved again, Oliver let himself take the tiniest of breaths. His eyes had adjusted to the darkness of the room, only a faint glow from the embers of the extinguished fire providing any light at all. Still, he could see that the snow in the room was melting.

He risked a look at the parlor door—the door that had been slammed shut by the will of the storm itself. His mind backtracked to the loud rattling of the windows, the explosion of the lightbulb and scattering of knickknacks onto the floor, the muffled thud of his own fall, and at last the slamming of that door. Where was everyone? Had no one in the house heard all of that noise or were they simply assuming his pre-wedding jitters had driven him into some sort of tantrum?

Collette. Where was Collette? Certainly she had not yet gone to sleep. In his mind he pictured the bedroom his sister still slept in when she visited their parents. All of the family's rooms were on the north side of the house and Oliver realized that it was entirely possible that, with their doors closed, neither his father nor his sister would have heard the sounds of discord from below.

His gaze ticked back toward the dim form of the winter man. *Good,* he thought. *They're safer if they stay where they are.*

Though the embers grew dimmer in the fireplace and the darkness gathered closer around him, Oliver took a step nearer the fallen man. If man was indeed what he was. He seemed almost transparent in the gloom of that room and he stirred not at all; not even to breathe.

A light gust shook the windows. With a sharp intake of breath, Oliver snapped his head up to gaze at the cracked glass and beyond. The snow was still falling heavily, though the wind had lessened considerably. Still, every bit of bluster against the windows was likely to make him jump.

Oliver turned his attention back to the figure on the floor.

The winter man was staring at him.

The last of the embers began to die and the room faded to black. Oliver felt as though he himself were frozen, swallowed by the cold blackness of that room—that room that had only moments before been his one retreat in his father's house. Quickly he shuffled backward several steps, trying to re-create the shape of the room, the placement of the furniture in his head. The love seat and chairs, the Gaudí floor lamp, the plants, the bookcases. He closed his eyes and took a steadying breath.

But inside his head he could still see those pale blue eyes staring at him in the glow of the fire's last embers.

"Oh, Jesus," Oliver whispered.

Something scraped the wood floor and Oliver snapped inside. He rushed for the parlor door, feet sliding in the melting slush beneath him, fearful that at any moment he would bark his shins on some forgotten table and fall over. He held his hands out in front of him and in seconds they struck the door; he jammed the index finger of his right hand and hissed in pain as he grabbed the knob and pulled the door open.

Dim light flooded in from the hall.

"Wait," a voice called from behind him. "Please."

His voice. The voice of the winter man. It was stronger now, or at least it seemed so, as though he spoke just beside Oliver or the air carried his words like snowflakes.

"Help me," he said again.

Oliver paused on the threshold. Slowly, he forced himself to turn around. The light from the hall cut a swath across the parlor and in that light he could see the winter man clearly. He was on his knees on the carpet, one clawed, frozen hand upon the wound at his side, the other supporting him as he struggled to rise.

"I ask for little enough," the winter man said, wincing with pain as he stood, icicle hair clinking together like wind chimes. "Safe passage from this house and to the ocean—"

"The—the ocean?" Oliver stammered, heart beating wildly. He was torn between the desire to flee and the plea of this proud being. Torn between terror and wonder yet again.

"It is Borderland," the winter man said. Then he shook his head impatiently, annoyed—though with himself or his host, Oliver could not determine. "If you will help, it must be now. I barely escaped the Falconer and dare not tarry."

Safe passage. Falconer. Borderland. With the pressure of the winter man's urgency, Oliver could not interpret any of it save the idea that this intruder wanted to get out of the house and to the ocean without anyone else seeing him.

Icy brows knit in consternation. *"Please."*

"Okay, okay, just wait. Just wait a second," Oliver said.

Father and Collette were in their rooms. It was late enough that Friedle had probably retired to the carriage house by now. Oliver shook his head, blew out a long breath, trying to collect his thoughts. *All right, get him out the back door and to the bluff. How hard can that be?*

What the hell am I thinking?

Oliver reached out and clicked on the hated Gaudí lamp, then gently shut the door, once again closing himself in the parlor with his unexpected visitor. The many colors from the glass shade cast a rainbow of antique hues upon the sharp facets of the winter man's frozen form.

"What *are* you?"

The winter man staggered slightly, dagger fingers still clamped to his side. He lowered his chin and glared dangerously at Oliver, an eerie fluorescent light in those pale blue eyes, now narrowed to slivers.

"I'll help," Oliver heard himself say, stunned by his own words. "I will. But tell me that, at least."

Carefully the winter man moved to the fireplace and placed a hand upon the mantel to support himself. He cast a glance at the windows, at the storm outside, and when he turned his attention again to the question at hand, Oliver thought he saw fear in those haughty, jagged features.

"I have many names, but by your custom, I am known as Frost."

Frost, Oliver thought. In his mind, something clicked into place. Tonight, this very night, had been the first snowfall of winter.

"Jack Frost," he whispered.

Frost nodded curtly. "Now you must aid me, or I shall have to attempt to reach the Borderland on my own. The Falconer—"

"But," Oliver interrupted, shaking his head, staring at the being he still half thought of as the winter man. "You're just a myth."

With a hiss, colors sliding over his translucent form, Frost lunged across the parlor at Oliver. The winter man did not so much leap as *flow*. Terror shot through Oliver and his heart thundered in his chest as Frost clutched him by the throat in a frozen grip, icy fingers like arrows embedding themselves in the wooden door, trapping Oliver there.

Frost sneered, showing glistening fangs like ice diamonds, and a polar wind seemed to wash from his open mouth as he spoke.

"Don't *ever* call me that again. Nor any other of my kin. Many of the Borderkind would slay you for that. I might have as well, another day."

Oliver felt his neck freezing, his skin sticking to the winter man's hand. He stared into those frozen eyes and swallowed hard.

"I . . . I'm sorry. I didn't know," he rasped.

Frost glared at him another moment, then pried his fingers from the wood and pulled his hand away, the ice tugging at Oliver's throat, leaving the skin seared by the cold.

"Will you aid me?" the winter man asked.

Oliver nodded.

Frost exhaled a blast of misty, frozen air and seemed to diminish somehow. His eyes—lashes tiny spikes of ice—fluttered lightly and his hand slipped away from the gouge in his side. Water spilled from that wound in a small cascade that spattered Oliver's pants. He could feel the freezing chill of that water, the winter man's blood, soak into the fabric and numb his skin where it touched.

The winter man slumped toward him. Stunned, Oliver reached up to support him and his hands slid on the creature's frozen surface, barely able to get a grip beneath his arms. Frost's body was so cold that it burned to touch him. It was as though only his fear and rage had kept the creature going and now, whatever he was, monster or myth, this thing who claimed to be Jack Frost had surrendered to injury and exhaustion.

"Shit," Oliver hissed at the pain in his hands. He spun around and propped Frost against the wall. "You've got to stand here. Right here, while I get . . . I don't know, gloves or something. A minute. Just one minute. I'll be right back, I swear."

Those frozen breaths came shallower, but Frost's eyes opened, still glowing ice blue, and he nodded. "Go. Quickly. I place my trust in you. What are you called?"

"Oliver," he said quickly. "Oliver Bascombe."

"Make haste, Oliver. Time is short. As long as I remain herein, you are in danger as well."

Not liking the sound of that at all, Oliver backed away from Frost, blowing on his frozen hands, then rubbing them together. *No way,* he thought. But the feeling was coming back into his hands, and with it, the pain. There could be no doubt that this was real. Which meant that this danger, this Falconer, Frost was talking about must be real as well.

Oliver opened the door carefully and stepped out into the hall. It was dark save for a lamp in a corner just outside the dining room and the soft orange glow of Christmas lights in the windows. He shut the door behind him, then rushed along the hall with as much stealth as he could manage. The house was silent save for the loud tick of a grandfather clock as he entered the main foyer.

Oliver allowed himself a tiny sigh of relief and cautiously opened the door to the large coat closet built in beneath the grand staircase. It took him a moment to find a pair of thick ski gloves and a wool scarf striped red, blue, and yellow.

"Hello? Oliver, is that you?"

Like a thief caught in the act he dropped the gloves and scarf and backed out of the closet. Collette stood at the top of the stairs, clad in red cotton pajamas that made her look younger than ever.

"Hey," she said with a sleepy smile. "What are you doing down there?"

"Nothing," he replied, perhaps too quickly. From her vantage point, at least, she would not have been able to see exactly what he had been up to in the closet. "Just trying to find this old leather coat I haven't seen around in a while."

"At this hour?" Collette said doubtfully. Even in the dim light he could see her smile. "You're not trying to find your Christmas presents, are you? I thought you'd outgrown that pursuit in the eighth grade."

A nervous laugh bubbled out of him. "Well, twelfth grade, maybe. But no, just remembered it had been a long time since I'd seen the coat. And I couldn't sleep, so—"

"It's natural to be nervous. I have sleeping pills if you want one."

"I'll be all right, but thanks."

For a long moment Collette only stood there. She was his older sister and knew him well enough to sense that there was more going on than he was prepared to reveal. Oliver could not imagine what she was thinking, but eventually she stretched and yawned and the moment had passed.

"All right. I just wanted to say good night. Don't stay up too late. Julianna might take it personally if you fall asleep at the altar."

Oliver chuckled softly. "I'm going to have a glass of milk, maybe some graham crackers, and then I'll be up."

"You and graham crackers," Collette replied, and then shuddered comically. "Good night."

"Night, sis."

Collette paused a moment, then glanced down one last time. "Ollie. If you really feel like . . . like you're going to be put in some kind of prison . . . you have to remember that no one's making you go. And if you decide not to, you know I'll back you up. No matter what."

He smiled. "Thanks, Col. Thank you. I love you. Go to bed."

She nodded once, then disappeared in the darkened hall at the top of the stairs. Oliver waited a full minute to be certain she was gone. At last he bent to retrieve the fallen gloves and scarf and snatched a thick green winter coat off a plastic hanger. Quickly he drew on the jacket and gloves and wrapped the scarf around his neck.

Even as he shut the closet door, Oliver was startled by a scraping sound behind him. He spun around to see Frost peeking around a corner. Jagged ice dragged across the wall, and though he knew the sound must be barely audible, it seemed impossibly loud.

The winter man said nothing. A kind of blue mist leaked from his eyes and his head bobbed as though he could barely hold it up.

Oliver shot another glance up at the top of the stairs but all that lingered in the gloom there were memories. All the magic he had believed in as a child had slowly bled out of him over the years. Now here it was again, all at once, rushing back to terrify and imperil him.

His face felt strange for a moment and then Oliver realized what it was; he should not have been, but he was smiling. Without further hesitation he went to Frost and slung one of the winter man's arms over his shoulder. Oliver could feel the cold emanating from the ice even through his heavy clothing but not so much that it hurt.

"You've got to be quiet," he whispered.

Frost glanced up at him, and Oliver was amazed to find gratitude in those frozen eyes. Together they started along the hall. The winter man was a troublesome burden, even though he bore some of his own weight. His feet scraped the wood floor and Oliver paused.

"Isn't there something you can do to help?" he asked. "The . . . the snow? You were . . . you were part of the storm at first."

"I am too weak for such feats," the winter man replied, his voice a rasp of frosty breath. "I tried to reach the Borderland myself, but fell short. I saw you . . . in the window. . . ."

This last was said with such effort that Oliver felt almost guilty for making him speak in the first place. But amongst his many questions, another rose to the surface.

"I don't understand any of this. What border are we talking about?"

They had reached the French doors at the back of the house. Oliver grunted quietly as he shifted Frost's weight and reached out to unlock them. Outside, the snow still fell heavily—at least eight inches, from what Oliver could tell.

The lock slid back. Oliver grasped the handle.

"The border that separates your world from my own. Your kind are trapped here. You cannot see beyond the Veil."

The way that Frost had said this last, the gravity in his tone, made Oliver pause again and regard him carefully. What was the Veil? Where did Frost come from? If this being, this winter man, was the source of the legend of Jack Frost, what did that mean for other myths and legends?

Frost shuddered and winced in pain. He glanced out into the snowstorm, eyes darting back and forth, anxiously searching the darkness.

"Please," the winter man asked again. "We must hurry."

There was so much that Oliver wanted to know, but the pain and fear in Frost spurred him on. If this was all he would ever know of the secrets of the world, it would have to be enough. Certainly it was more than most could ever hope for.

He opened the French doors and the storm rushed in. Snow swirled around them, the wind tugging at Oliver and making the winter man's icicle hair chime. Together they shuffled outside and Oliver managed to close the doors behind them. The click when they were shut seemed to echo.

"Come on. It isn't far," he told Frost.

It was almost as light outside as it had been within. The orange Christmas lights in the windows threw a queer glow out into the storm. Oliver was grateful for the scarf as the wind stung his cheeks, snowflakes pattering against his face and sticking to his eyelashes so that he was forced to blink his vision clear every few seconds. He cast his gaze down to get his face out of the wind and the driven snow and saw that Frost left no mark upon the snow. His feet passed through it, certainly, but it was as though his icy form flowed with the snow and it filled in instantly afterward. A ghost of December was passing through, and the storm—this storm Frost himself had started—barely took notice.

The chill breeze whistled past Oliver's ears as he bore Frost toward the bluff. His shoulder ached and pain shot through his neck; his legs felt like wisps of flesh and bone, certainly not up to the task of conveying the weight of the winter man any farther. But Oliver did not buckle. He gritted his teeth and grunted softly as the blizzard seeped into his bones. Between the cold and the burden, all of his questions were for the moment banished, and he focused only on the task at hand.

As they approached the cliff above the ocean, the surf crashing far below, Oliver hesitated.

"What now?" he asked, speaking loudly to be heard over the howling wind, for they were perhaps forty feet from the edge. "If we get too close, we could be—"

"This is your property?" Frost asked, voice like the cracking of ice on the surface of a lake in spring.

"My father's," Oliver replied, confused.

"No, this. Right here. This is not . . . public? Not public space?"

Oliver shook his head. The winter man scowled, showing those icy fangs once more. He winced in pain and when he clutched his side again, Oliver saw that despite the temperature, the water was still running from his wound.

"It's ours. The family's."

Frost snarled and a tremor of fear went through Oliver until he realized it was pain, not anger. Blue mist leaked steadily from the winter man's narrowed eyes now and he squinted even further, looking through the storm.

"You must take me to the edge."

Oliver stared at him then gazed again at the bluff, blinking snowflakes away. He could see the snow dancing in the high winds that buffeted the cliff face and recalled the way Frost had spun with the storm. He should drop the winter man, turn, and run back to the house. He could crawl from here if necessary. What the hell did he need Oliver for anyway?

But those pale blue eyes regarded him balefully. Oliver had said he would help.

"All right."

He pushed away the doubts that crowded in on him.

How many people touched real magic in their lives? Once more, he started for the edge. The winter man stiffened, head cocked at an angle as though he were listening for something.

"What do—"

"Hush!" Frost snapped.

Oliver listened with him. The wind nearly screamed. But after a moment he realized that it was not only the wind. Something else shrieked along with the storm, something hidden in the darkness and the driven snow.

"Move!" Frost snapped. "We must go now or all will be lost!"

It was lunacy. Complete and utter lunacy. Through the storm he could still see the Christmas lights on his father's house, the world he had always known and trusted. But he had the weight of the winter man against him and there was something more . . .

A change in the air. Snowflakes pelted his face as he looked around. A prickling sensation played across the base of his neck as he felt an ominous presence. The storm seemed to pull against him, but Oliver was keenly aware that it was his own fear that made him feel so sluggish.

"Please," Frost rasped.

At last he tore his gaze away from his home and turned to stagger with the injured myth through the driving snow. The edge of the bluff loomed nearer, and snow blew off that cliff in a cascade of white. If he went any closer he might truly fall. A strong enough gust of wind might end it for both of them.

"Now what?" Oliver asked, voice strained.

"Go on," Frost replied. "Just to the edge."

Oliver's mind flashed back to earlier in the evening, the moments he had spent there on the bluff, the pull of the edge, the temptation to throw himself over. It was as though he were being punished for that temptation now, as if the universe was determined to make him decide for real.

He shook his head sharply. "I can't."

But when he glanced at Frost, the winter man was not looking at him. Instead, those misting ice eyes were staring back over his shoulder. The myth looked terrified.

"The Falconer," Frost whispered, the words swirling up and away with the storm so that Oliver was not even certain he had really heard them.

But he knew what he would find when he turned. The hunter. Slowly Oliver turned.

Knee-deep in the snow of an extraordinary storm, a dark figure blotted out Oliver's view of the world he had once known. The hunter was eight feet high and half that across its shoulders. Its legs and arms were wrapped in strips of leather, chest and torso clad in hammered metal that looked pewter gray through the curtain of snow. It stood like a man, but its head belonged to a bird of prey and huge wings jutted from its back, pinioned to decrease wind resistance as it advanced upon them.

The Falconer.

In its right hand it held a long, thin blade, curved like a scimitar, and the scimitar was on fire.

"I am sorry," Frost said, a pained whisper in his ear. "He will kill you for coming to my aid."

Not real. It isn't. Can't be real, Oliver thought, gaping at it, forgetting to breathe or to blink or to allow his heart to beat.

But with each step he could hear the crunch of snow beneath leather-clad feet and the hiss as flakes fell upon that burning scimitar and melted. It paused and looked back and forth from Oliver to Frost as though trying to make sense of this new addition to its hunt.

"Oh, Jesus," Oliver said.

He thought of his family, and of Julianna, and he wanted to say good-bye to them all. He wished he could see the house, the Christmas lights, be in his mother's parlor again. But the Falconer was huge and terrible and blocked out the world. It opened its mouth and let out a bird-cry that pierced his ears, and Oliver shouted and clapped his free hand to the side of his head.

He felt like throwing up. He was prey, that was all.

Oliver shook his head violently. "No." He tore his gaze away from the Falconer, backpedaling toward the edge of the bluff, feet slipping on new snow. The wind shoved him with frozen hands and even over the pounding of his own heart in his ears he could hear the crash of the surf on the rocks below, could feel the empty void that stretched out over the ocean only a few feet behind him.

He reached up and grabbed the winter man's chin and turned the myth to face him. Wildly he stared into Frost's eyes. He could hear the Falconer screeching again.

"Do something!"

"Get me to the edge!"

"Fuck you!" Oliver screamed, frenzied, enraged.

The mist had stopped leaking from the winter man's eyes. The blue ice there seemed to have shrunk down to glistening, razor-edged diamonds.

"Get . . . me . . . to the edge!"

The Falconer shrieked loudly and raised the scimitar. Its huge wings beat the air and its feet left the snow and it *flew* across the bluff at them. Its beak opened wide, only darkness inside, and the fire of its blade gleamed dully upon its armored chest.

With what must have been the last bit of strength remaining to him, Frost thrust his right hand into the air, curved into a claw as though he could tear a chunk out of the sky. He ripped the air with icy talons and when he brought his hand down it was not merely air but ice, a massive blade forged of the storm itself. With a savage roar, voice like a raging blizzard, Frost swung the blade at the Falconer.

The hunter pulled up, wings struggling in the storm, and brought his blazing scimitar up in defense. It shattered, the fire doused, and the winter blade clanged off the Falconer's armored chest. The pewter-gray chest plate was scored deeply but the sword forged by the winter man shattered.

The Falconer stumbled and went down on the snow. But he stirred almost immediately and began to rise, even as Frost fell to his knees.

"No!" Oliver cried, reaching to steady him. He stared down into those ice-blue eyes, then glanced at the winter man's wound to find that the water that spilled from it was flowing faster.

The blue eyes began to close and again to leak cold mist.

"No," Oliver whispered.

In a panic he turned toward that sheer cliff that overlooked the ocean and the rocks below. Less than ten feet away. He could see the huge whitecaps the storm was driving in. Numb with fear, Oliver began to move toward the edge.

Head bowed, shoulders hunched, he braced himself against the wind that buffeted his back, urged him on toward that fatal tumble that lay ahead. No longer was

Oliver merely supporting Frost; he was practically dragging the winter man now.

Snow swept past his legs and out over the precipice. Oliver went down on his knees, two feet from the edge, Frost lying against him. The mist that leaked from the winter man's eyes was like cloud tears.

Frigid, frozen, filled with a kind of terror he had never imagined, Oliver turned one final time to glance toward home. A dim glimmer of Christmas lights was all he could see through the blizzard. The huge silhouette of the Falconer had risen, head and shoulders and wings a dreadful void in the heart of the storm. It opened its beak, this cruel hunter, raised its taloned hands, now empty of any forged weapon and yet no less terrible, and the Falconer shrieked once more.

"*You must come,*" Frost whispered weakly, and Oliver heard him as though the words had been spoken inside his head. "*Otherwise you will die.*"

Throat raw, Oliver stared down at the winter man, so still in his arms. Now he saw a glimmer of blue light in those diamond eyes.

"Where?" Oliver rasped, feeling as though to speak the word had cost him his final breath. Yet somehow he knew.

The Falconer shrieked and lunged, wings battling the storm.

The winter man grasped his arms around Oliver's waist with the last of his strength and kicked out with his legs, driving them both over the edge. They tumbled from the precipice and Oliver closed his eyes, a single warm tear burning his cheek as he went over. Together they fell. Oliver did not scream. He did not have the heart or the breath. He let go of the winter man but Frost clutched him all the tighter.

Oliver opened his eyes. The rocks were rushing up to meet him. The waves crashed against the base of the cliff, obscured by the curtain of snow, falling as Oliver and the winter man fell. They had become part of the storm, merged with the blizzard itself.

He turned over in the air and saw, above, that the Falconer had not given up the hunt. The thing streaked down after them with its wings pulled tight against its body, its arms outstretched, talons ready to catch them, capture them, tear them. But Oliver felt no fear. Instead, his entire body was filled to overflowing with one single, powerful emotion. He was crippled with regret.

The Falconer shrieked again but now it was far away, like a distant church bell, the ghost of a sound.

The scream of the hunter was cut off abruptly. Oliver cried out as a blue light erupted across the sky, enveloping everything. A spike of pain ripped through his chest as though something had been plunged into his flesh . . . or, more so, like something had been torn out. Blinded for the moment by the brilliance of that blue flare, he could see nothing. He could feel nothing save the arms of the winter man around him.

Together they struck water, sinking fast and deep.

But there were no rocks. And the water was warm. Frost let go and Oliver kicked out his legs, limbs heavy, winter clothes soaked through, dragging at him. Fighting that weight he struggled to reach the air, eyes still stinging from that light, mind awhirl with impossibility.

His head broke the surface and Oliver found that he could see again. But what he saw . . . a clear sky bright with the largest, palest pearl of a moon he had ever seen and stars too few, too large, too close. A snow-covered mountain rose up in the distance. Water, yes, but not the ocean.

There came a splash to his left and Frost appeared in the water perhaps ten feet away. They were in a huge lake, so enormous that on three sides Oliver could not see the shore and on the fourth, below the mountain on the horizon, he could only just make it out. With a sudden flash of terror he looked up at the sky again, but there was no sign of the Falconer.

"Where?" Oliver asked, and he heard the echo of his own voice, the word he had spoken only moments before, when the world was still real and solid and knowable.

Frost did not smile. Jagged-edged face above the water, the winter man stared grimly at him. "Home. We are on the other side of the Veil now. It was the only way we both might live. Yet by drawing you here, I have surely doomed us both."

CHAPTER 3

The night sky seemed to go on forever, stretching across the horizon as though it cradled the entire world and the sun would never return. A gentle breeze rippled the surface of the lake. The water was warm, proof that the sun had shone that day, but the wind was cool. Droplets of water slid down Oliver's face and the back of his neck from his wet hair, but he hadn't the strength even to lift a hand to wipe them away. The winter jacket he had put on . . . it seemed like days ago, somehow . . . was saturated and it began to drag him down. Oliver managed to unzip it, shrug out of it, and doff the gloves he had worn. At last he uncoiled the damp snake that his scarf had become and let that slither into the water.

Freed from those heavy clothes, he still had to contend

with boots he was too tired to remove. He could only float there, alternately staring at Frost and then glancing about at their surroundings. The land seemed preternaturally pure. Pristine. The air itself filled his lungs with a kind of tingle and his strength began to return.

"The other side?" Oliver asked. He glanced around once more, took in the snowcapped mountain in the distance, to what he gauged must be north, and the vastness of the lake to the east.

Frost did not answer. He was staring up into the night sky, moonlight gleaming off his frozen form, eyes narrowed with worry. After a moment he nodded to himself, seemingly reassured. Oliver was not thinking clearly and so barely recognized the purpose of the winter man's vigilance at first. Then a tremor of fear passed through him and he pictured their pursuer's flaming sword, the twisted image of the falcon's head on a human body ... wings spread out behind him.

"Do you see him? Is he—" Oliver said, glancing upward.

"No. His kind cannot cross the border. He will have to find a Door, and there are very few of those."

Oliver nodded as though he understood this far better than he did. It was enough, in that moment, to know they were not being pursued. Then another thought struck him and set off a fresh rush of alarm.

"But it's . . . wait, that thing is still back there? Collette's there. My sister. And . . . and my father."

"The Hunter will not trouble them. He would not dare reveal himself to ordinary humans."

"He revealed himself to me."

"Yes." Frost gazed at him, but he had turned now so that the moonlight threw his face into shadow.

There was such import in that single syllable that Oliver at last recalled the winter man's words only moments ago, when they had first burst up from the water. Frost claimed to have doomed them both. Oliver shuddered. There were so many questions he knew he had to ask. But the thought of the answers that might come in response sent dread spider-walking up the back of his neck.

He wasn't ready for the answers. Not yet.

Emotions skirmished in his heart. Terror was the undercurrent, but overwhelming it was a strange giddiness. None of this was possible. This could not be happening. He was getting married in the morning. Julianna was asleep at home right now, or maybe still fussing over her dress despite the lateness of the hour. His father had invited half the firm. *This isn't real . . .*

Yet he had felt Frost's icy claws on his throat, had seen the Falconer and felt the adrenaline surge through him, had careened off that ocean bluff with the winter man and tumbled down and down and down to the waves. He felt the water warm around him now, and his palms and fingers stung from where he had touched Frost bare-handed before. He smelled the air of this world, felt the rivulets of water running down his face. His tongue snaked out and he tasted it. *Salty. Like tears.*

"Oh, my God," he whispered.

He stared at Frost. The winter man did not seem to even be treading water but simply floating there, a dozen feet away. Now he raised a hand to push dangling spikes of icy hair away from his pale blue eyes.

"There are many gods here, you will find."

Frost seemed more alert, somehow restored by his return to this world beyond the Veil. *And I can't even believe*

I'm thinking in such terms, but what others are there? How else do I think of this and not lose my mind?

Slowly shaking off the lethargy that awe had wrought in him, Oliver began to swim toward shore. With his clothes and shoes on, it was slow going, but the lake was calm and the land was not far. He felt disconnected and unreal as he turned his back on Frost. The winter man did not speak or pursue him. Only after Oliver had reached a depth where his feet could touch the bottom and he had stood and begun to wade toward shore did Frost follow.

Oliver walked up onto the hard-packed dirt and scrub grass on the shore and sat down hard, not quite steady on his feet. Whatever the winter man really was, whatever these Borderkind were capable of, one glance around made it clear that there was no easy way out of here. Water in one direction and open land in the other. No vehicle, no sign of civilization. He glanced upward. They had tumbled out of the sky and into that lake, somehow slipped behind the Veil, behind a curtain between worlds . . . but there was no ledge up there, no ocean bluff, no house. They had just fallen out of thin air.

"There's no Falconer, either. That's a plus."

It was all surreal. The words themselves seemed to numb his lips as he spoke them. Yet a smile crept across his face, a mad little grin of amazement and of strange victory. Not only the triumph that they had survived, but that the tiny spark of hope he had nurtured all of his life, that somehow one day he would find a bit of magic in the midst of the ordinary, had been rewarded.

The winter man emerged from the lake. Whatever water clung to him froze on his icy skin, dripping not at all. Frost glanced upward as though to follow Oliver's gaze and then he turned his pale blue eyes upon his savior, spiked, frozen hair chiming.

"I told you. We've escaped him for the moment," said the winter man. "But we had best be moving on. If there is one Hunter after me, there will be others. I'd heard rumors that the Borderkind were in danger, but lent them no credence. If such sinister deeds are indeed afoot, there must be more trouble in the Two Kingdoms than I had realized."

"Others? What others? And what Two Kingdoms?"

"There are things you must learn if you are to survive here. But first, we ought not remain by the lake. One never knows what lurks beneath still waters."

Oliver stood up and brushed off the seat of his jeans as he glanced around again. Something splashed out on the lake in the moonlight, sending a circle of ripples rolling outward. He knew nothing about this place. Nothing at all.

Frost took a step and flinched, hissing through his teeth. He clamped a hand over the wound in his side, and when he took those jagged fingers away, the opening that had been there was sealed with new, bright blue ice. The gash was closed, and no longer weeping ice water . . . what passed for blood in the winter man's body. He was healing.

Oliver furrowed his brow and stared. Something inside him gave way in that moment. His mind had been turning over the events of the past—could it really be only minutes?—like a jeweler studying the facets of a diamond. He'd confirmed the reality of it, accepted it. Or, at least, he thought he had. But somehow in the back of his mind he had still perceived it all as some strange fantasy. Or lunacy. He was under stress, wasn't he? Getting married in the morning—*Jesus, in the morning! Julianna!*—to a woman he knew he was going to wed for all the wrong reasons. The pain was enough to tell him it wasn't a dream.

But he'd been lying to himself when he thought he'd really accepted the reality of his situation.

Until now.

Seeing the wound on the winter man's side now healing up, the blue ice so much like new pink skin that formed where a scratch had been, or a scar would be . . . that was the instant in which he really *knew* it was real. The feeling of surreality he'd had before evaporated.

"Shock," he said, laughing a bit madly. He stared right at Frost, marveled at the creature as though seeing him for the first time. Jack Frost. Jack fucking Frost. He might have veins that bled water, but he was made of ice and snow. He was . . . no matter how offensive the term might be to his kind . . . a myth.

Oliver's eyes were wide and he felt pain in his stomach, a basket of coiled snakes there that were nothing but manic laughter, wanting to spring up his throat.

"I'm in shock, I think," he muttered. "Maybe I should go back."

The winter man tilted his head and regarded him quizzically.

"I mean, this is . . ." He swept his arms wide, swallowing hard and feeling his throat burn with sudden emotion. His pulse raced and his chest pounded with the thudding of his heart. "This is fantastic. But I can't just . . . I'm glad you're all right and everything, but I . . ." He hated the sound of his voice even as he spoke the words that he had dreaded his entire life. ". . . I have responsibilities."

Jagged, frozen features refracted the moonlight as Frost tilted his head again.

"I'm sorry, Oliver. I had thought you understood." The winter man frowned, and though there was little detail in his eyes to reveal his intent, Oliver would have sworn there was real regret there, real sadness. "You cannot return. Even if I had the strength at the moment to make another border crossing, and I assure you that I do not, it would be nothing short of murder to return you to your home.

"You are marked, just as I am. They will be hunting us both now. Me because that is their assignment—and I mean to discover who gave it to them—and you because you are an Intruder. Humans get lost through the Veil frequently enough, but that is something entirely different. There are places and times when the magic in the Veil is unstable, and your people—sometimes individuals and sometimes whole villages—slip through. But once the magic that wove the Veil touches them, the Lost Ones cannot return home, cannot cross back through, not even through one of the Doors, for the magic that created them is all one and the same.

"You are considered an Intruder because you *can* go back. When one of the Borderkind opens a portal, it is a tear in the very fabric of the Veil's magic. You've crossed to the other side of the Veil without being touched by it. You can return, as long as you have a Borderkind to open the way. For the Lost Ones . . . not even a Borderkind can bring them back through. That is the nature of the enchantments used to create the Veil.

"But you are not Lost. You are an Intruder. And no Intruder is ever allowed to pass through the Veil and live. You will be executed the moment you are discovered. Unless we can keep you hidden."

Oliver took a ragged breath and pressed his eyes tightly closed. He pushed his fists against them as though that might somehow make it all go away.

"What are you talking about?" he demanded, opening

his eyes and staring at the winter man. "He's after *you*. Okay, I did you a favor, but I didn't want to come here, I—"

The winter man had seemed hesitant. Now all such hesitation fell away. Jagged ice and frozen eyes, he did not so much lunge at Oliver as slide toward him. Sharp blue-white talons snatched up the front of Oliver's wet shirt and frost formed on the fabric, crinkling as Frost clutched it tightly.

"That's enough!" he hissed, his breath frigid in Oliver's face. "I owe you my life, Oliver Bascombe. I shall not forget that. But a wasted effort it shall be if your foolishness keeps us here long enough for Hunters to arrive. The Falconer and his comrades will care nothing for your excuses. It is time that you—"

"No!" Oliver shouted at him. He plucked at his sodden shirt where it stuck to him and his boots squelched as he marched away. Panic thrummed in his chest. "I have to . . ."

He stopped. Swallowed. Reached up to pinch the bridge of his nose. "I have to go back," he whispered. Oliver shook his head. "Oh, shit. Oh, Julianna, I'm sorry."

The winter man must have sensed the change in him, for he stood back and waited, arms crossed. Oliver took several deep breaths. Where those snakes of fear had coiled in his stomach, he felt something harden. After a moment he took one final, shuddering breath. The breeze across the lake had kicked up a little and though the night was comfortably warm, he shivered in his wet clothes. The sweet air helped to wake him. The sparse trees rustled with the wind, but other than that, nothing moved.

Grim weight bore down upon his shoulders, but Oliver stood taller, managing it. "All right." His left eye twitched as he said it. "We're here. I still only have the vaguest idea where here is, and you're going to have to explain it all to me. All of it. But if we could be in danger, staying here, then you can talk while we go."

He ran a hand through his hair, mussing it up, trying to dry it a little. A little laugh escaped him. "Jesus. All right." Oliver glanced around again. "Which way? Toward the mountain?"

The winter man shook his head in consternation, icicles of hair shaking. "No. There is ice atop the mountains. That is the first place they would look for me. It would restore my power more quickly than I can manage myself, but I can't return home until this is ended. We'll go northeast to start, to get away from the lake, and then due east until we meet the Truce Road."

Oliver opened his mouth, but could summon no response. What was there left to say? He plucked again at his wet clothes where they stuck to his body. It would be an uncomfortable trek until they dried, and they had no supplies, no food at all. He wondered if Frost needed to eat, or would consider that Oliver did.

"What are we waiting for?"

Frost started off across the brittle grass on a diagonal path away from the lake. After a moment, Oliver followed him. He started to unbutton his shirt as he walked, thinking it would dry better if he let it wave in the breeze. But his mind was not on that task. Reluctantly, he turned to cast one final glance at the sky above the lake, the place where the Veil was thin enough for the Borderkind to pass through.

Lower, on the water, something caught his eye.

He had nearly reached that copse of trees—Frost had already begun to duck in amongst them, forging a direct path northeast—when he saw them. The surface of the lake had been broken by the emergence of small creatures, some of them still swimming but others wading onto the shore.

"Frost," Oliver rasped.

The winter man continued on, unhearing.

Oliver called again, more loudly, and his companion halted at last, turning to regard him with deep frustration. He seemed prepared to face another argument about their course of action, until Oliver pointed back to the lake and the winter man saw the monsters at the water's edge. Some of them had ambled out of the lake and begun sniffing at the place where Oliver had stood only moments before.

Their eyes gleamed wetly in the moonlight. The things were squat and rolled from side to side as they walked, long arms dragging beside them like chimpanzees. Their flesh was dark, but he thought he caught a hint of green in the moonlight, a putrid sort of hue. But as squat and ugly as their bodies were, their heads were far worse. Their faces were pinched, mouths pushed out like small snouts and eyes too close together. Worst of all was their skulls, which were concave on top, creating a strange kind of bowl out of their heads. Even those who had dropped to the ground to investigate managed to keep their heads upright. As they walked, shambling from side to side, their heads tilted back and forth to remain steady.

Otherwise the water in the bowl formed by their concave skulls would have spilled.

"We must go," Frost said. "I warned you that we should not linger. They must have sensed us from deeper in the lake. We've drawn their interest."

He reached out to grab Oliver's wrist. At the winter man's touch, Oliver hissed from the cold and pulled away.

"What are they?"

"Kappa," Frost replied.

Oliver frowned. "What the hell are—"

The Kappa seemed to notice them for the first time. Their heads all ratcheted around to stare and Oliver did not finish his thought. He could only stare back.

The creatures began to screech. The sound tore at his ears and he clapped his hands to the side of his head. They launched themselves across the scrub grass, some of them tottering along with their overlong arms raised high, and others running on all fours, reminding him once again of chimpanzees. Yet somehow they managed to keep their heads up, water sloshing in the strange bowls upon their heads but not tipping out.

Oliver had no idea what to do. He looked around at the trees to see if any were tall enough for him to climb, thick enough to support him. Would the little monsters be able to climb up after him? He started toward one of the trees, then thought better of it and turned to simply flee to the north, as fast and as far as his legs could carry him.

Icy fingers snatched him by the arm, painfully cold even through his shirt.

"Turn! Quickly!" Frost shouted.

Without thinking, Oliver complied. He spun around to face the things. Terror leaped in his heart, for now was the first time he noticed their mouths. Their jaws were wide and filled with tiny little razor teeth, row after row, like sharks.

"Oliver!" the winter man called.

Only then did he realize Frost had been talking to him.

The Kappa came on, and now he could hear the terrible sound of their clawed feet trammeling the grass, the shushing noise as the beasts rushed toward them.

"Bow!" Frost snapped.

Oliver frowned, breath coming too fast now, heart

thundering suddenly in his chest. He shook his head as if to deny what he saw.

"Bow down!" the winter man roared.

Oliver glanced over and saw that Frost had already done so. The winter man was bent at the waist in a deep, formal bow. Oliver hesitated only an eyeblink longer, and then he followed suit. What choice did he have?

The screeching stopped, all at once. There came a sloshing noise from just a few feet in front of him, and then a thump. Flinching, waiting for claws and shark teeth to tear in to him, it was only when he heard the sloshing noise again that he looked up.

The Kappa had all stopped screeching, stopped attacking. One by one they were bowing. But the three nearest him, the ones who had been nearly on top of him a moment ago, had fallen over on the ground. An instant later, he understood.

Oliver stared in astonishment as each Kappa bowed, and the water from their open, concave skulls spilled out onto the ground. One by one, as they did so, they slumped to the scrub grass, twitching, gleaming eyes roving wildly as though searching for something they could not see.

The winter man uttered a short, barking laugh so utterly unlike anything Oliver had heard from him thus far that the man jumped, startled, his terrified heart hammering once more.

Then Frost bowed once again. "Foolish demons. They should never stray so far from shore." The winter man grinned, showing sharp ice teeth, and turned to Oliver. "Now, run!"

This time there was no hesitation. Oliver did not even take a last look at the Kappa as he turned and fled with Frost. The winter man led the way, darting in amongst the trees. Oliver followed, his clothes stiff with dampness, and did not allow his discomfort to slow him. For several minutes they ran. His chest burned. From time to time Frost would brush past branches that became brittle with cold and snapped when Oliver pushed them out of the way. His breath came in heaving gasps and he was ready to plead with his companion to stop when they burst out of the small wood and found themselves at the base of a long, grassy slope. The snowcapped mountain was off to their left now, or near enough. They had been moving northeast all along.

Frost paused there and turned, still grinning, icy teeth gleaming in the moonlight. He laughed and threw up his hands and the wind gusted, twisting around him in a sudden maelstrom, and snow be-gan to fall from a perfectly clear sky. The warm night was abruptly chilled. Wet as he was, Oliver shivered.

"Quit that!" he snapped.

The winter man arched an eyebrow. Oliver had only seen him fearful and desperate and angry. This mischievous side to him was both endearing and somehow frightening.

With a single pass of frozen fingers through the air, the gust died and the snow evaporated. "You are alive, Oliver. Why don't you celebrate that?"

The admonition struck home, but Oliver could not push his fear aside so easily. "Those things . . . you called them demons."

"So I did. I told you that there were many gods here. There are even more demons."

Oliver tried to catch his breath as he glanced back the way they had come. His view of the lake was obscured by the trees. "Won't they come after us?"

The winter man tilted his head, and if Oliver was not mistaken, Frost actually rolled his eyes. "Those demons were from the land you call Japan . . . or they were, once upon a time, before the Veil was created. Their kind cannot refuse a gesture of politeness. We bowed. They were forced to bow. But without the water from the lake, they are too weak to attack. They would have to crawl back to the lake to get more, and even then, I doubt they would dare come so far from the water for fear of being stranded should it happen again."

"But you're not sure," Oliver said.

Frost shrugged. Strands of icicle hair hung across his eyes, but he did not push it away.

"We should go," Oliver told him.

The winter man smiled. "As I have been saying to you since you first drew breath in this world. Perhaps you've learned something already. Do as I say and we might both live a little longer."

Oliver knitted his brows. "Oh. That's comforting. Thanks for that."

"You are very welcome."

Hours passed as they trekked first northeast to the foothills of the mountains and then on a straight easterly course that brought them to a forest Frost said was simply called The Oldwood. It was a peaceful place, with twigs and pine needles underfoot and the trees spread apart enough that the moonlight shone through the canopy of branches and leaves above. There were no paths to speak of, but the going was easy enough. As they walked they heard animals moving through the brush and in the branches, and once Oliver was certain he saw a pair of deer in a clearing. They bolted before he could get a good look at them, but he had the idea one of them might have been walking on two legs.

The lake was far behind, and the Truce Road some-where up ahead. Morning was still hours away, but instead of feeling the exhaustion he knew ought to have overtaken him by now, Oliver felt exhilarated. Despite the horror that still fluttered in his heart when he thought of the Falconer, the strangeness of this world, and the knowledge that his life was in dire peril, every step away from the place where he had come through the Veil felt to him like another step into liberty. With no way to return to face his father or his fiancée or any of their expectations, Oliver Bascombe felt free for the first time in his adult life.

The irony wasn't lost on him.

For a time they walked in near silence. Now that they were out of imminent danger, Oliver had no idea how to talk to Frost. What did one say to a man made of ice and snow? It was almost funny, in the saddest possible way. All of his life he had wished that myths and legends were real, that he could meet a centaur or hear the song of the Sirens, like in the stories his mother had always read to him, the books he'd borrowed from her shelves. As a child he had imagined himself Odysseus embarking upon one great quest after another. His secret yearning to be an actor had been born of the same instincts and desires. Acting was a way to inhabit all of the things he wished he could believe about himself, but could never quite manage. On the stage he was heroic and noble, unique and courageous. Buckling beneath the pressure from his father to be responsible, to pursue his law career, had almost extinguished his creative spark. On the stage, he had hoped to keep that spark from snuffing out entirely.

Now he walked through a wild forest beside, and at

times a few paces behind, Jack Frost himself, and he didn't
know what to say. With his fear subsiding and a kind of
simmering wonder taking its place, he could not help but
feel awed when he looked at Frost. The winter man was
healed, though that line of darker blue ice where his wound
had been remained. His jagged, icicle hair sprang and sometimes clinked as he walked and each step left a bit of rime
upon the forest floor.

In time, though, as his muscles began to ache, Oliver's
focus began to drift. Even at night, with only the moonlight, he could see that this was not a forest like any other
he had seen. There was a primeval quality to the trees.
They were tall and ancient and of such variety that he felt
sure some of the species were unknown to the world he'd
come from.

The way was not always easy. There were hills in the
forest, and twice they came to steep ravines that had to be
circumnavigated. Oliver was sure that Frost could have
found his own way across without much trouble . . . he
wasn't sure how it worked, if the winter man could just become a gust of snow without a storm to work with, but in
any case he knew he was holding Frost back. Yet the winter
man said nothing, only kept walking, continuing doggedly
to the east.

They crossed through a clearing. On the far side was a
thick grove of tall shrubs that seemed their own forest in
the midst of the larger growth. Oliver pressed on. He was
about to forge through the shrubbery when Frost whispered his name, a chill little bit of voice that touched his
ears like a breeze.

Oliver paused and glanced at him.

The winter man crooked a finger and beckoned him to
follow. "We'll go around," he whispered.

With a furrowed brow, Oliver pointed to the greenery. "They're just shrubs."

Frost arched an icy brow. "Nothing is 'just' anything here. You are far from home, Oliver, in a place whose customs and people you know astonishingly little about. I am a poor guide, I fear, but the best you can hope for. If you wish to survive—"

"All right, all right, I get it," Oliver said, chastened. He followed Frost and they strode north across the clearing until they could go around that particular grove of shrubs. Only when they had entered the forest again did he speak up.

"Aren't you going to tell me?"

"What is it I am supposed to tell you?" Frost asked.

"We went around. I'd like to know why."

The winter man was several paces ahead and he glanced over his shoulder, mist fogging from his eyes. "You saw shrubs."

"How could I have missed them?"

"Yet they were not shrubs. They were Betikhan."

"Betty-who?"

Frost laughed softly and turned his attention back to blazing a path ahead. "Savage nature spirits. Before the creation of the Veil I believe they hailed from the part of the world you call India. Betikhan are benevolent creatures unless they are disturbed. Then they can be quite vicious."

Oliver ducked beneath a low branch and caught the toe of his shoe on an exposed root. He stumbled and caught himself quickly, surprising himself by laughing.

"Vicious shrubbery?"

His only warning was the chiming of icicles as Frost spun on him. The winter man bared needle teeth and a gust of frigid breath blew from his mouth. That blue mist crystallized around his eyes and then fell as a small dusting of snowflakes to the ground. Terror seized Oliver and he stood rigid, as though Frost had frozen him there. His breath caught in his throat, the cold air of the winter man searing his lips.

The fury in those eyes filled him with fear and shame.

"There is nothing at all humorous in our situation," Frost rasped. "In this world you will be surrounded by things that in your own would seem harmless. Make that presumption of anything here, and it could be the death of both of us."

He did not wait for a reply, but turned and continued on. For several moments Oliver only stood watching after him, remembering how to breathe. At last he hurried to catch up. For an instant he thought he had lost track of Frost in amongst the trees, but then caught sight of the gleam of moonlight on ice.

Something rustled in the underbrush off to his right. Already on edge, Oliver spun to seek it out and saw a long, slender fox in amongst some ivy. Its eyes gleamed and its fur was the color of rust in the light of the moon. For several seconds he stared at it and it returned the intensity of his regard, but Oliver was aware that Frost was gaining distance and at last he tore his gaze away and dashed through the trees after the winter man. He glanced back once, but the fox was gone.

"All right," he said quietly as he caught up. "I understand. As much as I understand any of this, I guess. I've been . . . uprooted. I'm lost. Do *you* understand? Lost in so many ways. All my life I've known all too well exactly what was going to happen to me tomorrow. Now . . . I don't have the first idea what'll happen in the next five minutes. All I do know is that I don't want to die. And that I have to get home."

Even as he said this last, there was regret in his heart. Did he really have to? But the answer was yes. Whatever became of his life, he couldn't just leave Julianna without explanation, couldn't disappear on his sister forever. He would not hurt them like that. Oliver wasn't sure what he had to go home to, but he cared too much for them to stay away forever.

Unless you die, he thought. But he put that thought into a mental box with all of the other unpleasant things that had come into his head since the impossible had taken over his life.

"So, explain it to me," he went on, trailing Frost by a few paces, trying to get abreast of him, to look into his eyes. "You've told me very little about this place. About the Veil. But we've obviously got nothing but time here. So talk to me. Please."

CHAPTER 4

O liver and the winter man walked on for a time with the request hanging in the air between them. *Talk to me,* Oliver had said. They came to a ridge of rocky ground that rose up from the forest floor like the spine of some massive beast. It would have provided a good view of the area around them and a path free of trees, but Frost stayed in the lee of the ridge and kept on to the east, and Oliver could do nothing but follow.

The winter man glanced up into the branches, and then surveyed the woods around them. He slowed a moment, peering off into the undergrowth, and Oliver wondered what he might have seen that could have unnerved him. But the thought was brushed aside when Frost looked over his shoulder and even slowed his gait enough so that they were walking side by side. The winter man's pale blue eyes seemed to shine with an inner light. Oliver thought it was probably just the moon, but it occurred to him that in this world he could not be sure of anything.

"To begin, you must assume that everything is real," said the winter man. "Every story, every fairy tale, every myth and legend. Of course, not all of them are, and most of the stories you know are only versions of the truth, tainted by the storytellers over the course of centuries and millennia."

Something rustled in the brush off to the left again and this time both Frost and Oliver turned to glance in that direction for several seconds. They continued on, however, and Oliver found himself studying the darkest places in the forest far more carefully, mindful of the tension in the winter man. The Falconer could not follow them this quickly, according to what Frost had said, but from his behavior it seemed this was little comfort.

"You've said as much before," Oliver replied. "So there's the real world, and all of the old legends are sort of walled up behind the Veil, but—"

Icy mist fumed from the winter man's nostrils and his brows knitted. "The 'real world'? That is precisely the sort of thinking that you must abandon. In the Once Upon a Time that starts so many of your stories, people understood that the magical and unusual existed just beside the mundane and the human, on the periphery of awareness. Then the world became more *civilized*. . . ."

Frost sneered the word.

"Industry grew and cities overran the world. The human cultures became more organized and the creatures of legend were demystified. Some hid away in caves and rivers and secret cities of their own—lost cities, to your history—

but others were hunted. Destroyed. Your kind was no longer afraid of the dark, or not enough for our protection. Humanity had lost its respect for magic and shadow, and that was dangerous to us.

"So we left."

Oliver glanced sidelong at Frost. There was such finality in those words that the winter man made it sound so possible, so real. Yet he was having difficulty imagining any of it, even in spite of the evidence all around them. He shook his head.

"Just like that?"

"Many of the tribes of legend, human and otherwise, have magicians amongst them. The most powerful of them gathered together and wove a spell that took years to complete. With their combined sorcery they created the Veil as a wall to separate our last sanctuaries from the mundane world. It is more and less than a wall, however. It will be easy for you to think of two worlds, layered one upon another, existing side by side, each imperceptible to the citizens of the other."

All of this Oliver had gathered previously, at least in a general way, but one thing Frost had said stunned him.

" 'Human and otherwise'? You talked before about the Lost Ones, but I'm having trouble with that. There are humans here?"

The winter man smiled softly, perhaps a bit condescendingly, as they continued to walk along the bottom of that ridge. "How many humans have mysteriously disappeared over the ages? And not only individuals. How many cities have been emptied of their populations, or perhaps disappeared entirely, down to the last stone? Entire civilizations are considered 'lost' by the mundane world."

So astonished was he that Oliver barely took note of

the change in the topography of the ridge, of the gray-white arches that emerged from the mossy earth. Flittering glints of light caught his gaze and he glanced up to see fire-flies darting to and fro in the air above the ridge, and in amongst the trees. He took all of this in but only with a part of his conscious mind. The rest was trying to digest what Frost had said.

"Are you . . . do you mean the Mayans? The Aztecs?"

Frost nodded. "And many others. Most of the legendary creatures—the faeries and boggarts and giants—live in the wild still, as is their preference. Humans make up a large part of the population of the Two Kingdoms—Atlanteans most of all. Though with their divergent evolution, some argue the Atlanteans are not really human."

That was enough to stop Oliver in his tracks. The winter man went on several steps before realizing he had fallen behind, and turned to face him. A dozen replies came into Oliver's head, all of them amounting to roughly the same thing—a scowl and some utterance of disbelief. *Atlantis?* He was supposed to believe that there had once been an Atlantis, and that no one had ever found any conclusive evidence of its existence?

But that was wrong, wasn't it? There were plenty of scholars who had theorized the existence and history of Atlantis, as well as its location. It was only that society did not take them seriously. And that was the purpose of the Veil. That was its magic. To keep secrets.

Oliver let himself fall back against the ridge and stared up at the moonlight streaming through the trees, trying to catch his breath, get his bearings. Exhaustion was a factor, but he knew that it was far more than that. He pressed his eyes tightly closed and wondered if when he opened them he would be staring at the ceiling of his bedroom.

Don't be stupid, he thought.

Then he whispered it aloud to himself.

He could hear the sounds of this mystical forest and feel the light breeze on his skin. The earth was rough under him but it smelled richly of soil and flora. The feeling of surreality tried to take hold of him again but he shook it off. Doubt was a luxury he could not afford.

His eyes snapped open and he sat up, glancing around. There was another of those gray-white arches sticking from the ridge only inches from him, and this close, he saw immediately that it was bone. Oliver jumped up and stumbled away from the ridge and then turned to stare at it with new perspective. Its shape took on new meaning in his mind, and those bones . . . he'd thought of the ridge as a spine before, and those were the ribs. They had been walking alongside the funereal mound of some gigantic, ancient beast.

"Oliver?"

The winter man gazed curiously at him, head tilted birdlike to one side, icicle hair swaying in the breeze. Frost clearly did not know what to make of him.

With a gesture, he urged the winter man to speak. "Maybe that's enough history for now. Just tell me about the Falconer. You said you were one of the Borderkind. I get that. How many of you are there? How many of these Hunters are after you . . . after us, do you think? And who sent them? If someone's trying to kill me, I should know who they are."

Frost frowned once more, glancing over his shoulder and peering into the deeper forest. When he turned to Oliver that icy mist was spilling from his eyes again. The night had turned humid and grown warmer, and as he spoke the moisture in the air formed ice crystals and drifted to the ground. His expression was grave.

"The Falconer is a Hunter. It no longer matters what he was in the history of legend. When the Two Kingdoms were at war with each other they employed Hunters. These assassins have never been content with peace and it would be a simple matter to compel them to kill again. I had heard that several Borderkind had been killed. Word of the murder of Julenisse reached me not long before my last journey to your world. Merrows and Selkies have been killed as well, but horrifying as that was, I'd thought perhaps it had been done for their skins.

"Most of the Lost and the legendary hate the Borderkind because we are the only ones with the ability to travel through the Veil without a Door. The Lost Ones, the humans, I've already told you, can never cross back. Once they've been touched by the magic in the Veil, they cannot pass back through, even using a Door. The other beings here, the legendary, could cross over, but the Doors are usually well guarded and it requires special authority to pass through."

Oliver frowned. "So, whoever sent the Hunters after the Borderkind, they're either really clever, or they've got some serious authority."

Frost nodded, troubled. "True."

"What I still don't understand is, why can the Borderkind cross?"

"It goes back to the creation of the Veil," Frost said. "At the time, there was great debate on whether some of us should be given that privilege. It was decided that those who desired that freedom could retain it, but only if there were enough people in your world who still talked about us, who still had a glimmer of belief in their hearts for us.

There are hundreds of Borderkind, but there will never be any others. Only those who became Borderkind at the time of the Veil's creation.

"Now someone is killing us, it seems. And most of the citizens of the Two Kingdoms will care not at all. Some will likely even cheer. The Hunters have likely been employed in secret, but even should word of their actions begin to spread, few will protest. We are only *myths*, after all," the winter man said, sneering the hated word.

A night bird cawed in the shadows of the branches above. In the bole of a nearby tree, Oliver was sure he saw the eyes of an owl.

"As to who is responsible, who has set these hounds upon my trail—and now upon yours as well—I fear I haven't the slightest inkling. We need to find a safe haven where we may rest and where we can see what other news can be discovered about—"

With a gust of frigid wind the winter man spun round and dropped into a crouch, fingers elongating into wicked talons. Something rustled back in amongst the shadows of the trees, far out of the moonlight. Oliver held his breath, wanting to ask what it was that had alarmed him so, but unable to form the words.

Oliver took a step forward and Frost shot him an abrupt look and then gestured for him to go, to run alongside the massive barrow. He snapped his head, indicating the urgency of their situation, and Oliver began to run. In three paces he found the winter man sprinting beside him and the two of them raced to the east with that ridge on their right and something rushing through the woods to the left, brush crashing and swaying.

Low branches seemed to reach for him but Oliver swiped them away. His stomach rumbled—a reminder of the hours since he had last eaten. His throat was raw, his chest constricted and his legs felt as though they were moving of their own accord. He caught sight of a fallen tree just in time to leap over it and glanced back to see it frost over with glistening rime as the winter man passed by. The finger of a branch scratched his forehead and he hissed but did not slow. He glanced over his left shoulder time and again, trying to catch sight of whatever paced them in the brush, but after several long seconds of running, the sounds from the woods ceased and he began to think it had given up the chase.

"What is it?" he gasped as Frost prodded him in the arm with an icy finger, urging him still onward.

"I do not know," the winter man said, his voice seeming to come from the breeze itself. "Something magical that does not wish to be seen."

That was enough for Oliver. If Frost thought they ought to run, he was not about to argue. They ran side by side, the legendary creature moving effortlessly even as Oliver got a stitch in his side. Still he forced himself on, feet pounding the soil. They had to put some distance between themselves and their pursuer, or at the very least find a clearing where it could not approach them unseen. All of these thoughts mingled with the fear in his mind and with thoughts of home, of people he was beginning to doubt he would ever see again. It was only physical and emotional momentum that carried him forward. He had nowhere else to go.

The ridge gradually sloped downward and soon he could see the tops of the trees on the far side. Ahead in the yellow light of the moon he could see that the forest floor seemed to flatten out again, and then beyond it there seemed a vast open space with no trees at all.

"There," he rasped.

"Yes," Frost agreed. "We can take our bearings."

In that moment, though, there came a snap of branches behind them. Oliver cursed under his breath and Frost bared his teeth and cut across in front of him. Oliver nearly stumbled before he realized what the winter man intended, but then they were both running up the steep ridge. It had diminished so much by then that the place they climbed up was less than ten feet high, and they scaled it without effort. Oliver glanced back even as they topped the rise and then he turned to catch a quick glimpse of the clearing that stretched out in front of them.

Oliver grunted in astonishment and flinched back as though he'd been struck. He teetered on that narrow ridge and his hands flew to the top of his head, holding the sides of his skull as though he was afraid there simply wasn't room in his mind for any more of what the world beyond the Veil had to show him.

The being that lay in the clearing ahead could only have been called a giant. He must have been seventy or eighty feet from end to end and his skin was a leathery, wrinkled brown. Yet size was only one of the facets of the thing that left Oliver speechless. Tatters of rough linen that once could have been considered clothes hung on the enormous creature, but the forest itself covered him now. The giant lay on his side, his knees and part of one foot buried in the ground, and saplings grew over them. A thick layer of moss had formed in crevices on the giant's body, where the sun rarely shone. It grew up in the crook of his neck and behind one ear. Weeds and mushrooms and flowers grew from the moss, and a bush with dark green and red-tinted leaves sprang from his ear.

All around the giant were the fireflies he had seen earlier, hundreds of them flitting from weed to flower.

Oliver narrowed his eyes.

They weren't fireflies.

"Oh," he whispered. "They're beautiful."

His feet seemed to move of their own accord and he started forward without making any allowance for the hill. He stumbled, tried to keep his footing, but the momentum tipped him over and then he was spilling end over end down the far side of the ridge. His shoulder struck exposed bone and he grunted in pain but could not arrest his tumble until at last he sprawled at the bottom, just at the edge of the clearing, perhaps forty feet from the giant's knees.

"Fool!" he heard Frost snap, above and behind him.

Oliver stood and brushed off the seat of his pants, which had dried long ago but were still stiff. He stared wide-eyed but found himself not looking at the giant, but the colorful things that fluttered all around. Unable to prevent himself from moving, he walked slowly alongside the enormous man. The giant's chest rose and fell in a slow, steady rhythm, and Oliver realized he was sleeping. *For how long?* he thought. *For the forest to grow over him like that . . . how long?*

He wondered what would happen if somehow the giant was to awaken, if his lost flesh would be restored, or if he would live as this half-decayed creature forever. Already he understood that there were many kinds of magic in this world, some far more sinister than others, but looking at the astonishing tableau before him, he was reminded how very much he had to learn.

A cluster of mushrooms grew from the giant's navel and more of those things, like fireflies, hovered around them.

Oliver watched as one of them, a pale thing that gave off a golden luminescence, flew toward the giant's face and into one enormous nostril. In the darkness of the giant's nose there were multicolored flashes of light. One of them flitted over to him, zipping toward his face, and Oliver gasped in surprise and fright and ducked back.

She tilted her head and studied him curiously, that tiny naked woman with her black eyes and hummingbird wings, a lavender light glowing around her as she danced in the air. The light came from a sparkling phosphorescence given off by her wings. He uttered a small noise of delight and shock when he caught the scent of her—a remarkable perfume that made him feel as though he had just woken from a long sleep. In fact, the air was filled with the mingling of many different scents, all alluring in their way, and he realized he had been smelling them since he had come over the ridge.

"*Les Bonnes Dames,*" the winter man said softly as he joined Oliver in the clearing of the sleeping giant.

"They're fairies," Oliver replied without tearing his gaze away from the tiny women.

Before Frost could reply, another voice came from behind them. "Peries, to be precise. Their ancestors were Persian."

Oliver turned to see a woman standing on the ridge from which they had just descended. In her way she was as breathtaking as the giant or the flitting Peries, for there was magic in every nuance of her aspect and yet she appeared entirely human. Her soft jade-green eyes seemed alight from within. Ebony hair framed a finely boned face with the distinct flair of the Orient. Her clothes were simple black garments but they were worn beneath a flowing, hooded cloak of copper-red fur. It struck him instantly that the night was too warm for such a cloak, but she seemed not to notice.

The winter man did not turn. "I knew it was useless to try to outrun you."

His tone made Oliver blink several times and regard this stunning woman anew. "You were the one in the woods. You were . . ." He stared at Frost. "Wait, is she one of them?"

With just a moment's hesitation, Frost did finally turn to regard her. A smile cracked the edges of his mouth and his jagged hair clinked together again.

"An excellent question," he said, staring at the red-cloaked woman. "Are you one of them? Are you hunting?"

She smiled in return, those jade eyes gleaming. Shadows seemed to coalesce inside her hood but it might just have been the angle of the moonlight.

"I am always hunting, kind sirs. But not for you. I was only walking, enjoying the night, the sounds and scents, and when I caught yours it made me curious. I decided to follow." She offered a small shrug. "Forgive me for intruding, but I thought to do you the courtesy of warning you not to wake the giant. The Peries put him to sleep and he is their home now. They would not take kindly to anyone waking him."

Oliver stared at her, dawning horror spreading through him. "This was deliberate? They *made* him this way?"

A strange smile came upon the woman's features. "They are beautiful, aren't they? But beauty has teeth and claws all its own. The Peries have made their home. Waking the giant would take their home from them, and they would likely tear your flesh from your bones if you were but to try. The giant would not thank you, either, for he would live in agony."

Nausea churned in Oliver's stomach and when he shot a glance at the rotting giant and the spritely things flitting in and out of his orifices and the holes eroded in his body, he could no longer see their beauty. All he saw were maggots, nesting in dead flesh.

The beautiful woman smiled and bowed low, red fur flowing over her as she moved. "I am Kitsune."

The winter man had stared at her from the moment of her arrival. "You are Borderkind."

"As are you, *Morozko*."

"I am Frost."

One corner of her mouth rose in the hint of a smile. "Of course you are." She inclined her head. "Your pardon. I mistook you for another aspect of your legend."

Oliver found himself mesmerized by the woman, even as he began to wonder what, exactly, she was. He was not surprised to learn that she was Borderkind. No human woman had ever exuded such magic. But here she was in the middle of this vast forest, seemingly alone.

"Are you hiding?" he asked, before he could stop the question from leaving his lips.

Her eyes narrowed as she turned those jade eyes on him. "What do you mean?"

Frost saved him from having to respond by holding up a hand to quiet him. "This is Oliver Bascombe. A friend. Your presence here has made him curious. He is not aware that Kitsune always travels alone."

For the first time her confidence wavered. She glanced away a moment and then walked nimbly down the hill to join them. Oliver was surprised at how small she was, the top of her head barely coming to his shoulders.

"At times it is unwise to be alone," she said softly.

The winter man continued to stare. "Then you are aware that we are hunted?"

"I have heard whispers. When I heard that you were in the wood—"

Oliver started. "Heard? From whom?"

Kitsune smiled indulgently. "There are many eyes in the forest. They saw you pass. I came to watch you. I know the Hunters are abroad in the land, but I have not seen any sign of them here."

Frost nodded. "That's good to know. You have my thanks."

She dipped her head so that for a moment her face disappeared beneath the red fur of her hood. "Where will you go now? To see the Sandmen?"

The winter man studied her warily. "Perhaps."

"Sandmen?" Oliver said, feeling more and more as though he had become invisible to these two, who were so different and yet of the same strange clan. "That's news to me."

"I told you we needed a place to rest. A sanctuary. The castle of the Sandmen is not far, just beyond the edge of the forest and a short way along the Truce Road."

Kitsune took several steps away from them. With her back turned she was completely hidden within her cloak, but Oliver thought she must be watching the Peries fly, their colors splashing the night, their perfume in the air. After several moments, she spoke without turning.

"I have not been through the Veil in years. They do not believe in me much anymore. Not even in their fantasies."

"That prevents you from crossing over?" Oliver asked.

A bittersweet smile touched Kitsune's lips. "No. But it certainly takes the pleasure from the trip." Her expression turned grave as she turned to Frost. "Yet no matter how infrequently I cross over, I am still Borderkind and the

Hunters will come for me eventually. I would travel with you, if you'd have me."

Oliver glanced over at the winter man. Suspicion was etched in his icy features, but he nodded slowly.

"If you wish."

"We'd be honored," Oliver told her.

Kitsune turned just enough so that she could look at him. In the moonlight, her entire face was suffused with a golden glow.

"Let us go, then. The forest is not safe for strangers, especially at night."

Oliver did not like the sound of that. He took one last, long look at the sleeping giant and the tiny winged women who flitted around him, and tried to imagine an entire world filled with such wonders. Whatever they encountered next, he was sure that he could not be any more astonished than he was now.

Yet it was not the first time during that long night that he had felt such certainty, and each time he had been wrong.

Drifting in sleep, Collette was gently roused by jazz music, playing soft and low. Her eyelids fluttered and she moaned with the pleasure of the warmth of her goose-down comforter, the feel of the flannel sheets beneath her, and the chill breeze that snuck in through the gap she had left in her window overnight. The jazz was from her alarm clock, which was still set to the same station she had always awoken to when she lived at home. It had been years, and yet while she snuggled there in her bed it felt as though she had never really left.

She opened her eyes and smiled, despite the early hour.

The sun had not yet risen, though the night had become that rich, dark blue that was not quite black. On her windowsills were the Christmas lights that her mother had always insisted upon, and their warmth only added to the cozy, little-girl feeling she had in that bed. Collette pulled the comforter more tightly around her neck and burrowed deeper. For half a minute she relished the feeling, and the music, but she had a full day ahead. Her little brother was going to be married.

Her smile faltered as she recalled the conversation she'd had with Oliver the night before. Everyone said it was natural to get skittish before getting married, but Collette wished she had listened to her own doubts before walking down the aisle with Brad. It would have saved her a lot of heartache. She hoped Oliver and Julianna knew what they were doing.

It wasn't her place to stir up trouble, though. She wanted to be there for her brother. That was the important thing.

Reluctant to leave her bed, she nevertheless forced herself to throw back the comforter and swing her legs over the side. Collette loved her job in Manhattan, really enjoyed living in the city, walking the streets that were so alive with light and energy. But at night when she went to sleep she could still feel the phantom presence of her husband beside her in bed. Not that she wanted Brad there with her. Not at all. But the comfort of having someone in her bed was something she missed. Yet, oddly enough, snuggled up in her childhood bed with that heavy comforter and the winter breeze coming in the window, she didn't miss that at all. She was supposed to head back to New York the morning after the wedding—tomorrow morning—but now she was thinking she might stay an extra day.

Tempted to retreat beneath the covers yet again, Collette stood and stretched. Gooseflesh formed on her bare legs and she grabbed a pair of flannel pajama bottoms that were draped across the footboard and slid them on. The window seemed to beckon to her and she went to it. Though the sky was beginning to lighten it was not quite dawn yet, and the Christmas light in the window made it difficult to see into the dark. The bulb was very hot from burning all night and so she used the front of her T-shirt to grip it and unscrew it.

With the light off, she could see outside, and the view made her smile. The blizzard had come and gone, and left a couple of feet of new-fallen snow in its wake. South of the house there were evergreens that were frosted with a coating of white. Out across the ocean the horizon was changing color, gleaming with golden light that was a harbinger of morning. It was breathtaking.

Collette knew that the storm would keep some of the guests from attending the wedding. The ones who had come from very far away, from Los Angeles and London and Houston, had already arrived in town, and the locals would make it without any trouble. But she expected some of the people who had planned to drive up last night from New York City to be no-shows. That was all right, though. The blizzard had seemed like a bad omen the night before, but this morning it felt to her like a blessing. It was beautiful.

It was going to be a perfect day. She could feel it.

She slipped on a thick flannel robe and cinched it around her waist, then left her bedroom. The urge to pee had snuck up on her and now the pressure from her bladder was fairly persistent. But she had priorities this morning, and before she did anything else she had to fulfill her promise to her future sister-in-law. She had to wake up

Oliver. Her brother slept like the dead. There were mornings even his alarm clock could not rouse him, no matter how loudly it was set. So Collette had taken on the job.

Quietly, not wanting to wake her father yet, she padded down the hall to Oliver's room and prepared to rap lightly on the door before entering. To her surprise, however, the door was open.

"No way," she whispered, a dubious smile lifting the corner of her mouth. Collette simply refused to believe that Oliver had risen before her this morning.

She did rap once on the open door as she went into his room, but then she paused, just inside, and stared in confusion at the bed. He had a down comforter as well, and four or five pillows. But Oliver was not in his bed, nor did it appear to have been at all disturbed since having been made the previous morning.

Unless he made it . . . she thought, before realizing how ridiculous that was. Her brother had never made his bed in his life. Collette sighed and smiled to herself. Oliver had been sitting up reading in their late mother's parlor the night before, anxious about the wedding. If he wasn't in bed, she assumed he had fallen asleep on the sofa in that room, in front of the fireplace.

"You're going to be stiff this morning, little brother," she said as she went back down the hall.

The house was quiet, dark, and quite chilly. At the top of the stairs she paused to turn up the heat, then started down. The foyer had a gentle gloom about it, the diffuse light of the pre-dawn sky giving her just enough illumination to see by. Collette turned left and went along the corridor into the south wing of the house, and to the room where only last night Oliver had expressed his doubts about marrying Julianna.

Her brother wasn't there.

A frown creased her forehead deeply as she backed out of the room. Confused, she returned to the foyer and then stood a moment, looking first up the stairs and then at the front door, wondering where Oliver might have slept last night if not in his own bed or in the parlor.

It took a moment for her to realize that something in the corner of her eye had caught her attention. Then her frown deepened as she turned to stare at the coat closet beside the stairs. The door was ajar by several inches. She opened it the rest of the way and saw an empty wire hanger lying on the floor just inside, amongst a pile of boots and shoes. Several scarves and gloves had spilled from the top shelf and one long wool scarf trailed serpentine down from above. Another hanger was pulled out and hung at a strange angle. Someone had gone out in a hurry. An image rose in her mind, a memory of the night before, when she'd heard Oliver up and about and come out of her room, half asleep, to see him poking around in the closet.

"Oh, no," she whispered. "Oliver."

Morning came quickly over the Truce Road, the sun rising in the east with unsettling speed. The sky was a richer blue than Oliver had ever seen, and the flowers that grew wild in fields along the way seemed painted from a palette of colors so vivid that nature could never have created them. It was not so much that things did not seem real, but that they seemed too real. Better. Richer. Even the air smelled sweeter to him than any he had ever known. The sensation had existed for him since his passage through the Veil, but it had taken the arrival of morning for him to absorb it. Thoughts about Dorothy and the rainbow were inescapable, for the change from his mundane life to this extraordinary place was jarring. It was more than he had ever imagined, and everything he had hoped for.

But what's that old saying? Be careful what you wish for. . . .

In all of his secret musings he had never wished to be hunted. The specter of the Myth Hunters hung over him as they continued on their journey, muting the astonishment he knew he ought to have felt at his surroundings. Now that morning had come, the threat seemed even more real. He wondered if this place beyond the Veil was truly as incredible as it seemed, or if it was simply the threat of imminent violence that made it seem so sharp, so vivid.

They had continued east through the forest and, as Frost had promised, soon come to its edge. Already the sky had begun to lighten and in that queer gray early-morning light the Truce Road had been easy to make out. There was a gently sloping hill with tall grasses that swayed in the breeze, carrying the scents of growing things, and at the bottom of the hill, running north to south, had been the road. It was little more than a dirt track, barely wide enough for a single car, though he didn't think there would be many cars on this side of the Veil. Carts, more likely. Buggies and carriages, drawn by horses, that sort of thing. Oliver had not bothered to confirm this suspicion with his companions, but he felt confident nevertheless. And the ruts in the road seemed to bear out his presumption.

Less than an hour had passed since they had come out of the forest and started their trek upon the Truce Road. As had been the case all along, Kitsune and Frost spoke intermittently, mostly in shorthand mutterings that he had listened to at first and then chosen to ignore. It was, he was disappointed to learn, the sort of conversation any two strangers might share. Where had they come from, what acquaintances did they have in common, where did they stand on the politics of the time. There were names of people and places that were unfamiliar to Oliver and though he tried at times to make sense of it, he found himself drifting away from the conversation even as he fell behind on the road.

He was an outsider. He did not belong here, but he had no other choice than to continue upon this path and pray that somehow it might be resolved.

The morning sun warmed the air and he thought it must have been nearly eighty degrees, but cloaked in her copper-red fur, Kitsune seemed unaware of the temperature. Several times while she spoke to Frost she glanced back at Oliver and caught him staring, and an indulgent smile touched her lips. Somehow her jade eyes gleamed from within even in direct sunlight.

For his part, the winter man was even less bothered by summer. The Truce Road was dusty and dry, but where Frost passed, his feet left moist, melting prints upon the earth. Oliver's own tread kicked up small swirls of dust behind them, but Kitsune's passing disturbed the road not at all.

Frost had been deeply suspicious of Kitsune upon their meeting, but there seemed a camaraderie now between the two Borderkind. It gave Oliver pause. She was no less beautiful by day than she had been at night, and he was no less taken with her, but as he hiked along behind them thinking mostly of his own mortality, of his chances of surviving to see another morning, he himself was less trustful of the mysterious woman.

They had something in common, the two Borderkind.

Oliver was just tagging along, and with every step felt the truth of that with greater intensity.

"Let me ask you something," he said, interrupting a conversation about someone or something called Gong Gong. Whatever the hell that was.

Kitsune glanced at him again, the fur cloak rippling on her as though it was knitted to her own skin. Even as she turned, the winter man looked as well—not at Oliver, but at *her*—and he realized that Frost had not lost his wariness of the green-eyed woman, but rather had hidden it. Oliver wasn't certain if the feeling that rose in him then was relief or only deeper anxiety.

"What is it, Oliver?" the winter man asked. The sunshine gleamed on his icicle hair, throwing prismatic colors on the ground behind him. Other than his blue-white eyes, his body was nearly translucent.

Oliver dragged the back of his hand across the stubble on his chin and quickened his pace, coming up beside them. His hands moved as he spoke, a trait he'd picked up from his mother as a child.

"I understand that the other humans here, the Lost Ones as you call them, can't go back because they've been touched by the Veil. And as long as I always cross over with you, or, I guess, with another Borderkind, that won't happen to me. So I can go back, and by the laws of the Two Kingdoms that makes me an Intruder. So I'm a fugitive."

The Truce Road curved slightly and now they found themselves striding up a long incline.

"True enough, Oliver. The Lost Ones are people who are called here, or lured, like so many of the old Faerie tales. You must have read them. Some aren't lured, but simply wander through the places where the Veil is thin or unstable. They are no threat to the Two Kingdoms because they can never go back. If the mundane world truly knew of our existence, believed in it, there's no telling what would come of it. War, probably, or at the very least piracy and interference. We can't have that."

"Fine, but why couldn't I just lie?" Oliver said quickly. "I mean, I could just say I was one of the Lost, that I was lured here. It'd be halfway true anyway. All my life I dreamed of escaping to some other place, something—"

Kitsune did not look at him when she spoke, but instead gazed out over the field to the east, where rough terrain had replaced the tall grass and flowers they had passed earlier.

"Pretense would not deceive anyone for very long. The Lost Ones are touched by this place. Just to look at them is to know that they belong here. You do not. And even if Frost can disguise you, the Falconer has seen you, and has your scent. No, the word will go out that there is an Intruder among us and you will be hunted not only by the enemies of the Borderkind, but by the agents and marshals of the Two Kingdoms as well."

Oliver felt numb.

The winter man glanced sidelong at him. "None of us wants to die, my friend. You saved my life. I will do all I can to repay that debt, to keep you alive and return you to your home."

His stomach gave a sickening twist. "Once upon a time I would never have wanted to leave."

Kitsune turned only slightly, so that just the tip of her nose was visible poking from her hood as he studied her profile. "No journey is ever complete until we come back to the place we began."

They walked in silent contemplation of the danger they

shared, trudging up the long, sloping hill. There were trees on either side of the road near the top, but they were scattered and small, with thin trunks and strangely contorted limbs. The turf here was all rocks and scrub grass, and those stunted-looking trees. Oliver thought he had once seen something like them in a dream, or a nightmare. In truth, the entire hill seemed familiar to him in that half-remembered way.

"Has it always been that way? The law, I mean?" he asked. "Have they always killed Intruders?"

"Always," the winter man said. "The only way to protect this world is to keep it hidden behind the Veil."

Oliver nodded. So that was the end of it. This was his journey and he would have to forge ahead. He would have to learn whatever he could about the Two Kingdoms if he intended to survive. There was no choice.

"What of Professor Koenig?" Kitsune asked, turning at last to look at them, one eyebrow arched.

The winter man knitted his brows so tightly that the ice in his forehead crackled. "Surely that's only a story. Our own sort of legend."

"Not at all," Kitsune purred. "I met him once, long years ago."

"Who's Professor Koenig?" Oliver glanced past Frost at Kitsune, but it was the winter man who answered.

"Just a man. A human historian, a folklorist, whose research led him to ask the right questions. The legend says he convinced a Borderkind to open a portal for him, so that he could explore our side of the Veil. That is, if you believe the tale. According to the story, he was the one Intruder who discovered our existence and was allowed to live."

"But why? Why him?"

Kitsune pushed back her hood for the first time since they had encountered her, and her black silk hair gleamed in the sun. "That part of the story I do not know."

"Well, that's what I need to find out," Oliver said, a rush of fresh energy filling him. "If I can find this professor, and learn why they spared him, maybe I can get them to forget about me, to leave me alone."

"He would be very old now," Kitsune said dubiously.

"But he could still be alive," Oliver argued.

"Perhaps," Frost said, nodding slowly as he walked between them. "You would still have the Hunters to fear, but that's a problem we face together. After we've rested at the Sandmen's castle, we shall continue on to Perinthia—"

"Where?"

"The capital of Euphrasia, which is one of the Two Kingdoms. In Perinthia, Kitsune and I will try to discover who has set these Hunters after the Borderkind, and we may be able to learn the whereabouts of Professor Koenig."

The winter man narrowed his eyes and gave Oliver a meaningful look, which Kitsune could not see. "If he is not only a legend."

"Haven't I told you he's real?" Kitsune asked. "How ironic that you, who so many believe a figment of the imagination, treat the existence of this mortal man just as his kin would treat you."

Frost said nothing at first, only walked along. At length he glanced over to regard Kitsune and she arched a mischievous eyebrow.

"We shall see," the winter man said.

But a spark of hope had been born in Oliver. If there was a chance he could be spared, no matter how small, he had no choice but to pursue it. If one man had gone through the Veil and lived, then it could be done again.

So involved was he in these thoughts that he did not notice at first that his companions had stopped, and he took two long strides past them before coming to a halt himself. They had crested the top of the hill with those ragged, bent trees on either side of the Truce Road, and he was about to ask what had prompted them to stop when he saw it. On the eastern side of the road the scrub brush gave way to sand.

Nothing but sand.

It stretched for nearly a mile, sculpted into large dunes that seemed almost like waves on an ocean, all of them leading up to the base of an enormous walled fortress, with a castle rising up from the keep at the center.

And all of it made of sand.

Against the blue painted sky, the sand seemed almost golden.

"It's . . . I never . . ." Oliver muttered.

But his awe was crushed by the winter man's next words. "This is troubling," Frost said, his tone as chilling as his touch.

Oliver began to ask what he meant, but as he did so he turned and saw that it was not the sight of the Sandmen's castle that had caused his companions to stop. Kitsune left the Truce Road, no trace of her passing in the dirt, and walked into the trees. As she stared upward, she did a curious thing. Kitsune raised her hood to hide her face.

Impaled upon a thick tree limb was a withered, gnarled old man clad in green so dark it was nearly black. Where the branch had burst out of his chest his shirt was torn and broken bones jutted out. Only there was no blood. Instead, sand had spilled from the wound. Even now, as the wind swirled around him, it sifted from his corpse and scattered the ground. There were heavy boots on his feet that seemed made of rough iron.

Kitsune dropped to one knee at the base of the tree and picked up something red. She spread it open with her fingers and Oliver saw that it was some kind of hat.

"What is it?" he asked, afraid that he knew the answer.

"One of the Sandmen," Frost replied, gaze shifting from the impaled creature over to the distant castle and then back again.

"So . . . what now?"

The winter man turned to him, then away. And then he started walking.

"We go and see if any are left alive, and give what help we may."

Oliver stared after him. He glanced at Kitsune, but she did not even look at him as she pulled her cloak more tightly around her and started after Frost.

"What if the Hunters are still there?" Oliver asked, for certainly that was what had happened here. The Sandmen were Borderkind. If one of them had been murdered, he couldn't imagine any other reason.

"Then there may be time to save some of the Bloody Caps. Every Borderkind who is killed is an ally we have lost. If the Hunters are still at the castle, then we must fight them."

An image of the Falconer swam into Oliver's mind and he felt sick.

"I don't suppose either one of you carries a gun."

Neither Frost nor Kitsune bothered to reply. They simply kept walking toward the sand dunes—that magical desert so out of place in this landscape—and the fortress beyond. Oliver wished he had a weapon. Any weapon. The last thing in the world he wanted to do was go up to that castle.

He glanced at the creature impaled upon that tree, and at the red cap on the side of the dirt road.

Then he ran to catch up.

CHAPTER 5

Not even a triple espresso could make Ted Halliwell happy this morning. Kitteridge, Maine, was a beautiful town, replete with both wealth and the culture that had made it an artists' colony for decades before the artists couldn't afford to live there anymore. Their work was still shown in the galleries, but the artists themselves lived inland, or much farther north.

This morning the town was more picturesque than he had ever seen it. It was, in his estimation, the kind of thing that would've given Norman Rockwell a raging hard-on, Americana at its best. The blizzard that had swept through the night before hadn't stuck around long enough to do serious damage, but it had made a hell of a mess. It wasn't even half-past nine yet and already there were kids all over town firing snowballs at one another—and at passing cars—building snowmen and forts and making snow angels. They were chasing one another, screaming with pleasure, faces red, brightly colored hats pulled over their heads. It was the *Saturday Evening Post* come to life. Ted was old enough to remember the *Saturday Evening Post*, though just barely. But there was nothing cheery about this excursion into Rockwell's America.

"You're awfully grumpy this morning, Halliwell," he muttered to himself. Fortunately, there was no answer. He had always told his wife, Jocelyn, that it was okay for him to talk to himself as long as he didn't get an answer back. When he started having a two-way conversation with himself, that would be trouble.

Once upon a time she had found that sort of thing funny. But Jocelyn had been gone from Halliwell's life, and from Maine entirely, for seven years now. His daughter, Sara, was living in Atlanta, Georgia, and he only heard from her every couple of months, at best. Ted Halliwell had just turned fifty-three, but already he was a cantankerous old man. It was an image he cultivated. It gave him a certain satisfaction. People in Wessex County knew him and remembered him. That wasn't much, but it was something.

The plows had done a poor job this morning and even busy roads were only wide enough for about a car and a half. The one positive effect of their sloppiness was that people were forced to drive slowly. With an inch or so of hardpack on the street that the plows hadn't been able to get up, and the sun already out, just warm enough to make it all even more slippery, driving fast would have been foolhardy. Even so, Halliwell cursed under his breath at the plow in front of him. Seemingly in answer, the lumbering truck started spraying sand and salt out the back, spattering his grill and hood like buckshot.

He had Harry Connick, Jr., singing Christmas songs from the car speakers, something that might have hurt his curmudgeonly image if anyone else were in the car. But Detective Halliwell had decided not to bother rousing anyone else today. Bad enough the sheriff had personally called him in, but Ted didn't want to ruin anyone else's day just because his own was shot to hell.

So he sipped his espresso and tried to let a little bit of Christmas cheer relax him, resisting the urge to pull his service weapon and fire a few rounds at the plow in front of him. When at last he came to Rose Ridge Lane, he cursed the plow driver's mother and father and took the right turn. Some of the houses on Rose Ridge Lane were visible from the street, but others were hidden in the woods, amongst the evergreens. The driveways were, of course, almost entirely cleared of snow. The people who lived on that street had the money to hire plows that would come to their homes first, and do an almost surgical removal, so that the snow cliff that was left on either side of the driveway was smooth and sheer as a concrete wall.

The last driveway on the left-hand side of Rose Ridge Lane—the ocean side—belonged to Max Bascombe. Halliwell had nothing against Bascombe. The one time they had met, the man had seemed fairly pleasant and not nearly as pompous as might be expected of the absurdly rich. But if Bascombe had a problem, it was a Kitteridge P.D. problem, not a sheriff's department problem. Bascombe, of course, didn't see it that way. He figured his money had helped get the sheriff elected and that meant he was owed a few favors.

Ted Halliwell had somehow become one of those favors.

Sheriff couldn't have sent the old man a hooker or a box of chocolates? he thought as he guided the car through a serpentine weaving of pavement.

He emerged from the tree-lined path and pulled into a circular drive in front of the house; the sort of thing one saw at hotels in the mountains or English manor homes. Halliwell put on the brakes and for a moment he just stared at the property. Both the enormous main house with its sprawling wings and the small carriage house that could be seen just to the north were decorated with Christmas lights. With the pristine new-fallen snow and those lights, and the ocean behind it, the place looked like a postcard.

How much money had Max Bascombe donated to the sheriff's campaign? Now that he'd seen the extent of the man's wealth, Halliwell had to wonder. Maybe enough that sending his primary detective off like some errand boy was a small favor in comparison.

"All right," he muttered as he pulled up in front of the house and killed the engine. "I can play the game."

Ted had been a Maine state trooper during his youth and had risen to the rank of detective there. Eventually, though, he had wanted to stay closer to the town where he'd grown up, and putting his skills to work for Wessex County had simply made sense. Folks out of state were often surprised to find that there even *were* detectives in places like this, and often assumed that they must not be very good at their jobs if they weren't working in some big city. Halliwell ignored such moronic attitudes. He was good at his job.

But today, his job was a waste of time.

He got out of the car and walked up to the front of the house. Before he had even reached the steps, the door opened to reveal a neatly put-together little man with soft, kind features. Even if Halliwell had never met him, there was no way he would have thought this guy was Max Bascombe.

"You're the detective?" the man asked, a European accent to his words that Ted couldn't identify. Swedish or something, maybe. He wanted to ask the man if the car had given him away. Instead he nodded and mounted the steps in three quick strides.

"Ted Halliwell."

The little man stepped back and opened the door for him to enter. "Thank you for coming, Detective Halliwell. My name is George Friedle. I work for Mr. Bascombe. He and his daughter, Collette, are in the kitchen. If you'll wait in the sitting room I'll let them know that you're here."

Halliwell thanked him and watched the man disappear into the back of the house. Then he blinked and glanced around, trying for a moment to figure out what the hell a sitting room was and where he would find one. He grunted in amusement and scratched at the back of his head, where his salt-and-pepper hair was buzzed down to a velvety scruff. A grandfather clock in the hall caught his attention and as he walked toward it he peered into the room beyond it, to the left of the foyer. There was a massive brick fireplace there, paintings of old frigates and schooners under sail, and heavy furniture in deep, rich colors. It was the type of room that ought to have been filled with a bunch of guys in tuxedoes, drinking martinis and smoking fat cigars.

"Detective Halliwell."

Ted turned toward the entrance of the room to see that

Max Bascombe had appeared alone. The little man, Friedle, had apparently gone on to do whatever it was he did in the house, and now it was just the two of them. Halliwell was tall. Bascombe was taller. The attorney was well into his sixties, if Ted's information was correct, but he did not look anywhere near it. He was broad-shouldered but trim, with serious features but an air of health that only came from regular exercise. And more than just a weekly stroll on the golf course. The detective wondered if he'd make that kind of effort to stay in shape if he had Bascombe's money. He doubted it.

"Mr. Bascombe. Good to see you again. Sorry it has to be under these circumstances." Exactly what the sheriff would have wanted him to say. Halliwell was relieved and disgruntled simultaneously.

The older man knitted his brow almost imperceptibly. "Yes. Thank you."

You don't have the first clue that we've met before, Halliwell thought. Not that he was surprised. He hadn't been running for office, after all. A sheriff's detective was beneath notice for a guy like Bascombe. Why bother with the help when he could buy the boss?

Bascombe gestured to a chair. "Have a seat."

It was more an instruction than an invitation. Halliwell did not take well to commands, but he was willing to cooperate if it meant getting back to his own life faster. He sunk into a high-backed burgundy chair. Bascombe came into the room but instead of sitting properly in a chair, he leaned on the arm of the sofa and looked at Ted as though the detective were a jury.

"What, precisely, did the sheriff tell you about the 'circumstances'?"

Halliwell hated lawyers. "Your son was supposed to be

married today. All I've been told is that no one has seen him since last night."

Bascombe nodded and took a deep breath. For the first time, Halliwell thought he saw some humanity under the lawyerly veneer. Sadness, disappointment, perhaps even embarrassment. Reluctantly, he reassessed Max Bascombe. It was, he allowed, just possible that though the man wore his lawyerly face often enough that he had forgotten how to behave around ordinary people, Bascombe was not entirely without a soul.

"My daughter tells me that Oliver . . ." the man began, then trailed off, sighing with regret.

"Oliver's your son?"

"My son. Yes." Bascombe shook his head. "But he was always more his mother's son than mine. Far more like her, God rest her. Sentimental. Lost in the clouds." He frowned and glanced up as though annoyed to discover that he had spoken these personal thoughts aloud. "My daughter, Collette, tells me that Oliver was having second thoughts about the wedding. First I'd heard of it, of course. God forbid he should have spoken to his father if he was troubled."

Halliwell waited for the rest, but the man seemed content to leave it at that. The detective leaned forward in his chair.

"Mr. Bascombe . . . I'm confused. Why, exactly, did you call the sheriff? Your son is an adult. It seems pretty clear what happened here. Awkward as it may be, he's perfectly within his rights to—"

"The hell with his rights!" Bascombe snapped, eyes narrowing angrily. "I want him found. And today. The wedding mass is at three o'clock this afternoon and Oliver damn well better be at the church by then."

Halliwell stared at him. "If there was any reason to

think something had happened to him, I'm sure we could—"

Max Bascombe stopped him with a glare, and Ted Halliwell hated that he could be silenced that way. It churned in his gut. There was nothing he would have liked more than to give Bascombe a lesson in the realities of police business, but though he probably could have found employment in any town in Maine, he enjoyed working for the sheriff's department. And Ted had no doubt that Bascombe could have him fired.

"I'm sorry," the dapper man said, surprising the detective. He offered a wan smile that seemed genuine. "I know this isn't what you signed up for. I'm sure it's not what you wanted to spend your day doing. But I need your help, Detective. Yours and the sheriff's. Oliver is going to regret this the instant he stops to think about what he's done. Forget the expense and the—how did you put it? Awkwardness. He's going to shatter this girl who loves him, and ruin his life. I just want to look him in the eye and make sure he understands this decision. As his father, I have to do that for him. I'm not asking you to cuff him and haul him back here. Just find him for me and I'll go to him."

Halliwell stared at Bascombe for a long moment. The man's candor—his sudden, revelatory reasonableness—was a surprise. The detective knew he had a chip on his shoulder and was willing to consider that Bascombe might really want what was best for his son. Or, what he *thought* was best. Either way, he didn't have much choice.

"I can't make you any promises, Mr. Bascombe. I can get a list from you of your son's friends and any places he likes to spend time. I'll move as quickly as I can and I'll be quiet about it. But we're talking *hours,* and if he doesn't want to be found—"

Bascombe halted him with an upraised hand. "Understood, Detective. You have no idea how much I appreciate your help." He stood up and walked toward the bay windows at the front of the house, but paused before he got there and turned to regard Halliwell carefully. "Do you have any children?"

None of your business, Ted thought. But he nodded. "A daughter."

He expected Bascombe to make some kind of comment, either regarding the irresponsibility of sons or just in general about the trials and tribulations of fatherhood, but the man only seemed to contemplate the response for a moment before offering a small shrug and heading for the exit.

"For Oliver's sake, I hope you find him quickly," Bascombe said.

Halliwell recognized his cue to depart and got up to follow the man. "I'll do my best."

In the foyer, Bascombe turned to look at him. "It's my understanding, Detective, that your best is pretty significant. The sheriff has a high opinion of you."

Halliwell had no idea how to respond to that. The two men regarded each other awkwardly.

"All right," Bascombe said. "Let me get Friedle in here, and Collette as well. Oliver's sister. The two of them will have a far better idea where he might have gone than I would."

As Max Bascombe strode away, Halliwell wondered if the man had any idea how very telling a statement he had just made. To look for Oliver Bascombe, he needed a list of the young man's friends and his hangouts. And his father did not have the first clue what to put on that list.

Not that Halliwell was in any position to judge. There

was a reason his own daughter only spoke to him every couple of months. Even back when Sara was in high school he wouldn't have been able to answer those questions.

A minute or so passed before an attractive young woman appeared in Bascombe's place. She was petite and finely boned, pale with a spray of light freckles across the bridge of her nose, and thick blonde hair that fell to her shoulders.

"My father said to tell you he had to take a phone call but he and Friedle would be along in a minute. I'm supposed to tell you where Oliver might be."

"That would help," Halliwell replied, studying her. The woman, late twenties or so, was deeply troubled, and not just because the wedding might not come off today. "You're his sister?"

"Collette."

"Ted Halliwell."

She crossed her arms and hugged herself as though she was cold. "You're a detective, right?"

"Yes."

Her scrutiny in that moment made him uncomfortable. "I'll give you the names and the places you want. But I know my brother. He might've gotten cold feet, and he was absolutely feeling some nervousness about going through with the marriage. But he loves Julianna. No way is Oliver going to just take off like this. He's not the kind of man who could ever do something like that. If he decided he couldn't go through with it, he would've gotten in his car and gone over to tell her."

Halliwell knew it was possible for people to hide their true selves, even from the ones who loved them most, but the woman seemed very sure of herself, and of her relationship with her brother. He didn't like the sound of it, either.

"What are you suggesting?"

She glanced back the way she'd come to see if anyone was within hearing distance. When she looked at Halliwell again, she seemed lost. "My father doesn't want to hear it. This is the sort of thing he would expect of Oliver, but Dad doesn't know him at all. Not really. So you're going to have to take the list and look. But I'm afraid that . . ."

Collette brought one hand up to massage the bridge of her nose, then slid it down over her mouth as though subconsciously wishing she could silence herself.

"I'm afraid, Mr. Halliwell. Oliver wouldn't do this. And before we all assume he would, that he'd just break Julianna's heart like this, maybe we should be asking how he got out of here? He was gone before the plow came this morning, and his car is still in the garage anyway. So, what? Did my brother just walk out of here in the middle of the night, in a blizzard?"

Halliwell stared at her. The Kitteridge police should certainly have been called into this thing, but Bascombe wanted it kept quiet and wanted it handled quickly. The local cops wouldn't start looking for Oliver Bascombe until Monday unless there was some sign of foul play. And even then it would be in every local newspaper.

But the sister was right to be concerned. Halliwell couldn't imagine anyone—especially a young lawyer who stood to inherit his father's wealth—going for a leisurely stroll in the storm they'd had last night. Unless he had someone on Rose Ridge Lane he could have stayed with, he wasn't going to get very far.

He would have to do what Bascombe and the sheriff wanted, follow up on the leads, try to track down the guy that way. At least until the church bells rang and the wedding ceremony was supposed to get under way. If he hadn't found Oliver Bascombe by then, Halliwell was going to take a very different approach to this case.

It had suddenly become very messy. Collette Bascombe was afraid for her brother, and Ted Halliwell was worried that she might have reason to be.

His morning, which had started seriously shitty, had just gone abruptly downhill.

The massive granite doors at the entrance to the fortress of the Sandmen hung wide open. The approach across the dunes and up the hill toward the castle had been difficult. Oliver's legs ached from the give of the sand beneath his feet, and the grit stung his eyes. The sun reflected off the dunes and raised the temperature twenty degrees over what it had been back on the road.

The night had been long and he was tired. It was catching up to him and he yawned in spite of the troubling sight of the stone gates hanging wide.

Just inside the fortress's outer wall they found the second of the dead Sandmen. Bloody Caps, Frost had called them. Now the winter man paused in the courtyard between the fortress walls and the castle itself and, as Kitsune and Oliver watched, his fingers grew long and sharp as butcher knives.

"I need a weapon," Oliver said, his voice a rasp.

Frost and Kitsune looked at him and then at each other. With her red-fur hood shading her face he could not see Kitsune's expression well, but her jade eyes gleamed in that shadow as she studied him.

"Yes. That would be wise. We shall have to find you something. For now, though, you must do without, and rely upon us to protect you if we can."

"That doesn't inspire much confidence."

Neither of the Borderkind bothered to reply. They started across the courtyard as though they wanted to be attacked. Oliver went more warily, glancing up at the castle and around at the interior walls of the fortress. It was all sand. All of it. Hard-packed so that it seemed almost like concrete, but he knew better. Sand blew across the court-yard and sifted against the walls, swirled up into dust dev-ils, and showered down when the wind died. But there was nothing in sight that he might have used as a weapon. Not a piece of wood or a rock, and sure as hell not a box of hand grenades.

Oliver drew his fingers across his eyes, smearing grit and moisture, and picked up his pace. Ahead of him, Kitsune and Frost had stopped at the tall castle doors. Even as he approached, Oliver was beckoned forward by the winter man. He was more translucent than ever as he turned toward Oliver and raised a hand to urge Oliver on with those dagger fingers. His blue-white eyes gave off a mist of frosty condensation.

"Do not tarry, Oliver. Not with so much death here, and the whereabouts of its bringers uncertain."

Kitsune had crouched in front of the partially open door. Her cloak rustled in the breeze, but not where it lay across her back or on her arms. There it simply rippled with the motion of her body, with the muscles underneath.

The castle doors were open only slightly, but in that gap was a third corpse, severed nearly in half.

When Frost pulled the doors open, dried skin and flesh stuck to the sides, and strings of it held on like spiderwebs, until at last the doors were wide enough that they snapped. It might have had sand instead of blood, but there were or-gans of some kind inside of it. Oliver averted his eyes. If he had looked at the remains for another moment he would have vomited.

He stepped over the dead creature so quickly that he nearly ran into Frost and Kitsune. He was so close to her that his face almost brushed the cloak, and he inhaled a powerful musk that rose off her. A sudden, stunning arousal raced through him and he took an involuntary step back, his heel landing atop the leg of the dead creature. Its skin burst like papier-mâché and it crumbled to dust. Or sand.

The winter man glanced back at him, danger in his eyes.

"You may want to find that weapon now, Oliver."

Kitsune moved aside, glancing around for any sign of imminent threat, and Frost stepped slowly into the vast, cathedral-like chamber that was the main hall of the Sandmen's castle. Oliver could only stare.

There were dozens of them. Perhaps hundreds. The Bloody Caps were all dead, strewn in bits and pieces around the floor of that massive cathedral and across the ornate staircases all around its circumference that led into other areas of the castle. Their clothes were shredded, skin and bones shattered and torn. Only their iron boots seemed intact. Untouched.

Kitsune moved in and out of the sunlight that streamed through the high windows, disappearing into shadows and then reappearing. The winter man's body glinted with refracted light and he moved with strange, unhurried grace as he examined the scene. Oliver stepped carefully over the broken corpses of the hideous little things. Sleep bringers and dream makers, according to myth. They were horrible, but Oliver could not help pitying them.

He glanced down and saw that the face of the creature below him had been savaged. When he could tear his gaze away, he saw the weapon in its hand. It was a knife of some kind, a dagger, but even as he reached down to pry it from the rough-textured fingers of the dead Sandman, he realized it was not metal, but bone. Or, perhaps, a tooth. As he brandished it before him he became certain that was what it was. A single fang, two inches in girth and at least seven in length.

What has teeth like this? he wondered.

The question only made him draw a long, measured breath and swallow once, hard. But the weight of the weapon in his hand lent him some comfort. He had taken fencing lessons throughout middle and high school. This was no fencing foil, but he had no doubt he could stab something with it.

When he glanced around again he saw that Kitsune and Frost had moved closer to the middle of the massive cathedral chamber. They were at what seemed to be the center of the carnage and were staring upward at something that thrust down from the ceiling. As Oliver walked toward them, trying to make out what had drawn their attention, things crunched underfoot.

Not sand.

He paused and looked down. Scattered across the floor of the castle were shards of what he first took to be crystal. He crouched and reached to pick one up, careful in case they might cut him. Only after the piece of crystal was in his hand and he had held it up, studying its intricacies and its beauty, did he realize that it was not glass that he held, but diamond.

"Holy shit," he whispered.

Standing, he started toward his companions again. All over the ground, mixed in with the gritty remains of the dead Sandmen, were shards of diamond, some of them tiny and others as long as his arm. He shook his head in wonder and stared upward again. Now he saw that the thing that had drawn the attention of Frost and Kitsune was the source of the diamonds. Something had hung there, a gigantic lamp or chandelier, from the looks of the structure of it. The top of it was still there, but it had been shattered in a thousand fragments or more, which had showered down to the floor.

"What was it?" he asked.

Kitsune slowly turned to him, her chest rose and fell with shallow breaths beneath her black tunic, and her expression was entirely open and unmasked. In her face and her eyes, he saw fear.

"It was the prison of the Sandman," said the winter man, his breath a cold mist. "The original Sandman. The monster.

"And now he is free."

Collette stood in the shower with her hands against the tiles and her back arched, letting the near-scalding water sluice down her body. The house was old and the winter tended to seep in, especially at night. In the cold air, steam billowed all around her and filled the entire bathroom. It felt good to breathe it in, to have the hot water pelting the muscles of her back, forcing her to relax after the day she had had. It may not have been the worst day of her life but it certainly felt that way.

She could still recall the contentment she had felt upon waking that morning. It seemed so absurd now, when she was filled with such exhaustion and regret and worry. Though she would have given anything to avoid it, the task of delivering the news to Julianna had ended up in her hands. The woman was not only her brother's fiancée but Collette's friend, and to see the feelings of betrayal in her face had been painful.

Julianna had cried, there in the back of the church, already in her wedding dress and more beautiful than she had ever been. Collette had held her hands, but could not escape the feeling that she was guilty by association, because Oliver was her brother. Still, she had stayed, twisting her bridesmaid's gown in her hands, and tried to convince Julianna that Oliver wouldn't ever have done this to her if he could have avoided it.

The words had felt hollow coming out of her mouth, no matter how strongly she believed them. When the priest had announced to the gathering crowd that the service would have to be postponed, and when the florist had come in with condolences, as though Oliver was dead instead of missing, and when the cellist had come in to say that the musicians would still need the balance of their fee—only to be nearly dragged from the room by Julianna's mother—Collette had stayed with her and tried to give her strength.

Never in her life would she hear the word *awkward* and not think of this day.

And yet, all along, as she comforted Julianna, her thoughts were of Oliver. For everyone else, the presumption that he'd gotten cold feet and run off superseded any fear for his safety; but not for Collette.

The detective from the sheriff's department, Halliwell, had phoned forty-five minutes before the church service to say that, though he had followed up on all the leads they had given him, he had come up with nothing. No one had seen Oliver today. No one had heard from him.

It had been what Collette expected. And yet to hear her

suspicion confirmed was a blow. Even now, so many hours later, standing in the shower smelling of apricot shampoo, she felt weakened by the memory of Halliwell's voice on the phone. She had told them Oliver would not have left Julianna at the altar like that. If he had changed his mind, he would have tried to comfort her as best he could, tried to blunt the sharp edge of the news. If Oliver was gone, he hadn't gone willingly.

She had seen him at the coat closet long after midnight, and in the morning found it in disarray. Perhaps he'd even taken out a coat and a hat, gloves and a scarf. It had been too long since she'd lived with Oliver to know what winter coat he wore, what hat he might take with him.

Collette did not believe for a moment that Oliver had just run off and abandoned Julianna. Something had happened to him, she was sure. But if she had told that cop, Halliwell, what she'd seen, he would have assumed her father was right, that Oliver had taken off. No matter how long she'd been out of this house, Collette knew Oliver better than anyone, and she'd looked in his eyes and seen the honor there. Regardless of his doubts, he wouldn't have run.

And where would he have gone, on foot, in the middle of a blizzard?

"Oh, God, little brother, where are you?" she whispered in the shower, and a spasm of fear went through her.

Collette turned the water off and ran her hands through her hair, squeezing some of the moisture out. She paused and took a deep breath, steadying herself and trying to push her worry away. It did not work very well. At least the police were actually looking for Oliver now and not just assuming he had jilted his bride. The Wessex County sheriff's department was working with Kitteridge police and the Maine state police. The cops had even interviewed poor Friedle to see if he knew anything about Oliver's disappearance. Ridiculous, of course, but they didn't know that. Collette was just happy they had not waited any longer to start looking for him.

She opened the shower door and reached for a towel, wrapping it around her head in a turban. Then she snatched up a second towel, an enormous fluffy blue thing, and quickly dried off. Her robe hung on the back of the door. She slipped into it and cinched the belt around her waist. The moment she opened the door—bright light and steam spilling out into the hallway—she shivered. The drop in temperature made her nipples hard and she crossed her arms over her breasts as the chill ran through her.

Though the heat was on very low—as it always was at bedtime—the pipes in the walls ticked with the effort of keeping it from getting any colder. The house creaked with its age and size, a venerable old thing whose emptiness seemed sad, as though the structure itself was mournful that it was just Collette and her father there tonight. There ought to be a real family in the house, she believed. Parents and children. Generations of family. Not just a distant, disappointed father and his apprehensive daughter.

The wood floor was cold beneath her bare feet and she hurried toward her open bedroom door. As she reached it, she paused and frowned deeply. A shudder went through her that had nothing to do with the thermostat. As a child Collette had often felt overwhelmed in this house. Often she had stayed awake long after her parents had gone to bed, and walking around the house late at night had been a terrifying adventure. Every night-black window seemed to hide in its darkness an unknown watcher. Padding toward the kitchen for a snack she would always have a strange, prickling sensation at the back of her neck, a tightening of the muscles between her shoulder blades, the certainty that someone was watching her.

That cold, familiar feeling touched her now.

But Collette was not a little girl anymore. She reached up to push the towel on her head up over her right ear and listened carefully to the moaning of the old house. Disdainful of her own hesitation, she glanced over her shoulder. There was a light at the top of the stairs that threw dim yellow illumination along the hall, but its reach was limited and there were shadows at either end.

"Dad?" she said, quietly. But that was foolish and she knew it. Her father was in his room, reading or perhaps already asleep, and if he had come out of his room, he wouldn't be wandering around in silence. Max Bascombe was, as she'd heard him say on more than one occasion, Lord-of-the-fucking-Manor.

Collette smiled derisively at herself and went into her room. The antique lamp at her bedside was on, its glass globes handpainted with roses and a white frost that cast a pink hue across the bed. The Christmas lights in the windows burned, and just being in the room let her relax a little. Perhaps the feeling she had had upon waking that morning, of being a child again, had affected her more than she had realized.

You're on edge because of Oliver, she thought.

Her thoughts were of her brother as she unwrapped her towel turban and began to dry her hair vigorously. She wasn't going to worry about blowing it dry tonight. After the day she'd had she had needed a shower, the heat and the relaxation of it, but in the morning she would take another. She would worry about her hair then.

Collette slipped off her robe and dressed in a clean pair

of thick flannel pajamas. She pushed her fingers through her damp hair and picked up the towel to do a better job of drying it. When she was through she took her brush from the top of the bureau and ran it through her hair. Her body prickled with anxiety. The shower had worked its magic on her, but now that she was out of it, her worries were seeping back in. How was she just supposed to go to sleep now, not knowing what had happened to Oliver? How had her father managed the feat?

Putting the brush down she went to her bed, picking up her book from the nightstand. She was reading Jon Krakauer's recounting of the tragedy on Mount Everest, *Into Thin Air*. It was a horrible story, but somehow an inspiring one as well. She hoped it would be enough to distract her so she could fall asleep.

Collette drew back the covers and started to climb into bed. As she did, that familiar feeling returned. Her brows knitted and she glanced at the door, which hung open half a foot. Though there was that small lamp in the hall, the light in her own room made it seem quite dark beyond the door. The urge to go and close it was powerful, but she resisted, chiding herself again.

Then something moved out in the hall.

Collette froze. "Dad?"

Her eyelids fluttered and a sudden sleepiness came over her, so strong that she swayed. Shaking it off, still trying to stare through that six-inch gap between door and frame, she reached up to rub at her eyes and wiped away the grit that was usually only there upon waking.

"Hello?" she said, and then she started toward the door. At first she walked slowly, but then she felt a flash of anger at herself and her father and at Oliver as well, and she strode over to the door and threw it open.

The light from her room cast its glow into the hall.

No one was there.

But someone had been there. Someone had been moving out there. She wondered if her father had wanted to talk to her and come down the hall, only to change his mind. Or if Friedle had come up from the carriage house for some reason. Collette could not help but wonder if whoever it was had seen her getting dressed, and she gnawed her lower lip angrily.

Then it occurred to her that there was someone else who might be sneaking around the house at night.

"Oliver?"

She had been afraid something bad might have happened to him. The truth was that without any way for him to leave the property by car, she had considered that he had called a friend and walked out to the road and been picked up, but her unspoken fear was that he had gone out in the blizzard and something had happened to him. The bluff overlooking the ocean was one of his favorite places in the world, and it had occurred to her a thousand times that he might stumble and fall . . . or jump. Not that he was suicidal, but there had been times when he was so forlorn that it concerned her.

Collette looked behind her, toward her brother's room, but nothing moved in the shadows there and no light came from under his door. Most likely it had been her father, much as she might have wished it was Oliver coming home, so she started in that direction. She passed the bathroom and directly beneath the light at the top of the stairs.

The next room on the right was the master bedroom. From within she heard the creak and rustle of her father moving around. A sad sigh escaped her as she realized he must be having just as difficult a time sleeping as she was.

In a way that pleased her. At least it showed that he was just as worried as he was angry. He must have come down to talk to her and then changed his mind. Her father hadn't spoken at all that night beyond a perfunctory conversation about dinner and then to wish her pleasant dreams.

"Daddy?" she said, vaguely aware that she had not called her father by that name for nearly twenty years.

Collette rapped softly and then opened the door. In the very same moment she felt a grit beneath her bare feet. The light from that hall lamp did not reach far into the room but there were Christmas lights in her father's windows just as there were in her own, and it was by their orange glow that she saw the grotesque tableau within.

Sand had been spread all over the floor. Max Bascombe lay on his back on the Persian rug, and above him loomed a gray cloaked figure whose very presence seemed to undulate like a swarm of a thousand bees. His skin appeared rough and the hue matched the sand on the floor. His features were impossibly, inhumanly thin, nose and cheekbones and chin sharply pointed, and his eyes gleamed a bright lemon yellow as he turned to her and grinned, revealing short, jagged teeth.

She had the inescapable feeling that she had seen him before.

"The past is a dream from which we never wake," he said, his voice a whispered scrape, like sleet against glass.

"No," Collette whispered, shaking her head with the denial even as hot tears stung her eyes.

Eyes.

One of her father's eyes was missing and the socket was red and raw, bloody tears streaking his face. Even as she entered and witnessed it all, even as the Sandman grinned at her, it used one knife-thin finger to pry out Max Bascombe's remaining eye. It ripped out with a sickening sound, trailing the torn optic nerve behind it like a tail, and the creature placed the eyeball delicately in its mouth and bit down. Fluid spurted from the eye to moisten and darken the sand on the carpet.

Her father was limp. Dead.

Collette was numb. Her breath hitched as she tried to free her voice from the paralysis of terror that gripped her.

The gray cloak seemed to embrace the thing as it flowed toward her across the room. It gripped her in those skeletal fingers and she felt herself swept off the floor, lifted up by rough, gritty hands, and its cloak began to enfold her.

At last, Collette began to scream.

It lasted only a moment, and then all of the strength went out of her. Her eyelids fluttered and she fell down and down into sleep, descending from one nightmare and into another.

CHAPTER 6

Hot wind whispered through the Sandmen's castle, scouring every surface. The sand moved with an almost living fluidity, a slow, inexorable crawl that, given time and a steady breeze, would erode and consume everything.

Oliver stared up at the remains of the diamond prism where the Sandman had been caged. *The original Sandman,* Frost had called him. The reference frightened Oliver because it was an unsettling reminder of how little he knew about the world beyond the Veil, and how much he had to rely upon the winter man if he was going to survive another night here, another day.

Kitsune was the first of them to move. She slunk amongst the bodies of the dead Bloody Caps, those ugly little goblins who had been torn apart by the Myth Hunters. Maybe *goblin* was the wrong word, but the classifications of the beings in this realm was something else he had to rely on others for. For a long moment Oliver watched the sunlight that streamed in the high windows of the elaborate sand castle shining on Kitsune's red-fur cloak, and then he turned to Frost. Nervous energy thrummed in his every muscle and he was waiting for the winter man to speak or act, to do something to indicate what their next move was. Anything to get out of there.

Frost knelt and scooped a handful of diamond fragments into his hand. They were almost invisible against the blue-white ice of which he was comprised. Mist steamed from the corners of the winter man's eyes and he seemed lost in thought. Oliver crossed his arms and glanced around again, bouncing one heel against the ground anxiously. Kitsune had paused in front of one of those tall, arched windows. In a crouch, she glanced over at them, her face lost in the shadows of her hood.

"We should go," Oliver said. "We shouldn't be here. How do we know the Hunters won't come back?"

The winter man turned to him with glacial slowness, as though drawing his mind back from wherever he had allowed it to wander. "How do we know they ever left?"

Oliver's throat went dry and he shook his head. He still clutched that long fang that he had picked up to use as a weapon and now his grip tightened. "Don't say things like that. Grim and mysterious are not qualities I have much appreciation for."

Frost's brows knitted with an almost inaudible crack of ice, and he turned to peer into the ruin of bodies, the dozens of Red Cap corpses strewn around the room, as if he had heard something shifting there.

"Nor I," said the winter man.

"We really should get out of here."

"No. We should do as planned. Rest. Recuperate. Plan. If there is danger here, it will most certainly follow us if we should leave. If not, then we may still find respite. The Sandman was not killed like these others. I wonder why the Hunters would free him instead."

Oliver watched Kitsune, who had started to move again: "You called him the original. What's that all about?" he asked, without taking his eyes off their companion. "And all of these dead things. What is it that we have stumbled into here?"

There came from behind him the familiar chiming of icicles clashing and Oliver turned to see Frost crouching beside one of the Red Caps on the ground. The creature's chest was a dry husk that had been cracked open, sand spilling onto the floor.

"They were not always like this. Red Caps. Bloody Caps. They were found all over Europe in times gone by, both in cities and in the country. All of them were mischievous, but some were savage and cruel. The nasty ones liked to hide in nurseries and orphanages and preyed on children's flesh. The Sandman considered children—all children—*his,* so he waged a quiet war against the Red Caps and eventually forced them to swear allegiance to him.

"Your modern legends are quaint, but the Sandman was a monster, a creature who stole into children's bedrooms at night in order to eat their eyes. If they were asleep when he arrived, he could not touch them. That was their only protection. Children all over the world huddled in their beds and hoped to be asleep when the Sandman arrived. Those that were unfortunate would never sleep again . . . or sleep forever thereafter, if the meaning suits you.

"With the Red Caps enslaved, he spread his influence, using them to harvest the eyes of children and to bring them to him. But the human world was changing. The Mazikeen and the Atlanteans were preparing to forge the Veil and these new little Sandmen did not want to be exiled forever from the castles and forests and alleys they loved. They knew they would be Borderkind only if they could alter the legend of the Sandman, make it something more benevolent, so that the stories would live on even after the worlds were severed by the Veil. They captured and imprisoned him. . . ."

The winter man picked up a diamond shard and glanced up at the roof of that vast chamber where the Sandman's cage had hung.

"He could not be killed, of course. Not by the likes of such creatures. But they could hold him for eternity, and such was their plan. The tales of Wee Willie Winkie and Billy Winker and the like grew from their efforts. Some of the dread surrounding the Sandman lingered, and lingers still, but their plan worked well enough that by the time the final magic had been worked and the Veil created, the Sandmen were Borderkind.

"Now the clever little Red Caps are dead, and the monster is free. The Hunters allowed him to live. I shudder to think why they would do such a thing."

Oliver shuddered as well. He had never even seen the Sandman but the legends alone were enough to unnerve him. He took one final glance around the castle and then started back toward the entrance, wary of every shadow and every whisper of wind and sand across the floor.

"All right. You two stay. I'm going outside. I . . . I'd rather sit in the sun and wait for something to come kill me than be in here with all this death."

The winter man said nothing as Oliver retraced their steps, but he had taken no more than a dozen steps when he stopped to look back. In this bizarre, impossible world, he was still the Oliver Bascombe he had always been, afraid to stay but even more afraid to leave. The realization of that sickened him, yet he could not pretend otherwise. He had saved Frost's life and the winter man had pledged to protect him in return, here beyond the Veil. Somehow he had expected to be stopped, to be told what to do and when to do it, in order to stay alive. He had expected to be treated the very same way his father had always treated him.

His grip on the fang-dagger tightened, his knuckles whitening.

"Maybe I ought to stay," he suggested. And then he nodded to himself. "I'll stay."

The winter man was focused on one of the many doorways on the far side of that vast central chamber and did not turn as he spoke. "That is probably wise."

"Fine. But we've seen all there is to see in here. Let's find somewhere else to rest. Somewhere with a door we can lock or barricade. If we're supposed to get to Perinthia, there are some things we're going to have to discuss."

"Agreed," Frost replied.

He lifted a hand and pointed a glistening, icy talon at the same door he had been studying before. It was at the top of a staircase sculpted from sand, an ordinary door—as much as any door could be ordinary in such a place—save that it hung slightly ajar.

"I have been here only once before, but I believe—"

From across that vast room came a noise like the surprised yelp of a dog. Oliver and the winter man reacted at the same time, twisting around and preparing to defend themselves. The sense of peril in this giant mausoleum was palpable. But the only thing moving in the castle was Kitsune. The lithe woman in her fox cloak leaped away from a small cluster of dead Sandmen and arched her back in the air. She landed on her hands and feet and quickly straightened up, eyes narrowed with suspicion, nostrils flaring as she stared at the dead creatures and then glanced at her companions.

"What is it?" Oliver asked, his voice low as he started cautiously toward her.

Kitsune paused a moment before taking several quick, almost delicate steps back toward whatever had alarmed her. She moved with a smooth grace that was not at all human, still sniffing the air.

"Something alive."

Oliver stared at the place where Kitsune had been, even as she stalked toward it again. Frost hurried to join her, though this revelation seemed to have made him all the more wary of their surroundings. Kitsune approached that cluster of dead Red Caps and dropped to all fours, her cloak sweeping the sandy floor. Her back arched as she crept nearer and then she simply stopped and raised one hand to point at something Oliver could not see.

The sunlight outside the windows dimmed, taking on a diffused golden hue. Oliver told himself that it was a cloud passing in front of the sun, but he felt his skin prickling with doubt. The wind died and in that moment it seemed the Sandmen's castle was an ancient tomb they had just unearthed, rather than the scene of a grisly slaughter that had occurred only hours earlier.

Frost paused a moment for one final glance around and then darted past Kitsune, who was on guard, and went to that cluster of bodies. Mist rose from his eyes and hands and when he reached for the nearest of the corpses, it crumbled at his touch, brittle as ancient papyrus. Oliver did not think it was from the cold. Frost scowled and shoved his hands beneath the remains, dragged the dead goblin out of the way.

"La Dormette," he said, his voice echoing around the chamber.

Then he was clearing away the other dead Red Caps. Kitsune darted over to help him. Oliver could not tell what they had found there in the death and shadows and so he went to join them. On the floor was a woman clad in snow white, somehow unblemished even in a place such as this. If it had not been for the elegance of her features he would have thought her a girl of nine or ten, so slight was she. Her hair was as white as her gown and her flesh the color of sand.

When Frost reached for her she whimpered and pulled her knees up to her chest. La Dormette had no visible injuries, yet her body spasmed every few seconds as though she were near death and she was either unable or unwilling to open her eyes.

"What is she?" Kitsune asked.

"La Dormette," Frost repeated. "An aspect of the legend of the Sandman. She was a nursery spirit for the children of France. The very opposite of her grim counterpart."

His features were carved from ice and yet there was empathy in his blue-white eyes as he gently touched the shoulder of La Dormette. Her spasms ceased and she became rigid, eyes pressed tightly shut, as though she waited for the killing blow to come.

"Take heart, cousin," the winter man whispered close to her ear, ice crystals forming in her hair. "You are not alone."

Kitsune drew her cloak and hood more tightly around her and her jade eyes gleamed from within. "Why would they leave her alive?"

Oliver felt a vicious twist in his gut, a terrible certainty. "She's Borderkind?"

"Of course," Frost replied, still preoccupied with concern for the injured myth.

"Shit!" Oliver rasped, glancing around the chamber, at the dead Sandmen and the shattered diamond prison, at the walls and windows and doors and the dimming sunlight. "They wouldn't, Frost! They've been set after you, all of you. They wouldn't leave her alive. Which means they haven't left. She's bait!"

Kitsune darted back toward the center of the chamber. Still, nothing moved but the wind and the sand that rasped across the floor. Oliver felt his throat go dry, and his muscles felt paralyzed. He forced himself to glance around and saw a shadow move across a window not far from the door through which they'd entered. This was not a cloud across the sun. This was something in motion.

Frost scooped La Dormette into his arms. But as he lifted her up, she screamed in agony, eyes snapping wide as she shook in the throes of death. Oliver gaped at the winter man and the tiny myth woman he held. Her left side, where she had been lying on the floor, was torn open, and sand spilled out as though from a broken hourglass. It was tinted red, a gritty dust of blood. On the floor, lodged into the hard-packed sand that was almost like concrete, were two long shards of diamond that she had been impaled upon.

The Hunters had started the job. Frost had unknowingly finished it.

"Dormette," the winter man said, voice heavy with regret.

"Kirata," she sighed as the last of her life spilled onto the floor.

Kitsune shouted at them both. Oliver barely heard her. He was staring at Frost and the lifeless myth in his arms. But their companion continued to call their names, to urge them to flee, and he finally tore his gaze away to look at her.

"We must go now," she said, and Oliver saw that she had no intention of leaving the way they had come in. Already she had moved toward the door at the far end of the chamber, the one that was partially open. The one that Frost had been staring at before.

Other shadows moved beyond the windows. First one and then another solidified into dark silhouettes, limned with orange from the sun that streamed around them.

"What the hell is Kirata?" he demanded, staring at Frost.

The winter man dropped the corpse of La Dormette and rushed at Oliver, grabbing his arm, ice numbing him to the bone.

"Run!" Frost commanded.

The advice was unnecessary. Oliver was already moving. In his privileged life he had experienced terror only in nightmares, hurtling headlong down dream corridors, breathless and beyond reason. But this was no dream.

Frost released him and then the two of them were running side by side. Oliver hopped over a shattered, withered Red Cap. Kitsune flitted across his field of vision just ahead, and beyond her he saw that slightly open door, the one that had fascinated both of the Borderkind since they had entered the castle. He risked a glance back and saw the Hunters leaping through the windows. They landed heavily, skidding on the hard-packed sand, and then let momentum carry them on. Sprinting toward the door and leaping over the Hunters' victims, he had only the briefest glimpses of them. Towering things, some on four legs and others on two, with massive shoulders and forearms. Shadows played across them and in the rush of his own flight and their pursuit it was difficult to make out their features, but they seemed to be cloaked much as Kitsune was, though their fur was a bright orange and black.

"Oliver!" the winter man shouted.

Too late.

He caught his foot on the papery corpse of a Sandman, boot crushing the husk even as he stumbled and fell to his knees. His heart clenched and he ceased breathing, certain that death was coming for him. With his free hand he pushed off the ground and he could feel it pounding with the stampede of the Kirata. The breeze brought a thick, animal stink and he nearly choked on the smell. As Oliver scrambled to his feet one of the things roared, a sound like the sky split with thunder, and the others joined in. He took a deep, terrible breath, filled with the aching, sorrowful certainty of his own death.

The steps to that open door beckoned, just ahead. Frost had stopped and now raced back toward him. Kitsune was on the stairs, hesitating. Oliver pistoned his legs, launching himself over another corpse and then throwing his entire body forward, sacrificing caution for speed. Off balance, he reached his arms out as though he might grab hold of something in front of him, some lifeline that could haul him from the grasp of the Kirata.

The winter man was fifteen feet away.

A Hunter slammed into him from behind, driving him to the ground. The heat and stink of the thing overwhelmed his senses. Utter, frenzied terror made Oliver twist and fight to escape the smothering weight of the beast. One heavy hand battered him, turning him onto his back, and then it slammed onto his chest, driving the breath from him, claws pricking his skin and drawing a trickle of warm blood.

Kirata. They did not wear robes. The fur was their own. From the name and the beast's face he was sure the legend was Asian, but he had never heard it before. They had the heads and upper bodies of Bengal tigers, orange fur striped with black, but their lower bodies seemed almost human. The Kirata's strength was terrible, and the vicious light in its eyes stole Oliver's last vestiges of hope. Its black lips pulled back from long, gleaming fangs and it roared, buffeting his face with rancid breath.

He dug his bootheels into the floor, trying to escape the deadly weight of the thing. It roared again and raised its other paw, claws out. But its fangs had his attention. One of them was missing. He felt the smoothness of it in the palm of his hand.

Oliver let out a primal, guttural scream as he drove that fang into the throat of the Kirata. It roared in pain and twisted back and away from him, and then he was free. But the others were there, nine or ten of them, stalking toward him.

The winter man appeared at his side, shouting at him to stand. One of the Kirata lunged and Frost lashed out with his left hand, driving the icy daggers of his fingers into the monster's abdomen, impaling him. The moisture in the tiger-man's body froze, his eyes icing over and crystals forming on his fur. The Kirata fell to the sand, dead or dying.

Something leaped over Oliver from behind, a streak of

fiery crimson. Scrabbling backward, afraid it was another Hunter, he jumped to his feet. His weapon still jutted from the throat of the first tiger-man and his hands clutched uselessly at the air. The thing that had jumped him crouched, seemed to brace itself there, and barked a warning at the advancing Kirata.

It was a fox. A single, ordinary fox.

When it glanced back at him, he recognized her jade eyes.

"Oliver, move! There isn't enough moisture in the air for me to hold them off very long!" Frost shouted, even as he extended his frozen talons and raked the chest of the nearest Kirata. A frigid wind began to whip around them all.

Kitsune the fox darted past one of the tiger-men and sprang up, transforming in mid-leap to the exotic woman he had first encountered. Her red-fur hood flew back as she sank her teeth into the tiger's neck and tore.

Oliver ran up the steps, momentum nearly causing him to fall again. He caught himself on a gritty railing of hard-packed sand and then he was at the top and the door was just a few feet away. It swayed in the winter wind Frost had crafted and the change in air pressure began to swing it closed.

"No!" he shouted, and lunged, hitting the door with both hands, banging it open wide.

Kitsune darted up beside him and wrapped her arms around him. He had crossed the threshold and she pulled him back. For just a moment Oliver resisted but then he let himself go, let her supple strength take him away from salvation.

She shifted so that she was beside him and she reached toward the doorway. The darkened corridor beyond wavered out of focus and Oliver squinted, unable to look directly at the flux in the air.

"Now we go," Kitsune growled, and she propelled him through the door with her. There was a momentary feeling of resistance, like walking into water, and then they were through.

The town center was astonishing, like a thing from a postcard half a century old. Oliver felt as though he had stumbled into Bedford Falls, the little town from *It's a Wonderful Life*. He and Kitsune had emerged in the middle of an enormous park in the middle of the snow-covered town. To one side was a picturesque train station with a genuine steam train puffing at the platform, awaiting passengers. To the other was a two-lane street with an old-fashioned movie palace, restaurants, a ski shop, a bakery, and a few clothing stores. Everywhere the trees were strung with a rainbow of Christmas lights that blinked warmly in the night. Giant wreaths were hung on each telephone pole along the street.

It was so utterly perfect a picture of Christmastime in New England that Oliver shook his head, not believing it. The little town square seemed even more unreal to him than the world beyond the Veil.

Shouts and laughter came to him through the trees and he caught sight of children playing in the park, hurling snowballs on the run and pelting them at one another. Beyond them, straight ahead, something yellow gleamed in the dark, low to the ground.

"Oliver. We should move on."

Her voice sent a shudder through him. When he looked into Kitsune's eyes he could only think of the fox he had seen. He would not even ask the question, for the answer was so obvious. Of course it was her. In the world of possibility he had discovered, it was the only reasonable answer. Her cloak was real fox fur, of course. Her fur, somehow. He remembered the press of her body against him as she had dragged him back from the doorway, forcing him to go through with her so that he would be able to make the border crossing, and the recollection of the feeling of her melded to him sent an electric tingle through his body. Her touch was sensual, even in the midst of danger. He wondered if it was part of the magic of her legend, or simply his reaction to her. Or perhaps—

"Oh," he said. "The border . . . Frost."

The winter man had defended their escape. Now Oliver spun to look for the door they had come through, but saw only the park and the trees and snow two and a half feet deep. Past that was an old brick building that he imagined was a school or courthouse or City Hall, or maybe all three of those put together. The Maine state flag flew beside the Stars and Stripes, so that answered some questions.

But . . . no door.

He turned to Kitsune, her expression hidden beneath her hood. "We have to go back for him."

A sudden gust of wind swirled up beside him, raising a cloud of snow. *I am here, Oliver.*

"Frost," Kitsune said with a smile that showed her oddly sharp teeth.

Oliver stared at the place where the wind and snow had danced. "You made it," he said. "But why are you like this? Can't you—"

Branches shifted in the large pine tree he and Kitsune were standing beneath. New-fallen snow showered down upon them, and in the snow, he heard Frost's voice again.

"*Of course. It is simply better to be with the winter, with the storm. It would be foolish of me to appear in my true state in a public park in the midst of a town.*"

"All right." Oliver nodded, rubbing his hands together for warmth. He needed a jacket. "Where to, then?"

"Another place where we might cross the border, but not too near to this one. We must be gone from here quickly, in case they should find a Door."

"So, wait, that wasn't a Door?"

Kitsune arched an eyebrow. "We passed through a door, but it was not a *Door*. Not the sort that you mean."

Oliver only stared at her.

She laughed softly. "There was a Borderkind portal on the other side of that door. The Sandman had created it, and not very long before. Frost and I both sensed it when we first came into the castle." All trace of amusement left her face then, leaving only a grave wariness behind. "When a Borderkind makes a crossing, it leaves a trace that others of our kind may follow. The trace dissipates in time, but we discovered it quickly enough."

Oliver felt a chill ripple through him. "So, wait, you're telling me he's here? The Sandman?"

Images of the horror they had described flashed through his head.

Kitsune tilted her head. "Perhaps. Or he was. Regardless, we must move quickly and be far from here if the Hunters should find a Door and try to catch up with us."

He tried to focus on that, on the next step. Getting out of here. If their journey beyond the Veil corresponded at all to their presence in this world, they were in far eastern Maine, probably not too far from Canada. If the Hunters came, they would begin tracking at this spot, so it was best to be as inconspicuous as possible. Kitsune wasn't made from ice, but a startlingly beautiful Asian woman in a fox fur cloak was not going to go unnoticed in a place like this. They were going to draw attention. He only hoped that the Myth Hunters would be as reluctant as Frost was to have direct contact with people.

Snow swirled around his feet.

"Hurry," Frost whispered.

"Going," Oliver replied. He glanced around again and decided to head toward the children and their snowball fight. There were bound to be adults there as well, and cars. And a parking lot. If there was a place to rent cars in this town, he had to assume they would not be open, but if they were lucky, perhaps there would be a taxi stand right here in the downtown. He did not relish the idea of becoming a car thief.

"We need transportation, and I need a jacket. Not to mention a phone."

Kitsune hurried through the park at his side, but at his mention of a phone she grabbed his wrist. "You cannot go home. You know this. They will find you there within hours."

"I know that," Oliver said. "It may take me a while to learn, but I'm not a fool. I can't go home, but that doesn't mean I can't call to tell them I'm all right. I was . . ."

Supposed to be married, he thought, and realized it had been hours since he had given Julianna and their wedding a moment's thought. Still, he knew she must have been brokenhearted and his father must be furious. He found it impossible to care if the old man was angry, but Julianna hadn't deserved this.

Oliver linked arms with Kitsune as if they were a couple out for a stroll in the park. He was surprised to see that there were only a few kids throwing snowballs and that the park seemed otherwise empty, save for a few people walking dogs.

Then he saw the skating rink, and he understood that the yellow flash he had seen before was the police tape that had been set up around its entire circumference. In the parking lot beyond the rink were several police cars, and four uniformed officers stood in a conversational cluster, clutching what must be cups of coffee in their hands.

"Hey, kid," he called to the nearest, a boy of fourteen or so whose face was bright with cold and exertion.

"Yeah?" the kid replied doubtfully, packing a fresh snowball in his gloves. His eyes scanned Kitsune, obviously impressed, and then he glanced at Oliver, perhaps trying to figure out what the two of them were doing together.

"What happened? What are all those cops doing here?"

A flicker of suspicion crossed the boy's face. "You seriously don't know?"

"We just got here," Oliver replied, shuffling closer to Kitsune to bolster the image of them as a tourist couple. "On vacation."

The teenager looked around, his ruddy cheeks not quite so red now. He seemed to want to be sure he was not overheard. Then his mouth stretched into an unpleasant grin.

"Some guy . . . some nut, right? Shows up in the park, walks right out onto the rink while people were skating, grabs this girl, and . . ." All the mischief went out of him as he realized his amusement was inappropriate. The kid shrugged. "He killed her. Right there in front of everyone. Right on the ice. People tried to stop him but he took off into the trees and they lost him. Shouldn't have, right? I mean, where the hell can you run in a town like this? There were a bunch of people around. No way he could've gotten out of the square without someone seeing him. You'd think, anyway."

Oliver shivered and crossed his arms, trying to warm himself from the cold that touched him now within as well as without. "The girl who was killed. She was pretty young?"

"Yeah, really terrible."

Kitsune moved nearer to him, lowering her hood. The kid was almost mesmerized by her nearness. "He removed her eyes, correct? That is how she died?"

"Yeah," the teenager said, nodding as though lost in an unpleasant dream.

The wind blew a flurry around their heads. "*The Sandman,*" Frost whispered.

Oliver did not have to ask for elaboration this time. The Sandman had taken his first child in centuries. And there would be more. He knew there was nothing he could do. That he couldn't stay, or the Hunters would catch up with him and his companions. But the urge was there to do something, to help, somehow.

Kitsune pulled at his arm and Oliver started away from the kid. But this was a bad idea. They were headed right for the police, two strangers walking out of a park where a horrible murder had occurred what must have been only hours earlier. And Oliver without a coat. They were going to notice him for sure. Talk to him. And if they became suspicious and wanted to speak to them in a more official capacity, that would mean they would be doing little more than sitting around waiting for the Hunters to come.

"This way," he said, turning toward the train station. The steam engine was still puffing in the station. No one used steam trains anymore, so he assumed it was some kind of local attraction. That didn't matter, as long as it would get them out of the center of town without running into the police. The forest around the town was probably state-owned. If he understood the laws of the magic used to create the Veil, that would be sufficiently public for the Borderkind to cross.

The station looked as though it ought to have been in the English countryside, not some quaint village in Maine. Smoke rose from fireplaces at either end. As they crossed the park toward the lot in front of the station, he could see people in line inside the well-lit building, but the line was moving, people boarding the train.

This is good. This will work.

"Hey!" a voice called. The kid with the snowball.

Oliver and Kitsune walked faster. Whatever mesmerizing effect her presence had, it clearly did not last.

"Hey, how did you know that? About Alice's eyes?" the kid called. "How did you guys know that?"

With a silent curse Oliver glanced toward the quartet of cops. All four of them had turned to see what the yelling was about. The question was whether or not they could make out the kid's words from that distance. Their reaction was gradual, one of them starting into the park, the others taking a few steps to peer at Oliver and Kitsune, but they were moving. They had heard. One of the cops went to the nearest police car and ducked inside, reaching for the radio handset.

The other three set off on a diagonal route across the park toward the train station. The kid kept calling after them, but now one of the cops—the first to have moved—began shouting as well. There was a hesitation in him and the other two, for they still held their coffee cups. Walking fast, but not running. Curious and guarded, but not alarmed. Not yet.

Oliver and Kitsune ignored them.

Police officers do not like to be ignored.

The one in front was the first to drop his coffee cup and start really moving. The other two followed suit. Oliver snatched up Kitsune's hand and began to run. For the second time in minutes, in two different worlds, they ran up a short set of stairs toward a door. Even as he grabbed hold of the handle and hauled it open, he could see that the last of the line had disappeared from inside the station, going out onto the platform to board the train.

Its whistle blew and steam blasted into the December night. People cheered. Oliver and Kitsune ran through the station. A woman at the ticket counter shouted at them not to run. An old man in a blue uniform warned them that they would need tickets if they wanted to get on the train.

As he pushed through the back door and out onto the platform, Oliver looked back. The cops were just coming through the front door and not one of them hesitated. Their eyes locked on him. The officer who had been first to react at every step reached down and released the strap holding his service weapon in its holster.

"Fuck," Oliver snarled.

A family of five were just beside them. The oldest girl gaped at him with obvious surprise while the mother glanced down at their toddler to make sure the word hadn't registered on the boy's ears. The father glared at Oliver with utter contempt.

"What's wrong with you?" the man demanded.

Kitsune went past him as though he wasn't even there, and Oliver followed suit. There were many more people than he'd imagined, all of them jockeying to be next onto the train. Most of them had coffee or hot cocoa and every other adult had a backpack or shoulder bag. He and Kitsune began to weave amongst them as quickly as they could, bumping their way through when they had to. They were cursed and derided and one man gave Oliver a shove, but it only propelled him in the direction he wanted to go, toward the front of the train.

But they were still on the platform. The train was still steaming, but it wasn't moving. People were still getting on board.

"This isn't going to work," he said through gritted teeth, glancing back to see the police sliding through the crowd. People got out of the way for the cops, especially when they looked serious, as these men did. Oliver understood that. He would be equally grim in the aftermath of a little girl's vicious murder. He wished he could stop and explain himself to them.

As if he could have explained anything at all.

They were nearing the engine. Steam churned out from beneath it, making the winter air warm and damp.

"What the hell are we going to do?" he asked Kitsune. She gripped his arm. "Hurry."

The steam from beneath the train turned cold and he realized the wind had kicked up. Snow swirled up from the platform. A powerful gust propelled them forward. He had meant for them to board the train, to escape that way, but they were out of time. Kitsune began to run, and Oliver kept pace with her.

"Stop! Police officers! Stop where you are and turn—"

The rest of their commands were drowned out by the scream of the winter wind that drove at Oliver's back, and a moment later they reached the edge of the platform. Kitsune was two steps ahead of him and he saw her jump. Knowing there was no other course, he followed suit, leaping off the edge of the concrete slab and landing in three feet of snow. But the police would not hesitate to come after them. He glanced around, saw that they were nearly at the front of the engine, and then he realized that this had been Kitsune's intention.

They ran through the snow, kicking the white stuff into a kind of cloud around them with every slogging step. The police were still shouting. One of them jumped down and Oliver was sure it would be the same man—the first to follow them, the first to drop his coffee, the first through the door.

"Faster!" Kitsune shouted, and when she took his hand it seemed to him that he did move a bit faster, that he was more agile. It might have been his imagination, or perhaps just the urgency of her touch, her power to influence.

Her cloak flowed out behind her in the snow.

Snow.

It was not just being thrown about by the wind now. The December night had been clear and full of brilliant stars, but now the firmament was obscured by heavy gray winter and snow had started to fall from the sky.

They rounded the front of the engine. In the bright lights of the cab they could see the silhouette of the driver.

The snow was even deeper on the other side of the railroad tracks and beyond them there was only woods. Lovely, dark, and deep. The cops kept shouting but their voices were muffled by the night and the storm.

As Oliver and Kitsune ran toward the woods, the wind struck them like a hurricane and the night was a blizzard, a complete whiteout, as though they were surrounded by a wall of snow that erupted from the ground and poured down out of the sky. The cold cut into Oliver and he could not move. Kitsune grabbed hold of him, wrapped him in her arms, her cloak enfolding him, and he felt the warmth of her fur.

And then the storm took them up in a cradle of snow and gale, and carried them away. Tossed in the night upon the wind and covered in snow, Oliver had never been so cold. He kept his eyes tightly shut, feeling Kitsune against him, and gave himself over to the winter man and the blizzard, wondering if he would ever be warm again.

CHAPTER 7

In recent years, sleep had been a reluctant visitor to the home of Ted Halliwell. Not, perhaps, so reluctant as his daughter, but near enough. Oh, he drifted off easily enough. Most nights he fell asleep during the eleven o'clock news, right between the weather and the sports, but by half-past two he would be wide-awake and staring at the ceiling or at the gauzy, dusty curtain that hung across his window, draping his view of the darkness and the stars. What happened in those lonely hours was not something upon which he liked to dwell. Truth be told, however, Halliwell saw ghosts in the wee hours of the morning, phantom shades of people who were not dead, but simply gone. The ghosts of his wife and daughter visited him as the night rolled toward dawn. He would gaze about the room at wisps of memory, of Jocelyn ironing in front of the television, of Sara using the bed as a trampoline, of lovemaking and Christmas morning and spring cleaning.

As the sky would begin to lighten, he often managed to tumble back into an uneasy slumber for an hour or two. Most nights he did not manage more than four hours of sleep in total. Halliwell had realized long ago that his house was haunted, but that he himself was the spirit wandering its halls. In so many ways, he was a ghost. There were days when he felt trapped in that house, just as if he were damned to haunt it forever, and other days when he felt free to leave and could not get out of there quickly enough to suit him.

On Monday morning, the day after he had been sent on a fool's errand by Max Bascombe, the sheriff woke Halliwell shortly after eight A.M. with a phone call.

"Hello?"

"Ted, it's Jackson."

"I'm not due in till two o'clock, Sheriff." Halliwell felt at home with the Wessex County sheriff's department. It wasn't the big leagues, not by a long shot, but it was real work with honest men and women who cared about the law. As comfortable as he was, though, he was not normally so abrupt with Jackson Norris. The man had hired him and told him often how grateful he was to have Halliwell around, but that didn't make them brothers, or even friends.

Ted Halliwell had played gofer for Max Bascombe yesterday on the sheriff's behalf, and it left a bad taste in his mouth. Waking up to the ringing of his phone after only a few hours' sleep had also put him on edge. If Jackson Norris was bothered by Halliwell's tone, he didn't let on.

"I'm aware of that, Ted. Sorry to say, your day's going to start earlier than you planned."

Something in the man's voice made Halliwell frown and sit up in bed. "What've we got?"

"Max Bascombe is dead. Murdered. The Kitteridge boys are following up right now, but it looks like the daughter is missing."

Halliwell swore, massaging the bridge of his nose. The heat had been working overtime during the night and the air in the house was so dry it had given him a headache.

"Is she a victim or a suspect?"

"That's what I want you to find out," the sheriff replied.

"Won't Kitteridge P.D. feel like we're stepping on their toes?"

"Stomp away, Ted. I'm going to have Bascombe's firm breathing down my neck. They have this impression that I owe them, and maybe I do. I can't afford to have them as enemies. I assured Bascombe that you were the best around, and now they're going to want you. Kitteridge P.D.'s idea of detective work is finding a stolen bike or filling out burglary reports so people can file their insurance claims. Now, get on over there before they've screwed the crime scene so badly that you can't get anything out of it."

The vote of confidence might have been genuine, but it sounded hollow. The sheriff needed him; that was the bottom line. And even if Halliwell was the best around, it was faint praise. It wasn't as though every department in the state had Holmes and Watson working homicide.

"On my way," he said, and hung up the phone.

Twenty-two minutes later he was on his way to Kitteridge. Snowdrifts were ten feet high in some places, and the mounds made by the plows were even higher. A supermarket parking lot had a mountain of white stuff right in the middle. They had nowhere else to put it. Some towns had managed to clear the sidewalks so local kids could go to school, but others had not quite gotten the job done.

When he arrived at Rose Ridge Lane he found two police cars blocking off the end of the Bascombes' driveway. The men standing sentry there were in uniform. Only one of them was familiar to him, a broad-shouldered, thick-necked cop with a crew cut who would have looked far more at home in a state trooper's uniform. His name was James Bonaventure, and he was the nephew of Kitteridge's chief.

"Detective Halliwell," Bonaventure said as Ted pulled up and held his I.D. out the window.

"Jimmy. Hell of a thing, isn't it?"

The cop nodded grimly. "Haven't even seen it, but from what I hear, I don't think I want to."

The other officer watched this exchange with curious eyes and a strange kind of disapproval. Whatever he'd heard about the rivalry between the local cops and the sheriff's department, it wasn't jibing with the friendly tone here.

"Want to let me by?"

Bonaventure smiled. "There a reason the county's interested?"

Halliwell did not return the smile. "Already my case, Jimmy. I spent all day yesterday looking into the disappearance of the DOA's son. Now the man himself turns up dead? The Wessex D.A. and the sheriff are going to want a hand in figuring out what happened here."

"All right, all right," Bonaventure said, holding up a hand to tell him to relax. "Don't have to get all righteous with me, Detective. I was just busting your balls. Tell you the truth, I think the chief's expecting you anyway. Someone with Bascombe's influence gets taken out like this, a lot of people are going to want to know how and why."

They moved the cars to let him through and by the time he reached the house at the end of that long, snow-walled drive, Chief Peyton Bonaventure was waiting for him in front of the Bascombe house. Halliwell waved as he pulled up behind the last of the police cars lined up in front of the house. There was a black van from the medical examiner's office and one other civilian vehicle, a sporty little Geo that he was damn sure didn't belong to anyone with the last name of Bascombe.

As he climbed out of his car, Halliwell felt oddly claustrophobic. There was something wrong with that, feeling more cooped up once he'd gotten out of his stuffy car than when he'd been in it. He took a deep breath and tried to brush off that strange weight, the oppressiveness of the moment. It was cold, the wind bitter, but the sun shone and the sky was a clear, crisp winter blue. He should have felt relieved to stretch his legs, to breathe fresh air. But somehow he could not manage it.

"Jimmy radioed you I was coming up?" he asked the chief.

Peyton Bonaventure smiled humorlessly. "Yep. Nice that *someone* let me know you were coming."

Halliwell took a deep breath and regarded the man evenly. "I had to play nice and diplomatic with Max Bascombe and his 'people' all day yesterday, Peyton. I'd like to think that you were above politics."

"As opposed to Sheriff Norris," the chief jabbed.

"Is that the way it's going to be?" Halliwell asked, disappointed.

"Nope." Peyton shrugged. "Just had to get that one in. You're welcome to come in and have a look around, Ted. Though I don't know what you're going to find. The care-taker or whatever he is, Mr. Friedle, told me about the whole wedding fiasco yesterday, the son disappearing. Got to figure he came back, right? Maybe the sister helped him, or maybe he did her, too, and threw the body off the bluff."

Halliwell nodded noncommittally. "Got to figure."

But he wasn't so sure. There were a lot of things that did not make sense to him and had not made any sense from the time he had arrived here on Rose Ridge Lane yes-terday afternoon. Collette Bascombe had not been angry at her brother for leaving his bride at the altar, she had been *afraid* for him, and dead certain he would not have just taken off without at least explaining things to his fiancée. Then there was the business of Oliver Bascombe's car. It had still been in the garage, and with the snow, there was no way that anyone had driven onto or off the property. So wherever Oliver had gone, he had been on foot. Unless someone had been waiting out on Rose Ridge Lane in the middle of a blizzard, with roads barely passable, to spirit him away. But Halliwell himself had followed up with the younger Bascombe's friends and come up with nothing.

It was a puzzle.

And now it had several new and vicious pieces.

Chief Bonaventure walked him inside. A pair of Kit-teridge detectives were still interviewing Friedle in the room off to the left, the same place Halliwell himself had met with Max Bascombe the day before. He gave them a nod of greeting but Friedle thought it was meant for him and shot back a hopeful look, as though he thought the sheriff's detective might rescue him from the scrutiny of the local boys. That was not going to happen. As far as

Halliwell was concerned, it was more than likely all three Bascombes were dead, and to his mind that would make Friedle a suspect, no matter what kind of alibi he might have.

Upstairs, they found Becca Green from the M.E.'s office still working on the victim's bedroom. Halliwell was relieved to see both Becca and the covered body of the victim through the open door. This is where the investigation would really begin. If anyone would have learned anything significant, it would be Becca. The chief rapped on the door frame and she looked up from scraping a sample of something viscous from the floor.

"Well, well, the gang's all here," Becca said with a wan smile. She was a small woman, no more than five feet, with an olive complexion and thick black hair. Taken individually, none of her features would have been considered admirable, but there was certainly something attractive about the whole. Halliwell thought perhaps it was the intelligence that sparkled in her eyes, or the mischief in her lopsided smile. He had no interest in Becca Green romantically—he figured that part of him was dead, or at least retired—but he admired the hell out of her.

"I see you kept Mr. Bascombe around for company," Halliwell said, gruff as ever. No matter how highly he regarded Becca Green, he had an image to maintain.

"He's a fascinating conversationalist. Much like yourself."

Chief Bonaventure sighed. "You two ought to take this show on the road."

"With or without the corpse?" Becca asked. Then she shifted gears, turning all business. "You want the rundown?"

Halliwell nodded. "Please."

Becca turned to survey the room. "I've got squat, actually. The chief will confirm no forced entry—"

Which means maybe the killer had a key, Halliwell thought.

"—and while there's sign of a limited struggle, there are no signs of a fight. Whoever killed Mr. Bascombe overpowered him almost immediately and was strong enough to hold him off the ground, presumably with one hand—"

"Whoa! Hold on, there," the chief said, actually holding up a hand to stall her report. "Where do you get that idea?"

But Halliwell was already looking at the floor and the rug. He saw the numbered markers that Becca had laid and was working it out in his own head.

"Marks on the rug from his feet. Blood spatter on rug and the wood as well," he said. Becca nodded in confirmation. "That tells you where he was and that his feet weren't on the carpet at the time of his death . . . but Becca, I've met Max Bascombe. This was a big man. I don't think I could hold him up more than a few seconds with both hands, never mind just one."

Which left out Collette as a suspect for certain, as well as Friedle, but not necessarily Oliver. Halliwell had never met Oliver Bascombe. He didn't know how strong the younger lawyer was.

"And where do you get the one-hand bit? What makes you say that?"

Becca looked at him grimly and raised the small tube she had just capped, into which she had placed the sample she had taken from the floor. "This, if I'm not mistaken, is vitreous fluid. From the victim's eyes. The perp was holding Bascombe off the floor when he ripped out his eyes."

Halliwell felt his pulse throbbing in his ears. His mouth

was open only slightly and he knew he was gaping like an idiot but could not help himself. He knitted his brows. Then he glanced past Becca to the thick shroud that covered the corpse, which was just waiting for the body bag that Becca would bring up from her van shortly. Ted walked over to Max Bascombe's body, careful to step around the areas with evidence markers, and drew back the shroud that covered it.

The man's eyes were gone, leaving only raw pits crusted with black-red blood.

"Cause of death is cardiac arrest. Trauma of the injuries gave him a heart attack."

"And his eyes?"

"Not here," Becca replied.

Halliwell let the sheet drop and took a deep breath. What the hell had he gotten himself into? His mind began to pursue every possible avenue. Last night he had begun to wonder if Oliver Bascombe had thrown himself off the bluff in the middle of the blizzard, or gotten drunk and walked off accidentally, snowblind. But now he was certain that was not the case. He wondered if, somehow, Oliver had never left at all, had hidden away waiting for the opportunity to do this. The pieces didn't all fit in his head, but at least it was a shape that had a certain logic to it. A rationale. And any kind of rationality was helpful at the moment.

Then he remembered the look on Collette Bascombe's face. Her sincerity and sureness.

"Tell me about the sister, Peyton," he said. "Any sign of foul play there?"

"Nothing," Chief Bonaventure replied. "She's just gone."

Like her brother. Halliwell felt something unpleasant niggling at the back of his brain.

"But her car is still in the garage, isn't it?"

The chief frowned and nodded. "Yes. But we figured her for a victim, Ted. Nobody's thinking the girl drove away from here."

No, Halliwell thought. *But her brother didn't drive away, either.*

"What about clothes? She take anything with her?"

"Far as we can tell, she was in her bathrobe."

Halliwell stared at Max Bascombe's corpse. The man had had wealth and power and kept himself remarkably, obsessively healthy. Halliwell had thought him a hard-ass son of a bitch, but nobody deserved to die like this.

"You've got A.P.B.s out on Oliver and Collette?" he asked.

"Statewide," Chief Bonaventure replied.

"All right. Let's see what turns up," Halliwell said, nodding slowly. "If he's still alive, I would dearly love to have a conversation with Oliver Bascombe."

He stared at the shrouded body on the floor, sure that even covered that way, even without eyes, the dead man was staring back.

Kitsune hardly left any tracks in the snow at all. Throughout the morning as they trekked northward through the forest in calf-deep snow, Oliver was drawn again and again to that observation. She seemed to walk on top of the snow, the only marks left by her passing a faint, indistinct impression and the occasional brush of her cloak on the new-fallen whiteness.

The memory of being carried away in the blizzard

Frost had become still left him breathless. The winter man was intimidating under ordinary conditions, able to alter the shape of his body and to control the moisture in the air around him to a certain extent, but in wintry weather, his power was simply extraordinary. He was not invulnerable; the Falconer had proved that. But in the cold and the snow, Frost was more than formidable.

Not that such exertion was effortless. To create that blizzard and to rescue them had sapped much of his strength. Fortunately, the snowy weather and the cold were restoring him quickly.

They had been walking for hours in what Oliver presumed was a state forest, though which one he had no idea. The previous night he had been unable to determine the name of the town into which they had emerged. This morning he was not overly concerned with their location, only that they continued moving northward and that they remained within the boundaries of the state forest.

The lands on the other side of the Veil corresponded with public space on this side, old space, owned by no human and unused, unspoiled and free. Public parks and state forests, open wilderness and the ocean itself. Such free land was tied inextricably to the wildness of the magic that had not only created the Veil but infused all of the legendary beings who resided on the other side.

With the greedy sprawl of humanity, there was less and less of this land as time went by. Oliver wondered what this meant for the people of the Two Kingdoms, but that was one of a thousand questions he had for his companions and he supposed he would learn all he needed to know eventually. One question at a time.

They kept on through the forest, trudging in the snow.

When they finally did cross back through the Veil, he wanted to be sure they had put some real distance between themselves and the Sandmen's castle.

His muscles burned with the effort of slogging through the snow and his feet were wet and cold. The boots were waterproof, but that didn't prevent snow from sliding down inside them and melting. What surprised him was how capable he was of accepting such discomfort. As children he and Collette had played in the snow for hours upon end and endured winds and temperatures that would have put them moments from serious frostbite, all without complaint. But as they had become adults, the resilience of childhood had left them. Or so Oliver had believed. Apparently, he was made of sterner stuff than he had come to imagine. It helped, of course, that the day was the warmest the region had seen in weeks—forty-five, at least—and the sun shone down amidst the bare winter branches and proud evergreens.

It was nothing short of a miracle to feel warm again. In the grip of the blizzard that the winter man had summoned to carry them away from the police, the cold had seemed all he would ever know. His mind had been muffled and numb, darkness closing in at the edges of his consciousness. Frost had swept Oliver and Kitsune away and into the woods, but even when they came to rest, it had taken long minutes for Oliver to shake off the chill that had dulled his thoughts and senses. He had his boots but no jacket—it had been left behind at the lake when he had first crossed the Veil—and his shirt was no protection from the elements.

Kitsune had been the one to find the cabin. Her senses were not at all human. They had struck out on a northerly course from the moment Oliver could manage to walk on his own, moving quietly through the woods until they were well outside the main area of town. Soon enough she was sniffing the air, and had located a small lake on the shore of which were spread half a dozen hunting cabins. Only one of them was occupied and enough distance separated them that it was half a mile from the most remote structure. That was the one they chose.

It had been all of the things he would have imagined of a real rustic cabin. There were two woodstoves but no other heat source, no electricity, and no running water. Instead of a stove, some enterprising and daring individual had rigged a barbecue grill with a propane tank just outside the rear door of the three-room cabin. It was crude as hell.

But there were beds and blankets and cans of deviled ham and SpaghettiOs in the cupboard. In a bureau, Oliver had found several sweaters and two old pairs of pants, and in the closet of the same room, a torn winter parka that must have been thirty years old. When he had slipped it on and found that it fit him, he laughed out loud with pleasure and relief.

Kitsune had woken him at dawn, the sensual scent of her musk filling the close air of the cabin's shuttered interior. Her jade eyes had glowed in the dim morning light filtering through the window. There had been no real conversation. Oliver had breakfasted on deviled ham and taken the last of the cupboard's old supplies—two cans of SpaghettiOs—and the can opener, and slipped them into the pockets of the musty-smelling parka. He'd gone out the back door of the cabin to piss in the woods, wondering where Frost had spent the night, and then they had set off.

Hours had passed. Oliver figured it was still morning, but based upon the position of the sun in the sky, it was sliding on toward noon. They had trudged for miles—or, rather, he had trudged while the other two moved through the snow without any difficulty whatsoever. A while back, as the day had grown warmer and the snow began to melt, he had removed his parka and now carried it slung over one shoulder. His feet were still cold and numb but his face and hands were warm enough and his body was heated by the exertion.

Every hour or so they paused to let Oliver catch his breath and lean against a tree for a few minutes, but he could see the restlessness of his companions. A dozen times he thought to press them on the source of that anxiety, but he was consumed by his own concerns and left them to speak in their own time.

Memories of his home haunted him. The scents and sounds and comfort of the house on Rose Ridge Lane accompanied him on that journey through the woods of northern Maine. Melting snow dripped off skeletal branches and the needles of pine trees, glistening in the sun, and he remembered a lifetime of Decembers in the house on the oceanside bluff in Kitteridge. In particular, his mind went back again and again to his mother's parlor, before the blizzard and the winter man. He thought of Christmas lights and gauzy, sepia-toned memories of his mother.

How could it be that his memories had more heft and substance and immediacy to him than the events of the past two days? Yet it was true. The world beyond the Veil had crystallized in his mind and he accepted the reality of it. It was fantastic, without question, but there was nothing dreamlike about his experiences there. He had felt the roughness of the terrain, the texture of things there: tree bark, the grit of the Sandmen's castle, the scratch of branches as he moved through the forest.

Now he was in his own world. The *real* world. He was still a target, still hunted, just as if he himself were one of the Borderkind, so he knew the danger involved in attempting to stay behind. Oliver had no choice but to forge ahead. The regret, the longing to stay here in the world he knew and understood, was sharp and profound. Though he relished the recent collision of his life with the extraordinary and the impossible, this exposure to the familiar made him hesitate.

Despite all of that, the world seemed surreal. The events of the previous night with the skating rink and the train station, with the murder of a little girl and their flight from the police, felt as though they had happened to someone else. It was one thing for him to pass through the Veil and witness the wonders there, but entirely another to be wandering the north woods on a December morning with an exotic shape-shifter and Jack Frost.

So he held on to those memories of his hometown and the house where he had grown up. As distant as they felt from him now, they were all that seemed real. And he needed that.

The longer they walked, the less real it all seemed to him. The forest was pristine with the recent snowfall, the sky a perfect blue. The colors were so rich and the air so pure that Oliver felt as though this was the world of magic and myth, that there was really little difference between what he knew and what existed beyond the Veil. As if he could pass through to the other side just by looking out the corner of his eye, by stepping at a certain angle past an ancient tree.

As tired as he was, it was not the ache in his legs that brought him to a stop this time. Kitsune was far enough ahead that he could only make out the shape of her, crouched upon the snow, and the sunlight on her bright orange-red fur. He could not have said, in that moment, whether she wore the form of woman or fox, and understood that it did not matter.

The winter man's blue-white eyes had been distant throughout the morning. Now he seemed to sense something beyond exhaustion in Oliver, for he tilted his head, icicles of hair cascading to one side with a strange December music, and studied his friend.

Friend. What a strange word. Oliver wondered if he and Frost truly were friends, or if only the debt between them kept the winter man at his side. He found he preferred not having an answer to the question.

"Are you all right?" Frost asked.

Oliver leaned against the nearest tree and put his head back against rough bark, dropping his parka on the snow. The question was vast, the possible answers infinite. But he knew Frost was not asking about his general well-being.

"I'm going to need a longer rest soon," he admitted, rasping his palms across the stubble on his cheeks, the friction connecting him more to the present and stealing him away from his musing.

"It should be safe to make a border-crossing now," the winter man replied. "It will be warmer there. And by now the Hunters have made their way to the village we visited last night and will be pursuing us here. If the Falconer is among them, they will have no trouble tracking us. If we are to stop for any length of time, it would be best to be on the other side of the Veil."

When the sun hit him at a particular angle, Frost was partially translucent. Oliver found it difficult not to stare at the beauty of it.

"Sounds logical," he replied, but his thoughts were elsewhere. With a frown he ran his fingers through his hair and held his arms against the sides of his head, mind going back to the skating rink from the night before and the yellow police tape roping it off from the rest of the park.

"What troubles you, Oliver?"

He glanced up at Frost. "At the moment?"

The winter man nodded.

"The Sandman." Oliver studied him. "He's here, somewhere. Murdered that little girl last night. The police up here aren't going to know how to contend with that. How can they, when they have no idea what they're up against?"

Frost took a deep breath and let it out in a plume of cool mist. "I see. You feel your knowledge makes you somehow responsible. That you have an obligation to stay. To help."

"Something like that."

"But you know the police would never believe you. And if you found yourself in the path of the Sandman, he would have your eyes. You know that even now the Hunters are searching for you."

Oliver knocked his head against the tree again. "Yeah. But it just feels wrong. We're talking about children here. There are going to be others."

"Perhaps," Frost allowed, those blue-white eyes clear and unforgiving. "Yet you have no reason to believe the Sandman will stay in this world. He has been a prisoner for a very long time. Predicting his actions now would be impossible. Even if he does stay on this side of the Veil, he isn't likely to linger in this particular area. If we were free to pursue him, I would join you in that quest. Perhaps it will come to pass. But at the moment all of our efforts must be dedicated to removing the sword of Damocles that dangles above our heads."

The reference was unfamiliar but Oliver understood the intent. Reluctantly, he nodded. "I get it. I never had any illusions that we had a choice in this. That doesn't make me feel any better."

A silence descended between them, broken only by the sound of melted snow dripping from the trees. Oliver had been doing his best not to think too much about how they were going to find Professor Koenig, if the man was even still alive, or whether he would be able to help even if they did find him. If he let himself ruminate on that subject, he would fall into a morass of distracting questions, and right now, distraction could be very dangerous.

"All right," he said, pushing away from the tree and bending to retrieve his parka, which was weighted down with cans of SpaghettiOs. "Are you ready to go?"

The winter man nodded thoughtfully, then glanced around for Kitsune. Oliver followed suit, his gaze automatically tracking to the last place he had seen her. There was no sign of her.

Oliver took the first step, casting a worried glance at Frost. Then the winter man fell in beside him and they hurried through the trees and the melting snow, following the path Kitsune had taken. They had progressed thirty or forty yards when Oliver held up a hand to halt the winter man.

"Shush," he whispered.

Frost frowned, ice crackling in his forehead. "What is it?"

"Engines. A road, not far off."

A gunshot slapped the sky, echoing through the trees. In the snow off to their left something dashed behind a berm made by a fallen maple and years of moss and detritus from fallen leaves. Oliver almost expected to see Peries flying around the dead tree.

Raucous laughter followed the gunshot, and then several hoots and catcalls.

"*Hunters,*" the winter man said, his voice the whisper of wind.

Oliver knew he did not mean Myth Hunters. The voices that reached them were entirely human, and he could not imagine the Falconer or the Kirata carrying shotguns. It was December, and the woods would be filled with men looking to bag a white-tailed deer but willing to settle for a few snowshoe hare or a coyote if that was all that could be found. Max Bascombe had gone on several hunting vacations while Oliver was growing up, but had never thought to invite his son. As much as the concept of hunting for sport unnerved him, Oliver would have gladly gone along if his father had wanted him there. He would have tried his damnedest to kill something, too, just to make the old man notice him. To make him proud.

The presence of hunters in the woods this morning was no surprise, but it was unwelcome for several reasons, not the least of which was the bitterness that swam up in the back of his throat at the associations they brought with them.

"We must find Kitsune," Frost whispered, and the two of them began to move through the trees, taking cover where they could.

"I'm sure she caught wind of them long before they would have noticed her," Oliver said. It felt true, yet still he worried.

Given the amount of noise they were making, Oliver thought the hunters had likely given up for the day and were preparing to head home. Together, he and Frost worked their way quietly through the snow, keeping to the cover of evergreens. They were moving up a slight rise and nearer to the occasional sound of car engines rumbling by on the road. Perhaps a hundred yards from the place they had been when they heard the gunshot, they came in sight of a man-made snowbank.

The voices of the hunters were just beyond the snowbank. They ridiculed one another good-naturedly and Oliver heard a loud, long belch before an empty beer bottle came spinning through the air over the top of the bank. Frost sneered at the discarded bottle and moved nearer, his passage over the snow utterly silent.

Of course. He's Jack fucking Frost.

Oliver followed, doing his best to match the quiet swiftness of his companion. Fortunately, with the snow melting there was no crunch underfoot and soon he was beside Frost on the snowbank, creeping up to get a look over the top.

It was a narrow, paved access road, just a few hundred feet from a moderately busy two-lane blacktop. Out on the main street, cars went by with a shushing noise as they kicked up some of the water that ran across the pavement from the snowmelt. There were two vehicles parked in the small circle at the end of the access road, an old Jeep Cherokee and a sparklingly new cherry red Ford F250 with a plow blade attached to the front. The hunters had plowed the access road themselves. There were four men, all in the requisite orange vests, though most of them had stripped off the thick coats and hats they would have worn when they went into the woods early that morning.

A dead white-tailed buck was strapped into the back of the pickup truck. From their vantage atop the snowbank,

Oliver could also see a brace of dead hares in the truck. He wondered which of the four men had bagged the deer.

Three of the men had gathered between the vehicles and were drinking bottles of beer from an enormous cooler. One of them, a thirtyish guy with thick, curly hair the color of rust and forty pounds he would have been better off without, was smoking a joint whose sweet scent only now reached Oliver's nose. The man took a long hit and passed it to another man, who might have been his brother, so similar were their features, only he was in much better shape and had his hair shorn down to a military buzz. They looked like the before-and-after pictures in some weight-loss commercial. The third sat upon the big cooler, sipping his beer and laughing about something Mr. Before had said that Oliver had missed. A hibachi grill was on the ground between them and fat sausages sizzled over the fire.

The remaining member of their troupe was standing at the rear of the Cherokee, the tailgate open as he zippered his shotgun into a leather case complete with shoulder strap and ammunition. He slid it into the back of the Jeep and then strode away from the group, toward the snow-bank on the other side of the road.

"Fish me out a beer, Gav. Just gotta take a leak," he said, unzipping his fly even as he walked.

"Goddamn it, Virgil, put it back in your pants!" said Mr. After with a shake of his head. He took a hit from the joint and tried to pass it to the guy on the cooler, who waved it away, so After had to pass it back to his brother.

"Fuck's sake, Virg, you've got a bladder like my grand-mother," said the guy on the cooler.

For his part, Virgil just swore at them all and started to piss, an arc of yellow that stained and melted the snow, steam rising from the hole he was making in the bank.

Oliver glanced at Frost, wondering what they were going to do. They could not wait forever for Kitsune to return to them and he had no interest in a run-in with these hunters, who would at the very least want to know who he was and how he had gotten there. They might offer him a beer and a sausage, which would have been welcome, but there would be no way for him to slip back into the woods without explanation. All in all, it would be better to go unseen. Better, in fact, just to get out of there entirely. He was concerned about how long Frost might be willing to wait for Kitsune, and how much time before those other Hunters—the ones they had to really worry about—might catch up to them.

Just as he was about to crawl back down the snowbank, Oliver was brought up short by the widening of the winter man's eyes. Frost stared in what seemed equal parts alarm and amazement at something on that access road, and Oliver dragged himself upward several inches to have another look. At first nothing looked different to him.

Then he saw the fox.

Kitsune darted along the access road at the base of the snowbank, doing her best to remain out of sight of Virgil and Gav and the Before-and-After brothers. At the back of the Cherokee, using the vehicle to hide herself, her fur rippled and flowed and she stood up. The transformation from fox to woman was as simple as that and Oliver had to blink several times as he tried to figure out what he had just seen and how it could be such a natural change. One moment the fur belonged to an animal and the next it was a cloak draped upon a beautiful woman.

With a peek at Virgil, who zipped his fly and started over to join the others, she ducked and reached into the back of the Jeep. In a single swift motion she slung the strap of the shotgun case over her shoulder and then she was darting for the snowbank, directly beneath the spot where Oliver and Frost lay in hidden observation.

Gav had a sausage wrapped in a roll, dripping mustard onto the ground as he went to take a bite. It was inches from his mouth when he glanced up and saw her scaling the snowbank with such delicate agility that she seemed to skate up its face.

"Holy . . . Virgil, she just . . . your gun! She's got your gun!"

He had only gotten out the first few words as he stood, pointing at the snowbank, when the others caught sight of Kitsune as well. Mr. Before spotted Oliver and their eyes met. Oliver could not help it. He grinned.

Then he was scrambling down the snowbank with Frost beside him and Kitsune leaped over the top, running so swiftly that she dashed past them. She cast a mischievous glance at Oliver, eyes alight with pleasure. The hunters were shouting threats and curses after them. He heard the sounds of them huffing up the snowbank. A beer bottle sailed through the branches of the tree to Oliver's right and then struck another, showering broken glass down into the snow.

"Do you . . . think . . . maybe it's . . ." he began, hardly able to catch his breath as he maneuvered through the trees, keeping abreast of Frost but unable to catch up with the fox-woman.

"Yes," the winter man replied, the icicles of his hair clinking together as they ran. "It's time we were gone."

The wind whipped up around them, driving the snow into a maelstrom once more. In moments the sky was gray and the sun blotted out and the shouts of the hunters were muffled. Kitsune paused just ahead as she realized what was happening. They caught up to her and she smiled, revealing those too-sharp teeth, just before the driven snow whited out all of their surroundings. The forest was entirely gone.

And Oliver felt the world *shift*.

CHAPTER **8**

The Whitney family lived in a Federal Colonial that
had been built in the last decade of the eighteenth
century for a sea captain by the name of George
Jensen. The seaman had been forty-one at the time of his
marriage to Ruth Anne Landry, twenty-year-old daughter
of the town's only baker. Her father had no dowry to speak
of, but with a wife as fair as Ruth Anne, Captain Jensen felt
he had all that he could ever have asked for.

The house had been built for her over the course of an
entire year, painstakingly constructed to meet the standards of the captain, who felt that his home ought to be
put together with at least as much care as his ship. Local
legend held that he had never slept a single night in his
own bed, that his last voyage ended in a storm at sea on the

very same day that the builders declared the house complete and announced to Mrs. Jensen, now heavy with child, that she could begin to decorate and move the couple's belongings into the sprawling home at her pleasure.

This was not precisely true. In fact, the captain had overseen the furnishing of his home and had spent several weeks there in his marital bed with his pregnant wife before sailing on that fateful voyage. The truth was less colorful but no less tragic than the legend.

On Monday afternoon, a small headache working through his brain like a burning fuse, Ted Halliwell sat in the parlor of the Captain Jensen House—as the plaque beside the front door proclaimed it—and listened to Marjorie Whitney tell the history of her home as she served him tea, smiled awkwardly, and did everything possible to postpone the moment when he would get what he had come here for: a meeting with her daughter, Julianna. The young woman Oliver Bascombe had left at the altar.

"That's a wonderful story, Mrs. Whitney. You must love being surrounded by so much history here." Halliwell sipped his tea, which tasted slightly of almonds, and then gingerly set the cup down. "But I really do need to speak with Julianna. Do you think she'll be much longer?"

From the moment he had arrived, Marjorie Whitney had evinced a sort of brittle pleasantry. Now there was a crack in it, no different, he imagined, than a crack in the china cup.

"She went to the health club a while ago, as I told you, Deputy—"

"Detective, actually."

The woman stiffened at the word. "I'm sure Julianna will be right down." Her nostrils flared as she took a breath and seemed to steady herself. "Oh, I've been remiss. I think

I may have some butter cookies in the pantry. Let me get some to go with your tea."

"That's all right. This is perfect," Halliwell told her.

"It's no trouble at all," Mrs. Whitney replied, and then she was up and fleeing the room as though she meant never to return. And perhaps that was true.

Halliwell took a second sip of his bitter tea, mainly out of politeness, and then let it sit. He clasped his hands on top of his knees and tried not to get too comfortable on the floral-patterned love seat where Mrs. Whitney had steered him upon his arrival. He wanted to get up, to wander around the room, but he did not want the woman to think he had been snooping if she ever did come back with those butter cookies. Despite his demurral, the thought of cookies made his stomach rumble and he had to try to remember the last time he had eaten.

Several minutes went by and he began to feel trapped on the love seat. He stared at his teacup and the tray that Mrs. Whitney had set out with a pot, cups and saucers, milk and lemon, and a ceramic strawberry that was actually a sugar bowl. When he found himself reaching for the teacup again, he knew it was time to get up.

He had just risen to his feet when Julianna entered the room.

"Detective Halliwell? Sorry to have kept you waiting."

"I understand. I was a bit earlier than we'd agreed. I appreciate you taking the time to meet with me."

Halliwell had been a cop for a long time. He knew better than to mention her aborted wedding, or even to offer his condolences, before they'd had a chance to build up to it.

Julianna was an attractive woman with fine, delicate

features that seemed out of place. It took Halliwell a moment to realize that it was her height that gave that impression. He figured her for five foot nine at least, probably taller, and her elegant features and stylishly cut auburn hair belied her formidable physical presence. He was vaguely aware that she worked at Bascombe & Cox, and thought that if she was a lawyer, she'd be the center of attention in any courtroom.

"It's no trouble at all," she said. The precise words her mother had used minutes before. But just as with her mother, it was a lie. He could see the pain in her eyes, the regret and grief. "I've known Mr. Bascombe my entire adult life. I can't imagine—"

She shook her head and one of her hands fluttered up as though pushing away whatever words would have come next.

"You know Collette Bascombe quite well also."

Julianna nodded. "Oliver's very close to his sister. Collette lives in New York now, and when she married they didn't get to see each other as often as they'd have liked. But, yes, through him I know Collette very well. She's a friend. I don't have any siblings, and she always treated me a bit like a little . . ." A wan smile lifted one corner of her mouth. "Like a little sister. So much for that."

Halliwell kept his expression neutral. "You don't think you'll be able to maintain a friendship with Collette, whatever comes of your relationship with her brother?"

"I'd like to think I could. But that's just wishful thinking. I love her, but she's still Oliver's sister. And it's going to . . ." She frowned, hesitating a moment as she focused on Halliwell. Her lips pressed tightly together, forming a white line, and then she let out a breath that was not quite a sigh. "Well, it's going to take a while for me to process all of what

I feel toward Oliver right now. I can't imagine that not affecting my relationship with Collette."

Halliwell slid his hands into his pockets and strode toward the window. He could feel her watching him but he gave her a moment without the pressure of his attention and instead looked out at the snow-covered lawn.

"Is there any word?" Julianna ventured at last, words catching in her throat. "About Collette, I mean."

The detective shook his head even as he turned. "Nothing yet, I'm afraid. But there was nothing at the house to suggest that Miss Bascombe's been harmed in any way."

Anger flared in Julianna Whitney's eyes. "What, other than her father's corpse, you mean?"

Then her jaw dropped and she blanched, covering her mouth in obvious surprise that the words had come out. "I'm . . . sorry. I know what you meant. I'm more than a little on edge."

"I understand. And I wish there was something I could tell you to set your mind at ease. Nothing about this situation is pleasant. Mr. Bascombe's murder is a horrible thing, but with both of his children missing, we can't even begin to get a picture of the time that led up to his murder. The only way for us to do that is to find Oliver and Collette. Is there anything you can think of that might help us with that? Anywhere the two of them might go together or anyone they would contact if they wanted to get away for a while?"

Her eyes narrowed in confusion. "I thought that Collette . . . well, that whoever killed Mr. Bascombe—"

"That's one possibility. We have to look at it from every angle, Miss Whitney."

Julianna shrugged. "All right. In any case, the answer is no. There isn't anywhere I can think of. I mean, their lives were spent in that house. I assume the police in New York have checked Collette's place there."

"It's covered. What about Oliver? Any place you think he would run to if he needed to think? Favorite childhood vacation spot? Great-aunt in Montreal? Anything at all?"

Her hand trembled as she reached up to push her hair away from her face. She stared at Halliwell as if he were some hideous new form of life that had just crawled out of the sea. "Run. You said run. Has Oliver got a reason to run? You can't possibly think . . . oh, Christ, you can't believe that he would . . ."

She could not even finish the sentence.

Halliwell did not flinch beneath her accusatory stare. "It's no secret that Oliver didn't get along well with his father, Miss Whitney. He hasn't exactly been acting himself lately, has he? You never thought he'd leave you at the altar, did you?"

He regretted the question the instant it left his lips, but could not take it back or temper the edge with which he had spoken. The hurt in her eyes had been deep enough, and now he had added to it.

"No," she said softly, horror and doubt creeping into her voice and her expression as she entertained the idea for the first time. Halliwell wished he could have spared her that.

"I'm sorry, but as I said, we've got to look at every angle."

His cell phone began to vibrate in his pocket. The ringer was off and the vibrate function always startled him. He flinched and then slid the phone out, flipped it open, and glanced at the incoming number. It was the sheriff's office.

"Give me a moment, would you?" he asked. Julianna

ignored him, staring off into the shadows of the parlor. He punched the TALK button on the phone. "Halliwell."

"Detective, it's Nora Costello. The sheriff wanted me to pass something on to you but he didn't want to do it by radio."

Halliwell frowned. All of the privacy of this thing was getting more and more under his skin. Max Bascombe was a homicide victim. The case would get investigated. It wasn't the first time the sheriff's department had gotten involved in a murder investigation in one of the local towns. But the sheriff was doing everything as quietly as possible, trying his damnedest to keep the Bascombe case out of the newspapers and out of local gossip as well. Halliwell figured it was a useless effort. The case was too big to keep anything private and the sheriff knew that. But the man was beholden to others who were going to try to control the flow of information and he had to play the game.

Ted Halliwell hated games.

"All right, Nora. Let's have it."

"Have you ever been up to Cottingsley?"

"Once. A long time ago. Cute little village in Aroostook County."

"A little girl was murdered there yesterday, right out in public in the middle of an outdoor skating rink. Her . . . it was her eyes, like the Bascombe case."

Halliwell held his breath. What the hell was this? Cottingsley was a hundred miles from Kitteridge, probably more. What were the odds that two murders could take place on the same day, share that ghastly similarity, and not be related? But that wasn't just around the corner. If the Cottingsley murder had happened during the day and the killer had then driven south to Kitteridge, it wasn't likely to be random, him showing up at the Bascombe house. On top of all of the other mysteries, not least of which was how Oliver and Collette had left their home in the first place, here was another.

"The sheriff wants you to go up there right away," Nora continued.

"Why? What's the point? Can't we just have them send down the crime scene report and the autopsy work?"

Nora hesitated. When she spoke again, she had lowered her voice. "We only learned about this killing because of the A.P.B. out on Oliver Bascombe. Last night, just hours after the murder, officers identified him as fitting the description of a stranger lingering at the crime scene. When they went to question him, he ran. That was last night. They're still searching for him. Apparently, well, he—"

"Disappeared," Halliwell said, a chill creeping up his back. "Again."

The more he learned about this case, the less it made sense to him. The only thing he could hold on to now was the absolute certainty that Oliver Bascombe knew more about his father's murder than the investigating officers did . . . and that maybe that knowledge was firsthand.

He thanked Nora and shut the phone, returning it to his pocket. When he focused on Julianna again he found her studying him with obvious suspicion.

"What was that about?" she asked.

"I'm sorry, Miss Whitney, but it's an ongoing investigation. When I have anything at all solid involving the whereabouts of either Oliver or Collette Bascombe, I'll personally call to let you know. Beyond that, there's not much more I can say. I thank you for your time."

He started toward the door and then paused. "Oh, and please thank your mother for the tea."

Julianna smiled. "It's awful."

Halliwell gave a gentle nod of agreement. "Well, for the hospitality, then."

"Detective, I'm sorry, just . . . do you really think that Oliver is responsible for all of this?"

He hesitated a long time before responding.

"I think he has a lot of the pieces missing from this puzzle. Beyond that, I wouldn't want to speculate."

During his first excursion beyond the Veil, Oliver had come to think that time passed more or less in sync on both sides. When they had left the Sandmen's castle and shifted back to his own world, however, they had gone from day to night. He did not think that more time had gone by in his absence but, rather, that both the days and the nights were longer in the world of myth. They had spent an entire night and most of a morning in Maine, but when they had passed through the Veil once more, the sky was just beginning to lighten.

Dawn in the Two Kingdoms. Or, in this case, in Euphrasia, for once Frost and Kitsune had gotten their bearings they had determined that they were far north of the Sandmen's castle, well on their way to Perinthia. Based upon Kitsune's sense of direction, they had struck off on a northeasterly path and within two hours had found themselves back upon the Truce Road at last.

"It may not always be safe to travel," the winter man had said, "but we ought to keep to it as long as we can, for the going will be easier and, some way, swifter, too."

Apparently there was magic in the road itself that shortened the journey. For his part, Oliver was dubious.

He wanted to find Professor Koenig as quickly as possible, and that meant hurrying to Perinthia. But he did not want to die, and even with the shotgun case slung over his shoulder—thanks to Kitsune's crafty thievery—he did not feel at all safe out on the road.

As they continued upon their journey, he realized that even more so than time, distance was quite different on either side of the Veil. He had thought that the land here would be exactly as large as all of the public areas of his own world combined, all pushed together in a sort of reverse continental drift. This was not at all the case. Distance was not equivalent.

Or so he learned when they came to the Atlantic Bridge.

They had followed the Truce Road through a dense wood and then up a rise that was part of the foothills of a mountain range to the west. The road turned due east thereafter and ran through a low, green valley where there were farms set at significant distance from one another. Cattle grazed in open fields and Oliver wondered how the farmers determined which animals belonged to which property. As the morning wore on toward midday they sighted several wild horses running along a ridge to the west and Oliver had to pause a moment to watch them run. The sight was among the most beautiful things he had ever seen. He didn't know a damn thing about horses, but had always admired the animals. Seeing them run free did something wonderful to him inside, but he knew he would never be able to put it into words, so he said nothing to his companions.

The weather was cooler this far north and it had grown colder over the course of the morning. He had been carrying the ancient parka with him but eventually he slipped it on again. One of the houses they passed, a rambling thing made of stone and mortar, had a plume of smoke rising from its chimney and the smell of the fireplace seemed to welcome them. Oliver was not a fool, however. They might deceive these country people, but there would be no real welcome for him, no respite, while the threat of death hung over his head.

"How much farther to Perinthia?" he asked, as they trudged up another rise in the Truce Road, which was broader now and spread with gravel.

Kitsune turned her jade eyes upon Frost, her cloak pulled around her so completely that her face and feet were all that was visible of her body. The winter man glanced at the sky, tracking the sun.

"Once we cross the Atlantic Bridge, half a day to the outskirts of the city. Even if we go on without rest all through the daylight hours, it will be night before we reach the city. We will have to camp and make our plan once night falls."

Oliver considered his words and then frowned. "How far to this bridge?"

"The *Atlantic* Bridge," Frost repeated, as though correcting him. "We're nearly there."

As they followed the Truce Road up that long rise, Oliver realized he could hear the river ahead. When they reached the peak and looked down into the river valley, he smiled in wonder. The river looked to be nearly a mile wide, and its current was swift and deep. The road went on a short way, down the other side of the hill, and then the bridge began. Small islands dotted the river and this place had obviously been chosen for that very reason. Stone pilings had been built upon the islands, and the bridge, a masterwork of stone architecture, spanned the entire river, touching down on each of those islands in turn, arching over the rushing water. Greenery grew thick upon those islands, and upon the one in the center there was an orchard of various fruit trees. From this distance it was difficult to tell how many different sorts of fruit grew there, but the colors were remarkably vivid. Oliver's stomach rumbled at the thought of that fruit and he recalled the tins of SpaghettiOs in the pocket of his parka.

"We might have to stop and have a picnic on the way."

"Perhaps," Kitsune said, slipping past him and starting down the road to the bridge. She glanced back, face partially shadowed by the hood of her fur, and smiled playfully. "Is this your first time across the Atlantic?"

Oliver and Frost followed after her, the rush of the river growing louder as they neared its banks. The sun glinted off the rough water, sparkling brightly. Out in the deep current something leaped from the water and splashed down again before he could get a good look at it.

"What do you mean, first time? I've never been here before. How could I have crossed the river?"

Beside him, the winter man laughed softly. It was a surprisingly gentle noise. "The Atlantic, Oliver. Kitsune is teasing you. The name of the river is quite literal. The bridge spans the Atlantic . . . which here is not an ocean, but this river. Breadth and distance are relative, depending upon which side of the Veil you are on. Nothing is exactly the same. In our world, Atlantis and Lemuria still exist. The Atlantic Ocean is merely a river. The English Channel in your world is, here, the Sargasso Sea. And it is vast."

They reached the bridge, and as they started across, treading upon bleached stone, Oliver stared toward the other side of the river.

"So, you're telling me that's Europe over there?"

Frost sighed. "Oliver, this isn't your world. You've got to understand that. While every place here corresponds with a location in the mundane world, the two are not the same. Not at all. They exist parallel to each other . . . but they are not mirror images."

Kitsune was ahead of them, hurrying as though she did not like being on the bridge—or perhaps she hated being above the water. Oliver ran his hand over the stone wall beside him, marveling at its smoothness. As he walked he looked down at the turgid water.

"But if this is the Atlantic, then when we reach the other side of the bridge, the land that we'll be standing on will . . . correspond . . . with Europe?" He laughed at the absurdity of it, at the marvel of it.

"Not precisely."

Oliver glanced sidelong at Frost. The winter man tilted his head, icicles cascading around his face.

"The United Kingdom, actually."

White birds dove and soared above the water, circling above the tiny islands in the river. The rush of the river and the song of those birds were the only sounds he could hear. With all the wonders of this place he had not properly appreciated that facet of Frost's world. The quiet. The peacefulness. Oliver could only take it all in and keep walking, musing to himself about what they would find when at last they reached Perinthia. In his mind he had built up certain expectations and he realized now that he would have to put them aside. It was a mistake to make any presumption at all about the world beyond the Veil and what he might find here.

His mind wandering, Oliver caught his foot on an upraised chunk of rock. He stumbled but managed to avoid falling. Looking back, he saw that some of the stones were buckled and cracked where something heavy had crossed the bridge. He glanced ahead and saw other such places and he wondered what monstrosity was so heavy that each of its steps would do that sort of damage. After thinking about it for a moment, he realized that there might be any number of things in Euphrasia that could be responsible, from giants to dragons to Heffalumps, for all he knew.

Oliver smiled at the thought and shook his head. Whatever it was, he didn't want to meet it.

As he hurried to catch up to Frost he saw that farther ahead, where the bridge passed above the largest of the islands it spanned, Kitsune had paused. Some of the fruit trees were so tall that they grew higher than the rail of the bridge and the fox-woman was standing completely still, her body arched as though preparing to strike at some unseen enemy. Yet seconds passed without her moving as Oliver caught up to Frost, and then the two of them made their way toward her.

Wary, Oliver kept far away from the trees that grew beside the bridge. Frost followed suit.

"What is it?" the winter man asked.

Kitsune's jade eyes flashed in the sun. She sniffed the air. "There. In the branches. Something watches us."

For long seconds the three of them stood silent and unmoving, peering into the treetops. Oliver felt a rush of heat prickling his skin even as a gust of cold wind swept across the bridge. His heart raced and he could hear it beating inside his head. Only the wind and the river made any noise. The birds that had been circling overhead had disappeared and nothing rustled in those branches. The trees were taller than any fruit trees he had ever seen. There were apples and pears, peaches and nectarines, and in the middle a trio of cherry trees, branches festooned with dark purple fruit.

"Show yourself," the winter man commanded.

A wave of cold emanated from him far more frigid than the wind. Oliver glanced over to see that Frost had his hands raised, fingers pointing toward the trees as though he meant to pluck some of that ripe fruit. Hunger rumbled in Oliver's belly. He studied the fruit more closely. Once upon a time, his mother had taken him and Collette to an orchard in New Hampshire in the early fall to pick apples. Most of the nectarines were gone by that late in the season but Oliver had passed a tree that had a single, perfectly ripe nectarine hanging from a high branch. It had been the sweetest, most delicious thing he had ever tasted. Fruit of the gods. Now that the memory had returned he recalled that it had been his father who had plucked that fruit down for him. How odd, he thought, that he should have forgotten such a thing. His father's presence on such an excursion would have been remarkable, even then. He had even shared a bite with his father and relished the warmth of the man's smile. The recollection of that smile, of that rare moment of unguarded fondness, sent a wave of regret through Oliver, but he brushed it aside.

He had always tried to be the son Max Bascombe wanted, no matter how miserable it made him. Now fate had intervened. The mundane world that his father so cherished had been revealed to be a sham. And instead of relishing it, Oliver had to focus on just staying alive.

"Are you sure, Kitsune?" he asked, shifting the strap on the shotgun case that he wore slung across his back. "I don't see—"

Still tasting the twenty-year-old memory of that nectarine, his eyes were on that particular tree. As he turned to glance at the fox-woman, though, he caught sight of eyes in the branches of the tallest of the cherry trees.

"Oh, fuck—" he snapped, stumbling back a few steps and slipping the shotgun case off his shoulder.

Kitsune leaped toward him, diminishing in midair, fur rippling as she transformed. She landed lightly on the stone bridge on fox feet and took up a position just in front of him, peering into the trees, trying to see what he had seen.

"What is it, Oliver?" Frost asked.

"The cherry tree," he replied, unsure if the words made any sense. He narrowed his eyes and looked again, searching for what he had seen before. The tree itself, or so it seemed. Something with the gnarled look of tree bark but the color of the ripest cherry.

"Show yourself, or I freeze the tree from peak to root," Frost warned. He stepped toward the tree, cold mist swirling from his hands.

Oliver started forward also, out of both fear for his friend and concern for his own self-preservation. Whatever was in that tree, its mere presence made him feel as though spiders were crawling all over his skin.

Kitsune uttered a single bark. Oliver glanced down at her, trying to understand what she wanted him to do.

Then the thing in the cherry tree spoke.

"I don't like the sun," it said. "And I like strangers even less. Strangers on the bridge." The voice was thickly accented and sticky, as though the speaker had difficulty prying the words from a mouth full of honey. "However, I have been known to be hospitable to Borderkind. Especially in times such as these."

The branches shifted as the thing in the cherry tree scuttled forward. At first he had thought it actually a part of the tree, but now as its weight bowed the limbs beneath it and it paused, sprawled across several branches only a few feet from the stone rail of the bridge, he saw it more clearly. Its arms and legs were so long and thin they might have passed for tree branches, if Oliver had not just seen the thing move. Its prehensile toes wrapped around its perch and its fingers were three times the length of a man's, with six or seven joints per digit. With that cherry skin, the texture of bark, it blended perfectly at the heart of the tree. Out amongst the leaves, however, it was out of place. Pink eyes like the bright, moist meat inside the fruit, were set deeply into narrow features beneath a smooth pate.

Kitsune barked again and Oliver flinched. He still clutched the shotgun case in his hands but had not even attempted to unzip it for fear of drawing the creature's attention. For the moment, it peered curiously at Frost.

"Your offer of hospitality is appreciated," the winter man replied, moving nearer the branches. The thing in the cherry tree studied him. "But I am afraid we do not have time to rest."

Frost let his gaze linger upon the thing almost in warning, then glanced over his shoulder at Kitsune and Oliver. "Move along."

The branches wavered again as the creature moved nearer, bending the limbs now so that it was only inches above the stone rail. The tips of its fingers had reached the sunlight and it flinched away a moment before grimacing and settling down once more. The wind shifted and swirled the smell of ripe fruit all around them.

"Do not be foolish," the thing said, spread like a spider upon the branches. "You may not be hungry, but I saw the lust in the human's eyes when he looked upon my fruit. He is desirous of a taste, and rest is always welcome. The river will replenish you, my shade comfort you, my fruit feed you."

It snapped off a cluster of cherries from the end of one branch and held them out toward Oliver. For the first time it really addressed him, and there was a cajoling kindness in its voice as though he were indulging a child.

"If you mayn't stop, at least have the sweetness of these cherries upon your journey. They are the fruit of the gods. Like nothing you have ever tasted."

That sticky voice was reassuring, despite its obvious exasperation with their distrust. Oliver slung the shotgun case back over his shoulder and went to take the proffered fruit.

"No," the winter man said sternly, a frigid breeze swirling around Oliver's hand as he reached for the cherries. Frost formed on their purple skin. "Take nothing. You are an actor. Have you never read the ancient plays? As a student of legend, have you never read the thousands of tales that warn against taking gifts from those you meet at the roadside? Are you so foolish as to accept food from the hand of a demon?"

In the shadows of the cherry tree's branches, the creature laughed. Leaves shook. It threw the cherries in its hand onto the bridge, where they lay in the sun, unclaimed.

"A gift freely given, then," the demon said. "Along with my name. I am Aerico. The fox is familiar to me. You are not. Some winter spirit, yes? Some cousin to Pelznickel?"

Frost glared at him. "Frost."

"Ah, yes. Jack Frost. Well, when you are through lecturing your friend you may want to reconsider your rudeness. So many of your kind have been slaughtered already. Father Christmas and Knecht Ruprecht and so many of your winter cousins. Krampus is too cruel and crafty to be taken so easily. But the others . . . the Strigae bring the whispers and songs each morning. The Hunters are abroad and the Borderkind are dying or disappearing. Roanes and Merrows slain and worn as coats. Jenny Greenteeth is dead. Even the gods of the Harvest are among the hunted. Appleseed has vanished, missing for days now."

"So many," Frost said softly, hanging his head.

Kitsune rubbed herself against Oliver's leg, orange-red fur alight with sunshine, and as she did she transformed again, growing to stand beside him as though she had been there all along. She had, of course, but the transformation was always startling. Her hood shaded her face, those exquisite Asiatic features, and her fur cloak clung to her body even as she moved, brushing the stone underfoot.

"You see, then, why we may not trust you," Kitsune rasped. "We must continue on. If you wish to be hospitable, give us not nourishment but information. Have the Strigae spoken of Hunters nearby? Have any crossed the bridge of late? Answers are a gift we would gratefully accept."

Aerico grinned, revealing teeth as black as rot, and the demon's fingers and toes curled around the branches to which it clung. Those deep-set eyes blinked several times and it extended its body forward far enough that the sunlight streaming through the outer branches dappled its smooth purple head.

"You are the only strangers I have seen on the bridge today. But there are others who are not strangers to me. And while they might not hunt such as yourselves . . ." One of those long, spindly fingers pointed at Oliver, who shuddered as though the demon touched his very heart. ". . . I'd wager they would not look kindly upon any who'd bring an Intruder through the Veil."

Kitsune darted forward in a single swift motion, leaping up onto the stone rail and perching there as she thrust her hands into the cherry tree's branches and wrapped her hands around the demon's throat.

Aerico choked, trying to withdraw into the deeper shadows of the heart of the tree. Kitsune held tightly.

"You shall say nothing of his—"

The demon twisted and kicked at her head, knocking her hood back. Kitsune lost her grip and nearly tumbled from the bridge. She kept her balance, but only barely.

"I will not have to say a word. The army comes even now!"

Oliver frowned and glanced at Frost, but the winter man had already turned. He was staring back the way they had come, pale blue eyes wide with alarm. Frost snarled in a guttural voice. If they were words, Oliver did not understand them, but he garnered their meaning well enough.

The first few soldiers of some kind of militia had just appeared over the rise in the west, following the Truce Road just as they had.

The winter man spun, icicle hair whipping around his head, and looked in the other direction, gauging their distance to the far side of the Atlantic Bridge. When Oliver sought Kitsune he found that she was transformed again.

"Are they after us?" Oliver stared at Frost's cold eyes.

"It matters little. The word has traveled. If they discover you, it will not go well." For just a moment he hesitated, eyes narrowing with suspicion as he glanced at the demon of the cherry tree. Then he gestured toward the trees.

"Hurry. Into the branches. Climb down."

"But—"

"We've no choice!"

A chill breeze encircled Oliver and urged him toward the stone rail. Frost was beside him. The demon scuttled back farther toward the trunk of the tree as the fox leaped from the bridge onto a tree limb. Oliver crouched on the rail and steadied himself on one branch, then swung down to find a foothold on a thicker limb below. Frost was there above him, red cherries like blossoming wounds against the white ice.

"Down, down, to the island, and quiet about it," Aerico said, a trace of gleeful hysteria in his voice. "I told you I was hospitable. The orchard will hide you."

Oliver paused in the lower branches of the massive cherry tree. He could see through the leaves that the island spread out around the stone footing of the bridge support, and there were far more trees than he had guessed. The orchard was dense and the fruit fairly glistened where the sun touched it.

"Wait. Be still," Frost said from above.

On a branch to Oliver's right, the fox sat watching him with her jade eyes. At the sound of marching boots, heavy and rhythmic as they crossed the bridge, she glanced up. All four of them gazed up at the bridge and waited. Oliver held his breath for long seconds and then began letting it out slowly, soundlessly. He had no idea what sort of creatures would be in the army of Euphrasia, or if they might have ears acute enough to hear him breathe. Or noses that might catch his scent, or those of his companions. Kitsune had been aware of the demon's presence. Oliver did not even want to think about what might happen if they were discovered down here. On this little island in the rushing river, there was nowhere to run.

The marching grew louder. Up on the bridge, an officer shouted muffled orders.

From this angle, Oliver could see nothing of the army save for upturned pikes bobbing and the helmets of soldiers who passed near the side of the bridge. Something massive lumbered by, shaking loose mortar from the underside of the structure, but he saw only the stooped shoulder or back of the thing moving past like the black, gleaming body of a whale breaching the ocean for an instant before sliding back beneath the surface.

The faux fur around the hood of his parka itched his neck and he felt heavy, clinging to the branches there. The shotgun case was like an anchor. He tried to catch Frost's eye and then Kitsune's, but both of them were staring up at the bridge and listening intently to the sound of boot heels on stone. Reluctantly he glanced around for Aerico and found the demon resting against the trunk behind and above him. The demon smiled, staring at Oliver with those sunken eyes, as though the fear that ran like mercury through him was all of the entertainment Aerico had ever desired. Oliver tore his gaze away and forced himself to stare at the masonry of the bridge, trying not to feel the eyes upon him or the nearness of so many who would kill him simply for existing if they discovered him there. He had never wanted to come here. . . .

But that was a lie. He had wanted to pierce the Veil his entire life, even before he had known that it existed.

A full minute passed as the soldiers filed by, and then at last the pikes and helmets were gone and the thunder of the march diminished. The demon made his skin crawl, but Oliver knew that Aerico had saved them a terrible encounter.

"Thank you," he said, hoping he hid his reluctance as he forced himself to look up at the cherry-tree demon again. Aerico was sprawled across branches, fingers and toes curled round them like a sloth, studying him with great interest. The demon was no longer smiling.

"Oh," it said. "You are quite welcome."

Oliver recoiled from the menace in its voice, readjusting his grip on the rough bark, parka and shotgun weighing on him. His left foot slipped as he backed away from the demon and he looked past Aerico, past branches and thick leaves and bunches of cherries, hoping for intervention from Frost or Kitsune.

The fox was curled in several branches, captured by them, one of them prying her jaws open as she tried a muffled bark.

Beside her the winter man had been impaled on a half-dozen tree limbs. They had spiked through him, burst from his neck and skull and torso, and where they had emerged, fresh clusters of cherries grew. These were no longer the illusions of wounds.

"Oh, you fucker," Oliver whispered. He felt faint, felt as though he would lose his grip and tumble from the tree. But as he tried to move his hand it was held fast to the branch.

Frenzied, he swung his head around to see what had grabbed hold of him, thinking the branches would capture him as they had Kitsune. But this was far worse. The branches were not moving. Instead, the bark of the cherry tree had begun to grow up over his fingers, spreading. A cherry blossom bloomed on the bark that covered his hand.

The demon laughed and whispered something, dangling from the branches above him. He thought it was one word.

Hospitality.

CHAPTER 9

The demon's pink eyes gleamed wetly in the shadows among the tree's branches. Its smile split the cherry-purple flesh of its face to reveal those black, rotting teeth again.

If I don't get out of this tree, I'm dead. Numbed by shock and dread, Oliver felt a grim coolness settle upon him. He did not spare another glance at his companions, could not afford to consider their fate before his own.

"Bascombe," Aerico said, reaching down toward him with one hand, those spindly digits stretching as though to caress his face. "That's the name on the warrant. There's a reward for your life, do you know that? Oh, word gets around quickly enough. The Strigae are wonderful that way. Now, Bascombe, we shall sample some of *your* fruit."

All thought of strategy left Oliver then. Animal fear overrode logic and he reacted like a wolf caught in a trap. Pain did not matter. Only freedom. Oliver grabbed a branch above him and shook it fiercely, trying to set the cherry-tree demon off balance. Holding on to that branch as an anchor, he twisted his arm around, trying to tear his fingers from the bark that was growing up over them. It was attached to his skin somehow and his flesh burned as he worked it loose, as though he was tearing off the upper layer.

Aerico held fast to the branches that supported it and sneered at his efforts. "Oh, I think not. You'll just stay here until I get my reward. Or most of you will." The demon ran his long, thin black tongue over those disgusting teeth and it reached out to grab Oliver's arm.

Oliver flinched back. The cherry-tree demon's fingers only grazed his wrist, but where it touched, bright red blisters erupted. It occurred to him then that the demon was toying with him, that it did not consider him a threat and so had attacked the Borderkind first.

When the demon reached for him again Oliver shouted the filthiest obscenities he could think of as a kind of battle cry and threw himself backward, simultaneously tearing his hand away from the bark that had grown over his fingers. His skin burned. Pain drove up his arm and for a moment it took his focus, so that he barely felt himself dropping through the lower branches of the tree, branches and leaves and cherries whipping past him as he fell. He struck a thick branch and his weight and momentum broke it, the parka helping to blunt the pain of the impact.

He crashed to the island on his back, grunting in pain as he landed on the shotgun case that he still carried. The wind was knocked out of him and he struggled to breathe, face flush with pain and panic, his shoulder and spine aching as though he'd been struck with a baseball bat. Above him he heard Kitsune begin to bark, and somewhere in the midst of his agony and terror felt a small spark of relief that she was alive. Twined in those branches, she could not transform or the constriction might be the death of her. But for the moment, the cherry tree had not killed her.

"Oh, yes, Mr. Bascombe. If it is a game you desire, I will play." Aerico clambered down through the branches toward him.

Oliver stared up at the demon as it descended. His fingers were scraped raw, a hundred pinpricks of pain. He took in long, ragged gasps of air, steadying himself. The ache in his back was so brutal he thought there was a chance it might be broken, and that he would then lie here like carrion awaiting the vulture's arrival.

Except for the times he had played one on stage—and perhaps that was why he enjoyed acting—Oliver Bascombe had never been a hero. Not even the hero of his own life. In his own mind. He had studiously avoided conflict. But he was more terrified of dying than he was of fighting.

He rolled over and staggered to his feet, muscles in his back protesting. Unsteadily he backed away, staring up at the cherry tree, and swung the shotgun case around so that it hung in front of him. Aerico laughed softly in that sticky voice and dropped to the lowest limbs of the cherry tree. Oliver shot back the zipper and reached in, hauling out the gun. There was more ammunition in the case, but the shells already loaded would be all the chance the demon would give him. He let the case fall to the ground and swung the shotgun barrel up.

Aerico leaped out of the tree. Oliver tracked him with

the gun and fired. The blast resounded across the island, bouncing off the masonry of the bridge and echoing out over the river. Leaves flew and cherries exploded and a branch cracked and hung toward the ground. But the demon had not been lunging at Oliver at all. The branches of the next tree swayed and Oliver's stomach twisted as he realized Aerico had made the leap from one to the next like some flying squirrel.

"Shit," he whispered, backing away from both cherry trees.

The demon did not like direct sunlight. Oliver had one shell remaining in the shotgun. He swept the barrel from side to side, trying to sight Aerico in the trees and knowing that he had little chance. The demon's natural camouflage, the texture and color of his skin, meant only the motion of branches could give him away . . . and every time he saw branches moving and tried to get a closer look, the demon was already gone.

Oliver fled.

But Aerico was correct. There was really nowhere to run.

He darted beneath a pair of apple trees, past dangling pears and ripe nectarines whose sweet fragrance would normally have pleased him and now sickened him. His head turned in a frenzy as he sought to make certain the demon did not surprise him or get behind him.

He nearly fell into the river. Erupting from between two pear trees he turned, watching the trees, backed up, and accidentally shot one foot off the island's shore and into the water. The current tore at him, trying to unbalance him. His arms pinwheeled and he managed to regain his balance, still holding the shotgun with one hand.

Spinning, certain Aerico would use the moment to drop

down upon him, Oliver gripped the shotgun firmly again. His scraped left hand sang with pain and he bumped it with the gun. Oliver gritted his teeth and cursed at his own stupidity.

His right hand trembled with the urge to pull the trigger, to have the satisfaction of blowing a hole in the cherry-tree demon.

The sunlight shone on his back. The river rushed past. There was no sign of the army up on the stone bridge. Somewhere in that small orchard he heard Kitsune begin to cry out in pain in the voice of a fox. Images flashed through his mind of the winter man, speared through with cherry-tree branches, cherries blossoming through his body.

Off to his right, up in the trees in the shadow of the bridge, branches swayed and leaves rustled.

Oliver swung the barrel of the rifle and his trigger finger twitched. He was certain he saw the demon crouching in the tree, but he forced himself not to fire. He had one more chance. Only one.

Now the sound of Kitsune's pain became even greater and he faltered. He had never intended to leave his friends to die, only to survive himself and find some way to help them if he managed to destroy the demon. But he could not hear that sound, could not endure her pain, without attempting to aid her.

Back to the water, gun aimed at the branches above, he began to circle the small island as swiftly as he could manage. He stumbled over roots and stepped into the water several times, for the trees grew nearly right up to the shore. Oliver had worked his way perhaps a third of the way around the circumference of the island and Kitsune's cries continued, yet he had not seen any further trace of Aerico in the orchard.

What if he went back to them? He could be killing them, even now. Or Kitsune. Frost is probably already . . .

He didn't finish the thought. Instead he stood, breathing heavily, pain still there but receded, overridden by adrenaline. He could jump into the water and let the current carry him, try to make his way to shore downriver. Or work his way around the outside of the island to the bridge and try to climb up to the stone rail before the demon could get to him. But either way, he would be alone beyond the Veil, hunted by the army and every citizen with a taste for whatever reward would be given for the head of an Intruder. Without his companions—his friends—he was as good as dead.

There were more noble reasons why he could not abandon Frost and Kitsune, but survival demanded only one course of action.

He surveyed the branches of every tree in sight, peaches and apples and pears, but nothing moved there. Above the island, far above the bridge, birds flew in formation above the sky. There was no sign of Aerico.

Oliver hesitated not a moment more. He gripped the shotgun and ran into the trees, ducking under branches and working his way around the largest apple trees, making a direct course for the trio of cherry trees he knew were on the other side, just beside the bridge. The skin of his left hand stung. It was bright red where it had been scraped raw by bark. His right wrist was covered in blisters from the demon's touch. But his hands were steady now and he watched the branches above him as he ran, gaze sweeping the orchard.

There was a small clearing ahead. A spot of sunlight.

Beyond that, through the screen of the branches of a pear tree, he saw those gigantic cherry trees. His own heartbeat filled his head. He could barely take a breath, and when he swallowed it hurt his throat. The man he had always been would not have recognized this guy running through the trees. A voice he recognized as his own, as the professional voice of Oliver Bascombe, lawyer, screamed at him to stop this foolishness, to run and pray for a miracle. But the voice of his heart and now his head as well, the voice of the man he was onstage, projecting to the back of the audience, shouted it down. There was no room for sheepish, unassertive Oliver here. He had to be the man he always wished but never believed he could be . . .

Or he would die.

Leaves rustled and a branch cracked above and to his right. He swung the shotgun that way even as he backed away to the left, darting around a copse of apple trees, pushing through the dense tangle of branches between them. He turned to continue toward the cherry trees and his friends.

A figure loomed in front of him, up in the branches of an apple tree. There was no time for thought or hesitation.

Oliver fired the shotgun and it blew a massive hole in the chest of the creature up in that apple tree.

But the thing did not move. The tree swayed, but it remained where it was. Branches were wrapped around its arms and legs, strangling its throat, plunging into its eyes and mouth. And now, even as Oliver stared, more of them rushed in to slide into the gaping wound the shotgun blast had just made, and apple blossoms began to flower there.

It was a dead man, a brown leather pouch slung over his shoulder. He was taller than any man Oliver had ever seen, but a man nevertheless. In death, one of his hands had been closed into a fist, and now with the jerking of the branches invading his flesh, the fingers loosened and the hand opened slightly.

Spilling out apple seeds.

Aerico had mentioned him before. Appleseed.

Johnny Appleseed.

He had not been caught by the Myth Hunters, but murdered by the demon of the cherry tree, perhaps trying to appease them.

Oliver staggered backward. A familiar, sticky laughter chuffed in the tree just behind him. He spun, but too late.

The demon was upon him.

If Kitteridge was Norman Rockwell's wet dream, the kind of New England town that bespoke another era, a purer piece of Americana, then Cottingsley was the source of Rockwell's passions. It *was* that other era, that purer Americana. Kitteridge was quaint, but it was a twenty-first-century town, complete with Starbucks and an Internet café. Driving into Cottingsley was a journey back in time.

Twelve days before Christmas and with a blanket of crisp, white snow upon every roof and tree and lawn, the town dredged up whispers of old memories in Ted Halliwell. The detective nurtured his grumpy exterior, but inside somewhere was still a boy who had grown up in a town very much like this one. There were wreaths on every street lamp and lights on every house. Kids threw snowballs at one another in the yard of a red brick schoolhouse as he drove past. Passing through the center of town, with the old train station and the skating rink in the park, he saw a couple strolling along the sidewalk, laden with the bags and boxes from their Christmas shopping, the man wearing an old-fashioned dress hat of the sort his uncle Bud had always favored.

It was, he thought, much like living inside a snow globe.

If he had come here in summertime he was certain he would have seen kids in simple, neat clothes having a catch on the town common or playing baseball in the schoolyard. There would be horns and strings played every Saturday night on the bandstand in the park, with crowds and balloons and ice cream, perhaps even fireworks. Driving into Cottingsley unsettled Halliwell, touching a part of him that he'd long forgotten. Though the experience was bittersweet, he found himself pleased to be there. Such feelings had not been roused the last time he had visited Cottingsley, but he had been a younger man then, and had still had his wife and daughter in his life. He had not been alone.

How strange it was that in this place, frozen in times past, where he knew no one at all, he found himself feeling less lonely than he had in years.

Then he saw the blue glass ball on the post in front of the police station up ahead and the sense of well-being that Cottingsley had bestowed upon him evaporated. This place had been tainted by violence, just like every other town in the world. If it had ever really been the pure dream of another age that it seemed on the surface, surely those days had passed long ago. Whatever remnant of innocence the town had managed to retain would have been destroyed by the hideous public murder of Alice St. John.

Halliwell pulled into the lot behind the police station and slid his Wessex County sheriff's department I.D. plate onto the dashboard. When he stepped out of the warmth of the car he shuddered and zipped his coat. It was less than two hours farther north from his usual stomping grounds, but it felt colder up here.

Or maybe you're just getting older, Ted. Older by the hour.

A cute little redheaded girl was sitting behind the reception desk inside the station. She looked up from a hardcover book when he came in and smiled politely. Halliwell figured she had to be eighteen to have the job—out of high school—but she didn't look quite that old.

"Can I help you, sir?"

He hitched his belt, self-conscious as he caught himself doing it, and pulled his I.D. wallet out, flipping it open. "Afternoon. I'm Detective Halliwell. I have an appointment with Detective Unger."

There was that smile again, warm and heartbreaking. Halliwell imagined boys promising eternal devotion to God to have those eyes twinkle for them just once. A curmudgeon he might be, and old enough to be her father, but he couldn't imagine any man immune to that smile. The receptionist thumbed a button on an intercom on her desk.

"Daddy," she said, "Detective Halliwell's here from the Wessex County sheriff's."

"Thank you, Sarah," came the crackling reply. "Send him back, would you? Actually, on second thought, I'll be out."

Halliwell raised an eyebrow. "The detective's your father?"

Sarah Unger gave him an uncertain look, as though wary of disapproval. "Yes?" she asked, the *What of it?* clear but unspoken.

"Must be nice for him, having you around." Halliwell said it without thinking, just voicing his gut reaction, but the words echoed in him and he slid his hands into his coat pockets and let out a long breath as though he were deflating. He tried not to calculate the number of days since he had last seen his own daughter. His Sara. That this girl shared the name sent regret stabbing through him.

The girl's brows knitted—she sensed something had upset him—but she said nothing and a moment later a man appeared from the door behind her, which was set into a broad wall of smoked glass. It looked more like a lawyer's office than a police station. The man was tall and thin with a narrow, hooked nose and piercing eyes. He wore a thin white mustache and his hair was little more than wisps of salt and pepper.

"You're Halliwell?" he asked as he slipped on a long wool coat. Once again, more like a lawyer than a cop.

"That's right. Detective Unger?"

Unger put his hand out and Halliwell shook it, thinking that the man reminded him more than a little of a gunfighter from some old spaghetti western.

"Pleased to meet you. I've got an appointment later so I thought we should just get on to business, if you don't mind. I'll walk you over to the crime scene and we can have a look around, give you an idea of what happened. If that suits you."

The man had been all activity from the moment he'd appeared, putting on his jacket and then checking the gun in his shoulder holster, as if he expected armed resistance to their outing. As he spoke, he went to the reception desk and flipped through several messages his daughter had written down. When Halliwell didn't respond immediately he glanced up, eyebrows raised.

"That'll be fine," Halliwell said.

Unger nodded and put the messages back down on the

desk. He bent over it to kiss his daughter on the forehead—an act that seemed out of place with his overly businesslike demeanor—and Halliwell decided he liked the hawk-faced man. Unger slipped a thick scarf and a wool cap off the coatrack by the door, earning Halliwell's envy, and then led the way back outside.

They had less than an hour of daylight left and already the world had a gray twilight pall about it. As they strode around the front of the police station and then started down the street back toward the center of town, Halliwell caught Unger up on the circumstances of Max Bascombe's murder and the disappearance of his children.

"Well, we know Oliver Bascombe's alive, at least," Detective Unger said, his small blue eyes glancing sidelong at Halliwell. "Or he was last night."

"No doubt about your witness I.D.?"

"None. Three different kids picked him out as having been in the park last night. Half a dozen people who were in the train station identified his picture as well. The officers who tried to chase him down didn't get within twenty feet of him, but the lead officer, Morgan Dubay, was close enough. It was him, all right."

They reached the town square and crossed the street in front of a small pub called Two Dogs. On the other side of the park, smoke rose from two thick chimneys that jutted up from the train station.

"Never really doubted it, considering the way the girl was killed."

Unger grunted, lowered his head and stared at the ground a moment, and then narrowed his gaze as he peered at Halliwell again. "What do you make of it, then? The son do it? He unhinged or something? Or is he running and whoever killed his old man and the St. John girl is chasing him?"

Ted Halliwell rubbed his hands in front of him, blowing on them to warm them as they started through the park on a path that led amongst tall evergreens, past a playground that was closed for the winter—all the swings missing—and toward an outdoor skating rink still roped off with yellow crime scene tape.

"There's a lot that doesn't make sense about the Bascombe case," he said, without glancing again at Unger. He didn't want to have to try to put into words the unease that took him when he considered the unusual way first Oliver and then Collette had vanished, Oliver in the midst of a blizzard, and both without any obvious clue as to the mode of their departure.

"But do you make the son for the killings?"

Unger had asked a direct question. Halliwell couldn't avoid answering it.

"I don't figure him for a killer. But you never know, do you?"

There was a pause in the conversation as Unger took in the question, which Halliwell had purposely posed with a weariness he knew the other detective must share. That was the price of the job they both worked, a dulling of blind faith in humanity.

"No," Unger agreed. "No, I guess you don't."

As they approached the rink—and the train station beyond—Unger stopped and pointed south to where the evergreens were more plentiful and grew together in a dense little wood right in the middle of the park.

"According to the kids, who were the first to see him, Bascombe came out of those trees there with an Asian woman in some kind of fur coat with a hood."

Halliwell frowned. "First I've heard about her."

Unger shrugged. "The A.P.B. was for Bascombe. Anyway, point is, all the witnesses to Alice St. John's murder had the killer showing up the same way. Guy in a black or gray cloak—sounds like the Grim Reaper from the description—rushes out of the woods, grabs the nearest kid, and—"

He grimaced and shook his head. "Poor little thing. My wife had Alice in her kindergarten class six, seven years ago. Cute as a button."

The details of the girl's murder were in the preliminary coroner's report and Halliwell felt no need to press Unger on them. The little girl's murder had been hideous, her eyes gouged out, the cause of death blood loss and trauma. But there were things about the report that were unclear and he could not avoid addressing them.

"I'm sorry, Detective. It's a hell of a thing."

Unger nodded grimly.

"The preliminary report says the investigating officers never found her eyes. Is that still—"

"Not a trace," Unger replied in disgust. "You believe it? The guy kills her right out in public, mutilates her like that, and keeps them as . . . as trophies or whatever. It's inhuman."

Halliwell started toward the skating rink. He didn't bother ducking under the police tape. There was nothing to see but ice. New-fallen snow had covered up any trace of blood or the markings the local cops had made to note the position of the body. There were no evidence markers. Nothing but that bright yellow tape. Still, he found himself staring at the spot where he imagined it had happened. Two kids were making snow angels in the park not thirty yards from the site of the murder, but there weren't any others in sight. He wondered how many parents were keeping their kids under lock and key this week. Most of them, he imagined.

"My officers were at that end of the park," Unger continued, pointing north. "They spotted Bascombe and the woman talking to some kids here. Then the two of them started for the train station and one of the kids shouted after them. According to the kids, they seemed to know about Alice's murder. Anyway, the officers were suspicious and went after them, thinking to question them, and Bascombe and the woman took off. They ran into the station."

As he spoke, Unger led Halliwell across the paved drive that separated the station from the park and up the stairs of the train station. They went through and out onto the platform. There was no train in sight.

"It's a tourist thing, the train. Scenic railroad. They serve hot chocolate and sing Christmas carols and pretend they're riding to the north pole. The kids love it, apparently. But it's nice that they can make some money to keep the old trains running and the station in decent shape. It's a historic landmark and I'd hate to see it end up replaced by more shops."

Halliwell nodded. "It's a beautiful town. You could live your whole life here and never have to think about all the crap the rest of the world deals with every day."

Unger laughed. "That's the hope." He gestured toward the tracks, beyond which there was nothing but winter forest. "The train was here. The officers pursued Bascombe and the woman through the crowd. The suspects jumped off the platform and ran around the front of the train to the woods on the other side. By the time the officers got around there, they were gone."

Gone. Halliwell wasn't sure how to express his thoughts to Unger, so he kept them to himself, but that was the thing that kept coming back to him. The killer appears out of nowhere, a tall, imposing guy, fairly conspicuous in his cloak or whatever. He kills a girl in broad daylight yet somehow manages to disappear without a trace. Then Bascombe and this mystery woman appear, also seemingly out of nowhere, only to vanish. Others might have made assumptions about the Cottingsley P.D., figured they were incompetent. Halliwell knew better. One cop, sure, but an entire police department incapable of tracking three strangers in their town—strangers who appeared to have no vehicle and no other means to leave the town—was impossible to believe.

So, what, then? That was the thing he kept coming back to. How had the killer—not to mention Bascombe— slipped in and out of Cottingsley undetected? Likely the same way Oliver had left his family home back on Rose Ridge Lane in Kitteridge. But Halliwell hadn't figured that part out yet, either.

Arms crossed, teeth almost chattering with the cold, he stared at the snow-covered woods behind the train station.

"So where did they go?" he asked, mostly to himself.

"North, for starters," Unger replied.

Halliwell cocked his head. "How do you know that?"

"A bunch of hunters saw them. Well, saw the Asian woman in the fur. Fox fur, according to them. She stole a shotgun and some ammunition from the back of one of their trucks and then ran into the woods."

"That's new information," Halliwell said.

"As of a few hours ago, yes," Unger confirmed.

"And let me guess. They went to chase her, but she vanished into the woods?"

Unger nodded.

"Shit," Halliwell muttered. He scratched his head, staring again at the snowy woods across the train tracks.

"There is . . . one other thing," Unger said.

Halliwell turned to regard him, but the other detective studiously avoided his gaze. He had his hands clasped behind his back and was looking south along the tracks as though he expected the train to arrive at any moment.

"Yeah?"

"Something that wasn't in the preliminary report. And . . . won't be in the final one, either."

"I don't like the sound of that," Halliwell said.

Unger continued to pretend to wait for the train. "The officers on the scene reported a substance left behind in Alice's . . . in the victim's eye sockets by the killer. The coroner confirmed it. Just—" The detective shook his head and blew out a long breath. "Just packed in there, somehow. None of the witnesses saw it happen, apparently. I mean, they saw him mutilate her like that, take out her eyes, but nobody saw him filling the empty sockets back up."

There was a hollowness in his voice that would haunt Ted Halliwell for a very long time.

"With what?" he asked.

At last Unger turned and stared at him, nostrils flaring in what might have been anger or grief or horror. When he spoke, he flinched as though the words physically hurt him.

"With sand."

Oliver smelled cherries.

The demon lunged from the branches overhead and laughed as he fell upon his prey. The shotgun was empty, but instinctively Oliver swung it up and drove the butt of the weapon into Aerico's face. The demon's spidery fingers scratched Oliver's throat and he felt a terrible itching—sure that the same blisters and splotches that had appeared on his wrist before were spreading across his neck. But he ignored it. The butt of the shotgun split Aerico's cherry skin. Beneath it was the same moist purple flesh as the fruit.

Aerico squealed with pain and tumbled to the ground, but quickly scrambled away, turning around to face Oliver in a crouch. One of those impossibly long hands was clasped to his split cheek and his pink eyes flared with fury.

Then the demon laughed again and lowered his hand. Where the wound had been, cherry blossoms had grown, knitting the flesh together. Aerico would heal. The image made Oliver shudder as he recalled the fate that had befallen Frost in the cherry trees, with branches speared through his icy form and cherries growing from his wounds.

Must be some magic there, more than just the injuries. He's Jack Frost. He's a storm shaped like a man. Oliver thought of the poison touch of the demon and was certain that had something to do with it. Somehow Aerico had paralyzed Kitsune and the winter man, and ambushed them first because they were a danger to him. Too powerful to combat without subterfuge.

"You're a coward," he said suddenly, speaking the realization aloud.

The demon stopped laughing. In the shadows of the orchard he started forward again, careful this time and eyeing the shotgun Oliver was using as a club, but preparing to attack nevertheless.

"I don't like you, Bascombe," Aerico sneered, the smell of cherries stronger than ever. "I may fill you with seeds, with my seeds, and see how many new trees will grow from your flesh, roots burrowing from your back into the soil . . . and see how long I can cultivate you and keep you alive while it happens."

Oliver was in so much pain from the welts and blisters and scraped hand and the injuries to his back and shoulder that his fear seemed far, far away. He had distanced himself from it. Exhaustion and pain seemed to smother him, and now he was only angry and impatient.

Across the orchard he could still hear Kitsune barking in pain.

He waved the shotgun as though it was a baseball bat and just nodded, urging the demon on. If he'd been a different sort of man he would have summoned up some pithy quip, some macho riposte, but Oliver wasn't wired that way. He just wanted to survive.

Aerico scuttled nearer to a pear tree and reached long arms upward, spindly fingers wrapping around the lower branches. The demon meant to return to the trees, to attack from the shadows. Oliver amazed himself by rushing forward, not wanting to give Aerico another chance at such an attack. He raised the shotgun.

But never swung it.

Even as the demon tried to pull himself into a tree, the ground seemed to whisper and then green and brown shoots pushed up through the dirt. Tree roots wrapped around Aerico's legs, cutting in to tender cherry flesh. Stalks of corn and wheat burst from the ground with a dry, rasping noise and ensnared the demon's arms and throat, weaving themselves around him. Aerico screamed and tried to tear himself away, but he was held fast.

The ground rumbled as entire corn plants grew from nothing and other crops pushed up from the island—

wheat and barley and rye. A small tree grew in the midst of those farm crops and soon it was clear it was an apple tree. As the cherry-tree demon struggled and mewled pitifully and Oliver watched in astonishment, his injuries throbbing, the apple tree grew quickly to the height of a man.

It *was* a man.

Oliver saw that it had a face and its branches were arms and it pulled its trunk from the ground and had legs. It did not so much as look at Oliver, but walked past him, apples and leaves rustling on its branches, and stood staring at the corpse of Johnny Appleseed dangling from another tree.

It wept, and its tears smelled of fresh-cut apples.

The crops were so thick in the clearing of the orchard and around the bases of the trees that at first Oliver did not see the other things moving amongst them. Then the stalks and shafts moved with the passage of these new arrivals and he held his breath as the figures emerged. A wolf, a stag, and a creature built like a man, but whose entire body was formed from corn husks. Even his face was shaped like a human's, right down to the indents where his eyes ought to have been, but there were only pale green corn husks.

And then he spoke in a voice that was the rustle of the wind across the corn rows.

"Behold the gods of the Harvest."

CHAPTER 10

Oliver could hardly draw breath as he stared at these things that called themselves gods. There had been a moment where he had thought he might be able to defeat Aerico. But now his stolen shotgun was empty and he was alone against the four new arrivals. The massive wolf lowered its head and sniffed the ground. The buck stood and regarded Oliver with clear, intelligent eyes, its huge, intricate antlers casting complex shadows. The apple-tree man paid little attention, his focus on the corpse of Johnny Appleseed. Yet the one that disturbed him the most was the thing—the god—that had spoken. It watched him as though it had a real face, and eyes to see with, but there were only corn husks indented as though they were eyes. The Kirata and the Falconer had terrified him, but this was something else entirely. Some ancient part of him at the base of his brain and the pit of his stomach shuddered at the alienness of it, and he wanted to scream.

On the ground that separated him from the gods of the Harvest—and the new crops that had grown up around the trees in the orchard—the demon from the cherry tree struggled against the corn and wheat stalks that seemed to be pulling it down into the soil. The air was sickly sweet with the smell of overripe cherries. Yet none of them bothered to even glance at Aerico as it was subsumed by the ground. Consumed. Its cries were muffled by the vegetation that grew over its mouth.

Oliver pretended not to notice, awaiting some word or action from the gods of the Harvest. Long seconds ticked by, perhaps more than a minute, as the corn-husk man stared at him and the wolf sniffed the ground.

Then the wolf raised its head. It made no sound, but some kind of signal had been given, for the stag trotted several steps closer and the man—or whatever it was—covered in corn husks emerged further from the crops.

"You are the Intruder all of the whispers are about?" said the corn-husk man in a sandpaper voice, his mouth a dark, toothless hole.

Oliver felt so obviously out of place that he saw no point in lying. "I am."

"Your name?"

"Oliver Bascombe."

With a ripple like the wind in the crops, the corn-husk man bowed. "We are well met, Oliver Bascombe. You fought bravely against the demon. But we must be going if you are to avoid the Myth Hunters. Aerico slew Appleseed for them. Undoubtedly they will come for his remains."

Oliver was keenly aware of his own breathing. He

stared at the corn-husk man as though he had no idea what the creature was talking about, yet he thought he had understood quite well. It was just difficult for him to believe.

"You're . . . going to help me?"

The Harvest god glanced at the buck and then at the wolf, husk rasping against husk. "The demon could never have been trusted, but we understood that. It was his nature. We must all be true to our natures. Yet by murdering Appleseed, he betrayed us."

He said the words as though they were an answer to Oliver's question. And perhaps they were. When he had finished he turned and started through the new crops that had thrust up from the freshly turned earth and then into the thicker part of the orchard.

Oliver frowned in confusion. Where were they going? What was to become of him now? What of his friends?

Then the apple-tree man moved to the corpse of Johnny Appleseed and began tearing him loose from the tree where he had been killed. The smell of apple cider—or of fermented apples—filled the clearing, and Oliver decided he did not want to bear witness to this process. He set off after the other gods of the Harvest. Though he gave the apple-tree man and his slaughtered kin a wide berth, the creature did not even glance at him as he passed.

The deep rushing sound of the river filled the air. From above came the cawing of birds, but none of them soared down to roost in the trees on this strange island. There was just the wind in the trees and the gods of the Harvest moving through the wood ahead of him. He followed them by the sound of their passage amongst the branches and leaves, and also by the shoots that sprang up from the soil after their passing. Wheat and corn and rye had begun to grow up like sparse grass.

Oliver picked up his pace, both afraid to lose them and afraid that the apple-tree man would catch up to him with that cider-smelling corpse in its branches.

Only when he saw the buck stopped up ahead, its antlers indistinguishable from the branches of the trees above it, did he realize that the gods of the Harvest had paused . . . and that he could no longer hear the muffled, pained yelping of Kitsune the fox. Then Oliver ducked beneath the low-hanging limbs of a peach tree and realized he had come full circle, back to the trio of towering cherry trees in the shadow of the Atlantic Bridge. The river flowed nearby, the dark stonework of the bridge echoed its rushing voice into the trees, and the smell of cherries was overwhelming.

The buck once more stood silent, as though it were the sentinel on alert for any threat to present itself. On the rough ground in the triangle formed by the three trees, the Harvest wolf stood over Kitsune, who lay sprawled in a tangle of fur and limbs, no longer a fox.

As anxious as he was at the presence of these self-proclaimed deities, Oliver hurried past the buck and went to kneel by her side. The wolf inclined its head as though in invitation—or permission—and took a step back. Kitsune seemed to have been dropped to the ground like an abandoned marionette. Her ebon hair was feathered across her face and he reached out to brush it away, to see her eyes.

Kitsune growled and bared her teeth.

Oliver froze with his fingers only inches from her. That low growl continued for a moment and then abruptly ceased. Her nostrils flared and she sniffed the air. A kind of mewling sound came from her throat and she stirred, pulling herself up into a fetal curl on the ground just beside him. Her hair fell away from her face and as he watched, her jade eyes fluttered open.

"Kitsune?"

"Hello, my friend."

"Are you badly hurt?"

"It is passing," she said, the perfect bow of her mouth offering amusement and irony. "We were foolish, ignoring our own warnings. We might have been better off taking our chances with the soldiers."

Oliver shook his head. "I thought the trees were killing you."

"As did I, at first. But no, these cherry trees are his and there is poison in the touch of their wood. He was holding us, but I do not know for what purpose."

Poison in the touch. Oliver rubbed at his wrist. With Aerico's death, the welts had begun to heal. Even his scraped fingers did not sting as much.

Oliver glanced over at the buck and then up at the wolf. "Actually, that makes sense. He was waiting for the Hunters to come. He must have intended to give you to them alive. And me as well. Apparently there's a reward. He's already killed—"

A frown creased his forehead. In his relief at finding Kitsune alive and recovering and disoriented by his melee with the cherry-tree demon and the arrival of the gods of the Harvest, he had been mentally adrift, just reacting to whatever came. Now he uttered a small laugh of mingled hope and disbelief.

"Wait a second," he said, glancing around, and then upward.

The corn-husk man stood in the lee of the bridge, now twice as tall as he had been before. His torso had stretched so far that his chest and abdomen measured at least nine or ten feet. New stalks of corn grew from the island soil, wrapping around his ankles and legs and anchoring him to the ground. He reached into the branches of that cherry tree nearest the bridge and with the dry rustle of husks his arms lengthened as well.

Where spears of sunlight found their way through the canopy of the tree, ice glistened. Frost was still there, speared through by branches and with bunches of cherries growing from the wounds. The frozen form of the winter man did not move. As far as Oliver knew he had not moved since those branches had impaled him, cracking the ice of his body, branches growing inside of him.

He's not dead, Oliver thought, as though trying to convince himself. *Frost isn't . . . he doesn't have a body, really. He's just ice. Winter. A walking blizzard. Poison couldn't affect him.*

He stood, and, smiling slightly, he moved nearer that tree, tilting his head and trying to get the best view up at Frost. As the corn-husk man grabbed hold of him, Frost shook and the icicles of his hair clinked together. That familiar winter chime caught Oliver's breath in his throat.

Aerico was a demon. Any poison in him was demonic . . . magical. Perhaps it could affect Frost, after all.

Oliver watched, nodding as he silently urged the corn-husk man on. The creature grabbed hold of Frost and began to pull, exerting more and more force, attempting to tear him away from the branches that had been forced through him. A crack sounded, and then another, and Oliver held his breath, unsure if it was wood or ice that was cracking. Cherries dropped off Frost and fell to the ground below, ignored.

There came another loud crack. Oliver flinched and began to speak, to warn the corn-husk man to be careful.

And Frost shattered, practically exploding in a shower of chunks and shards of ice that rained down through the branches to the ground around the cherry tree. Several pieces struck Oliver, one of them stinging him as it made a tiny cut on his cheek.

"No!" he shouted. "What did you do? What the hell did you do? You idiot!"

He shoved a branch out of his face and started around the tree toward the corn-husk man. With a growl, the wolf leaped into his path, back arched and yellow teeth bared. It was as tall on four legs as he was on two and his heartbeat faltered with his step. Shaking his head in grief he stared up at the corn-husk man even as the creature—deity, whatever—began to shrink. Its torso contracted with a whisper and rattle of crops. But if he thought he might understand the thing, might see some emotion that would explain, he had forgotten for a moment about the blankness of its features, about those pale green husks across where its eyes might have been.

Defeated, his shoulders slumped and he stared around at the fragments of the winter man. Some of them were large enough to be recognizable—a forearm, a shoulder, a foot—but most were just chunks of ice.

Oliver lowered his head in sadness, staring now at nothing.

A familiar scent reached him and then he felt the soft brush of Kitsune's fur against his hand. Her fingers touched his shoulder.

"You misunderstand," she said.

It occurred to him, at those words, that maybe Frost

had already been dead, after all. That was the only possibility that made any sense to him at all.

Until he felt the chill breeze that danced around the trees, caressing his face and ruffling his hair. Leaves fluttered to the ground as though it was autumn. A sprig of cherries fell from a branch and landed at his feet.

There was ice on them.

The wind picked up, whipping into a frenzy that focused on a place roughly at the center of that triangle amidst the cherry trees. The pieces of ice, the shards of the winter man, began to tumble toward that vortex, some of them sucked up into the air and drawn right into the midst of that miniature storm. At its heart there was snow.

Oliver laughed, covering his mouth in amazement as he watched the blizzard take form.

The wind died.

Frost stood in their midst, unharmed, as the gods of the Harvest began to gather around him.

"Hello, Frost," said the corn-husk man.

"Konigen, I am in your debt," the winter man replied.

Kitsune stepped toward them, glancing quickly back at Oliver with a playful grin before nodding in gratitude to the corn-husk man.

"We ought to be going," she said.

Frost nodded. "Indeed." Then he looked over to Oliver. "Coming? I would very much like to hear how it is you are still alive and Aerico is no longer with us."

"Coming," Oliver agreed, unable to stop smiling.

He joined them there, amidst the cherry trees, and he realized that he had never really believed there was a chance he might reach the end of this nightmare alive. Until now.

Frost and Kitsune had been his traveling companions,

but this trial on an island in the middle of the Atlantic had made of them something more. They were bound in a way he did not entirely understand, though he felt the power of those ties.

A long journey still lay ahead, but he would not face it alone.

The terrain on the eastern side of the Atlantic Bridge was rough and inhospitable, as though once upon a time the land had been sown with salt like the ruins of ancient Carthage. Nothing grew there save low, twisted shrubs and scrub grass that looked to Oliver more like steel wool than something alive.

Ahren Konigen did not accompany the fugitives, but rather remained behind upon the island that had been the domain of the demon of the cherry tree. The apple-tree man—whom Oliver had learned actually was referred to, even in myth, as the Appletree Man—remained with Konigen. Nothing was said, but Oliver understood that they would travel back to their own lands in some way other than traversing this dead landscape, working their way along underground from root to root, perhaps.

Only the Kornwolf and the Kornböcke, as he learned they were called, traveled with them on the Truce Road through that rough terrain. The road itself was little different on this side of the Atlantic Bridge, though it was rutted in places from many long years' passage of cart wheels. The wolf trotted far ahead, sniffing the road and pausing at the crest of each hill to peruse the horizon, seemingly on guard against the return of the soldiers who had passed earlier. The stag followed behind, aloof as ever, and if Oliver paused to glance its way, the animal would halt and raise its rack of antlers, staring coldly at him until he started onward once more. It was unsettling, yet he never felt threatened by these strange creatures.

They had saved his life, after all. He had no idea why, but they had put themselves in dire peril on his behalf. The thought was not as comforting as he would have expected, for it reminded him of the weight of the threat against him and his companions.

After the initial relief of finding that Frost and Kitsune had both survived, Oliver had asked a number of questions, learning the names of the Harvest gods that had intervened on their behalf and that they were only a few among a seemingly infinite number of such deities.

Now, with the Atlantic Bridge miles behind them and the day growing warmer with the persistence of the sun, it was Kitsune who brought his inquiries to a halt. She threw back the hood of her fur cloak and glanced at Frost, her jade eyes strangely wide.

"Remarkable as it seems, there is a question Oliver has not asked," she said, more than a hint of exotic accent in her voice that he had not heard before. "Is our destination much farther?"

The winter man frowned with concern, head tilting, icy hair clinking as he regarded her. "I'd thought you were healing?"

Oliver saw now how pale Kitsune seemed. Her hands were at her sides but they seemed to waver as though she was afraid at any moment she might lose her balance, there on the road.

"Healing, yes. But not healed. I need only a little time to rest and something to eat to restore myself." Kitsune glanced away as she uttered this admission.

Frost scanned the land around them, looked at the

Kornwolf and then back at the stag, who had stopped but took no notice of them, like some subway commuter doing his best not to recognize the presence of anyone else on the train. Oliver decided that he did not like the Kornböcke. Not even the littlest bit. Regardless of what it and the others had done, he could not help feeling that the stag thought them beneath its own station.

"At our current pace it will be another hour, at least, before we enter the domain of Ahren Konigen."

A pained look rippled across Kitsune's face.

Oliver scratched the back of his head, unsure if the thought that rose in his mind would be welcome. But the way Kitsune trembled, he could not remain silent.

"I could carry you."

All trace of mischief was gone from her. Kitsune smiled softly at him but shook her head. "You are weakened yourself, Oliver, and did you not hear Frost? It's an hour's walk."

He shrugged lightly and gestured to her. "Well, I couldn't carry you like this. But . . . as a fox . . ."

The wind tousled his hair and blew up dirt from the road. Kitsune stared at him and he felt himself hushed by her beauty, by the clash of delicacy and viciousness in her. Those jade eyes so often seemed to be laughing, but now there was only tenderness there.

"I . . . it's just that Frost is ice, and if he carried you—"

"I could carry you both in a storm," said the winter man, long, sharp fingers waving toward the sky, "but I am also weakened. I don't know how far we would get."

"We dare not risk it," Kitsune rasped, her voice like a little growl in her throat, without taking her eyes away from Oliver. "But if you are truly willing . . ."

Her words trailed off but the inquiry remained in her eyes.

Oliver nodded. "Of course. We all need to rest, somewhere safe. I wasn't sure if the suggestion would offend you."

She arched an eyebrow but without any trace of a smile, so that the expression was profoundly enigmatic. Just as Oliver was trying to puzzle it out, Kitsune reached up and raised her hood. The fur rippled across her back and along her arms and then she diminished, transforming from woman to fox in that strangely fluid metamorphosis that Oliver knew would never cease to astonish him.

He set down the shotgun case—which he had retrieved, along with its ammunition, before they left Aerico's grove—then took off his parka and tied it around his waist as tightly as he could. Despite the sun, the breeze was cool, but the effort of their journey would warm him. With the shotgun case slung across his back once more he turned to Frost and Kitsune again.

Ahead of them, on a rise in the Truce Road, the Kornwolf howled low. Oliver frowned and glanced at the Harvest god, but the wolf did not seem alarmed, only impatient.

The fox walked to him. An image flashed through Oliver's mind of her trapped in that cherry tree, and the way its branches had captured and violated her. He shuddered as he crouched to pick her up. In his arms, the fox made to climb up one shoulder and he stood steadily, wondering what Kitsune had in mind. In a moment she had wrapped herself around the back of his neck like some kind of living stole. Her body was hot and her fur soft against his skin. The extra weight was not going to make the walk any easier, but he felt sure he could handle it.

"Are you sure about this?" Frost asked, a mist rising from his blue-white eyes.

"I can manage," Oliver replied.

The winter man turned. "Then let's be off. I don't want to be on the road longer than we have to. After we make it to the Harvest Fields, we'd be better off from now on traveling at night."

Before Oliver could reply, he was startled by the presence of the stag close behind him. It was so close he could smell its breath, damp and earthy like home-brewed beer.

"Move along," the Kornböcke ordered.

Oliver frowned. He wanted to tell the otherwise silent deity to go fuck himself, but he had a feeling that might undermine the help they were receiving from the gods of the Harvest. Even so—

"We're doing our best," Oliver told him.

The stag only glanced around pointedly to remind him that they were still in danger. Oliver got the message but decided that if the stag thought no words were necessary, that was a policy he would also pursue. Without another glance at the creature he started off. At first Kitsune was restless on his shoulders and he could feel her heart beating too fast against the back of his neck. But then she seemed to settle down and lay her head upon her paws on his right shoulder, copper fur tickling his cheek.

Some time later—perhaps Frost's predicted hour, though Oliver thought it longer—they came over a rise and a valley lay before them so green and lush that Oliver could only think of the Garden of Eden. He thought that Kitsune might have fallen asleep on his shoulders and he held her fore and rear paws gently just in case she might be jostled from her perch. When he spoke to the winter man, who strode beside him with that gait that often seemed like a flamingo across the surface of a lake, he did so in a voice just above a whisper.

"I don't understand. All of the land we just crossed, from the river to this valley . . . how can it be so barren and this so fertile?"

"There was a war there, once, before the Truce," the winter man said, as the two of them hurried to catch up with the Kornwolf, who had sped up once they came in sight of the Harvest Fields. "The lands of the Harvest gods were untouched because they were neutral. No soldier was welcome there."

Oliver nodded. They had always been rebellious and independent, these things of nature. "That's good to know."

As exhausted as he was, Oliver felt his spirits lifted and some of his strength returned as they entered the valley. There were groves of trees in spots but most of what he saw, extending out before him all the way to the crest of the farthest hill, were crops. Corn and wheat and cabbage and squash all grew there, regardless of the season in which they were meant to peak. When they passed a pumpkin patch, Oliver actually laughed softly to himself. For some reason, that sound seemed to be the one to wake Kitsune, and soon she tensed to leap down to the road. She did not resume her human shape immediately, but kept pace beside him on silent paws.

The wolf and the stag disappeared into a vast cornfield and Oliver saw the stalks rippling as they passed.

Just as he began to wonder where they would find Ahren Konigen, three figures moved from the crops and out onto the road ahead of them. They were women, petite and lovely, with bronze skin and black hair tied in braids. They were naked save for leaves that at first Oliver assumed had been woven into some covering. But upon closer inspection, he realized that the leaves were growing from their flesh.

As Oliver paused, fascinated by these new Harvest creatures, Kitsune moved past him. Between one step and the next she stood up from the four legs of a fox, copper fur like a banner unfurling in the breeze as it became a hooded cloak once more. She touched Frost on the shoulder and he paused, allowing her to take the lead. Kitsune favored Oliver with a momentary glance before turning her attention fully to these ambassadors—for that was what they seemed, a kind of greeting party sent out of the fields to meet them.

The three women stood waiting as Kitsune approached with a respectful air about her. She put her hands together and bowed her head a moment, speaking in a low voice in what Oliver believed was Japanese. He was only vaguely familiar with the language through some of the law firm's clients, and the only words he knew translated into either basic greetings or colorful profanity. The three women were nearly indistinguishable from one another but the one in the center seemed by virtue of body language alone to be the leader amongst them. The others clearly deferred to her and it was she who replied to Kitsune, briefly and softly, after which all three of them inclined their heads in one shared motion.

Yet the language the women spoke was not Japanese. It was not any language he had ever heard.

Kitsune returned the respectful bow and backed up two steps before turning away from them and striding toward Frost. The winter man had borne witness to this exchange without word or gesture. Now he turned and beckoned for Oliver to join them. For his part, Oliver had been lulled by curiosity into the role of observer and was almost startled to be drawn back into that of participant.

"They are Deohako," Kitsune told her companions,

"guardian spirits of the Harvest in the legends of the Iro-
quois people."

"But you spoke to them in Japanese," Oliver said.

Her jade eyes sparkled. "True. There is an aspect of
their legend in Japanese stories. They understood well
enough." To the winter man, she added, "We are to follow
them."

Frost nodded and Kitsune turned to face the Deohako,
who did not hesitate but immediately started into the tall
rows of corn. Momentarily that strange parade was making its way along a path that arranged itself before them—
crops moving aside to let them pass—and then closed up
behind as though to conceal their passage.

Oliver was glad to know their trail would not be visible
from the road but he was deeply unsettled by the overall effect, the knowledge that there would be no easy departure
from the fields. The feeling persisted as they were swallowed deeper and deeper by the crops until they came to a
clearing where the rich brown earth yielded to the heavy
print of his boot but where not so much as a sprig or blade
of grass was rooted in the soil.

A moment later, they began to grow, just as they had on
the island in the midst of the river where the cherry tree
demon had nearly killed Oliver and his companions. There
were perhaps a dozen of them, some effigies of animals
like the Kornwolf and the officious stag, others the shape
of humans, but still others little more than oddly shaped
stalks of corn, contorted trees, and even a massive squash
plant whose growths bore slits that might have been eyes
and mouth.

The Appletree Man and Ahren Konigen were the last to
arrive. The others shifted through the rich soil to yield
to them. The afternoon light was growing long, throwing

distorted shadows across the branches and stalks of the Harvest gods, and in that slant of light the Appletree Man barely seemed to have a face at all. When the tree stopped moving save for the breeze in its branches, it seemed to have been there forever. The others might have deferred to both of those deities, but it was Konigen to whom they all looked now. Konigen who spoke.

Konigen who glanced around as though he had eyes instead of mere indents layered with corn husks. He regarded the visitors to the Harvest Fields and a quiet came over the clearing, disturbed only by the wind in the leaves.

"We know that you desire rest and sustenance. We will parley, briefly, and then you will be given to eat of our crops, the sweetest fruit and most delicious vegetables you have ever eaten. The fox shall be encouraged to run amongst the roots and rows and trap whatever mice or voles might be found here."

The muscles in Oliver's legs burned with exhaustion but he thought it would be bad form to collapse there in the clearing. He was tired, his attention span short, and yet Konigen's declaration startled him. There was something vaguely cannibalistic about even considering eating the provenance of the Harvest Fields. It was no garden, but a kind of city unto itself, a settlement of legends from dozens of cultures.

Neither Frost nor Kitsune seemed to react to this pronouncement, however, and the fox-woman's expression seemed to brighten considerably at the mention of her hunting in the fields. The idea was faintly repulsive to Oliver, making him think of cats who dragged birds and mice home to leave their broken, bloody bodies on their master's threshold as some sort of offering.

Konigen spread his arms with the rasp of husk against

husk, and regarded the others gathered there. "Appleseed is dead. Aerico destroyed him. Withered him."

There was a rattle of leaves and branches that had nothing to do with the wind.

"Most of the Harvest are not Borderkind, and the Myth Hunters have ignored those amongst us who are . . . until now," Konigen continued, focusing on Frost. His expression darkened with a crinkling of the husks that composed his face. "But along the wayside and in the fields and orchards we have heard the stories of dark deeds. Of murder. Julenisse, Nicolai Chudovorits, Sinter Klaas, Pater Cronos, all of them dead."

The winter man had been remarkably silent for some time and Oliver wondered if his injuries had taken a greater toll on him than he was willing to admit. Now he brought a hand to his face so quickly that the sharp edges of his fingers scraped ice upon ice and shaved off a sprinkle of frost that drifted to the dirt. The icicles of his hair fell over his forehead and he shuddered, hunched with grief.

"Devils," Frost whispered.

Kitsune stood in the midst of the clearing, almost regal in her cloak, jade eyes looking out from beneath the hood. "The Sandmen are dead as well. And La Dormette. The original, the root of the legend, escaped. We have heard of others who have been killed. Selkies and Merrows and other of my distant kin."

Ahren Konigen nodded slowly. "This is true. Even Hu Hsien. Your cousin, Coyote, is alive, however. He has hidden himself well."

The fox-woman sneered. "Yes, that will solve everything, won't it? Hiding? He ought to be ashamed."

"La Llorona is among the dead. Eshu and Anansi as

well. Several aspects of Herne the Hunter have been destroyed, but other variations of the Wild Hunt have gone beyond the Veil. They will be forced to fight before long, when the Myth Hunters find them."

"Are there many among the Myth Hunters now?" Frost asked, a frigid hatred in his blue-white eyes, in the very mist that plumed from them.

"Far too many," Konigen replied.

The winter man nodded gravely.

"We only know what we have heard. Appleseed knew his fellow Borderkind better than those amongst the Harvest who are bound on this side of the Veil. It may be that some of those we have heard are dead yet live, and it is likely that many more have been killed and we are not yet aware of it. What is clear is this . . . whoever has set the Hunters after the Borderkind, they must be stopped."

A rime of ice had spread on the soil around Frost's feet. When he spoke, a chill wind swept through the Harvest Fields. The gods must have felt it, but none seemed to notice.

"That is our intent," the winter man said. "Any aid you can provide—"

"With regret, we cannot risk the health and safety of the Harvest with an open alliance," Konigen said, and Oliver thought he glanced away in shame, though as he had no eyes it might have been a trick of the late-afternoon shadows upon the husks of his face. "We can only offer sanctuary."

Frost was silent for several long moments, mist still pluming from his eyes.

Kitsune stared around at the gods of the Harvest. Her fur cloak rippled as she moved nearer to her companions, standing now between Oliver and Frost.

The winter man nodded. "Of course. And we are grateful. Though sanctuary may be the totality of our future, from here on. The Borderkind who still live will be traveling just as we are, seeking safe haven. It will be difficult to mount a defense without allies."

Oliver astounded himself with the sound of his own voice.

"You don't need a defense."

The entire congregation stared at him. He fidgeted beneath the weight of their regard, but he forged on.

"It's what you've already said. Someone has set the Hunters after the Borderkind. You can escape the Hunters if you're smart and quick and strong enough. But your situation is a lot like mine. The only way to survive is to get whoever's calling the shots to order them off."

Kitsune drew back her hood. Her silken hair blew in the breeze. She smiled at him.

"True, Oliver. But we haven't any idea who commands the Hunters. The question that will lead us to our real enemy, of course, is who benefits from the destruction of the Borderkind? But until we answer that question, we are in the dark. Meanwhile, given that we've got only a handful of Hunters after us, and you've the whole of this world ready to kill you, for the moment we'd best concentrate on getting you to Perinthia and attempting to have the mark of death lifted from you."

His stomach gave a lurch, and Oliver shivered. "You say that as though it's the simplest thing in the world."

"A simple goal, but a complex journey," Kitsune said, inclining her head.

"Yes," Frost agreed. "One thing at a time. Though if we can learn anything useful in Perinthia . . ."

The Kornwolf stalked from amidst several other

Harvest creatures. "If you mean to pass through Perinthia, this one must find clothes without the look and scent of his world. There is a settlement of Lost Ones on the way to the city. They have no love for any authority on either side of the Veil. They will help."

"Yes. Excellent," Konigen said. And then he stepped forward with that same shushing sound of husk against husk and approached the three travelers. The Harvest king—for that was surely what he was—acknowledged Frost and Kitsune, then reached out a hand to Oliver, who hesitated a moment before holding out his own.

Konigen dropped a waxy green seed into his hand.

"If all else fails, you may use this. Depending upon where you are, it may take root and help you. Or it may not."

Oliver stared at the seed and then at this being, the tall, shifting effigy made of corn husks. Konigen seemed entirely less human up close.

"Thank you. But . . . I'm not sure I understand . . . why? Why would you take the risk involved in helping us? In helping me?"

The clearing was filled with a flutter of leaves and a creaking of branches. Oliver could feel the presence of Frost and Kitsune, but was only barely aware of them in that moment, as he felt the gods of the Harvest confer all of their attention upon him for the second time that day.

The husks over Konigen's eyes moved, revealing slits of darkness. The void there, the hollow inside, was more dreadful to see than anything this world had presented to him thus far.

"There is peace in the Two Kingdoms, and *structure* to the Veil," Konigen said. "*Order.* And whoever has sent the Hunters out to slaughter the Borderkind is an enemy of

Order. We oppose them. And if that power wishes you dead, then we are pleased to be able to aid you in whatever small way that we can."

Oliver closed his hand around the seed.

It was warm to the touch.

CHAPTER 11

Halliwell had returned from Cottingsley shortly after six o'clock and hadn't bothered to go into the sheriff's office. Instead he had retreated to his home, where he went about the business of an aging bachelor with the numb gravity of a somnambulist. The world had been dulled, his senses diminished, by his visit to that quaint little village whose charm had been perverted by the grotesque murder of a little girl.

He cooked himself a late meal, a shrimp étoufée that his elevated cholesterol transformed into gastronomic idiocy. His doctor would have scolded him, and with reason. Halliwell had been unmoved by the thought. Like an inveterate drinker, he had been well aware that he was doing himself a disservice when he bought the stuff. And just to relish the point, he'd fixed himself a Seagram's 7 and 7-Up to go along with the étoufée. Creole food went best with whiskey, he'd found.

It tasted like nothing. No spice, no bite, no pleasure.

Of course. For how could he take any pleasure in his meal, or in anything else, this night? Images of the corpse of Alice St. John—of the gaping hollows where her eyes had been—lingered in his mind and surfaced whenever he was not on guard against them.

He had thought of Sara, his only child. His daughter. How long had it really been since they'd had more than a perfunctory conversation? How long since they had connected on any level at all? A terrible suspicion had grown in him as he tipped whiskey and ice to his lips that the answer might be never.

Sara. And the girl at the reception desk at the Cottingsley police station had been Sarah. Halliwell was not the kind of man to believe the Powers That Be were trying to send him a message. He was not truly certain he believed in the Powers That Be in the first place, so placing cosmic significance on something so mundane it barely qualified as a coincidence was beyond him. Yet he had found himself dwelling on the girl at the reception desk, Sarah, and on Alice St. John, and on his own Sara as well.

As he stumbled through his evening, trying to find solace in the simple task of preparing his meal and cleaning up after himself, he had been unable to accept these nonexistent connections. At rest in the leather recliner that his ex-wife had bought for him a dozen years earlier, he stared at the television without focus. Had someone asked him in that moment what it was he was watching, he would have been forced to guess were it not for the CNN logo in the bottom corner of the screen.

From outside the living room window there came the glow of multicolored Christmas lights, but they were not his own. His next-door neighbors, the Ochse family, always did things up big for Yuletide. The lack of any such lights, or any holiday decoration at all, made his own home seem pale and unreal.

It was late now, though he could not have said exactly how late. Even with the television on, he could hear the ticking of the clock on the wall. It chimed at the hour and half hour. Halliwell hated the fucking thing but left it up there in defiance of himself. It was a part of the life that had slipped away from him, the life of husband and father.

He swirled melting ice in his glass and wondered how many whiskey and sodas he'd had. Only one or two, surely. But he'd had dinner hours ago and somehow the ice was still there in the glass. It would have long since melted to water if he hadn't added fresh ice. And what was the point of fresh ice without a fresh drink?

Perhaps two was conservative. Three, then?

Halliwell rose to make himself another drink, Alice St. John's mutilated face still haunting his mind. He thought he might want to be very drunk tonight before going to sleep, otherwise he would surely dream of her, and he didn't want to be all alone inside his slumber with that dead girl.

He found himself picking up the portable phone in the kitchen. Setting his glass in the sink, he thumbed the TALK button and began to dial Sara's number in Atlanta. As he listened to the ringing on the other end he leaned against the counter and closed his eyes, tasting the whiskey in his mouth and feeling it move through him. Halliwell had already been numb when had had come home from

Cottingsley, but it had been the wrong sort of numb. Now he had replaced it with another kind.

"Hello?"

"Hey, sweetheart. It's Dad."

"Dad?" Sara rasped sleepily, followed by a tired little groan. Looking at the clock, Halliwell was sure. "Do you know what time it is?"

He did not. Frowning, he glanced at the television. CNN had it as 11:37 P.M. He remembered many nights when he was still waiting up for her when midnight rolled around and she was out past her curfew. Time changed everything.

"I woke you. I'm sorry, Sara. The night kind of got away from me."

"You all right?" his daughter asked, and he told himself there was genuine concern in her voice.

"Bad day on the job."

"What happened?" Beat. "Wait, you haven't been shot or anything?"

Halliwell chuckled drily at that. "Nope. Still unperforated. I just . . . I'm sure your mother already has things planned out and I know you don't want your life complicated, but I was just sitting here thinking how nice it would be to see you on Christmas, just once, you know? It's been almost the whole year since you made it up this way."

"Dad, don't . . . you know how little time off I have. I can't be bouncing around from state to state. I don't want to go anywhere for Christmas. If Mom would ever let me hear the end of it, I'd stay in Atlanta."

He nodded with the phone in his hand, just as if she could see him. Several seconds passed in which he found it hard to breathe, then Halliwell shoved himself away from the kitchen counter and went to the window.

"I know it's a lot, sweetheart. I'm not saying every year. Just once, you know. Or, hell, let's get ambitious. Once a decade, you come see your old man at Christmastime. Doesn't even have to be on the day. I'll pay for your ticket, if money's an issue, and—"

"You know that isn't it. I don't have that kind of vacation around the holidays. The agency doesn't like us to . . . we've talked about this, Dad. It just isn't feasible."

Feasible. The little girl whom he'd held all through the night, T-shirt stained with her snot and tears, was telling him it wasn't *feasible.*

"Your mother could do without you this once," Halliwell said, staring out the window at the Ochses' front lawn.

"Don't do this to me, Dad, please. I'll come up for Valentine's, all right? And we'll talk about next Christmas, maybe, okay? But not this year. It's a week and a half away. I've got my plane tickets. I've got a four-day weekend for Christmas, that's it. I just can't—"

"All right," he said, his voice low, embarrassed at the emotion choking him. "Okay."

"Dad," she pleaded, though he'd said nothing more.

"It's okay, Sara. I'm okay. Just one of those days, you know?"

You remember, he wanted to say, but he didn't dare. Why remind her of the times when the job had gotten to him, when he had been dour and cold? Now the shittiest days on the job had nearly the opposite effect. Instead of pushing away people who loved him, he wanted to hold them close.

But you pushed away so hard, there's nobody left.

"Listen, you have a wonderful Christmas, okay. Give that boyfriend of yours a hello from me, and please, sweetheart, try not to work so hard. Life's for living, right?"

"I'll talk to you before then, Dad. And I'll call on Christmas."

As if it was some kind of negotiation.

"All right, Sara. You take care." Halliwell wanted to say he loved her but the words were spoken so rarely that to speak them would be awkward, and he'd had enough of awkward tonight.

He thumbed off the phone and set it on the mantel as he went by on his way to the recliner. The chair creaked beneath him and he settled in comfortably, understanding without conscious choice that he would fall asleep there, as he did almost every night, before moving to the bedroom sometime in the wee hours of the morning.

The numbness had seemed to abate while he spoke to Sara but it was waiting for him the moment he relaxed. The whiskey and the horror of Alice St. John both set quietly and diligently to work on him. He stared at the television again, attempting to make sense of what was on the screen. Highlights of the biggest news stories of the day flashed by. The top of the hour, then.

Midnight.

He let himself read the crawl at the bottom of the screen. The little snippets of news—of entertainment and sports and politics—were always fascinating to him in the way they painted a picture of the American worldview. Which often led him to contemplate what sorts of things would be enormous news in other countries but did not even make it to the footnote of the crawl across the bottom of the screen of a twenty-four-hour news channel.

His eyes ached, staring at the screen. He felt the exhaustion of the day begin to slide into the pleasant sluggishness that preceded sleep. The chair was home to him, in so many ways. Halliwell was reading but only half aware of what he read on the crawl. Something about the governor of New Jersey. A bit about the estate of late actor Marlon Brando.

And then this:

FRENCH AND US AUTHORITIES SEEKING CONNECTIONS IN PARIS, SAN FRANCISCO MUTILATION MURDERS, VICTIMS BLINDED IN KILLINGS POLICE CALL "IDENTICAL"—AP

Halliwell sat up.

They snuck into the village of Bromfield under the cover of night. Even at first glance, however, Oliver thought the word *village* was understating things. They had traveled east along the Truce Road for several hours, beginning at dusk, and when they came in sight of the place Oliver at first thought they had somehow gotten onto the wrong road, for this was a village of cottages and shops. Oil lamps lined the Truce Road where it ran through Bromfield, and light flickered inside several of the small homes along several narrower streets that intersected it, striking off to north and south for parts unknown.

Once in sight of the village, they left the road and moved as surreptitiously as possible across grassy fields, taking cover where they could in copses of trees. In the distance, the moon and starlight showed several farms to the north of the village and a silver line of water that wound its way amongst the farmland, not quite a river but more than a stream.

Frost led the way. Ever since the injuries the demon Aerico had inflicted upon him, he had been unsettlingly silent. Conversely, the normally quiet Kitsune had taken to traveling beside Oliver and engaging in conversation that seemed designed to educate him more about this world without making him feel too ignorant. He was used to her mischievous side, but this gentle guidance was a facet of her that he had not expected.

Her cloak rippled around her, catching the moonlight, as they followed the winter man far out of the way so that they could come up to a stone cottage at the edge of Bromfield from the rear. Oliver heard someone playing the violin inside, a sweet and lilting sound that surprised him in this setting, but soothed him as well.

They moved along behind the homes on the north side of the Truce Road, most of which had healthy gardens growing. In some of the cottages they could see people going about their evening, enjoying dessert or playing parlor games. In one house, which seemed to be lined with books, a man with thick black hair and a long face sat in a high-backed chair, reading. It made Oliver think of home, and he felt a twinge of melancholy. He envied that man the peace that came from a comfortable chair and an old book.

"Oliver," Kitsune whispered, her breath warm in his ear, her fur cloak brushing his hand. He turned to her and her jade eyes were wide and sincere. "Do not tarry. We may have friends here, but certainly some of the people will be tempted by the reward Aerico spoke of."

He nodded and pulled himself away from the back of that cottage. Kitsune started after Frost, who had moved on without them and was now two cottages ahead. She reached back a moment as if to take his hand and Oliver blinked in surprise. Her hand was gone as though it had never been there, lost inside her cloak, and he wondered if she had merely been stretching, or gesturing, or if he had not seen it at all.

Frost had paused behind a cottage larger than those they'd already passed. The moonshine glinted off a thousand angles on his icy form as though he wore a constellation of tiny stars, and Oliver worried, not for the first time, that it would be the presence of the winter man that led to their discovery. But as he considered it he realized it was a foolish concern. He was Jack Frost, after all, and had spent centuries moving through the winter landscape of Oliver's world, avoiding the eyes of the curious.

The winter man beckoned to them.

Oliver and Kitsune hurried to join him, moving swiftly behind a cottage whose owner had a pair of cherry trees in the backyard. The reminder of their terrible morning was unwelcome, and Oliver shuddered as he passed the trees. He had put his parka back on and the shotgun case slung over his shoulder made a kind of shushing noise, scraping across the jacket as he ran.

Kitsune, as always, moved in total silence.

Even before they reached Frost, Oliver heard the slow clap of horses' hooves out on the Truce Road. They came up beside the winter man and peered around the corner of the cottage to see a wagon passing by, but the beasts yoked to it were not horses at all. Their bodies were similar to a horse's, but each had a head like a giant eagle, and what appeared to be wings pinned at their sides. A man sat on the wagon's seat, but he was larger than any man Oliver had ever seen. Not a giant by the standards of this world, but huge just the same. The back of the wagon was loaded with barrels, and atop one of them sprawled a dark, twisted-looking creature, a goblin or something very like it. From this distance—and, Oliver suspected, perhaps even upon closer examination—it was impossible to discern the goblin's gender. It was dressed in ragged clothing, hairless, and its skin was a sickly green that glistened in the lamplight out on the street.

The cart rattled by and Oliver turned to Kitsune, so many questions in his mind. She placed a finger to his lips to hush him, giving a little shake of her head. A little friction spark jumped at the contact but he did not flinch. For a moment he only stared at her and then he pulled himself away, wondering at the way she so easily derailed his thoughts. Her beauty was captivating, but he did not think that was the explanation. Nor was her mythical nature the sole reason, he thought. There was something else.

Laughter came from out on the Truce Road. A trio of seemingly ordinary people came sauntering down the street with an easy camaraderie, a man and two women. Their clothing was old-fashioned but, Oliver was pleased to see, not entirely archaic. The man wore blue jeans and heavy boots with a thick jacket of the sort his mother had always called a "peacoat" and which had been popularized by sailors in the navies of countries around the world. Dark blue wool.

The parka would have to go, but Oliver thought perhaps it wouldn't be as difficult to blend in here as he'd thought.

When the road was clear again Frost gestured for them to follow and continued on. They passed behind another small cottage and then came to a two-story house with a sloping roof that had several small dormers, little windows like eyes set in to what was probably the attic.

The house was dark.

The structure beside it was alive with light and music.

From the drone of voices that came from within and the laughter, Oliver felt sure it was a pub or bar.

"The Wayside Inn," Kitsune whispered, as if she'd read his mind. Her breath was warm and moist, close by his ear.

Frost stared at the Inn for a few seconds, then glanced at the house behind which they huddled. When he faced them at last, one corner of his mouth lifted in a kind of smile and his brow crinkled with amusement.

"Soon the bar will close. Guests of the Inn will go up to their rooms, but others are already beginning to leave. We must hope to find a man on his own, perhaps one who has had too much to drink. At the least we must have a shirt and coat, for such things are roughly made here and factory-made things will draw attention. If we can find shoes and trousers that fit you, Oliver, so much the better."

"You're enjoying this," Oliver whispered in amazement, but also with relief. Frost had been so quiet and grim all through the night that this was a welcome change.

"It's a beautiful night, and at the moment no one is trying to kill us," the winter man replied.

Oliver grinned.

Kitsune lowered her hood, silken hair framing her face. One of her eyebrows arched. "You know, I could go in and lure a man outside, alone. We are hunted in secret, you and I. There is no reward for our death or capture, only for Oliver's. I have been here before. Travelers always pass through on the way to Perinthia."

Frost nodded. "Yes, that would certainly make it—"

His eyes narrowed and he stared beyond them, back the way they had come. Kitsune frowned as she sniffed the air, suddenly alert, but the wind was blowing from the east and Frost was looking west. Oliver's mouth went dry as he spun around, memories of the Falconer and the Kirata flashing across his mind.

But it was only a man. He stood perhaps fifteen feet away in the night shadow of the house, where the moonlight could not reach him. An enormous swell of laughter came from within the Wayside Inn, and someone began to play thunderous, roadhouse piano, badly out of tune. The sound of the Inn's door creaking open and banging shut came to them from out in front. Someone called good night to a companion and the reply was more bark than words.

Throughout all of this, Oliver, Kitsune, and Frost only stared at the man. Kitsune growled, low in her chest.

"You know," the man said from the night shadow. "Before indulging in assault and robbery, you might consider borrowing what you came to steal."

The man's tone was bemused, but Oliver's heart was hammering in his chest. Discovery would destroy their plans. It could even cost them their lives.

"Show yourself," Frost commanded.

"As you like, sir." Without hesitation or fear the man approached them. When he came into the moonlight Oliver saw that it was the man with the thick, shaggy black hair and long face he had seen through the window several houses back. The man whose cottage was full of books.

His accent was British and his features showed little emotion, save for his eyes, which were alight in that pale face. If anything, he seemed merely curious, studying both of the Borderkind and then focusing on Oliver's parka and the shotgun case over his shoulder.

"Kill him," Kitsune snarled.

Oliver flinched, darting his gaze toward her. "Wait a second."

"Oh, no need for that, love, surely," said the man unhappily. "What sort of reward is that for a Samaritan only looking to do his good deed for the day?"

Frost looked first at Kitsune and then Oliver before taking a step nearer the man. To his credit, the Englishman did not appear frightened.

"We've heard far too much talk of rewards today. What sort of reward is it that you seek?"

How the man could ignore the ominous presence of the winter man looming so close, Oliver did not know. Yet instead of addressing Frost, or even Kitsune, he directed his reply at the only other human in that gathering.

"No reward, truly. My old mum raised me right, didn't she? But in exchange for more suitable clothes and a cup of tea by the fire, I confess I'd dearly like to have word of home. Most of the Lost Ones don't like to admit it, but I miss it. Too many years have passed since I saw the other side of the Veil."

He nodded politely to Frost but stepped around him and held his hand out.

"Oliver Larch, at your service."

Larch was as good as his word. Once he had them all safely ensconced within his little cottage with the curtains drawn and the fire stoked high, he set out a tea tray for Oliver and Kitsune. Frost did not partake. There were scones as well, and though they were not fresh, smeared with raspberry jam they were still delicious. Oliver had not expected to be hungry after the largesse of the Harvest gods, but the jam persuaded him.

While the two Olivers talked, Frost wandered the cottage, quietly perusing some of the books on the shelves that lined the walls, picking up a small framed photograph from a writing desk in the corner and then a jar of ink Larch used for writing.

Oliver barely paid attention to the winter man's seeming disinterest. It had startled him, somewhat, not only to find a man willing to help them in this place where so many seemed determined to kill him, but also to have that man share his own name. He could not escape the idea that here was an Oliver who had found himself in this place and made a home for himself amongst myth and legend, a simple life that was both extraordinary and entirely unremarkable. Oliver and Oliver.

When all of this was through—providing he managed to remove the order of execution that had been sworn against him—he wondered if he might actually stay here. The idea quickened his breath, like that of a little boy dreaming of running away to join the circus. Yet this was no dream. It was his reality.

Kitsune sat on the floor by the fireplace, legs curled under her, but her jade eyes were alert and she listened to every word the two men exchanged.

Larch knew many people who had been the forgotten of their societies, who had slipped through the cracks. Homeless people and runaway teenagers whose parents were glad to see them go. But far more often, he claimed, there were incidents like his own. On a clear night in the fall of 1973, sixteen-year-old Oliver Larch had heard voices outside his window, beneath an ash tree that had always made his eyes itch when the wind blew just right. When he went outside to investigate, he saw someone behind the tree and called out to them. Receiving no answer, he went around the other side of the tree . . .

. . . and pierced the Veil.

Simple as that. He had looked for a way back, of course. If there was a hole there—and there must have been—surely he could find his way home again. In all of the fairy stories his grandmother had told him when he was a small boy in Derbyshire, those stolen away by the fairies eventually made it home again. But not Ollie Larch. He was never going home. He'd stumbled into a place where the Veil had, for a few nights, worn thin and become unstable, and he'd unknowingly pushed through it.

Its magic had touched him. He couldn't go home again. Not ever.

At first it didn't help at all to learn that he was in good company, that there were thousands upon thousands to whom the same thing had happened. But time changed his perspective. He met children whose pictures had ended up on milk cartons and men whose wives were sure they had taken off with another woman . . . not to mention women who were presumed to have been killed by their boyfriends or husbands. Of course, all of those things really did happen, but amongst the many such reports around the world each year, a small percentage had actually ended up here.

They were the Lost Ones, and whatever lives they had were left behind. New lives had to be built here.

"You don't look old enough to have been sixteen in the early seventies," Oliver told him.

Larch had smiled. "Ah, but that's one benefit of living on this side, yeah? Longer days. Longer nights. Longer years. A body adjusts, after a while." He took a sip from his teacup, frowned, and set it down to stir in a bit more honey before picking it up again. "Really, though, folks like myself are Newcomers. The Originals look down on us a bit. More than a bit, I'd say."

"Originals?" Oliver asked.

"The descendants of the old lost races—the Atlanteans, you know? The Mayans and Incans especially, which is why I settled here instead of Yucatazca. Those of us who come over alone have to make do, make friends, start over. It's different for the ones who come over en masse. Way back when there were the Roanoke Islanders, but there've been so many others, from the Norfolk battalion to those three thousand soldiers from Nanking. Not to mention the ships and planes and . . . well, it's just I think it'd be easier not to have come over alone."

The Englishman's expression had become melancholy and Oliver wished he could have thought of something to say to comfort him. He could think of nothing that would not sound hollow even to his own ears. After a moment, he pushed the conversation onward.

"You know what makes little sense to me? The timing of everything. Atlantis disappeared long before the Mayans, and even they vanished before the Veil was created, if I'm understanding the history here at all."

Kitsune stirred by the fire.

"You make too many assumptions," she said. "There have always been worlds unseen, secret places and peoples. But once upon a time things were more fluid, passage back and forth simpler. The Veil came later . . . it was a . . . joining of many things, not only a barrier."

"A line in the sand, really," Larch added. "You stay on your side and we on ours, that sort of thing."

Kitsune nodded solemnly and went back to lounging. She had startled Oliver by removing her fur cloak—something he had not imagined possible—and laying it over the back of a chair, and the black cotton clothing she wore outlined her lithe form in such a way that he could not fail to appreciate it. It took an effort to draw his gaze away.

"But there are crossings."

"For the Borderkind, yes," Larch said. "No one else is supposed to cross. Their rights were sort of grandfathered in, you could say. And we Lost Ones, of course. But we never wanted to come here and we can never go back. That's the way the Veil works. Perhaps not for you, though, yeah? What's your story, then?"

Oliver hesitated. He was perched on the edge of a faded sofa and now felt like retreating behind it. Still perusing the books in the cottage, near an archway that led into a small kitchen area, Frost paused and glanced over in concern. Kitsune perked up from her place by the fire, obviously curious how he would respond.

"Oh, come now," Larch prodded. "I saw you skulking about and heard enough of your conversation to know that you're not meant to be here, and I'm certainly aware what that means. If I'd had any interest in exposing you, I'd hardly have snuck after you in the dark."

Oliver laughed and settled back into the sofa. "There's that, true enough. All right, I'll give you the story. But first . . . doesn't it seem a remarkable coincidence that the one person who sees us, the one who invites us home for tea, is the one person who's willing to help? Who isn't looking to turn me over to be executed? And who happens to share my name?"

Larch lifted a finger. "First, I'd say you share my name, as I'm appreciably older than you are, my young Oliver." Another finger. "Second, I'm hardly the only person in the village who'd be willing to help. I daresay you'd have plenty of allies here, though just as many enemies. That's simply the way people are, as you know. Though on second thought, most of us are too apathetic to help the law . . . but nobody in Bromfield is going to fight for you, either. I'm happy to put you up for the night, give you some old clothes to help you go unnoticed, but if there are soldiers coming your way, I'm not going to chain myself to you to keep them from taking you away, right?"

He raised a third finger. "Coincidence? I'd call it luck."

"I have a question," Frost said, his breath pluming in the warmth of the cottage. His body glistened, reflective in the light from the fire. He held up a slim leather book. "Books are not easily come by on this side of the Veil. How did you manage to gather all of these?"

Larch sprang from his chair with childlike enthusiasm. "They're wonderful, aren't they? It's been my main occupation since I first accepted that I would live my life here. Some of them I got from other Lost Ones, mostly Newcomers like myself, folks on shipboard who managed to have some of their belongings with them when they pierced the Veil. But most, I confess, I've bartered for over the years with Borderkind. Another reason I'm so pleased to meet you, Mr. Frost. And you, Miss Kitsune. I hope if the opportunity ever presents itself for you, you'll consider . . . acquiring a book or two while you're on the other side."

Oliver gazed around the room, smiling at Larch's infectious glee. He had not given the books a second thought, but put into perspective, the amassing of such a large collection was singularly impressive.

"You must know a lot of Borderkind," he said.

Larch's expression collapsed with regret. "Not so many as I did once."

They all stared at him.

At length, it was Frost who spoke. "Then you know?"

"About the Hunters? There are rumors. Once again,

apathy reigns supreme. So far, any violence has been far from the cities. The truth is, if you're going to Perinthia, that's probably the safest place for you."

Larch shot a glance at Oliver. "Provided Mr. Bascombe can pass for a Newcomer." He smiled. "Now then, you were going to tell me how you came to be here."

"It involves the Hunters, actually," Oliver replied. "One in particular."

As he told his story, Kitsune rose from the hearth and went to Frost. Larch seemed barely to notice them, so enrapt was he with Oliver's tale of a wedding averted and the arrival of the Falconer, and the man shuddered when Oliver began to speak of the demon in the cherry tree.

When he had finished with the story, Larch thanked him and rose from his chair, determined to get them settled in for the night as comfortably as possible in the small cottage. He had extra blankets for Oliver, he said, and for Kitsune if she desired it. There was only the single bed, in his own room, but his guests were welcome to sleep on any piece of furniture they deemed suitable. He did have pillows and cushions to spare, and he hoped they would be helpful.

The travelers accepted his hospitality graciously, but Oliver could see that whatever had passed between Kitsune and Frost was preoccupying them both. It was only when Larch had picked up after their late-night tea and prepared to retire to his bedroom that Frost spoke up.

"Mr. Larch, have you any idea where in Perinthia one might most readily find a Mazikeen?"

Larch crossed his arms almost petulantly. "You don't want to mix with the Mazikeen, Mr. Frost. If you're attempting to avoid undue attention, that's hardly the way to go about it."

Kitsune tilted her head so that her hair fell like an ebony velvet curtain across her face. "We will need their help. The risk is unavoidable. Can you help us?"

The man seemed as though he might continue to argue the point but Kitsune's gaze either won him over or unsettled him enough that he surrendered with a shrug.

"There are places where trouble gathers in Perinthia. As there are in any city, in any world. The Mazikeen are trouble. Go to Amelia's, well after dark. If you're looking for trouble, it'll find you there."

CHAPTER 12

O liver sits in his mother's parlor, drinking cocoa with whipped cream on top. On the floor by the fireplace, Julianna curls languidly, relishing the warmth of the blaze. She lays her head upon her outstretched arms and gazes up at him with jade eyes. Something about this is not right. Several somethings. Her hair is tied back into a ponytail but in the firelight it has a rich reddish copper hue, like the coat of a fox.

Also, his mother is in the room, standing by the Gaudí floor lamp and reading from a tattered Agatha Christie novel, open in her hands.

"Mom?"

She turns to him, a curious smile on her face. There is

intelligence and love and humor in her eyes, and he misses her so badly that his dreaming heart breaks.

No, he won't think of dreaming.

"Should you be here?" he asks.

His mother chuckles softly, shaking her head and rolling her eyes just a little, as she'd always done when her son had surprised her with his precociousness.

"Where else would I be?"

"It's . . . I'm so happy to see you."

Oliver tries to get up off the sofa but he cannot. He looks down and finds that his lower body has been frozen in a block of jagged ice. The fire blazes and he can feel its heat, but the ice is not melting. Out of the corner of his eye, he sees something move by the fireplace, darting across the edge of his vision, but when he glances over, there is only Julianna. She has not moved, but her expression has changed.

Her lips are peeled back, revealing black gums and long yellow teeth, rows of deadly fangs.

"Julianna?"

"You ruined it all. My life. Did you think I'd just hide in my room and cry? I'm going to hurt you the way you hurt me. And then I'm going to forget you. What are you, after all? You're not Oliver Bascombe, you're just Max Bascombe's son. I can't believe after the life you've lived, you don't see that."

Pain sears his chest. Oliver hisses and looks down to see his shirt is torn. Blood seeps from fresh claw marks that have striped his flesh.

"Oliver."

He turns to face his mother, shaking his head in confusion.

"Drink your cocoa," she says indulgently. "Drink up."

He shakes his head again, mumbling some rebellion, and

glances back to find that Julianna is gone. The fire is out. Snow falls in the empty fireplace, hissing on cinders.

Oliver is startled by a sudden banging at the window and as he looks over, the glass shatters but does not fall. Instead it turns to snow and a winter wind blasts into the parlor, swirling it around. The room is dark now. No fire, no Gaudí lamp. He seeks his mother in the darkness but she is not there.

The ice that had held him down is gone.

He staggers to his feet, squinting against the storm that blasts into the room, and stares out at the darkness. At the blizzard. It is not the bluff overlooking the Atlantic he sees, not the yard in which he and his sister played as children.

Outside there is only sand.

Some distance away, his father stands and stares at him. Oliver feels trepidation at the sight, and a kind of dread that he has not felt since he was a small boy, curled up beneath his covers, eyes moist with fear at the scratching of a branch against the window and the sounds of an old house shifting.

Max Bascombe has been altered, somehow. Oliver expects him to sneer, to shout and proclaim and dismiss, but even from that distance he can see that his father is doing none of these things. Instead he is pointing. He is cupping his hands to his face and crying out to his only son—yes, their eyes meet, and Oliver sees that his father is trying to communicate with him—and yet his words are lost in the storm, in the snow that swirls in the air and never seems to touch the endless, shifting sand.

His father is sinking, the sand slowly swallowing him, but he seems not to know this. He only cries out to Oliver, fearful, as though trying to warn him.

Something moves under the sand.

Oliver wants to go to his father, to tell him to watch for

whatever circles, sharklike, under the cascade, but he is trapped by his father's urgency.

At last, dread trembling in him, he begins to realize that there, in the darkness, he is not alone. His mother is gone. Julianna is gone. His father cannot reach him.

Something touches his shoulder, needle fingers digging in, and begins to turn him around.

The snow blowing through the window is sand now, and the grit of it fills his eyes, stinging him.

Close them. He knows he must close them.

But the thing in the darkness is pulling him round to see now, and he wants to see. And, after all, he does not feel sleepy at all.

"Oliver."

"Oliver."

He awoke, sucking in a deep breath as though in his sleep he had ceased inhaling, and his eyes snapped wide. In the darkness a cloaked figure loomed over him and he could still hear the dream echo of its voice in his head, saying his name. An outstretched hand reached down toward him and only then did he break free of the lingering effects of the dream.

"Get away!" he shouted, scrambling back over the arm of the sofa, fumbling, then falling onto the wood floor with a thump. His elbow thwacked the ground and pain shot up his arm as he tried to crab-walk backward.

The cloaked shadow sprang through the air. Oliver opened his mouth to scream again, chest thundering with his racing heartbeat, but a powerful hand clamped over his mouth to silence him. Its weight bore down on him and he stared up . . .

Into jade eyes.

"You *must* be silent," Kitsune said, and then she tossed her head, throwing back her hood, and her raven hair glinted in what little light filtered into the cottage from outside.

Oliver shook with relief and then nodded, pressing his eyes tightly closed a moment.

Kitsune removed her hand.

"I was ... it was a nightmare," he whispered. "But it seemed like more."

Even as he spoke, it occurred to him that there were other things to fear than his nightmares. Kitsune was poised and alert, head cocked as she listened for something he knew he did not want to hear. Oliver extricated himself from beneath her and climbed to his knees, reluctantly glancing around the darkened cottage.

"What is it?" he asked, voice barely audible.

A shiver ran up his back and gooseflesh rose on his arms. A breeze had rippled through the room, and without turning he knew that Frost had joined them. When he did look, he found the winter man holding out to him a pile of neatly folded clothing.

"Quickly, Oliver."

He took the shirt and pants, only then really aware that he wore only a T-shirt and underwear. In the dreadful tension of that moment, however, there was no room for the indulgence of embarrassment. The pants were some kind of wool-blended trousers and he stepped into them even as he glanced around at his companions again.

"Would one of you tell me what's up? What time is it? How long have we—"

"Hush!" Kitsune growled quietly, baring fangs at him.

There was a hint of pique in her eyes that confused him, but he was used to being puzzled by her.

As he slipped on the thick white cotton shirt and began to button it as quickly as his sleepy fingers would allow, he turned pleading eyes upon Frost.

The winter man gestured for him to hurry. "You slept only a few hours. Not enough, but it will have to be. The Kirata are here, in the village. Even now they will be searching for our scent, checking every home and business."

Oliver swore softly as he reached for his own boots. They had rubber soles, and he could only hope they would not be so modern as to draw attention. Certainly many of the Lost Ones had modern clothing that they would have been wearing when they pierced the Veil. The boots would have to do.

As he bent to tie them he caught motion in the periphery of his vision, near the door, and he jerked back, ready to fight. It was Larch, who had been standing in the darkness, peering out a front window throughout their exchange. In the dim glow from outside his eyes looked desperate.

"Please, hurry!" he said, the words almost a whine. "You can't be found here. I tried to help you, now you've got to help me by getting out of—"

"We're doing our best, Mr. Larch," Kitsune growled, the words darting across the darkened room.

Oliver fumbled his way through the near-dark to the darkened fireplace—shards of his dream returning—and grabbed the shotgun case where it rested on the mantel. He spun around, narrowing his eyes to get a better look at Larch.

"A coat. You said you had something for me."

Larch raced into his bedroom and came out almost

instantly with a long, thick gray woolen coat. "Take this. But you can't leave the other here. Nor your clothes. Get rid of them somewhere else."

"Kitsune, the back," Frost whispered.

The fox-woman slid through the shadows to the back door and opened it quietly, slipping out into the night, disappearing beyond the gleam of moon and starlight. Oliver stared at that open door, holding his breath as he pulled on Larch's coat and slipped the shotgun case over his shoulder. Frost grabbed up his parka and discarded clothes and went to the front of the house, glancing quickly out the window before rushing toward the back . . . following Kitsune.

"No sign of them yet. But they will be prowling. Could be anywhere."

The winter man hesitated only a moment before following Kitsune into the dark. Oliver paused and looked at Larch, and he wished he could stay. In a way he had found all he'd ever really wanted when he and Frost had tumbled out over the ocean and through the Veil. Magic. Freedom from the expectations of the life he'd known. Part of him wished he could just sit awhile, get to know this village, explore.

He cast a yearning glance at the shelves and shelves of books in Larch's cottage and felt another pang of envy. At last he took a deep breath and nodded to the Englishman, then stepped out the door.

The chill was bracing. The fire in Larch's hearth had died hours earlier but the cottage had held much of its warmth. Outside, the wind whipped along behind the little house and made his whole body feel brittle. He buttoned the wool coat and turned up the collar, and that helped.

Frost was off to his left, Kitsune to the right, both of

them on watch. When he emerged, the winter man rushed to him, an arctic breeze accompanying him, and together they hurried to where Kitsune waited. Frost still carried Oliver's cast-off clothes. After what Larch had done for them, they wouldn't leave the clothes so close to the house, even though Oliver was certain that if they entered his home the Kirata would smell the presence of their prey. He hoped it didn't come to that.

Morning was only a few hours away and the village was silent but for the whistle of the wind through the gardens and the eaves of the larger houses. They moved swiftly to the east, past the Wayside Inn and behind a building that might have been some sort of marketplace. Just ahead, the Truce Road was intersected by another, much less impressive thoroughfare. Little more than a dirt cart path, really, it branched off the main road and was lined with houses that seemed far less well kept than their counterparts there.

As they passed silently between houses, Kitsune sniffed at the air. Her fur cloak gleamed the color of fire in the moonlight. She started to move again, slipping through shadows like water. At the corner of the large house, where a flower garden had been planted—and Oliver tried not to think about how some of these flowers could grow in such weather—Kitsune went rigid and still.

Frost seemed not to notice at first, so intent was he upon surveying their surroundings, and by reflex Oliver thrust out a hand and clutched his arm. The ice seared his flesh with cold and he hissed as he withdrew his touch.

But it was enough. The winter man turned to glare at Oliver, and in doing so caught sight of Kitsune, paralyzed as though Frost himself had frozen her there. Yet this was no attack, only caution and fear. Her eyes were wide and her chest rose and fell rapidly.

"We're not going to make it, are we?" Oliver asked grimly.

She bared her fangs, his voice—or perhaps his words—snapping her out of whatever trance she'd been in.

"They're close," Kitsune whispered, focusing on Frost. "At least one just ahead. Perhaps two. And others close by. Is there no other way?"

The winter man shook his head slowly so that the icicles of his hair did not clink together. His eyes misted white-blue and the little clouds swirled around his face.

"There can be no running. Only death or survival. And our path lies ahead of us."

She nodded solemnly and took another deep breath of the air that breezed around them—of the scent of their enemy. Then Kitsune slipped over beside Oliver and tapped the strap of his shotgun case.

"A sword in its scabbard is not weapon, but decoration."

Oliver nodded and set the case down, opening it and removing the shotgun. It was loaded. He pulled out a handful of shells and pressed them into the pockets of his wool coat, then nodded to indicate he was ready.

Kitsune raised her hood, her jade eyes lost within. "Be careful."

Even as she turned she changed, diminishing as she dropped to the ground. It was as a fox that she slipped out in front of the house and darted across the narrow, rutted road that led to the northern farms. The street lamps on the Truce Road were out, leaving only celestial light, pinpoint glimmers of gold in the night sky. Kitsune was a dark shape, moving low to the ground. From their cover, Frost and Oliver watched her slip into the deeper darkness between two cottages across the way.

The winter man turned to Oliver and nodded gravely. The wind picked up, dancing around them, and stole Frost away. The entire substance of him was carried away on the wind, crumbling to snow and sleet that spiraled up into the sky above Oliver's head. In the darkness up there, above the height of any cottage or house, the winter man would storm briefly across the night and then pause to wait for him on the other side of the road.

All along he had realized that he was a burden to them, but now Oliver realized precisely how significant a burden. *It's me,* he thought. *I'm going to get them killed.* With the cherry-tree demon, he had taken a hand in saving their lives, but now he knew that his companions would not have been in that predicament were it not for him. Kitsune had stealth and cunning, Frost the ability to disappear into the night, into the wind. Oliver had only a weapon with which he was hardly an expert.

So why bother with me? he thought. By now, Frost surely owed him nothing, no matter what he might believe. They were all fugitives, and that created a kind of kinship. But they would be better off if they left him behind.

They were allies, certainly. But were they also friends? Could it be that simple?

All right, then. We stick together. But that means not getting them killed. Not being a liability.

As these thoughts crossed his mind he slipped the strap of the shotgun case over his head so that it was across his back and would not fall or get in the way of his aim. He held the cold metal of the shotgun firmly in both hands and left the cover of the house. In the silence of the sleeping village, the noise of his footfalls seemed incredibly loud in his ears. He breathed evenly and hurried without running, scanning north and south. To the north the road continued past perhaps twenty or thirty cottages and then there was no more village, only the farms in the distance.

To the south was the Truce Road and the intersection that could only be the center of town. In the square there he could see a horse stable and a two-story building with what appeared to be a general store in the windows of the first. A sign squeaked as it swung in the breeze. Somewhere, real wind chimes sang their strange, lonely melody.

The village square was empty.

His throat had gone dry without his realizing it. Oliver ran his tongue out to wet his lips and his step faltered. The barrel of the shotgun swung in an arc in front of him as he scanned the street, the houses in plain view, and the village square.

The street was empty.

Nothing moved but the wind, that creaking sign in front of the general store, and the weathervane on top of that very same building. Some dust blew up from the road and the grit was in his eyes. He blinked it away as he swung the barrel again, blinking at the impossible. Kitsune had their scent. The Kirata were *here.*

Hunting them.

He made a complete circle on that very spot. As he glanced around, the collar of the wool coat rasped against his unshaven cheek and an image leaped unbidden into his mind, a tinted home movie half drained of color, little Oliver standing on top of the toilet lid watching with furious scrutiny as his father shaved, wondering what that was about. When he had been very small, his father had loved him. Had picked him up and blown raspberries on his belly and tickled him and held him tightly, and on the weekends when he would go without shaving, the stubble had sometimes scraped the boy. Sometimes it had hurt. But he had never minded.

His nightmare returned. His mother in her parlor, and his father out across the shifting sand. Most of the dream was lost now, but he remembered those things. And something in his father's face. Fear. But not for himself.

Oliver knew he had to get home. Even if he could find a place for himself in this world, he owed Julianna and Collette—and even his father—some word to indicate that he was all right, so they would not have to worry.

Bitterness rippled through him and lifted the corner of his mouth. As if Max Bascombe would worry. The old man might be frustrated, furious, and profoundly disappointed. But he wouldn't worry.

Oliver shrugged off these phantoms of his mind that had come to plague him at the most inopportune time. He looked into the darkness between cottages, where Frost and Kitsune undoubtedly waited for him, though he could not see them. For a moment, he scuttled sideways, letting the shotgun barrel linger in the direction of the village square.

Then he was in motion again, somehow quieter and more focused. The shotgun felt more comfortable in his grip. He would feel better in the company of his friends.

As he reached the edge of that glorified cart path, the front door opened on a cottage off to his left and a Kirata stepped out into the night. The monster had to duck to get out, and its fur was bright stripes of orange against the night, for the black stripes were lost in the darkness. The effect was troubling, making the creature seem ethereal.

He was downwind, but it didn't need his scent. It saw him.

The Kirata opened its jaws in a roar that seemed a gruesome promise, and suddenly it was all too real. An answering roar came from the south and he twisted round as he ran to see another of the Hunters coming around the corner in the village square. It wore filthy, matted pants that came down only halfway to its ankles, and no shoes, for its feet were more like large paws and the muscles in its legs stood out as it sprang along the street toward him, leaping at first and then breaking into a run.

Oliver never slowed.

As he passed between the two cottages, following the path his friends had taken, he gripped the shotgun more tightly, its case bouncing against his back. As he sprinted into the backyards, still heading east, he saw no sign of Kitsune or Frost. He searched the sky for a gust of winter weather, frantically sought a glimpse of the fox slipping through a garden or beneath shrubs. But they were gone.

He was alone with the Hunters.

The roar of the Kirata echoed all around him, some distant and some much nearer. Over his shoulder he caught sight of the two he had seen out on the road as they gave chase, barreling between houses and into backyards, clawed feet tearing up flower beds and vegetable gardens. One dropped on all fours and came on even faster, and Oliver forced himself to look ahead, afraid he would stumble, knowing he could run faster if he bent himself to it.

He could practically feel their claws tearing his flesh.

Ahead of him, behind a small, simple building whose tall windows suggested a schoolhouse, there was a playground. A slide and a wooden swing-set and a trio of see-saws, all in a row.

Two more Kirata stood there, the wind ruffling their fur. One, taller and more lithe than the others, was white and black. Oliver glanced around, looking for some exit. To the left was only farmland, and beyond that, open country. To the right were cottages and the Truce Road, where he would be completely exposed. But it couldn't be more dangerous than the situation he was in, so he diverted toward that opening, feeling the vulnerability of his unprotected back even more.

Images he had seen a thousand times on television flashed in his head, big jungle cats bringing animals down and tearing at them, dragging their bloody viscera through tall grass.

Screams built up at the back of his throat but he could not set them free. His legs ached and his chest hurt with the pounding of his heart and his fingers were white with terror where he gripped the shotgun.

The Kirata closed in.

A roar split the night above him.

Above him.

Oliver staggered to a halt and stared upward at the Kirata that perched on the roof of a cottage. The tiger-man tensed to spring. Oliver swung the shotgun barrel up, set the stock against his shoulder, braced his feet, and pulled the trigger.

The blast blew a hole through the tiger's upper torso. It hit the ground a corpse and its blood rained down, spattering Oliver, the copper stink of it filling his nostrils. His hands shook, but his grip on the shotgun never loosened, even as he muttered something that was half curse and half prayer.

The way out to the Truce Road was open, but he knew that there must be more out there and there were probably others on the way. Those giving chase were almost upon him. He had nowhere to run. Trapped in the space between two cottages, he turned and cocked the shotgun, wishing he had a better weapon, or that they would wait patiently while he reloaded.

It was a twelve-gauge. Five shots. Then he was dead. And that was if the Kirata even let him get five shots off.

He took a step toward the Truce Road, turning in jerky motions, knowing there were no options left. The two Kirata who'd first spotted him came tearing around the corner of the cottage on his left. Oliver was surprised to find his breathing steady as he crouched into a firing stance and pulled the trigger. The shotgun bucked in his hands and the blast echoed off the cottages. The Kirata running upright was taken in the shoulder, fur and blood and bone flying as it spun around with a roar of pain almost as loud as the shotgun itself.

Three rounds left.

But the second Kirata was on all fours, running low to the ground and faster than the first, tearing up grass and soil with its claws as it knifed toward him through the night. The other two had come around the cottage on his right, but they were an afterthought. A low growl like a car engine rumbled from the throat of the tiger-man as it bore down on him.

Oliver tracked it with the barrel of the shotgun, trying to get a bead. He misjudged its speed. The monster was too fast, and the realization sent a shiver through him. He pulled the trigger and the ground a foot to the right of the Kirata thumped with the impact, throwing up clods of dirt.

Then it was upon him. Too late to fire again, he lifted the shotgun up in front of him with some vague intention of defending himself, using it as a club or even jamming the stock into its jaws. It would buy him only seconds of life, but he found in that moment that he wanted to wring every possible second out of it.

"I'm sorry," he said softly, not sure to whom the apology was directed. Perhaps Julianna. Perhaps his family. Perhaps himself.

The Kirata leaped, claws snickering through the night air and jaws wide. He thrust the shotgun out in front of him.

The fox struck the Kirata from the side, appearing as if from nowhere, looking tiny and insignificant next to the thunderous locomotive power of the tiger-man. But Kitsune had been stealthy and quick, and her jaws closed on its throat in midair. The moment seemed eternal and he saw her twist in the air, paws pressing against the beast's head, using leverage and tearing. The Kirata's throat ripped open and blood fountained from the wound. The two animals crashed to the ground together. Kitsune rolled and was up almost instantly, springing back on her four legs in defense, copper fur glinting in the moonlight, ready for more.

The Kirata staggered as it tried to get up onto two legs. Its eyes were putrid yellow in the night and gleaming with predatory lust. A flap of skin and fur hung down from its throat and blood ran from that ruined flesh like rain from an overflowing gutter. Then it faltered, and collapsed.

Oliver could not breathe as he looked at her. Kitsune barked, her focus not on him at all, and he spun to see the other two—including the white tiger—racing toward them, both upright.

He leveled the shotgun and fired, and the orange and black Kirata's leg gave way in tatters and broken bones. It went down, but the white tiger came on. Oliver had one shot left and he knew he had to make it count.

Which was when the blizzard hit, gale-force winds and driving snow that existed only in that space between cottages. The Kirata roared in surprise and perhaps even fear as the wind drove it backward. It dropped to all fours to combat the wind and shook snow from its eyes as it started toward Oliver and Kitsune again.

The winter man took form just beside it, reached out with his left hand even as the blizzard died, and grabbed a fistful of its fur and skin. The Kirata grunted and turned, claws coming up to attack ... and Frost drove the elongated ice dagger fingers of his right hand into its face, puncturing its eyes and thrusting deep into its brain.

It fell dead in a light dusting of snow.

The wind ceased, save for the ordinary nighttime breeze.

Oliver opened his mouth to shout something, but Kitsune was beside him, woman now instead of fox, and she clapped a delicate hand over his mouth. With her other hand she was already propelling him forward. He fumbled with the shotgun, trying to get a better hold on it, and he lost his grip. It hit the ground at his feet and he tried to stop, tried to go back for it, but Kitsune would not even allow him to slow down.

"Run," she said, a whisper harsh upon his ear. "Marra has come."

The winter man led the way, and they were running again. As they left the space between those two cottages Oliver took one glance back at the Truce Road and saw several Kirata gathering, starting after them. A guttural voice called to them and they stopped and turned, giving up the chase at the command of a new arrival. The figure that joined them in the street was taller than a man, perhaps seven or eight feet, and seemed to have a human body, but its head was that of a ram, heavy horns blacker than the night.

Then Oliver was around the corner and still running. Kitsune was beside him and she reached out and grabbed hold of his free hand, practically dragging him along. Up ahead, Frost had stopped and grabbed the reins of a pair of saddled horses, and suddenly Oliver understood where they had gotten off to in those moments when he thought he had been abandoned, when he thought he was going to die.

The privileged life he had led had prepared him, in some strange way, for this. Once upon a time it was common for people to know how to wield a sword or shoot a gun or ride a horse, but in the modern world such pursuits were only for the wealthy. Until today, he had only ever shot skeet. And he had never ridden a horse out of need. But he could get himself in the saddle quickly enough.

He mounted the horse in a single swift movement, gripping the reins in both hands, cursing himself for having dropped the shotgun. Kitsune climbed up onto the mare beside him.

"Ride east for Perinthia. Stay off the road!" the winter man rasped in the darkness. And then Frost was gone, disintegrating into snow and wind and sweeping up into the sky.

A roar erupted behind them. A second came from the roof of a house just ahead and Oliver glanced up to see a Kirata up there, preparing to jump.

"Ride!" he called to Kitsune, and he snapped the reins.

The horses were swift and the terrain familiar to them and they galloped as though they had been waiting all their lives for such a flight. The tiger-men gave chase, but they could not keep pace with the horses, and in moments

Oliver and Kitsune were riding east into the night, away from the village of Bromfield and toward a city where every citizen would likely be on the lookout for him.

Yet exhilaration made him shout and he glanced over at Kitsune, whose hood had been thrown back by the wind. Her hair blew behind her like the wings of a raven and she laughed at his exuberance, her smile, for once, entirely without guile or mystery.

On the eastern horizon, the black sky had a tinge of cobalt, a whisper of dawn.

CHAPTER 13

Halliwell had fallen asleep in his chair and slept there all night, shifting uncomfortably while CNN droned on in the background of his dreams. The light of day and the stiffness in his aging body had woken him shortly after eight o'clock, and the long, uncomfortable night had conspired with his old bones to make him feel ancient. He was not on the clock until the afternoon shift, which began at two, so he had taken his time showering and making himself an egg, cheese, and bacon scramble for breakfast, a treat he gave himself once a week.

And he had watched the clock.

It was unlikely a sheriff's detective from Wessex County, Maine, was going to get much cooperation from the Paris police, but if he could be patient until eleven or twelve, he figured the San Francisco P.D. might be slightly more co-operative. The Paris cops might cooperate once they understood that he had a pair of killings that also included blinding as their primary feature, but then, he didn't speak a word of French, and what little experience he had with the French suggested that they had an attitude about that sort of thing.

So he had eaten breakfast and kept an eye on CNN for more news. There was a brief report, but it told him only that both victims had been children. No gory details. Blinded how, exactly, he wanted to ask. But first he needed to find someone who might actually have an answer.

It was only as the clock ticked toward noon and Halliwell went to pick up the phone, prepared to dial information for San Francisco, when he realized the call would cost him. Other than Sara, with whom he rarely spoke, there wasn't anyone he called out of the area. He had the minimum long-distance coverage and it seemed foolish not to let the sheriff's department pay for the call, especially if he was going to be on awhile, trying to get the information he needed.

As he made this decision, Halliwell had an odd sensation. He was tempted to eat the cost of the call, just so he could make it from here and not have to answer questions from Jackson Norris. The sheriff had every right to get an update on the investigation. Hell, it was the sheriff's investigation, really. But Halliwell now realized that there was more to it than just the job. Somehow, without him being aware of it, the case had become very personal. The mystery of what had happened to Oliver Bascombe and his sister Collette, how they had seemed to simply disappear—the brother twice now—was getting under his skin. The witnesses who'd seen Bascombe with a woman in a fur coat had said she looked Asian, but he'd considered the possibility that they were mistaken, and that it was Collette with him.

He would have given anything to talk to either of them, but mostly the brother. Oliver Bascombe would have been able to solve a lot of mysteries for him. Most important amongst them, of course, was the identity of the man who killed Alice St. John and Bascombe's own father. It could be a coincidence, these murders in Paris and San Francisco. After all, how could it be anything else? All the news would say was that the victims had been blinded, but that didn't mean their eyes had been removed. And even if the murders in Maine were identical to the others, they couldn't possibily be the work of just one man. The odds were absurd.

Halliwell needed answers, and he was starting to realize that he needed them for himself, not just for the job. On the other hand, he couldn't get all proprietary about it. Whatever he discovered he would have to report to the sheriff anyway.

Shaking his head, bemused by his reluctance, he grabbed his thick winter coat from the rack by the door and slipped it on, double-checking that his service weapon was properly strapped into his holster and that he had his identification and keys.

When he arrived at the office, he was ninety minutes early for his shift, but he managed to make it past the front desk and the deputies' break room without anyone taking note. Halliwell shared a large corner room with tall windows and a clanking iron radiator with two other detectives, but at the moment it was empty. He went through the paperwork and mail in his in-box, some of which would require his attention later, then shoved it all aside and picked up the phone. The wooden chair creaked beneath him, as he imagined it had even on the day, decades earlier, when it had first been purchased for the department. He dialed information and asked for the police department in San Francisco, California—homicide division, if they had a separate number—and scribbled it on the corner of his desk pad with a pencil so depleted it ought to have been used to score miniature golf.

Turned out San Francisco homicide did indeed have a separate number. When he dialed, it rang only once before being picked up. The cop on the other end was a detective named Beck. Halliwell introduced himself.

"What can I do for you, Detective Halliwell?"

"Before we go any further, you might want to call me back, look in to it, so you know I am who I say I am."

Halliwell had been through this before. Reporters would say anything on the telephone, try to trick someone into revealing information that nobody else had. Whatever it took to get the scoop.

"No, we're good," Beck replied, his voice a low rumble, yet so clear it was as though he were standing in the same room. "Caller I.D. said Wessex County Sheriff. Two-oh-seven area code is Maine. So what've you got?"

"I'd like to ask you some questions," Halliwell said, "but this will go faster if I just tell you what I'm working on. We've got a victim here, adult male, fifties, murdered in his bedroom. Perp removed his eyes. The next county over there's another one, a little girl this time, same m.o."

A little sigh of disgust came over the phone line, and then Beck cursed, more quietly but just as clear. "Jesus."

"You can guess why I'm calling—"

Beck laughed humorlessly. "You saw our case on the news and wanted to find out how our vic was mutilated."

"Pretty much. CNN said the subject was blinded."

"All right, Detective. Here we go, then. The best part. No sign of forced entry, no witnesses, no strange cars in the driveway, anything like that. Just a random kid, a quiet nine-year-old boy with a touch of autism, middle-class family, father's a cameraman at the local ABC affiliate. Only the mother was home at the time, but we've got her 911 call on tape and nobody figures her for the crime. But if not her, then how, right? The house was locked up tight. It was bedtime, but Jason was giving his mother a hard time. He begged for another half an hour to finish reading a chapter in a book called *The Wolves of Willoughby Chase*. Heady stuff for a nine-year-old. When she goes in, he's lying on the bed with blood staining the pillow under his head, running down from his eye sockets.

"So, yes, that was the mutilation. The perp tore his eyes out. The medical examiner is still trying to determine what he used to remove them, but it was not done with any delicacy, I can tell you that. My partner and I caught the case. It looked like the guy had used a grapefruit spoon and just . . . dug around in there. Cause of death was heart failure. In a nine-year-old boy. That was the trauma and pain of it. The little guy had a heart attack."

There was a catch in Beck's throat and Halliwell felt a chill travel through him, a grim shadow over his heart as he thought of Alice St. John.

"Any leads at all?" Halliwell asked hopefully.

Beck paused a long while. When he spoke again, there was a new wariness in his voice, as if he was thinking maybe he should have checked up on Halliwell's I.D., after all.

"Not much," he said at last. "No physical evidence. Like I said, no forced entry. We were starting to look at the mom because we had no other choice, and then the desk sergeant here brought in an *L.A. Times* his wife had picked up when she was down visiting her sister. She pointed out a tiny little piece in the international news about the murder in Paris. The circumstances—the child at bedtime, no forced entry—sounded similar enough that I checked on it. They were too similar."

Ted Halliwell had been a cop a long time. There were hesitations in Beck's voice that told him the man was leaving something out. He could almost hear the empty spaces in the story. And he had a feeling he knew what was missing.

"He took them, didn't he?"

"Pardon me?"

Halliwell sighed. He knew he was right. It couldn't be, but he felt it powerfully. He told Beck about Alice St. John's murder, how it had taken place in public and so was vastly different from the Paris and San Francisco cases. Max Bascombe's murder, however—though the only one not involving a child—fit the m.o. perfectly. He gave Beck what little description he had, knowing it would provide nothing. And then he went back to the question.

"The killer took them. He did, right? In both of the cases here, Bascombe and the St. John girl, the eyes were removed from the scene. Locked doors and all."

The silence told him all he needed to know. Halliwell drew a deep breath and leaned back in the chair, letting the familiar squeak cry out to the empty room. Questions fired through his mind, echoing around without encountering any answers.

"How can that be?" Detective Beck asked, but Halliwell was sure the man was not speaking to him, but to whatever cosmic force he believed might be listening. "Can you hang on a minute?" he asked. And then, before he put the line on hold, Halliwell heard him calling out, "Lieutenant? We've got another one."

The words echoed in his mind for every second of the nearly two minutes he was on hold, so that when Beck at last returned to the line, he nearly shouted at the man.

"Another one? What's that about, Detective Beck? The way you said that, it sounded a hell of a lot like—"

"You're not the only one who's called."

Halliwell narrowed his eyes and stared at the blank, dark face of his computer screen, as if expecting it to flicker to life and provide some kind of explanation. "How many?"

"One definite in Prague. One in Toronto. Two that may or may not be related in Louisiana. And an orphanage in Germany, just outside of Munich."

Nausea roiled in Halliwell's stomach and he leaned forward, elbows on the desk, running his free hand through his thinning hair. "At an orphanage? Was there more than one—"

Beck had anticipated the question. "All of them. Twenty-seven, ranging from eighteen months to eleven years old."

Halliwell slid his hand over his mouth and stared across the room at nothing.

"Hello?" Beck prompted.

"I'm still here. I'm sorry. It's just . . . a lot to take in. I've been doing this a long time, but twenty-seven kids—"

"Thirty-three, if you count them all, including yours. Plus one adult. That seems odd, doesn't it?"

Halliwell laughed, the sound hollow in his ears. "Odd? What the hell is odd, in this context? There's no way one guy is doing all this. That means there's some kind of conspiracy. Maybe it's Internet-based, a bunch of psychos sharing ideas in a chat room or something, going out and doing this and then reporting back to one another."

"Maybe." Beck didn't sound convinced. "I'd almost be happy with that as a solution. Except in every case there's no sign of entry, no physical evidence. Your situation is the only one I've heard about where there are any witnesses. If there were multiple perps, you'd expect at least one of them to screw it up, to leave something behind that the investigating officers could use."

Halliwell couldn't argue with that logic. Neither one of them wanted to admit that they were baffled, but it was obvious in the conversation. It was only a matter of time before other agencies became involved, including the FBI. Once it began to look like a serial killer and the case involved more than one state, the Bureau would get into the fray. Halliwell would normally have bristled at the idea, but at this point, he thought he might welcome anyone who might be able to help.

And he knew that eventually they'd get around to focusing on him and the Wessex County sheriff's department. Their case was the only one involving an adult, and the only one with witnesses. There were also missing persons to consider, an aspect that seemed unique to the Bascombe murder.

Yes, Oliver and Collette Bascombe seemed to disappear at will, with no known means of transportation, and in the brother's case, in the middle of a blizzard. In that way, they were like the killer, leaving no trace of themselves behind.

When Halliwell was through talking with Beck, they exchanged information and he hung up. Sheriff Norris registered only a flicker of surprise when he knocked on the man's door and quickly entered. Jackson had been getting several phone calls each day from Max Bascombe's law firm, the man's partners in the firm pushing hard for results from the investigation. Those lawyers wanted a quiet inquiry and quick results, and they wanted Jackson Norris to make sure that was what they got.

They were not going to be happy.

At the edge of the city of Perinthia, a patch of the world was on fire. It was not quite morning, nor even dawn, when Oliver and Kitsune rode toward the darkened towers that loomed on the horizon, thrusting up from the Euphrasian soil without any suburban preamble. There was only the Truce Road bisecting grassy plains and then the eruption of shadowy spires and formidable edifices whose shapes all combined in the dark to present themselves as a sort of wall or massive gate. Yet Oliver was surprised to discover, as they drew closer and the indigo sky lightened to cobalt, that there was no wall around Perinthia, only a series of watchtowers spaced perhaps a quarter of a mile apart from one another.

South of the road, twice that distance from the city's edge, was that patch of fire. The earth was a volcanic pit there, black and riddled with cracks that glowed with the hellish red of burning magma. Streams of liquid fire shot upward with no warning, and all around the edges, where no grass grew, the circumference was a ring of flame burning several feet high.

A mile out from the city, Oliver let the horse canter to a stand of trees and then pulled the reins up to halt the beast as Kitsune joined him on her own mount. The horses snorted conspiratorially to each other as though decrying their treatment these past hours by the thieves who'd stolen them away.

"It's nearly dawn, Oliver. We cannot afford to rest now. Once the sun rises we haven't a hope of getting into Perinthia without being noticed," Kitsune told him.

Her eyes were wide and alert and her face flushed with the exhilaration of the ride. The wind had blown her hair into a wild tangle that spread across her hood and over her shoulders. Though her tone was cautionary, there was that familiar light of mischief in her eyes, as though she couldn't help it, despite their circumstances.

Oliver felt only trepidation. "I don't think we have a chance in hell of going unnoticed. The watchtowers are too close. This is impossible." He shook his head, but could not stop his gaze from drifting back to that patch of infernal, volcanic earth.

"And what the hell is *that* anyway?" he asked, gesturing toward the burning earth in the distance, troubled by the sight.

Kitsune knitted her brow impatiently. "I'd thought Frost had explained all of this to you. On this side of the Veil, nothing can exist unless it does so in a space parallel to public land on your side. When public land is sacrificed to development, it devastates portions of the land here. Our world diminishes. Often such destruction leaves a fragment of scorched ground behind, a wound in the Veil. Such wounds heal in time, but the world is diminished afterward."

The horse shifted beneath Oliver, chuffing softly, as if something had unsettled it. He pulled the reins taut in his hands, surveying the dark, brooding shape of the city on the eastern horizon. The tallest of the towers were silhouetted now with diffuse light, the sun flirting just at the verge of showing itself. At this distance it was impossible to be sure, but the watchtowers seemed still.

"Shall we?" Kitsune asked.

Oliver nodded, but then he frowned and glanced around. "All right. But where is Frost?"

The leaves in the birch trees where they had taken cover rustled with a gust of wind and Oliver shivered as cold air swirled around him. He could see his breath, and a few flakes of snow fell as though shaken from the trees. The two horses stamped their feet and one of them sneezed.

"Here," Frost said, even as the wind began a small, frigid twister of ice and snow. It subsided, and the winter man stood before them.

Kitsune pulled her cloak closer around her against the chill of his arrival. "I wondered when you would return. I thought perhaps you had abandoned us."

The winter man fixed her with a hard look, mist rising from his eyes. Then he glanced at Oliver, the familiar chime of his icy hair tinkling together welcome after his absence.

"I went ahead to determine our best point of entrance. We'll need to make our way around to the south side of the city." Frost turned to Kitsune. "The guards change shift at sunrise, so that will be our best hope. But it means we must move now. And without horses."

Oliver let out a breath. "Is that wise? What if we have to run?"

"Our approach will be less conspicuous on foot."

"Don't you mean *our* approach?" Kitsune said. "You can drift in on an errant breeze with no risk at all."

"True enough. But once within the walls, the two of you will have to do some of the advance work. You might blend in in Perinthia. I will not."

Oliver grabbed the pommel of his horse and dismounted. "Quit bickering. We've got maybe twenty minutes before the shift change. We've got to get going."

The two Borderkind looked at him as though surprised he'd spoken so curtly to them. Oliver was amused. As amazed as he was with everything around him, including his companions, the awe he had felt upon first piercing the Veil was lessening with every hour. He figured that would be helpful. Awe might cause him to hesitate at the wrong moment and get him killed.

Kitsune laughed softly and climbed down off her horse. She leaned in to whisper something to it, and though he was curious Oliver didn't bother to ask if she and the horse could understand each other.

The winter man stayed with them as they set out from the trees and across the grassy plains toward Perinthia. They took a diagonal path that cut across the Truce Road, moving as quickly as they were able across that mostly open space. The only sounds were Oliver's footfalls, the occasional chime of Frost's hair, and the wind. Their path took them right up behind the patch of burning, volcanic earth, and a sulfurous stink rose from that pit so powerfully that Oliver had to breathe through his mouth—and even then wished he could have stopped entirely.

All three of them watched the city as they ran, keeping low and moving through the areas of the tallest grass. More lights came on, the early risers greeting the dawn. Still the watchtowers were dark and quiet.

They'd been approaching at an angle but now with a gesture Frost turned them on a direct path that would take them between a pair of watchtowers perhaps a quarter of a mile apart from each other. The sky continued to lighten and Oliver thought he saw a dark figure in the upper window of the tower to their right. At the left, nothing stirred, but suddenly their error struck him.

"This is idiotic," he whispered. "Both of you can be far less conspicuous than this. You don't have to protect me right now. We're going to get caught."

"Oliver," Frost cautioned.

"Get out of here. Kitsune, you too. Running is going to draw attention. Trust me. Just go."

But he had not even finished speaking and already the winter man was gone, a swirl of snow and ice eddying away on the breeze that stirred the tall grass. Kitsune raised her hood and in a single fluid motion she transformed, shrinking down to disappear herself into the grass as a fox.

Oliver was alone, one hundred yards from the edge of the city, and the sun was beginning to rise.

Ignoring the watchtowers, he turned up the collar of his coat against the wind and bent against it, hurrying but not running—just a man out for a walk and regretting it. Not for a moment did he think any guard bearing witness to this would be convinced by it. There was no one else outside the city and no one on the road, so it was clear this sort of casual stroll outside of Perinthia was uncommon. The question was how emphatic the authorities had been about the search for this Intruder.

It would be better simply to not be seen at all than to rely on such a question, of course, so he kept his head down and he hurried and he prayed. His whole body tingled with the feeling of eyes burning into him, though that might only have been paranoia. His cheeks were flushed and his hands clammy where he'd shoved them into his pockets.

Despite the cold wind, he began to sweat. His throat

felt constricted and his pulse raced. He ran out his tongue to wet his lips, staring at the ground, and it took him a moment to realize it when his boot heels first hit cobblestone instead of grassy sod. A surge of tentative hope sparked in him but he kept on for a count of twenty more steps before allowing himself to look up.

Oliver found himself on a street lined with well-kept row houses, mostly brown stone with granite steps and high, arched windows. There was an old European flair to the neighborhood that did not speak of any one country, though the roughness of the stone exteriors and the flower boxes outside many of the windows put him in mind of Holland. Their scent was so pleasant it stopped him in the middle of the street.

Lampposts lined either side, but they had burned out now.

The sun was rising, throwing a line of bright morning light on the left side of the street and casting the right side in shadow. Oliver longed for the light, but kept to the shadows.

From that street he could only see the tops of the watchtowers he had passed on the way in, and could not see the windows at all. He was tensed, alert for any shout or sign that he had been seen and was being pursued, but nothing came. When a door opened across the street he was startled, but took deep breaths and started walking again, alone on the streets of Perinthia, at least for the moment.

The woman who came out of the row house was old and stooped, dressed all in mourning black. Her nose was long and hooked and her eyes, when she glanced toward him, were tiny beads of white. Oliver shuddered to see them, and to be seen by her.

Her expression was less a smile than a sour twist that made Oliver swallow hard, throat dry. He was sure that she would speak to him, ask him what he was doing on her street—there were only homes here, so he had no reason to be here unless he was a resident or a thief—but she only eyed him curiously a moment and then tottered away northward, deeper into Perinthia.

Oliver slowed his pace so as not to catch up with her.

At the end of the street he found himself at an intersection not only of streets, but of styles. To the west was a narrow street, little more than an alley, between two pagoda-like buildings. Between them he saw a courtyard splashed with dawn's light, where dozens of people knelt to face the rising sun. Some were women in pure white gowns with patterns in the fabric. Some—and this quickened his heart—wore the heavy garb of soldiers. Most of the people gathered there seemed to be Asian, but not all of them were. And there were those among them who were not people at all. At first he took the huge lizard with its strangely furred face and tiny wings to be some kind of statue, it was so still.

Then the sunlight reached it, and it moved, ever so slightly.

There were other things amongst them, too, stumpy little men whose mouths opened as though on hinges as they sang some kind of morning chant, and there were cats. A great many cats. He found himself staring despite the presence of those soldiers, and on second thought he had to wonder if they had any official capacity here or were somehow ceremonial for the little enclave he was spying upon.

The rattling approach of a carriage drew his attention. The driver up on the high seat was an ugly little man wearing a green felt fedora. A pair of midnight-black horses had

been harnessed to a vehicle that seemed an antique to him.
But then, everything here was of another age. He could see
along streets to the north and east from here, and with the
sun coming up, some of the taller structures were more
readily visible to him. A clock tower chimed the hour,
claiming it to be seven in the morning, but he was unsure
how they kept time here, given the length of the days and
nights. The city that spread out before him seemed a tapes-
try sewn from different regions and ages of history, a little
Victorian Europe, a pocket of ancient Asia, and more than
a little of America in the twenties and thirties.

Down the northern road, to his astonishment, he saw a
Model-T Ford go by, engine banging and popping as its
tires rolled across the cobblestones.

"Wow," he whispered under his breath, smiling in spite
of himself. All of the fear that had raced through him only
minutes before drained from him, surrendering to the
wonder of the place.

In the back of his mind he knew he had to find Kitsune
and Frost, but he started along that northern road regardless. It was still early, but more people were stirring now. A
trio of massive, shaggy-haired creatures whose gender was
a mystery passed him, going the other direction. They were
easily a dozen feet tall and the third one pulled a wagon
as though it were a rickshaw. Upon it were barrels and
wooden boxes full of various fruits and vegetables. There
were winter pears and bananas, the reddest apples Oliver
had ever seen, bunches of carrots and onions and buckets
full of peppers.

Going to market, he thought.

As he continued down the road he saw other oddities.
A goblin in a full-length jacket, a formal shirt, and no pants
wandered dangerously across the road, singing in a drunken

slur and doing his best to stagger out of the sunshine and into the shadows that the early-morning light provided. Beautiful, graceful, lithe creatures no higher than his knee and clad in clothes like Gypsies darted up and down the street, playing some sort of game with what appeared to be merely a piece of paper, save that the paper itself changed shape constantly, like some kind of remote-control origami masterpiece. A handsome man with massive antlers strode by, hooves clicking on the street, tiny little devilish-looking things swinging from the twisted rack upon his head. One of them made obscene gestures toward Oliver and the others all laughed a high little titter.

Yet most of the people he saw on the streets of Perinthia were human, and ordinary enough to look at. Their mode of dress varied wildly, as did their race, but none of them took any notice of their differences. They went about their business in so mundane a fashion that he was set at ease.

At the next intersection he stood back to watch the city come alive at morning. He had reached a main thorough-fare now and there were shops all along the street, as well as bars and restaurants. One building off to his right was enormous enough that it might have been a cathedral, but he saw that the door was set in to another, much larger entrance, at least thirty feet high, and he understood that this was either the home or business of giants. Larger by far than the ones he'd seen going to market.

"Apparently, no one finds you particularly out of place."

A tiny sound emitted from his throat and Oliver twisted round, ready to defend himself. It was only Kitsune, standing beside him with the hood of her copper-furred cloak thrown back and the sun on her face. He had not even realized it, but he had given up trying to hide himself in the shadows.

Oliver glanced around to make sure they had not drawn attention. Then he rolled his eyes.

"Don't do that to me. You're going to give me a heart attack."

The sun gave a milky hue to her jade eyes. "I doubt that."

"And what did you mean by—"

But then it dawned on him what she had meant. He had been wandering the south side of Perinthia for fifteen or twenty minutes and no one had taken any special interest in him or even looked at him very closely, save the crone in black who had been the first person he'd run across.

"So we're all right."

Kitsune frowned. "For the moment. It's unlikely the citizens will know what you look like, but the police will. Wandering around wide-eyed as a child is not the best way to remain at liberty."

Oliver nodded. "I can't argue. So what now?"

"There's nothing we can do until tonight. We need a place to be out of sight, particularly for Frost. He can't remain incorporeal forever, and he also cannot be seen in the city. Word will get back to the Hunters."

"I take it you have a place in mind?"

Her eyes twinkled. "I do."

CHAPTER 14

Oliver clutched the heavy iron key in his hand as he climbed the stairs to the third floor of the Hotel Fleur de Lis. It was an old building in classic Parisian style, three stories of guest rooms around a central courtyard filled with fountains and flowers and benches where one might sit and read in enviable peace. The soft swish of Kitsune's fur cloak followed him and she moved silently into place at his side when he paused at the top of the steps.

"This way," she said, moving into the corridor, passing through splashes of sunlight from the exterior windows.

Some of the rooms faced the street, but Kitsune had asked for one that looked down upon the courtyard. Now, as he followed her to room 36, Oliver pondered just how fortunate he and Frost had been to encounter her in the woods that night. It seemed so long ago to him now. Could it really have been only days? Kitsune had reason to ally herself with them. As Borderkind, she was a target of the Myth Hunters, just like Frost. But she had proven invaluable, not only in a fight, but this very morning. Kitsune had chosen this hotel from previous experience and had been the only one among them to have any Euphrasian coin.

At the door to their room she stepped aside to make way for him. The weight of the key in his hand was reassuring and Oliver took pleasure in the familiarity of the moment. He unlocked the door and pushed it open, letting Kitsune precede him out of courtesy and habit. Shutting the door behind him, he slid the dead bolt and chain into place, and put the heavy key into his pocket.

A weary smile touched his lips as he took in the room. Curtains little more than chiffon wisps were tied back on either side of the three tall windows and the wood floor gleamed with diffuse golden sunshine. There was a kind of honeyed sheen to the entire chamber, a softness gifted upon the place by the indirect daylight. The head- and footboards on the bed were intricately carved, and there were several paintings of fairy glens and dragon hoards mixed with the afternoon-at-the-park and still-life-with-fruit sort of thing he'd always found in ordinary hotels.

So pleased was he with the room that Oliver had scarcely noticed Kitsune slipping through a sliding door that separated bedroom from bath. The squeak of a faucet and abrupt knocking of pipes and the sound of running water took him entirely by surprise. A nearly absurd happiness filled him as he turned.

"Running water?" he asked in disbelief, as though the sound might have been some cruel trick. He'd not even considered the possibility that there might be a real bath or shower in Perinthia, though he ought to have, considering some parts of the city were up to at least early twentieth-century standards.

"Why do you think I chose this hotel?" Kitsune called to him.

Oliver smiled and went toward her voice. He came in sight of the open door, and then his smile faded with an unconscious exhalation of breath.

Kitsune stood on one foot, the other raised behind her as she bent to test the temperature of the water. She was entirely nude, her long, lithe body finely sculpted. Her breasts were small, her nipples tiny brown berries, and her silken black hair spilled across her face while she let the water run over her fingers. Oliver found that he could not breathe. There was no sign of her clothes, nor of her copper fur cloak, though he presumed there must be some dressing area in the bathroom. He'd thought for so long that the fox in her, the transformation she underwent, was the part of her he found magical. But there was utter enchantment in the effect she had on him in that moment. He shook a little, just looking at her.

Satisfied that the water was warm enough, she stood up straight, catching sight of him out of the corner of her eye. Through the curtain of her hair she watched him a moment, making no attempt to shield herself from view. Her smile was a whisper of suggestion and amusement as she pushed her long hair back and gazed at him boldly.

"The soap is perfumed," she said. "I have been dreaming about this place since yesterday." As if there was nothing at all unusual about the moment.

She stepped into the bath and drew the curtain and he

heard a kind of ticking from the pipes, to which the staccato spray of the shower replied. Oliver stood staring at the curtain, the image of Kitsune's bronze form, every curve of her, etched into his mind.

It was several moments before he realized that there was another sound, a rougher noise, like gravel pelting glass. He turned to see water dripping down the right-most window, though the courtyard was still bathed in sunlight. The window rattled in its frame and tiny pellets of hail whipped against it in the wind.

Frost.

Oliver hurried over and opened the window, staggering back as a powerful gust of icy wind blasted inward. Snowflakes danced in the air and twisted in a dizzying whirlwind as the gust slid across the room to a corner out of sight of the windows.

Inch by inch, they constructed the winter man.

Frost was all sharp edges and glistening icicles. Icy mist drifted from his eyes as he gazed past Oliver at the open door, the sound of the running shower filling the room. A hint of emotion, possibly disapproval, flickered across his face and then was gone.

"I've been to Amelia's and had a look about the place. Unseen, of course. It is closed now, and dark. We must limit the possibility of Kitsune being recognized by someone who might inform the Hunters, and your exposure to the city. Anyone who is obviously new to Euphrasia is likely to fall under suspicion of being the Intruder who is wanted by the authorities. The less you talk to people, the better. We'll stay here until dark."

Oliver scratched the back of his head and glanced at the windows. "That's a long way off."

"There's nothing to be done about it. You and Kitsune

rest. Eat. The kitchen will bring food up if she asks. They will think you lovers, wishing to indulge in each other."

Heat flushed Oliver's face and he kept his gaze locked on Frost, steadfastly refusing the temptation to glance back at the open bathroom door.

"We'll make do," he said. "Is Amelia's far from here?"

The winter man shook his head. "Not far at all. Four blocks. Perhaps five. The neighborhood is less than desirable, but perfect for a place like Amelia's. The character of Perinthia changes with every corner turned."

The conversation continued for another minute or two. When Kitsune emerged from the shower, wrapped in a thick white cotton robe that seemed stark and bright against the café au lait hue of her skin, it was obvious she wore nothing under it. As the two Borderkind discussed the necessity of waiting out the day in that room, Oliver did what he could to avert his eyes from her, afraid he would stare. The memory of her nakedness was vividly replaying itself in his head.

Later, after they'd eaten—the staff of Fleur de Lis had been just as accommodating as Frost had predicted—exhaustion took over. Oliver had been cognizant of the fact that there was only one large bed and no sofa or any other surface comfortable enough to sleep on by choice. Even so, he'd intended to make up some kind of space on the floor with an extra blanket he'd found and one of the pillows from the bed. Kitsune would not hear of it.

Had she remained in just that cotton robe in which she had emerged from the bathroom earlier, there was no way he would have gotten into bed with her. Not that he thought anything might happen—he was just some ordinary guy, after all, and she was exotic and . . . hell, she was supernatural—but even so, the awkwardness would have crippled him. Not to mention thoughts of Julianna. The marriage had never happened, but she was still his fiancée. And with Frost in the room, his embarrassment would have been that much worse.

Not that their eventual compromise was much better. Kitsune wore the black top and pants she'd had on throughout their adventures thus far and she insisted that he climb beneath the covers while she spread her fur cloak over herself and burrowed into the bed. She seemed to find his discomfort amusing, but only for the minute or two that it took her to fall into a deep sleep.

Oliver was not so fortunate.

While Frost stood watch over them, entirely still in the darkest corner of the room as though he were truly frozen, Oliver lay turned away from Kitsune, wide-awake and staring at the wall. He had showered after they'd eaten and the clean linens felt wonderful against his bare arms, but every nerve ending seemed to be alive and aware. From time to time he drew deep breaths and forced his eyes closed, trying to will sleep to claim him. An echo of his nightmare in Oliver Larch's house remained in his mind, and thoughts of this only added to all of the thoughts that troubled him.

His eyes were shut tight when he felt the cold air against his face. When he opened them, Frost was crouched beside the bed, watching him intently. His hair chimed as he tilted his head like a curious bird.

"What haunts you, Oliver?"

He stared into those blue-white eyes, trying to find the words. A shiver ran through him from the nearness of the winter man, and perhaps from his own thoughts as well. Throughout their journey, their flight from those who would have taken their lives, Oliver had exulted in the discovery of magic and of the ironic freedom bestowed upon him by the intrusion of violence, terror, and the supernatural into his life. But his dreams had been dreams of home.

"I've been gone too long," Oliver said, keeping his voice low so as not to rouse the gently purring Kitsune. "That night you came to me, with the Falconer hunting you, my wedding was supposed to be the next day."

"Those events were not in your control. You did not abandon your fiancée willingly."

Oliver's stomach gave a sour twist. "No. But I was glad. I'd been doubting the decision to marry since the day I first proposed."

"Do you not love her?"

"I do. I think I do. But it felt like I was . . . surrendering to the future my father had mapped out for me. Julianna was going to marry that guy, the one my father had groomed so perfectly, and then I'd have to be him forever. I wished I could just break out of that, be more of what I wanted, and then if she still wanted me . . . but I was too well trained, wasn't I?" He laughed bitterly. "I was a good puppy. Doing just what my master wanted."

Frost tilted his head ever so slightly and a blast of frigid air swept through the room.

"Some would say that is the role of a good son."

Oliver stared at him, wondering if that was Frost's belief, or simply one he had observed in the ages he had spent as harbinger of winter in the world of men. "A good son, I guess. But what happens when the son isn't a boy anymore? Someday he may have a son of his own, and then what?"

The winter man smiled. The ice of his face cracked, chips drifting to the floor. "That is the question at hand, is it not? And if you survive the piercing of the Veil, you will have an opportunity to answer it."

"I can't wait that long. My father will be embarrassed as hell by my going AWOL for the wedding. Julianna, too, I'm sure. But Collette would have been worried the first day. And by now, she and Julianna have probably both gotten to the point where they think I'm . . . that if I haven't come back yet, then I'm dead in a ditch somewhere."

Talking about the conflicts inside of him was like releasing steam from a pressure valve. As he began to relax, at last Oliver began to feel as though he might be capable of sleep.

"I've been gone too long. I know it would be dangerous for me to be around them, but I can't just let them stay in the dark. I've got to at least let them know I'm alive."

Frost opened his mouth slightly, revealing jagged, frozen teeth. It wasn't a smile or a laugh, but Oliver wasn't sure how to read the expression beyond that.

"How do you propose to do that?" the winter man asked.

Oliver watched him closely. Kitsune was warm beside him, even though she was not under the covers, but the chill coming off Frost seemed even more frigid.

"Could you take me across the Border? Just for a few minutes? Half an hour, at the most? I've got to call them, Frost. I have to let them know."

The winter man's brows crackled. "What would you tell them that they would believe?"

"Only that I'm all right. That I'm in some trouble and I hope to be able to come home soon."

Slowly, Frost nodded. He stood from a crouch, unfolding with such fluidity it was as though he were a storm himself and each motion was a gust of wind. This was not far from the truth. Yet Oliver could not admire the beauty of the winter man. Instead he was troubled by Frost's demeanor.

"What is it?" Oliver asked.

"I will do this for you, Oliver. I have pledged to aid you because it was saving my life that imperiled your own. But you must wait until we have found a place where I believe we can cross swiftly and safely, and then you must make haste. We will not spend even one night in Perinthia, if I can help it. At sundown we go to Amelia's. If we are not able to learn the location of Professor Koenig there, I know of other places we might ask such questions. And then we leave."

"Of course," Oliver said. "The Hunters could find us at any time. Got to keep moving."

The winter man spun on him, eyes furiously narrowed, features shifting now into slivers, chin and cheeks and nose all long and sharp. The mist that drifted from his eyes eddied around his head and he took a step back toward the bed, arms raised, dagger fingers curved as though he meant to strike.

Oliver's mouth dropped open but he could not move or speak. The cold caressed him, but it was fear that had frozen him, not the power of the winter man.

Frost dropped to one knee and reached out to tap a fingertip—a needle of ice—against Oliver's temple.

"Think. You must begin now to imagine a world beyond yourself. You seek your life's path, and I do understand. But you must also see that far more is at stake here than your one fragile, mortal life. It is not for myself that I fear. Not even for the Borderkind alone, though this conspiracy seems aimed at us. It is not enough to ask who is attempting to slay the Borderkind, but why. Have you given no thought at all to the greater powers at work here?"

Oliver hesitated, feeling more than ever like a child as he lay in bed with Frost looming angrily above him. He'd thought the Borderkind his friend, but just then his heart thundered with terror and his breath caught in his throat.

The winter man snarled. "No. I suppose you haven't." He shook his head. "I have been watching for the Hunters, wondering why they haven't made more attempts to kill us. I have come to the conclusion that it is because they have been spread too thin. There are many Borderkind, you see, far more than there are Myth Hunters."

He spat the word *myth* like it was poison on his tongue. "They are busy, the Hunters. Out across the Two Kingdoms, killing. And when I ask myself why, I cannot think of a single answer, except that whoever is responsible has a larger plan, and wishes to make sure the Borderkind are not able to interfere. Perhaps our secret enemy dreams of conquest, and the freedom of the Borderkind to travel where we wish makes us dangerous to him. But that is mere conjecture. The rest is mystery. But my life and Kitsune's life and thousands of others' rely upon my solving that mystery.

"So I will take you through the Veil to make your phone call, and I will get you to Professor Koenig because that is what I promised. But every minute that passes ticks us closer to the extermination of the Borderkind, and that I cannot forget."

Oliver wanted to say so much. He wanted to show his gratitude and swear his loyalty to Frost, to vow that once he was no longer marked for death he would remain in this world and fight at their side and do whatever he could to unravel the savage conspiracy that was closing in around them.

But the glint in the winter man's eyes kept him silent.

When the winter man turned away and went back to the shadows in the corner of the room to wait out the rest of the day, Oliver let himself breathe again. Laden with fear and guilt and frustration, he was certain he would never sleep.

Soon enough, however, he did at last slide down into a troubled slumber, into dreams that spanned two worlds, in both of which he felt alone.

Night in Perinthia was vastly different from morning. At dawn the streets had been well nigh deserted, but just after dusk, they were bustling. Carriages rattled over cobblestones, but they were hardly the only traffic on the streets. There were cars as well—most of them ancient, noisy, oil-stinking things from the early days of the twentieth century. Others, however, were bizarre incongruities: an old sedan, complete with running board, that looked as though it might once have been driven by John Dillinger, and a 1970s-era Ford pickup truck with faded green paint on what small areas had not already been eaten by rust.

Those were the metal beasts. There were far more of the other variety. Black dogs of immense size and a startling variety loped along sidewalks and stalked amongst the crowds. Some had blazing red eyes, and others, though smaller, seemed to walk several inches above the ground, paws never quite touching anything solid. There were creatures of every persuasion, most of which seemed to have been put together from the component parts of other animals. A rooster's head on a lizard's body, with a scorpion's tail. An alligator's head on the body of a lion, with eagle's wings. Some he thought he knew from mythology: a gryphon, a harpy, a Pegasus. But most were a puzzle to him, a menagerie of legend and story.

Massive horses clomped slowly along the stone roads, not moving aside for carriage or auto, most of them carrying dark riders in leather armor, some of whom had no flesh on their bones and only a skull for a head . . . while others had no head at all. There were giants of differing size, demeanor, and sophistication. Boggarts and goblins and trolls—though often it was difficult to tell the difference—and nymphs and fairies from around the world, some of them flitting wisps with shimmering wings of color, and others lithe men and women of ethereal beauty and the cool reserve and calm of the deepest ocean before a storm.

And there were monsters, of course. Staggering things covered in filth that seemed to have dragged themselves from swampland or sewer, beautiful dead-faced things with mesmerizing eyes and a reach just long enough to snatch their prey, and deadly, razor-toothed things low to the ground and almost faster than the eye could follow.

Amongst them all, far more numerous than the beasts and the fairies and goblins and the monsters put together, were the humans. Generations of Lost Ones who had slipped from one world into the next—the children of Roanoke and Norfolk, of Shanghai and Tunguska, of the ill-fated passengers of a thousand ghost ships. A city full of men and women and children to whom this was all no more than ordinary, who linked arms with romantic intention and gazed in shop windows as they walked, who sampled the wares from merchants' carts and laughed at the antics of street performers of all persuasions.

Music and laughter and shouting filled the air in jarring conjunction with hooves on stone and rattletrap engines. From restaurants, pubs, and cafés there rose a mélange of richly textured aromas, of spices and herbs and sweets that created the recipes of a hundred cultures that had once hailed from North America, Europe, and Asia, some of which had long been forgotten in their native lands.

This was the city. Perinthia at night.

Oliver Bascombe was giddy with awe at the wonder of it all.

Frost remained unseen, drifting along high in the air above, riding the winds of the Euphrasian night. Kitsune was at Oliver's side, however, and from the moment they had stepped out of the Hotel Fleur de Lis, her fingers had been twined with his as though they were lovers. Less conspicuous that way, she had said. And he knew she was right, but still his face flushed and his skin prickled with the pleasure of her nearness and the memory of her body, and he forced himself to remember that it was Julianna he longed to see, Julianna whom he had already hurt so much.

Hand in hand they arrived at Amelia's, a place with darkened windows and no electricity, its sign illuminated by gas lamps, flames brightly dancing inside glass. Music poured from within, a big-band sound with horns and thumping drums, and smoke wafted out the open door, pipe and cigar and cigarette and sweet homegrown herb all drifting together.

Yet confronted with all of that, it was the sign that caught Oliver's attention as they approached the door. Upon it was carved the name of the place, with a painting of an old airplane and the stark, plain face of a woman.

"Amelia's," Oliver said in a hushed voice.

Kitsune gripped his hand. Her brows were knitted with concern. "What is it?"

He smiled. "Amelia's . . . it's Amelia Earhart." A soft laugh escaped him. "I guess now we know where she went."

Kitsune made a soft, warm sound in her throat. "She was a good woman. Kind to all breeds. Her daughter owns this place now. Or is it her granddaughter? The years mean so much less to us than to humans. It is easy to lose track of generations."

The melancholy air of this statement startled him and would have lingered longer in his mind had not the door opened just then and a man emerged in a wash of louder music and more voluminous smoke. At second glance, Oliver determined that this was no ordinary man at all. He was no giant by mythical standards but well over seven feet tall, and half as broad. His beard had once been the color of rust but was now run through with gray streaks and he wore a wide-brimmed hat that cast his eyes in shadow. His long coat was well made, neat and immaculately clean, speaking of a certain refinement, and in one of his enormous hands he clutched a walking stick that was intricately carved and topped with a bronze figurehead.

A fox.

Upon his emergence, Kitsune stepped nearer to Oliver. She might simply have been moving aside to let the huge man pass but it felt like more than that to him.

"Little cousin," the man said, a smile spreading across his face though his eyes were still lost in the shade of his hat. He reached up to thoughtfully stroke his beard. "It's good to see you well. The wind blew ill whispers of your fate into Perinthia."

Kitsune did not throw her hood back but rather seemed

to retreat beneath it as though she wanted to transform herself, to become the fox and slip away into the alleys of the city. He felt her stiffen as she forced herself to stare into the shadows of his face.

"I am grateful for your concern, Mr. Smith. Though I confess it surprises me."

The man startled Oliver then by reaching up and removing his hat with a wide, sweeping gesture. He offered a slight bow and when he stood, there was only kindness in his gray eyes.

"Kitsune, I am a smith. If I arm Huntsmen and shoe their horses, it is my work, not my heart. When Herne and his wild boys chose you as prey, I did not ride with them, and I was pleased when the hunt was called off without success. Now the riders of the Wild Hunt are all dead or fled, for there are more dangerous Hunters about, as you well know. And for those I would not make so much as a chamberpot. I wish you luck, my dear. You and all your kind. And if you ever have need of me, I shall hope that I am up to the task."

All of his charm and apparent sincerity did nothing to thaw her. Kitsune only offered a small bow in reply to his words.

The man she'd called Mr. Smith wore a resigned expression when he turned to Oliver. "Good evening to you, Mr. Bascombe. Have a care in Perinthia. It is easy to get lost here, but also easy to be found. Stay not a moment longer than you must."

Oliver stared at him. "How do you know my—"

Mr. Smith raised an eyebrow, a small smile on his face. He put his hat on, casting his eyes in darkness again. "Don't be ridiculous, sir. You're a wanted man. That is public knowledge. And anyone who knows what is being done to the Borderkind, and hears the whispers, will know who you are the moment you are seen with Kitsune." He glanced around as though waiting for something. "I'm sure our friend Mr. Frost is not far away. I wish you all a safe journey."

With that he clutched the bronze fox head of his walking stick and set off down the street. Oliver and Kitsune watched him go for a few seconds. A gust of frigid wind swirled about them and Oliver thought he heard Frost whispering something on the air, but could not make out what it was.

"Come. He's right about one thing," Kitsune said. "We must not linger."

Oliver sought out the departing man again but had lost sight of him amidst a throng of people and creatures roving through the street. "Who the hell was that guy?"

"Wayland Smith. A single man for a thousand myths. We'll speak of him another time, perhaps. Tonight we have other things to attend to."

Kitsune lowered her hood, the fur cowling on her shoulders, and stepped through the front door of Amelia's, into smoke and the blare of big-band music. Trumpets and trombones and skittering drums. After glancing round in search of any sign of Frost, and finding nothing, Oliver followed.

The first thing he noticed was that the percentage of non-humans was far higher in Amelia's than it was out on the street. Though there were only gas lamps outside, there was electricity within. Behind the bar a neon sign for Champale, which he'd never heard of, flickered as if on the verge of being extinguished. On the left were booths and high cocktail tables and on the right was a long mahogany bar that ran forty feet toward the back of the place. At first glance, it was a dive. At second glance it became clear that it wasn't just a bar.

Amelia's was a nightclub.

Past the cocktail tables and the bar were stairs that led down into a much larger room with high ceilings and a broad, gleaming dance floor surrounded by tables that were attended by waiters and waitresses in black tie. The juxtaposition was startling. The brightest lights were on the band, perhaps because many of the creatures inside Amelia's preferred to be in the dark, or at the very least the shadows.

Not merely goblins and fairies and the like, but other things. Unique and unfamiliar . . . at least unique in his experience. In one corner of the bar were two creatures that might have passed for men in bad light, were it not that they were twice as tall as a man and had long bat wings that furled around them like a grandmother's shawl.

"Keen-Keengs," Kitsune whispered, nodding toward them. "Australian legend."

As they worked their way through the bar she continued to identify many of the creatures they encountered, though there were many she did not know the proper name for. A giant, hideous cannibal called the Kinderschrecker unnerved him the most. Then he saw the Hsing-T'ien, which had no head at all, but a wide, vicious-looking mouth in the center of its chest. It stopped him in his tracks and Kitsune was forced to drag him deeper into Amelia's.

Hanging from the ceiling were chains with perches that in another place would have served for birds. Here they provided a place for Jaculi to roost, the fierce winged serpents coiling round the wooden bars, their tails hanging down almost far enough to touch the heads of those below.

Some of the patrons clearly recognized Kitsune, whispering behind their hands, but others actually seemed to know her. Oliver felt oddly comforted when she raised her hand to wave to a tall, painfully stooped creature with pale green skin and arms that reached nearly to the floor. With him was a humanoid serpent with arms but only a snake's body below and a face that was not quite a man's and not quite an asp's.

The long-armed creature made his excuses to the serpent man and made his way through the bar to join them. Oliver glanced around to see if they were being observed, but no one seemed to be taking any particular interest in his and Kitsune's arrival.

The fox-woman hugged the hideous creature, whose flesh had the texture and gleam of a frog, and Oliver couldn't suppress a small shudder at the sight. Her smile revealed far too many sharp teeth. The sight always unnerved him and yet somehow it no longer detracted from her beauty.

"Grin, this is Jack," she said, gesturing to Oliver. It took him a moment to realize that *he* was Jack, which meant the creature was called Grin.

"Jack, meet Grin. An old friend."

"Another Lost One named Jack," Grin said, his voice a quiet burble. "Isn't that odd how so many of the humans who find their way here are called Jack? I wonder if there's anything to that?"

Kitsune cocked her head and looked at him. "You have become a philosopher in my absence?"

Despite its grotesqueness, the creature managed to look sheepish. "Not quite. Just odd, I thought." Then he gave a surreptitious glance around. "Anyway, I guess you're not here for a drink, eh? Looking for other Borderkind, yeah?"

Kitsune nodded. Oliver moved in to try to shield their conversation from a group who were drinking and talking around a nearby cocktail table.

Grin got a bit twitchy then, gaze darting back and forth between the two of them. Those long arms swung around nervously. "Lailoken's down in the club. Got a girl with him. There are Stikini here as well, four of them together, but you don't want to talk to them." The creature nodded toward Oliver. "They'll eat your Jack."

Kitsune gave him that slight, mischievous grin. "That would be bad."

"Word's getting out," Grin said in that sticky, burbly voice. "A lot of the travelers are dead. Not a lot of killings in Perinthia yet, but the Borderkind in the city have heard and most have gone underground."

"We're going to need to find them," Kitsune said.

A flutter of alarm went through Oliver. He frowned and watched her closely. They were supposed to be looking for a Mazikeen—from what he understood, a kind of sorcerer—but she was asking about Borderkind. His conversation with Frost earlier in the day came back to him now and he had to wonder if his companions were abandoning him to the more pressing concern of the conspiracy against the Borderkind. He supposed he wouldn't have blamed them, except that his life depended upon them.

Oliver spoke up. "We also need to find a—"

"Hush, Jack," Kitsune growled.

It startled him so much that he did fall silent, glaring at her. Grin laughed wetly.

"Bloke's not housebroken yet, I see. Ah, well, you'll get him sorted. Anyway, you want to find some of those that've gone under, you'd best talk to Jenny."

Kitsune flinched visibly. "Jenny? I'd been told she was dead."

The pale creature frowned at that. "Nobody's told her, apparently. You didn't see her at the bar?"

"I suppose I did not think to look, given that I'd thought her dead." Kitsune put her hands together and bowed her head. "My thanks, Leicester Grindylow."

"Not at all, Kit. Least I can do."

Kitsune slipped her hand into Oliver's and he was surprised by how warm her touch was. She pulled him along as though he really were her pet, dragging him toward the bar, weaving in amongst people and monsters who did not look as though they would give way for a petite little woman no matter how beautiful, yet she managed to make a path for them without trouble. A pair of hairy, stinking trolls narrowed their eyes and snorted at Oliver and looked as though they were going to make trouble, but then a breeze from nowhere pushed them a step backward and a rime of ice formed on their beards and eyebrows. Their eyes lit up with alarm and they turned to seek out trouble elsewhere. Trouble they could control.

The way she glanced back at him, tugging on his hand as though to show him off to her friends, Oliver felt like he was back in college, at some bar in Boston with Jessie Colbert, a girl he'd dated for about a month. The dissonance between then and now was jarring and he felt disoriented. The smoke and the music didn't help at all.

At the bar, Kitsune nudged a pair of ordinary-looking men out of the way. Beyond them, Oliver saw the Jenny that Grin had been talking about. He hadn't made the connection between the name and Kitsune's insistence that she was dead. Now he did. The bartender wore a faded red corset and a gauzy slip instead of a skirt or pants. Her skin was sallow and pockmarked and she looked like some dead thing who had drowned in a lake or a pond and been dredged up days or weeks later. Her eyes bulged from her face. Even in the dim light of the bar and the haze of smoke he could see that her hair was a stringy, unwashed green. But her most striking feature was her mouth. It was far too wide, going almost to the bottoms of her ears, and she had a mouthful of fangs stained with mossy sludge almost as green as her hair.

Jenny Greenteeth.

She was pouring a whiskey when Kitsune bumped up to the bar with Oliver in tow. He made polite murmurs to those he had to sidle up beside to join his companion. A trace of an icy breeze brushed the back of his neck and it was reassuring to know that somehow Frost was with them.

When Jenny Greenteeth glanced up and saw Kitsune, her hand shook so much that she spilled whiskey on the bar. Then she hid her surprise beneath her reaction to the spill, cursing and grabbing a towel to wipe up the mess, apologizing to the customer who'd ordered it. Kitsune obviously wanted to speak with her but Jenny shook her head once, curtly, and then gave a tiny nod to indicate that they should follow. She whispered something to a Keen-Keeng who was bent over the counter sipping at a foamy stein of beer, and he climbed unceremoniously over the bar to take her place.

"What the hell—" Oliver began in a whisper.

Kitsune grabbed the front of the jacket Larch had given him to replace his parka and hauled him along behind her once again.

Working her way out from behind the bar and then through the crowd, Jenny paused at the top of the steps that led down into the nightclub, making sure that they were following. But she didn't wait for them. She went down the stairs. The band was blasting out an old Glenn Miller song, but there was a sitar player bopping along with the horns. At the bottom of the steps, Jenny turned hard left and made a beeline for a door that swung wide as she approached, disgorging a waiter with a tray that was loaded with plates of steaming food.

Jenny never reached that door. Instead, she stopped at another, on her left, that looked as though it doubled back underneath the bar. Oliver thought it was odd that he hadn't noticed the door, like it wasn't even there until Jenny reached for it. She glanced at them again and then disappeared through that heavy door made of wooden planks and iron bands.

"Wait, wait," Oliver whispered, fighting the temptation to look around to see if they were being watched. "How do we know this isn't some kind of trap?"

Kitsune's upper lip curled back in a silent scowl.

Chastened, he said nothing more and strode with her to that door. When Kitsune opened it, he preceded her into the gloom beyond.

CHAPTER 15

As the door closed behind them Oliver felt the icy draft of Frost passing by and shoved his hands in his pockets, wishing for the warmth of Kitsune's fur. The club had been so bright that it took his eyes a few moments to adjust, after which he saw that they were in a long, downward-sloping corridor. A bare bulb hung forty feet or so along, where it was clear the hall diverted to the left.

Backlit by that distant light, Jenny Greenteeth faced them in the corridor. For the first time, Oliver noticed how brutal her hands looked, with long talons and pale, translucent webs between her fingers. For a moment he was frightened of her. And then she spoke, and her voice was so heartbreakingly sincere he could no longer fear her.

"Kit, love, what am I supposed to do with you?"

"You might begin with a hug," Kitsune replied archly.

Jenny shook her head, relief seeming to overwhelm her anxiety, and wrapped her arms around Kitsune, fingers plunging into the fur of her cloak. Oliver felt a strange pang of jealousy that made absolutely no sense at all. He was focused on getting home, on trying to repair the life he'd left behind, on easing Julianna's worries. Or he should have been.

"I'd heard you were dead, Jen."

The water boggart, Borderkind like Kitsune, smiled slyly as she stepped back from the hug. "Wishful thinking on someone's part. I haven't left the neighborhood. If the Hunters want me, they know where to find me."

"They will come eventually," Kitsune said. "No Borderkind are going to be spared. They're killing Selkies. What is more harmless than that? But they've been slaughtered just the same."

All the pleasure left Jenny's features. "I know. There are a lot of us trying right now to identify all of the Hunters that have been sent out, and to figure out who's behind it all. Officially, both Kingdoms deny any knowledge of the Hunt. Unofficially, we've heard from the inside that the kings are clueless, that neither of them ordered this."

"Nor do they care, am I right?"

Jenny nodded, and the Borderkind shared a moment of kindred revulsion.

"What's happened with you? What are you doing here? Did you have a plan?"

Oliver felt like a spectator. Neither of them really noted his presence with more than a momentary glance. But this was a reunion of friends, and he was willing to hold his tongue.

Kitsune smiled. "The Wild Hunt were after me again. The real thing, not these Myth Hunters."

"Herne is such a prick," Jenny spat.

"Oh, he's getting a taste of his own medicine now, I'd think. While they were after me, the Myth Hunters went after them. The Manticore, I'd guess, from the smell, and some others as well."

Manticore. Now there was a monster with whose legend Oliver was familiar. Just the word conjured images that raised gooseflesh on his arms.

"So, they actually saved you from Herne and his hounds?" Jenny asked, incredulous.

"Not purposefully, you can be assured. I was simply not their target that day. I wandered the woods awhile afterward and then found Frost and Oliver, and now, well, we're all in trouble, aren't we?"

At the mention of his name, both of the women looked at Oliver. Kitsune smiled, but Jenny appraised him doubtfully.

"All of this fuss over you?" she said, and then rolled her eyes. "Well, at least it distracts them from the Borderkind for a while." Jenny glanced around and then frowned, baring her fangs. "Where is Frost, anyway?"

"*Here,*" came the voice of the winter man.

Jenny shivered as though his tone chilled her more than his presence. She turned and all three of them saw the eddy of wind and snow that constructed itself into a familiar face, a form of shadow and ice.

Frost stared at Jenny Greenteeth as though he was not quite sure if he could trust her. Kitsune had been so quick to do so that Oliver felt ashamed by how easily he had gone along with that.

"The Grindylow told Kitsune many Borderkind had

gone underground. We must speak to them immediately, those that we can reach. And we must find a Mazikeen. I owe a debt to Oliver, whom you've just met, and it must be repaid quickly—for his own sake and for ours. And I would discover what is being done about the Hunters."

Jenny smiled and executed a formal bow. "At your service, my lord Frost. When Grin said underground, he meant it literally. And Amelia's has always opened its arms to the lost and the fugitive. Just down this way."

She pushed past him and led the way down that corridor, which had wood and masonry and slabs of granite in its structure. At the hanging lightbulb—which gave off enough heat to mist the air around it when Frost passed by—Jenny took that left turn.

Oliver paused and would not continue, staring back up the way they'd come at the door.

"What is it?" Kitsune asked, suddenly closer to him than he'd realized, her breath warm on his neck.

"Isn't this a little conspicuous?" he asked. "I mean, the whole club could have seen us come in here. If this is where the Borderkind are hiding out, it isn't exactly safe, is it?"

Frost glanced at Jenny, icicle hair swaying, crackling, mist rising from his eyes. "There are Mazikeen here, yes?"

She nodded.

The winter man turned back to Oliver. "They are sorcerers. If this is where they have chosen to hide, they will have put a glamour on the door. No one will see it unless they know what it is they are looking for."

Oliver remembered that he hadn't noticed the door until Jenny had pulled it open. He was not entirely convinced, but if Frost wasn't worried, he supposed he had to have faith.

They continued downward, the corridor turning yet

again and the walls becoming more rough-hewn as they descended. If his sense of direction was functioning, he thought they'd come back to a point where they were directly beneath the nightclub stage, though they must be quite deep, for there was not even the most distant whisper of music. And still Jenny Greenteeth led them on. Another hundred yards or so and they reached a new door, this one entirely cast from iron, with the sort of wheel latch that Oliver had seen on submarines in old movies. Jenny opened it, waited for them all to pass through, then closed it tightly behind them.

On the other side was the sewer. The stink hit Oliver immediately and his stomach lurched. He pulled the collar of his shirt up and covered his nose and mouth, but made no complaint. This was the way they were going. Whining about it would accomplish nothing.

Light filtered in through gratings a hundred feet or more above. The walls were stone and every fifty feet was a complex archway, complete with decorative stone carvings and statuary. Oliver was both amused and impressed that anyone would make such an effort to build elegance into the sewer system. It looked like ancient Rome down there in those vast tunnels, echoing with dripping water. There were walkways on either side, and in the center a river of diluted filth.

Dry wings fluttered in the shadowed eaves where the light from the gratings did not reach. Oliver peered into the darkness but could see nothing. The stench of the place had him disoriented, though he kept his face covered and breathed through his mouth. As they walked through the sewers, he thought of the catacombs beneath Paris that he had always wanted to visit but never found the time.

Jenny Greenteeth led them along the gently curving

tunnel, all of them careful to keep to the walkway above the effluent waste burbling below. For long minutes they followed her, turning several times into estuaries that led off beneath other neighborhoods. Oliver thought that in reality they had not come far at all from Amelia's, but it seemed an eternity to him down there, nearly suffocated in stink.

When Kitsune paused in front of him he nearly collided with her and imagined the two of them careening off into the sewage. She clutched his arm to steady him and only then did he see what had made her stop. Less than a minute before they had crossed a narrow iron walkway above the trickling river and then turned into a right-hand tunnel that was significantly smaller than the cavernous and elegant hall they'd traveled to that point. The ceiling was perhaps fifteen feet high, with shafts up to much smaller gratings at ground level far above, and there was much less light. The noises that came from the darkness seemed not those of rats or other vermin, but of the shifting shadows themselves.

Jenny had paused, but at first Oliver did not see the door. He realized that like the one in the club, the Mazikeen must have enchanted it, for when she reached out to knock softly on the echoing metal, it resolved itself in his vision. At the edge of the stone ledge perched Frost like a spider carved from ice, his hair strangely jagged, daggers instead of icicles. He stood as though prepared to lunge at the door.

They waited. Oliver's stomach roiled as though it might finally revolt at the stench. There was no sound from the other side of the door. When a response came, it was not from that iron entry, but from the shadows above them.

"Who goes there?" a gruff voice asked, thick with an accent of the Far East and punctuated with a snicker.

Frost twisted toward the voice with such speed that he seemed to slice the air. Kitsune bared her teeth but did not dare try to catch a scent in the sewer; Oliver had not thought of it, but knew the stink must be agony for her.

"Gong Gong, love, there's no time for games," Jenny said, brow creased in annoyance. "Enough rubbish. We've kin here, in trouble and on the run. They need our help and soon enough we're sure to need theirs."

Another rasping snicker drifted from the darkness, followed by the sudden beating of wings, and a shadow drifted down from the others. The creature was reptilian, its hide black as crude oil, with tassels of gray beard upon its chin and a tuft of silver hair on the crown of its head. It had a narrow body, almost serpentine if not for the four limbs with their deadly-looking talons and the charcoal wings jutting from its back. Its eyes were as gray as thunderheads, and sparked as if those clouds were pregnant with lightning.

Gong Gong was a dragon.

Three feet high.

At the end of its tail was a puff of hair the same silver as that of its head, not unlike a well-groomed poodle.

Oliver chuckled. Even through the shirt over his mouth, the sound was audible.

It snarled at him. "Kin? That's human."

Jenny moved to defend him but Kitsune was already there, sliding between Oliver and Gong Gong, her fur cloak brushing against him. "Our fate is 'twined, Black Dragon of Storms. He is not kin, but still we're bound."

Frost pointed a sharp finger at the little creature and a swirl of chill wind brushed through the tassels of his beard. "Waste not a moment more, cousin. The enemy's clock ticks away the minutes until our end."

Gong Gong sneered at Oliver, glaring up at him with those lightning-flecked eyes. "Monkey," he muttered, then marched to the iron door and scraped a talon across it, tapping so softly Oliver could not make out the rhythm.

It scraped heavily open, and a sudden gust of icy air swept out into the sewer. Frost shuddered at its touch and stood back a moment, letting it caress him. A smile touched his razored lips.

Gong Gong and Jenny went in first and Kitsune followed. Oliver waited on Frost, concerned that something might be wrong with him. But then the winter man nodded to urge him forward.

"Black Dragon of Storms?" Oliver asked in a whisper.

The winter man's blue-white eyes narrowed. "That was foolish, what you did. Never take the unfamiliar lightly, no matter how it appears. Heed that advice, or your life will be forfeit the next time. You were lucky."

Oliver blinked. "Lucky?" he whispered. "He's three feet tall."

Frost glared at him. "He is not always so small."

The winter man went through the door and for a moment Oliver forgot that he was alone in the sewer tunnel. Then the shadows seemed to whisper again and he took a quick, anxious glance around before hurrying after Frost. Once he was on the other side, the door swung shut of its own accord.

More Mazikeen magic, he thought. *And what does that mean, the little shit's not always so small? How big could he get?* He wondered what it meant to be the Black Dragon of Storms, what kind of power that entailed, and decided he would heed Frost's advice and do his best not to piss Gong Gong off any further.

Beyond the door was a platform and then a circular stairwell of the same iron, descending downward. Gong Gong's wings made a sandpaper rasp as he took flight, eschewing the stairs and gliding down ahead of them instead. Jenny and Kitsune followed, though the fox glanced back to check on him, which lent Oliver some comfort. Frost paused and stared a moment at the iron door they had come through.

"What is it?"

The winter man gave a small shrug. "I trust nothing of late."

"Makes sense to me."

Frost smiled and any tension between them was gone. Oliver started down the stairs, reminded of the time as a boy that he and his sister had climbed the endless steps of the Statue of Liberty in New York. He had descended perhaps a hundred steps before he realized that he had stopped covering his face as soon as they had left the sewer, and though the smell lingered in his clothes and his nostrils, for the most part it was gone. It only smelled cold down inside that strange tower of metal stairs.

And faintly of flowers.

At the bottom of what seemed like hundreds of stairs was yet another door, this one carved of light wood and flanked on either side by oil lamps in sconces. Gong Gong paused at the door and looked back up the way they had come as though counting heads. Then the lightning-eyed dragon bent over and seemed to whisper something to the wood, and the door swung open to admit them.

The chamber they entered was so entirely different from anything Oliver might have expected that he stood just over the threshold, staring stupidly at the room laid

out before him. It was constructed like an outdoor courtyard, with a pair of marble fountains adorned with statues
of angels, pure water cascading around them. The stone
tiles of the floor were run through with rich mineral colors, like something in a villa in Tuscany, and all around the
sides of the chamber, where sloping walls curved upward,
there were gardens filled with wildflowers. It should have
been impossible for such flowers to grow down there so far
beneath the ground, so far from the sun, but this was
Perinthia, after all. The smell of flowers was intoxicating.

There were torches set in to the walls, but there also
came a wash of light from the ceiling high above that could
not have been genuine sunshine but replicated it nearly
enough.

On the other side of that quaint courtyard two pair of
French doors were set in to a wall as though they led into a
house, and Oliver thought that perhaps they did. Perhaps
this was a home, far beneath the streets—the mansion of
the Mazikeen. For some of those gathered in the courtyard
must have been the sorcerers they had sought. There were
half a dozen beings that Oliver could see and half that
number were tall wraithlike creatures in gold-fringed black
robes with an almost priestly elegance. They were impossibly thin and they moved with a fluid grace as though they
were dancing underwater. Though their faces were hidden
in the shadows of draping hoods, their hands were visible,
and seemed ordinary enough save for their skeletal thin-
ness and the length of their fingers. The flesh had a pur-
plish tint, as though lightly bruised.

At the center of the courtyard, roughly between the
two fountains, was a hand-carved mahogany table surrounded by only three chairs. None of the creatures in that

underground sanctuary were seated, however. Two of the Mazikeen stood together as though in silent communication on the far side of the chamber and did not so much as glance up as the newcomers arrived. The third stood by the table and faced their three guests.

"Come," Kitsune said, startling Oliver, for he had not even realized she had come back to get him.

There was no mischief in her eyes, only urgency. Her hood was thrown back, and in that strange subterreanean daylight she seemed oddly vulnerable. She nudged him with a shoulder and together they approached. Gong Gong flew ahead and landed at the center of the table. All of those gathered around it had turned to watch the approach of these new arrivals with cold curiosity.

The Mazikeen presiding over the group at the table bowed to Frost, and the winter man returned the gesture. Fear rippled through Oliver as he tried to peer beneath the wraith sorcerer's hood. This creature did not look like an ally. It looked like something that would send him screaming up out of a nightmarish sleep.

"Frost," the sorcerer said. "Kitsune. I am pleased that you were able to come to us. There is much to be done if any of us are to survive."

"Jenny and Gong Gong saw to it that we found you," Kitsune replied.

The Black Dragon of Storms snorted and the thunderclouds in his eyes seemed to roil with menace. "I was watching the door. That's all. Don't bring me into this."

The Mazikeen made a short bow in response to this muttering, but otherwise ignored it. Its head moved, draped in that hood, and Oliver could feel the sorcerer studying him, taking his measure. He fought the temptation to stand taller, to force a grim expression onto his face.

"This is the Bascombe?"

Frost nodded, and Oliver realized that Kitsune and the winter man had flanked him, standing on either side as though presenting him for some kind of judgment. "Indeed. An ally, to whom I owe my life."

Kitsune's fingers brushed against his where he had his hand hanging at his side, and a rush of warmth swept through him, lending him strength to bear up under the sorcerer's regard.

"Oliver Bascombe," he said, inclining his head in respect.

"I am Mazikeen," the creature said, confusing Oliver for a moment until it gestured toward the other two who seemed almost entranced together. "We no longer have names as you would understand them. We are all simply Mazikeen."

But Oliver doubted there was anything simple about it.

Introductions followed. He had arrived with Jenny Greenteeth, Kitsune, Frost, and the troublesome Gong Gong. Aside from the Mazikeen, there were three others in that bizarre courtyard, all standing round the table.

One of them was an ocher-skinned man in loose, rough clothing with three bright blue feathers tied into his long hair. Though his clothes were more old European, his aspect was that of a Native American, and the feathers did little to dispel this impression. He was called Blue Jay, and Oliver faintly recalled stories he'd read in college surrounding this myth, about a devilish trickster and shapeshifter. Blue Jay said nothing to him when introduced.

Beside him was a wild-looking man who seemed not quite flesh and not quite wood, with small branches growing in a sort of crown around his head and tiny flowers and leaves on his face and exposed arms. He was tall enough—

nearly ten feet—that Oliver would once have considered him a giant, but now he'd seen real giants and this creature was almost of ordinary height in comparison. The towering forest man had brown hair that hung halfway down his back and a beard that fell nearly to his knees. He wore only a single garment like a Roman toga, tied round his body with vines. The Mazikeen introduced him as Lailoken, of Scotland, and the forest man thrust his hand out with a cordial, if slightly crazed, grin. Oliver shook his head, pleased that at least one of them was willing to be friendly to a human being.

With all that he had seen, not least of which were the extraordinary and intimidating creatures in the courtyard of the Mazikeen, very few things surprised Oliver more than the final member of that rebellious troupe of Borderkind. He had been aware of her since the moment they entered and his curiosity was rampant. Her hair was like spun sugar and her diaphanous gown was the blue-white of Frost's eyes. The gossamer fabric clung to her curves in breathtaking fashion.

Yet her flesh was ice.

Nothing about her was jagged or sharp like Frost. Instead, she was smooth as the finest porcelain, but translucent and radiating a familiar chill. Her gaze was brazen as she took in Frost, and even when she was introduced to Oliver there was a predatory hunger there. She reached out and touched his face and his cheek stung with frostbite, a stinging pain that lingered for long minutes afterward.

"Yuki-Onna," Frost said, embracing her with the perfunctory duty of a member of the family. "Queen of Snows. It is a relief to find you well."

"And you, Frost. Word carried on the wind that the Falconer had found you."

"Indeed he did," the winter man grimly replied, and then he gestured to Oliver. "If not for this man, only legend would have remained."

Yuki-Onna graced Oliver with the most beatific smile he had ever received. She nodded her head in silent gratitude and then turned her attention back to Frost. They held each other's hands like reunited lovers and abruptly and simultaneously dissolved into wind and snow and ice, swirling into a blizzard perhaps four feet across and eight high, cold air sweeping around them yet somehow without withering a petal upon the flowers in the courtyard of the Mazikeen. Oliver caught his breath as he watched those winter spirits, saw the beauty of this strange melding, as the two storms were momentarily one and it was impossible to see what was Frost and what Yuki-Onna.

Just as quickly as it began it was over, the snow settling and building the winter man and the Queen of Snows, though their hands were no longer linked.

Kitsune brushed his hand again. "Did your mother teach you nothing?" she whispered. "It is rude to stare."

With a quiet laugh he tore his gaze away from the winter spirits and looked at the fox-woman. Her expression was impossible to interpret, though he was sure he'd heard amusement in her tone.

"You are all welcome here," the Mazikeen spokesman said in a reedy voice from within its cloak. "If we are to unravel this conspiracy against the Borderkind and strike back against its perpetrators, we must stand together."

Gong Gong snorted derisively, spreading his leathery wings. "Stand together. Good idea. Tell Coyote and other cowards who run and hide."

Oliver saw Kitsune stiffen. Based upon things she had said the last time Coyote had been spoken of, he was apparently a closer relation than Wayland Smith and these other creatures she called "cousin." He had the idea that all of the Borderkind, regardless of how outrageously different from one another they might be, considered one another cousins.

Frost cocked his head to meet the gaze of the Mazikeen, false sunlight gleaming upon his sharp features. "And we will stand with you. First, however, I have a debt to repay. The Borderkind are being hunted in secret, but Oliver is wanted by the Crowns of Two Kingdoms and there is a price on his head. With respect, my friends, we must first locate Professor David Koenig, the only human Intruder to have discovered a way to pierce the Veil and to be pardoned for the crime. Like Koenig, Oliver is not Lost. The Lost Ones are trapped here. They cannot return, even if they wished to. But because he was carried through the Veil and can return to speak of it, the authorities will not suffer him to live. Oliver hopes to learn how Koenig managed to secure a pardon. And I have vowed to help him in that quest.

"Only when I have fulfilled my vow will I be free to join you in our fight against the Hunters and their masters," the winter man said, eyes misting. "I have been told that the Mazikeen will know where to find David Koenig. Will you share this knowledge so that I may aid Oliver and then return here to join this insurrection?"

There was a lengthy pause that quickly grew uncomfortable for Oliver. Neither Kitsune nor Frost seemed even aware of the awkwardness of it, but he saw the way Jenny Greenteeth glanced at her feet and then shot her gaze round the courtyard without looking at anyone. Yuki-Onna closed her eyes a moment with a trace of melancholy in her porcelain features but then only nodded once. Blue Jay and the Scottish wild-man shot spiteful gazes at Oliver and then turned to the Mazikeen, whose eyes were on Kitsune.

Yet it was Gong Gong who spoke up. "And you, fox? You'll go, too?"

"I've said so," Kitsune replied calmly, the fur cloak rippling along her back as she stood to her full height. "And so I must. You wouldn't have me break my word?"

"Bloody hell, Kit," Jenny sighed. "They're killing us."

Kitsune gave the smallest twitch at those imploring words, but then pressed her hands together before her and inclined her head in a minimal bow. "Our fates are twined with his. Should we abandon our promises and leave him to die?"

Gong Gong drew his wings tightly around him as though they were a blanket, only his lightning-studded thunderstorm eyes visible above the black skin. "Better him than you, cousin."

Kitsune stared at him with utter contempt.

The Mazikeen rapped its spindly hand upon the table. "That is enough. Time slips past. Frost, the name of Professor Koenig is familiar to me. His present location is not within the sphere of my knowledge, but we are Mazikeen. Give us a moment and we may discover what you seek."

It bowed to the winter man and then in a more general fashion to the rest of those gathered around the table, after which the Mazikeen withdrew and strode to join the other two of its kind, who still seemed locked in some motionless conference in the shadows of a far wall. On either side of them were flower gardens, rich explosions of color and scent. Oliver knew little about flowers beyond roses and carnations, but he had the vague impression that this array was unusual. Some of the flowers that grew there were unlike anything he had ever seen.

The moment the Mazikeen who had been their de facto host approached the other two, they stirred. Their faces were still hooded but they turned to watch the other. As he joined them, however, they became immobile once more, and now the one who had spoken joined them in that strange meditative paralysis.

With a somewhat relieved sigh and a shy smile—revealing even more of her hideous teeth—Jenny slid onto the table, legs dangling beneath it, almost like a little girl.

"So that's it, then? You find out what you need and then you're off to wherever?"

Lailoken scowled in disgust, muttered something in a guttural tongue entirely unfamiliar to Oliver, and stalked away. They all watched as he went to a set of French doors, flung them open, and then disappeared into the home of the Mazikeen, not bothering to close the doors behind him.

"Quite a temper, don't you think?" Blue Jay asked.

Kitsune nodded solemnly.

Blue Jay narrowed his gaze. "You did not answer Jenny's question."

Gong Gong shook himself as though to dry his ebony skin and took flight. He circled once above their heads and then found a place in the face of the wall where tree limbs grew through a hole in stone like bonsai trees on a mountainside. He perched there, and the enchanted sunlight that warmed that courtyard seemed to dim as though a cloud had passed over.

"We must go as quickly as we can," Kitsune said, both to Blue Jay and to Jenny. "There isn't time for—"

"There is one thing we must do first," Frost interrupted, the look in his eyes a challenge to anyone wishing to contradict him. "Oliver's family does not know what has become of him. I'm going to take him through the Veil so that he can call them."

Kitsune blinked in surprise. "Now?"

"Now?" Jenny echoed.

Blue Jay traced a finger along his own jaw and studied Oliver closely. The mischief went out of his eyes and his gaze was cold. "Yes, now. He may not have another chance. Of course. You must," the shape-shifter said, and for the first time Oliver thought he could almost see the bird in the Borderkind's face. The blue feathers tied in his hair seemed to dance and sway of their own accord.

"Yes," Frost agreed. "While the Mazikeen confer. You'll remain here and learn whatever more there is to learn of this conspiracy?"

"If you wish."

"I would be grateful. We should not be gone long."

Blue Jay and Jenny Greenteeth sat side by side on the table. Oliver wondered if anyone ever used the mahogany chairs in the courtyard. Kitsune glanced at him, brow furrowing.

"Be careful," she said. "Much of the mystery was gone from your world forever when the Veil was created, but some still remains. And there are times when only a little mystery can be quite dangerous indeed."

There was something in her eyes and in her face that made him want to stay, to remain with her and not be parted. But from the moment Frost had mentioned taking him back through to make contact he had been thinking of Julianna, and of Collette, and the longing to hear their voices and to soothe their fears was stronger.

"I'll keep an eye out."

Blue Jay wore a smile, but Jenny's expression was dark

with foreboding. "Go on, if you must. But hurry, yeah? This is all happening too fast."

The winter man flowed up beside Oliver with a bone-chilling gust of wind. He nodded. "Come here."

Oliver followed him to the fountain on the opposite side of the courtyard from where the Mazikeen conferred. Frost gestured to the water that sprayed into the air and it became snow. Winds buffeted Oliver as the snow became a small blizzard in that spot alone, even blotting out the false sunlight from above. And through the snow, he could see an opening.

"Go," Frost told him. "I will be with you."

Oliver stepped through.

It was midday in London, mothers pushing babies in prams through the park, when Oliver appeared from nowhere, stepping out of nothing and back into the world of his birth. He knew the city immediately by the red double-decker bus he saw rumbling by far across the green grass and over the tops of bushes and a wrought-iron gate that went round the park. A gust of frigid air was the only sign that Frost had accompanied him, and when he looked down he saw a sprinkle of icy rime upon the lawn, like frozen dew.

"Mum!" a little girl shouted. "Mum!"

Oliver turned to see her, a pretty little thing with a ribbon in her hair and her coat buttoned up tight. It was nearly Christmas . . . how many days away he was not certain . . . but there was no snow in London. It snowed rarely in the British capital, though that had not always been true. With an oversized mitten she pointed at Oliver.

"Mum! That man!"

The mother peered suspiciously at Oliver and then turned to her daughter, her voice lower but still audible. "What of him, Ellie?"

"He just . . . un-vanished! Wasn't there a minute ago!"

Heart hammering in his chest, Oliver gave the mother and child a warm, indulgent smile. Isn't she the cutest little thing, he hoped his smile would say. Her mother smiled back and rolled her eyes a bit before taking the girl by her mitten-clad hand and walking away.

Oliver let out a relieved breath and looked around, trying to orient himself. He'd spent a semester living in London during college and it had been one of the greatest experiences of his life. He'd taken a classical drama class and gone to see more plays in a handful of months than he'd seen in the cumulative years of his life to that point. He'd become passingly familiar with the city, but did not recognize this park at first glance. He could see a lake to his right and far off to the left a bandstand at the bull's-eye center of the walkways that threaded the park. A sign beside the path had arrows pointing in several directions he might walk to find a Children's Zoo and a Deer Enclosure, amongst other things. Another for Sub-Tropical Gardens. Distant memories flickered across his mind, and then he put it together. This was Battersea Park. He had never been here before, but had heard about the variety of attractions it offered.

Public land. So a part of the world beyond the Veil was made up of a mirrored version of Battersea Park. The Borderkind had a gift, that much was certain.

For a moment he just breathed in the damp, chilly air of London. It was warmer and the sky clearer than he would've expected as the year drew to a close in the United Kingdom, and he felt fortunate just to be able to feel the sunlight of his own world. It was the first time he had been on his own in many long days, however, and he felt exposed. Frost was somewhere nearby, he knew, perhaps riding the frigid winds that blew to England all the way from the Russian steppes. But still he felt vulnerable.

And the clock was ticking. He was frightened for his own life, but he was now equally concerned for the danger his friends faced. Several times during the quiet confrontation in the courtyard of the Mazikeen he had considered releasing Frost from his vow. The other Borderkind needed him, and they had to find out who it was that controlled the Hunters. But the truth was that he had saved Frost's life, not once but twice, and Kitsune's once as well. It wasn't so much that he felt they owed him their loyalty, but that he had pledged his to them, even if they were not aware of it. Presuming he was able to find a way to get the order of death lifted from him, he knew that he would not abandon them to their fate.

"Okay, okay, clear your head," he whispered to himself.

A slim, bald man with glasses and a cigarette dangling from his mouth gave him an odd stare as he passed, but did not stop. Oliver surveyed the park again, no longer focused on his location or the people who were enjoying the unseasonably pleasant December day. He was searching for only one thing. Not finding it, he began walking toward the fence in the distance and the road beyond. The path curved and he followed it out to a gate.

On the sidewalk just outside, he finally found a phone booth, one of the red-painted boxes that spoke of London tradition. He felt shaky and oddly warm in the rustic peacoat Oliver Larch had given him. Taking a deep breath, he opened the door and stepped inside, and a kind of happiness touched his heart. He was not out of danger, but at least he could make contact. He could hear the voices of the people he loved. Julianna must be furious with him, and he could not blame her. Even now he was not sure that missing the wedding was a bad thing. But all of those considerations had to wait. Regardless of how much shit she might give him, he had to at least let her know that he was all right.

Oliver plucked the phone from the cradle and dialed for an operator, then asked for international help. His awareness of the crisis beyond the Veil made him impatient as he went through three different people before an operator could help him make an overseas call and charge it to his credit card. It was probably shortly after noon, which would make it pretty early back home, maybe seven o'clock or so. But the call couldn't wait, and he doubted anyone would want him to wait.

Yet at home, there was no answer.

The operator indulged him by trying the number a second time, but there was nothing. Not even the answering machine.

A ripple of unease went through him. He had no idea what day it was, but there ought to be someone there at this time of morning. Oliver wanted to think that Collette would have stayed in Maine after his disappearance, but he wasn't sure how many days had passed at home and eventually she would've had to go back to New York, back to work. But even if she was gone and their father was out, there ought to be a machine. Or Friedle ought to have been there.

His anticipation turned to uncertainty, he gave the operator Julianna's number, not at all sure how he would begin to explain. It took half a minute of odd noises on the line before he heard it start to ring on the other end.

On the third ring, she picked up.

"Hello?"

"Jules?"

He heard a tiny gasp and a muttered "Oh, my God."

"Julianna, I'm . . . listen, I'm okay. I can't even begin to imagine how much you must hate me right now, and it's going to be a while before I can get back home, but I wanted you to know that if there'd been any way . . . I mean, I would never have left that way if I'd had a choice."

"Oliver," she said, as if she was only just beginning to believe it was him.

"Yes. Yeah, sweetheart, it's me."

He could hear her crying. "Where are you, Oliver? Where the *fuck* are you?" The curse sounded almost like a growl.

"I'm . . . look, I'm in London. I can't explain it to you right now. I'll be in touch again soon. I just wanted to let you know, and let Collette and my father know, that I'm alive and in one piece and—"

"Your father? You don't know about your father?"

The question, uttered in stark disbelief, put a chill in him far worse than the winter man's touch. "What do you mean?"

"He's dead, Oliver. While you were hiding out, or going walkabout, or whatever the hell it is you're doing, trying to sort out your life, someone murdered your father . . . mutilated him! God damn you for not being here! Though if you ask the police, they're not sure you weren't."

Oliver had never felt so numb, or so cold, or so hollow. In his mind he was one of those chocolate Easter bunnies with only air inside, the kind that crumble almost at the lightest touch.

"He's . . . oh, Jesus, don't say that. Don't say that."

Her voice turned softer then, revealing the anguish beneath her fury. "He is, Oliver. Oh, baby, I'm sorry, but he is. I've been so afraid. I thought you were . . . at first I thought you'd left me, but when they found your dad like that, I was afraid you were dead, too. Are you really okay? You're in London? You've got to come home, Oliver. You have to come home now."

He shook so badly he could almost not get the words out, and when he did they were a quavering rasp. "I can't, Jules. Honey, I can't right now. But soon, I promise."

"Are you in danger?"

Oliver flinched. She sensed it, obviously. Or had figured it out. Why else wouldn't he come home?

He ignored the question.

"You said . . . he was mutilated. What . . . how was he . . . what happened?"

The silence that followed was far too long. Oliver began to feel as though he would throw up just thinking on his father's murder and imagining the worst.

"His eyes. His eyes were . . . taken." Julianna seemed to swallow that word. "The police have nothing, Oliver. Not a lead. There wasn't a fingerprint. No sign of an intruder except for what he'd done and—"

"Collette," Oliver said. "I tried calling the house. I need to talk to her, Jules. I only have a minute and I need to call her right now. Where is she? Do you know?"

He could hear that she was crying, and he wished he could have been there to wipe her tears away. Whatever they might one day be to each other, or not, he wished he could at least do that.

"She's not with you?" Julianna asked, incredulously, as though it was the hardest question she had ever put into words. "Collette's gone, too. Vanished, just like you did. On the night your father was killed. No one's seen her since. She's just . . . gone."

Oliver's mouth opened and closed, but no sound came out. He shook his head, fingers clutching the phone so tightly that it hurt him. His mind could not process this final piece of information. And as he tried, he heard muffled screams coming from the park.

He turned to see the winter man, manifested in the morning sunlight on a busy street corner in Battersea, London, rapping icy fingers on the glass.

"Oliver. We have to go. Right now!"

The fury with which his mind rejected this demand overwhelmed him. His grief was too much. He prepared to scream, to shove the door open and rail at the creature who had drawn him into this peril, who had pulled him away and left his father to die at the hands of some savage while his sister was spirited off, perhaps to her own slaughter.

Then he looked past Frost and saw Kitsune staggering through the wrought-iron gate, her face spattered with blood, cradling her left arm, which dripped crimson tears onto the concrete path. Beyond her, Blue Jay came at a run, a miniature black dragon cradled in his arms, unmoving.

"I love you, Julianna," he whispered into the phone, barely aware that he was speaking. "And I will come home. I promise."

He hung up on her questions and her tears.

CHAPTER 16

Collette came awake reluctantly, even her unconscious mind filled with a dread of what she would
encounter upon waking. Exhaustion had eaten its
way into her very bones, yet much as she might wish to retreat for endless, blind hours into the sanctuary of sleep,
her rest was fitful at best. Even in her dreams, she was
starving. Even in her dreams, her body was scoured by
sand.

Now her eyelids fluttered and her brows knitted together in an attempt to stave off wakefulness for just a few
more minutes. In that half-dozing state she could imagine
herself still in her bed, still in her father's house, still in the
world she had known. But the grit of sand was everywhere
on her, a thousand tiny itchings beneath the soft flannel of

her pajamas. She wore nothing else, not even underpants, and she was barefoot. The sand was warm enough, but its intrusion into every crevice of her body and its clinging, scraping scatter inside her pajamas was torment.

Once upon a time, she would have thought it enough to drive her mad. But she understood more about madness now than once she had.

With her eyes fully open, no longer able to deny that the world around her was real, her face contorted with hopelessness and she shook for several moments. Forcing herself up, she took a deep, shuddering breath and then swallowed her despair. Her right hand came up and she wiped at her eyes. She felt as though she would cry, but no tears came. There was sand in her mouth, tiny pieces of grit that she could not rid herself of. Dehydration was having its way with her, and she hadn't enough saliva to summon a wad of spit.

Collette hugged herself and simply sat there in the sand, aware that some had sifted into the legs and arms of her pajamas as she slept but not yet able to muster the motivation to do anything about it. What was the point? There would only be more. Really, there wasn't anything here *but* sand.

She took a long breath and forced herself to look around. The round chamber she was in—she never thought of it as a room, and it was too airy and open to be a dungeon—had no door, but a dozen windows all around the circumference. They were tall, arched windows with no glass and during the day the sunlight flooded in and heated the chamber. But the windows provided no hope for exit. They were twenty-five feet from the ground and the walls were made entirely of smooth, hardened sand.

It was all sand.

The floor was the soft, shifting stuff of dunes and lonely beaches. The walls were as hard as cement, but it was the same material in a different form. This had been her prison for days, though how many she could not have said. Time seemed to move torturously slow here.

While the sun shone, her prison was not only lit, but heated. By afternoon it often grew so hot that the sand seared her bare flesh and she had to keep to the shadows. Midday was torture. Food and water were often brought to her while she slept, and if it was the same fiendish thing that had imprisoned her here that delivered her meager meals, she had never seen it again. Not since that first night.

Not since it slaughtered her father and tore out his eyes.

"Daddy," Collette whispered. Still seated, she hugged her knees against her chest and lay her cheek atop them.

She closed her eyes and let the night breeze caress her. For it was dark now. There was no way for her to tell how long she had slept, but it had been hours. When she had drifted off in the cool shade of afternoon, night had been distant. Now evening had come. Later it would grow cold there in that sand prison, but for now it was only the breeze that hinted at the dropping temperature. The sand beneath her still retained the accumulated warmth of the day.

The windows were still visible, the moon and starlight turning them into portraits of the night sky, but in that chamber the darkness was deeper. More intimate. Collette had been alone there too long, however, and that intimacy had become part of her prison. She wanted someone to talk to. Someone to shriek at. Anyone upon whose shoulder she might weep. Company, even in her misery.

A dry laugh escaped her lips. *Misery loves company.* It

took on an entirely new meaning in her mind. She was going to die. Of that she was certain. Having witnessed the mutilation murder of her own father, there was no room for doubt in her mind. But for a woman with only the faintest, little girl's impractical hope, there was still something about the solitary nature of her imprisonment that was a separate sort of hell.

Where was she? What was the dreadful apparition that had brought her here? Where had it gone, and when might it return? Such questions occupied her waking mind for every moment that she did not spend in anguished grief for her father and for her own predicament.

And what of Oliver?

That question returned again and again, and with it both dread and that one tiny spark of hope remaining. More than ever, now she was certain that Oliver's disappearance was not of his own volition. Something had happened to him. He had been abducted, or led astray, or driven somehow to leave the night before he was meant to marry Julianna. And Collette believed—she had to believe—that there was some connection to that creature, to the murder of their father, and to her own captivity. If the thing had murdered Oliver, why not leave his corpse?

If he wasn't dead, on the other hand . . . was it impossible to think this world was the place to which he had vanished?

There was another question, however. One that she avoided as much as possible. When her mind drifted there she would do whatever was necessary to obstruct its progress. The question was: *Why am I still alive?* The demon—if that was what it was—had torn out her father's eyes, slain him in his own bedroom, but the only physical harm it had done Collette amounted to cuts and bruises sustained when it had abducted her.

Now it imprisoned her. Fed her. Kept her alive.

If she spent more than a few seconds wondering its purpose, the question would cripple her.

"Oliver," Collette whispered, running her tongue over her dry, chapped lips and staring at the night sky through the windows high above, wondering if her brother could see them as well. "Where are you, little brother?"

A breeze swirled around inside that round chamber and she shivered a bit, though it felt good. Sweet. Collette took a breath and looked into her mind's eye, as she had done during every period of wakefulness since she had been taken, and thought of movies. In her head there was a collection of all of her favorite films, many of which she'd seen a dozen times or more. She knew them well. Well enough to visit them now, when she needed the escape they provided more than ever. If she focused enough she could replay the key scenes from all of these films in her mind, and she had found herself in some way she didn't quite understand able to wander into the worlds those films created. Not as an actor, nothing so imaginative. But as a tangible observer, as though the events were unfolding around her. *The Philadelphia Story. October Sky. Field of Dreams. Casablanca. An Affair to Remember. Heaven Can Wait. Say Anything.*

"We'll always have Paris," she whispered in the dark, feeling the abrasion of sand on teeth and tongue.

She could see the inside of Rick's Café Americain with utter clarity; the screens and the drooping leaves of plants, the lazily turning fans, the beautiful women and shady men all breathing in an air of danger. And at the piano, Dooley Wilson sang. Not "As Time Goes By," but some other tune she was not old enough to recognize. A contest of wills arose at the bar, eyes flashing angrily, and then Bogart entered, eyes heavy with melancholy and gravitas, to resolve it.

No, not Bogart. Rick Blaine. Not Dooley Wilson, but Sam the piano player, the weapon Rick and Ilsa will use against each other.

The music is sweet. The wine is dry as bone. As sand. Standing in the midst of the café, Collette hears a whisper, a voice like parchment paper, the words too soft and muffled to make out.

"Your eyes . . . he's going to take your eyes . . . maybe not today, maybe not tomorrow, but sooooon."

With a sudden, sucking breath, Collette snapped her eyes open, wrenching herself from the trance state to which she had retreated. The whisper had not been a part of the scenario she was painting for herself. It had come from outside.

The chamber seemed lighter, though not with approaching dawn. It was only that she was more acclimated to the night now, and the moonlight and the glimmer of stars seemed to reach more deeply into that prison.

She reached out to touch the wall with her fingertips, another movie scene flashing across the silver screen in her mind. Dorothy in Oz, tapping the heels of her ruby slippers together and saying, in that sweet, lost voice, "There's no place like home. There's no place like home."

Collette wished she were Dorothy, that she could tap her heels together and just be home.

And even as this thought occurred to her she felt the wall begin to give way. She stared at it and saw that it no longer seemed quite solid. The real solidity of the wall had given way and it was almost as though she were pushing her fingers into warm water, with currents tugging at her hand. Her eyes still saw the wall, but her fingers seemed to pass through it into some darkness beneath, as though she might have passed right through.

Beyond the wall, she smelled something entirely out of place and it took a moment for her to recognize the scent. Pine trees. Sap and needles.

What the hell?

Off to her right came that rasping whisper again. Collette started, breath coming in short bursts, heart thundering like the bombastic promise of a summer storm. She drew her fingers back from the wall and when she realized what she'd done and touched it again, it was solid and unyielding. For a moment it had seemed there might be some escape, but now again she was trapped. Her skin prickled as her eyes searched the hills and dips and crenellations of the sand in that chamber. The whisper was real, yes. But the words? That must have been her imagination, her memory of her father's murder driving her subconscious. It must have been.

The noise came again, this time above, and she looked up.

A small sphere of glittering light hovered near the top of the chamber. It seemed to dance in the air, a hypnotic series of gentle glides and darting zigs.

"*Collette,*" the whisper came again. "*The problems of two little people don't amount to a hill of beans.*"

The sandpaper rasp of that voice came from above, as though from that sphere, and after those words that used the famous dialogue of her best-loved film against her, there came a dry chuckle that seemed tinged with almost parental indulgence.

Collette shook, eyes wide, staring at the light. It terrified her, and yet it also had a sublime beauty that she could not ignore, a purity that touched something inside of her.

There came another sound—this from behind her—a shifting of sand and a soft thump. She gritted her teeth and forced her eyes closed and kept her back turned. Collette did not want to see any more, did not want to know what else might be down in that doorless chamber with her. All of her unspoken prayers had been pleas that she would be freed, or at the least that she would find some relief for her loneliness. Now she would have given anything to be alone again.

"It is called Vittora" came a new voice from behind her. A child's voice.

Slowly, steadying her breathing, she turned and opened her eyes. In the shadows of her prison was a small boy, no more than nine years old by the look of him. His shirt and pants were colorless, leeched by moon and sand of any character at all. The rest of him was equally bland and ordinary, save for one terrible detail.

He had no eyes.

Where the boy's eyes would have been, set in to an entirely unremarkable face, there were only dark, hollow pits that might have gone on forever. He took a step nearer and Collette flinched, drawing back half a foot. A smile touched his lips and he turned his face upward, catching more of the light from the Vittora, and in that glow she could see that a trickle of sand slid like hourglass tears from the ragged holes where his eyes ought to have been.

In his hands he held a small silver tray upon which sat a glass bottle full of water, an apple, a block of cheese, and several thick slices of bread.

Collette was not aware, at first, that she was screaming.

Every muscle in her body was tensed and her fingers dug into the soft, shifting sand beneath her. When she at last heard the sound of her own fear and realized it came from her own mouth, she fell silent and could only stare. The child made no further move to approach her, and the light . . . the Vittora . . . paused in the air above her, trembling just as she was, as though they were connected.

"The Vittora is your guide . . . it is the luck that stays with you throughout your life, only manifesting itself when it prepares to leave. Most people never see it, but here . . . anything is possible."

She refused to stare into those empty eyes, instead watching that tremulous light. "Why is it . . . leaving?" she managed.

"The Vittora leaves when it senses that its host is soon to die."

Collette felt as though some part of her gave way, some central bit of her structure, and she collapsed in upon herself. She wanted to weep, but dehydration would not allow it. Her tongue moistened her chapped lips.

"Why?" she wailed. "Why are you doing this to me?"

"The past is a dream from which we never wake," he said. Words she had heard before.

The boy moved two steps nearer. She cringed but did not bother to move away. She was crippled by anguish, but also by the knowledge that she had nowhere to run. Still she refused to look into those hellishly empty eyes.

"You should scream more," the boy said.

The Vittora sighed and whispered, but she could no longer make out the words.

"Really, you ought to. That will bring things to a conclusion more quickly. If you scream enough, perhaps your brother will sense you, and he will come. And that will bring the end."

"My . . ."

Collette went cold, entirely numb. She turned and faced the eyeless, colorless boy. "What do you know about my brother?"

The child's voice became a kind of sigh. "Olllliver." He smiled, laughed quietly, and sand spilled from his ragged sockets. "You asked why. He is the reason you are here. They freed the Sandman, Collette, do you not understand? Your father's murder was a message, and you are the lure to bring Oliver here. They sensed something about him from the moment he passed through the Veil. They sense the same thing in you. And I can feel it as well. You both must be eliminated. And so he will come here, for you, with his traveling companions, and you will all be destroyed."

She shook her head in denial, revolted by these dark intentions, plans she barely understood. And yet a part of her was gleeful. Oliver was alive, just as she had believed.

"So we shall wait for him. And while we wait, the Sandman visits your world . . . and he plays."

With a grin that showed jagged teeth like broken concrete and sprinkled sand once more from the hollows in his face, the boy reached into both pockets and brought forth two handfuls of wet, gleaming, bloody eyeballs, each trailing a slick nerve tail.

Collette could not even scream. Instead she just scrambled away from him on the sand until her back hit the solid wall. Grit showered down from above, sliding down the back of her shirt. The floor of the chamber buckled and heaved and hands thrust up from the sand, more children crawling from the ground beneath her, all of them eyeless like the first.

But the Vittora, the light of her luck and life, was still there. It flickered weakly, but it had not yet abandoned her.

She held her breath and tried to look away but she could not. There were four children now, two girls and two boys, all nearly featureless, blanched, and dry. When they moved it was a dry rasp, and now they stood together, staring at her without eyes.

And in their midst, a figure began to rise. A figure she had seen before, cloaked in shuddering gray, body flowing, features thin and jagged, eyes that terrible lemon yellow. He grinned with those tiny, jagged teeth.

The Sandman.

He opened his arms, smiling at her, and then he reached out and touched the children one by one, and one by one they collapsed into nothing but piles of shifting sand. Nothing but sand.

"*I see you,*" he said, tapping one long finger just below a sickly yellow eye. "*Oliver will come soon. And then we play.*"

Even after he was gone, she could not tear her gaze from the place where he had stood, from the little mounds of sand where the children had been. In the dark she was sure she could still see those lemon eyes.

Above her, the Vittora gleamed dimly, and its soft whispers rasped like the breeze across the sand.

Oliver kept his hand on the phone for a moment, Julianna's voice ringing in his ears, word of his father's murder knitting a stitch in his chest. He stared in disbelief through the red-framed glass panes of the phone booth at Frost. His mind was disconnected from the sight. This was London. The real world. It was early morning maybe a week before Christmas and there were people all over the place. The sight was so visually dissonant that he felt locked in that place, trapped in the phone booth, though perhaps that was his secret wish, that he might hide there.

But there was to be no hiding place.

A scream tore the air on that fine, crisp morning, loud enough that it penetrated easily through the walls of the phone booth. Oliver's senses came alive, his skin prickling with awareness, his gaze sweeping the world around him. Kitsune was limping toward them, bloodstained hand clutching her abdomen, a spill-trail of crimson behind her. Blue Jay followed with the still, ebony form of Gong Gong in his arms. The dragon looked like some kind of carving, a statue in the trickster's arms.

A mother pushing her child in a pram had turned a corner and nearly run into Kitsune as she staggered out through the gate of Battersea Park. The woman had almost hit her and as Kitsune passed, the back of her fur cloak had brushed across the blanket covering the baby's legs. On the blanket now was a bright red stain of fresh blood. The woman knelt by the pram, tugged the blanket away and threw it to the ground. She stared after Kitsune and Blue Jay, shouting angrily.

Others were beginning to pay attention. A pair of men who'd been doing work on the electrical box on a lamppost twenty yards along the sidewalk were walking quickly toward the corner now, their attention on the woman. But in seconds that would change.

Jack Frost stood like an ice sculpture in the midst of that London neighborhood, quite obviously alive, his eyes filled with frustration and anger, his mouth split open to reveal those jagged frozen teeth.

None of this was supposed to happen. The Borderkind were not meant to be seen like this. The world would not believe in legends anymore. Whatever came of it would be ugly, and it would stop him from getting to Professor Koenig . . . never mind figuring out what had happened to Collette. If he ended up in a cell somewhere, the Myth Hunters would find a way to get to him. He'd be a bloody smear on concrete.

"No," he whispered, and then he was moving.

Oliver slammed out the door of the phone booth hard enough to shatter two of the glass panes. Kitsune was nearly upon him. The pain etched in her face hurt him, but he turned to Frost.

"Can you close her wounds?"

The winter man frowned but he nodded, icicle hair clinking. The sky had begun to darken, the sun obscured by a gathering storm that might have been the onset of Frost's wrath or the power of the Black Dragon of Storms.

"She'll heal on her own," Frost said. "She needs only a handful of minutes."

"Oi! What the fuck you doing?" shouted one of the electrical workers.

"Come on, Keith," the other said, trying to pull his mate away. "Some kind of television bollocks, yeah? Don't get involved."

Oliver ignored their continued comments and the people who had obviously seen the Borderkind go by and were emerging cautiously from the park, gathering like curious birds, whispering to one another. The mother with the pram left the bloody blanket behind and began to retreat . . . but then she paused and pulled a mobile phone from her purse.

"Oh, shit," Oliver growled, shaking his head. He shoved a finger at Frost's face. "We don't have a minute. She needs to stop bleeding right now."

The anger that flickered across the winter man's face was gone in an instant. Frost stepped toward Kitsune and pulled her into his chilling embrace. She grunted and hissed through her teeth in pain. The winter man slid a hand beneath her cloak and she let him touch her wound. Ice spread across the fabric of her black tunic, the blood that soaked it freezing solid. Kitsune hissed again but the pain in her face seemed to ease.

"This will do more damage at the moment, but it will stop the bleeding for now."

"Numb," Kitsune managed. "Thank you."

Blue Jay joined them, carrying Gong Gong as though it was the most ordinary thing in the world. More people were shouting at them. There had to be a dozen just outside the gate to the park and three or four behind the electricians, as well as a pair of elderly women standing by the young mother with the pram. Cars began to beep angrily as motorists stopped to get a glimpse of the impossible unfolding in Battersea Park.

"Look here, what the hell d'you think you're doing? What *is* that thing?" snapped the fiercely red-faced electrician.

"Keith," his partner cautioned.

But Keith wouldn't be swayed. He started toward them, something nobody else gathered around watching the freak show was willing to do. Maybe he just couldn't believe what he was seeing, thought Frost was some kind of illusion or gimmick. That didn't mean he wasn't afraid. In his way, perhaps he was more afraid than anyone else . . . so afraid that the only way to combat that fear was to confront it.

"Oliver—" Frost began.

"No," Oliver snapped, staring at him, forcing the winter

man to look him in the eye. "This is my world now. None of this can happen. We can't afford it, not any of us. You need to be gone. Right now. *Gone.*"

The winter man might have given the slightest nod, and then he was, indeed, gone. Icy wind shook Oliver where he stood and a trace of snow swirled around his feet.

"Bloody hell, did you see that?" called another man.

But it was women's voices that cut in to Oliver's thoughts. He heard them chattering to one another and several of them cried out in surprise and alarm. Several people smiled, thinking it some kind of trick, or a show. Oliver considered playing off that, trying to make it seem like they were street performers or something, but it was only a glancing thought. There had been too much blood.

He took Kitsune's arm to help her stand up straight and she grimaced but managed to walk beside him. Blue Jay wore an amused expression, somehow enjoying the chaos, and still made no effort to hide Gong Gong from the crowd. The three of them began to walk away from the crowd gathered round the phone booth. The light had changed but cars were still stopped. Horns honked. The trio of strange arrivals to this neighborhood crossed the street as hurriedly as Kitsune could manage.

"Hang on! Where you think you're off to, now? There's blood back here!" the electrician called.

Persistent, he started across the street after them. Some of the people at the park's exit began to move as though they might also follow. Oliver wasn't having that. He snarled over his shoulder.

"Fuck off, Keith!"

The man actually recoiled at hearing his name come from this stranger. It gave him pause. Oliver used the moment to get them out of there. He started walking north with Kitsune and Blue Jay and he could see the bridge over the Thames River not far off.

"This day only gets more interesting," Blue Jay said.

Oliver glanced over his shoulder and saw that several cars were pacing them, people gawking out the windows in paparazzi-like fascination. He cursed under his breath and tried to get Kitsune to pick up the pace.

"I'm sorry, but if we aren't a lot less conspicuous by the time the police show up, this is going to get even messier."

"It's all right," she muttered, taking long, slow breaths. "Already I'm starting to heal."

"Hello! Hello!" shouted a voice from a passing car. The passenger hanging out the window had a camera.

Oliver turned his face away. Saw Gong Gong again, so still in Blue Jay's arms. Then he glanced up at the trickster. "Is there anything you can do? A glamour or something, make them see something else, make us invisible to them?"

The feathers in his hair blew in the cold December wind and for the first time Oliver realized that it had begun to snow. Flakes dotted Blue Jay's thick black hair and rested upon his narrow shoulders.

" 'These aren't the droids you're looking for?' " Blue Jay asked with a smirk. "That sort of thing?"

It jarred Oliver to hear those familiar words come from the Borderkind's mouth, but he nodded. "Something like that."

"Not a chance. I'm no sorcerer. I know a few tricks, that's all," Blue Jay said. As he walked, he shifted the burden of Gong Gong into his left arm and reached with his right hand to touch Kitsune's bloody cloak. He ran his fingers down over her fur.

When he pulled his hand away, the blood was gone.

Oliver glanced down and saw that her blood-soaked tunic was also now restored.

"Just a trick," Blue Jay said, and now there was no more amusement in his face, but a kind of stoic regret.

"Is he dead?" Oliver asked, nodding toward the dragon.

Blue Jay frowned and glanced up at the dark sky, snow flying past his face. "The storm gathers. He will be all right. Others were not so fortunate."

Kitsune broke away from Oliver, managing to keep up with them. The blood was gone and she had said she was healing, but still she clutched a hand to the place her wound had been and her face was contorted with pain.

"The Hunters came, Oliver," she said.

And when she reached out to brush her fingers against his, he could not mistake it for anything but purposeful. There was a sweet melancholy to her expression that made him want to hold her. He remembered how she had looked in the Inn in Perinthia, stripped naked as she prepared to shower, and he shivered. Julianna was his fiancée. Whatever was to happen between them, he still loved her. That much, he was almost certain of. Almost.

"I figured as much. What . . . I mean, did anyone else get out?"

The bridge over the Thames was ahead.

"There were Kirata," Kitsune went on, her eyes distant as though she was seeing it all unfold in front of her. Her lips curled in disgust. "And Marra was there."

Oliver shivered as he remembered the unsettlingly demonic goat-headed man whom they had seen only for a moment in Bromfield, just before they had fled. The cold intelligence in the creature had troubled him, and Marra had lingered in his mind like the memory of a nightmare.

"At least two of the Mazikeen were killed. One of them

might have escaped, but not with us. Lailoken and Yuki-Onna are dead," Blue Jay said. He lowered his head as he walked. "I have not yet had a chance to tell Frost that his sister is gone."

Sister. Oliver's stomach did a sick twist as he thought of Collette, and realized what Frost had lost.

"Surely he will have felt it," Kitsune said. "He knows."

Oliver felt the seconds ticking by like an itching at the back of his neck. Already he'd let this go on too long. They had to get somewhere they could have a real discussion and figure out what to do next, get away from the people staring at them before the police arrived, which could be any moment. But he could not go. Not yet.

"The Mazikeen . . ." he began, and then sighed, shaking his head. "I'm a dead man. How the hell do we find this professor now?"

Kitsune touched his elbow, a pained smile at her lips. "Oh, no, Oliver. They located him before the attack came. Koenig is on Canna Island, off the coast of Scotland."

It was like a spike of adrenaline to his heart. Oliver glanced around, feeling that he could even sense the approach of the police. But now that he knew Koenig was alive, and that Kitsune knew where he was, there had to be a plan. They had to get out of London and there was no way they were crossing the Veil again to do it.

"We've got to split up," he said hurriedly. "All right, look, Blue Jay, I don't know what you can and can't do, but I do know that you can't carry Gong Gong around and not draw attention, never mind the way you're dressed. Word will get out about what just happened."

Oliver ran his hands through his hair as though he might tear it out. "Do either of you know this city?"

"I have been here once before, long ago," Blue Jay said.

Horns beeped. People shouted. Oliver struggled to think.

"All right, look, there's a place called Trafalgar Square. There's a statue of Admiral Nelson there. Ask if you have to—but not with the fucking dragon in your arms—cover him up or something. Meet me at noon at the base of the statue."

"What are you going to do?" Kitsune asked.

"Fix this," Oliver said, laughing a bit wildly, feeling hysteria overcome him. "I'm going to fix all of this shit."

He said nothing of his father's murder or of his missing sister. Now was not the time. Later there would be an opportunity. At the moment, all that mattered was getting out of London without further trouble.

They had reached the bridge and started to walk over it. From behind, there erupted a braying police siren. Oliver spun and saw a police car stopped at the corner where he had called Julianna, where the Borderkind had appeared in front of Battersea Park and likely shaken the faith those people had in the world around them.

"They're coming. Any minute." Desperate, he looked to Blue Jay. "You've got to get out of here with *him*."

The trickster smiled. "We'll see you at Trafalgar Square."

Then Blue Jay dumped Gong Gong over the bridge. Oliver shouted but could not stop him. As he fell, the dragon seemed to awaken, twisting his body around, trying to spread his wings. He hit the water like an anchor and sank.

"What the hell—"

Kitsune grabbed Oliver's hand. "He will be all right. He is the Black Dragon of Storms. He needed to sleep to heal. He saved our lives. Now he will wake."

Upon those words there was a crash of thunder across

the sky so loud that Oliver scanned the storm clouds for some sign of catastrophe. It sounded like the whole world was cracking open. Lightning played up in the clouds but did not reach its fingers down toward earth. The snow sped up, falling more heavily now. It had been a clear day not long before and now it was growing steadily into a blizzard.

Oliver looked down over the bridge to where Gong Gong had hit the water and saw a ripple on the surface of the river and a shape moving beneath, an enormous thing that seemed to make the water heave upward. Then it was gone.

"Until we meet again," Blue Jay said.

It was not the blink of an eye, but a fraction of that. Blue Jay vanished, and where he had been was a small bird with the same cerulean feathers that had been tied in his hair. The bird flapped its wings and darted out over the Thames, weaving through the snowstorm as though at play.

Kitsune twined her fingers with his.

"We will be all right now," she said.

The braying siren—so different in its grating wail from those in America—moved closer. Oliver glanced over and saw that the traffic had started to move, stubborn gawkers reluctantly giving way to the police car.

He shook his head. "No, Kitsune."

"We'll walk hand in hand," she said, wincing slightly as she touched her abdomen again, then smiling weakly. "They will think us lovers."

He stared at her. "You don't understand, you're unmistakable. A beautiful Asian woman in a fox-fur cloak. It might not matter, but if they ask you for identification and you don't have any, they might want to question you about whatever those people back there saw, and we can't afford that. If you're being held, and the Hunters come for you—"

She held up a hand to cut him off. "I'm not thinking clearly. I shall see you at midday at Admiral Nelson's feet."

Oliver would never watch her transformation without holding his breath in astonishment. The cloak flowed around her. He watched those jade eyes as her face became the narrow, cunning face of the fox and copper fur enveloped her. The woman was gone. At Oliver's feet was the small, lithe fox.

The police siren warbled.

Kitsune darted away across the bridge, northward through the falling snow, a small limp to her walk.

Oliver started to walk after her, taking his time, wanting attention to remain on him as she disappeared into the storm. A passing motorist shouted something at him. Then the voice was drowned out by the police siren and he heard the squeak of brakes in need of fixing as the car rolled to a stop beside him, engine rumbling. A door opened.

The siren cut out.

Back along the way Oliver had come, just at the beginning of the bridge, electrician Keith watched warily, keeping well back as though afraid a battle might break out.

"Oh, thank God!" Oliver said as the officers got out of their car and came toward him. He gave them no opportunity to ask questions. "You know, in the States we have a saying, there's never a cop around when you need one. I'm so glad to see you guys."

"That right?" said the larger and older of the two, his cap pulled down snugly over his thinning silver hair. "Got the impression you'd rather avoid us, sir. We've got a few questions for you."

Oliver blinked in feigned confusion, remembering the

exhilaration he had felt the first time he had ever stepped onstage as an actor. The freedom in it. There was freedom in this as well, for it was just another sort of performance.

"Okay." He shrugged, mystified, brushing some snow out of his eyes. "Whatever you say. But, look, I really need some help. I was walking in the park and stopped to make a call. When I came out of the phone booth I had my organizer out—the one with my British money and my passport—and this guy, this fucking guy, he bumps me and then takes off running. Looked like an Indian, that's the weirdest thing. Native American, I mean. Feathers in his hair and everything."

The older cop crossed his arms and stared doubtfully through the snow.

"Right, I'm sorry, you're saying this Indian nicked your billfold?"

They both tensed as Oliver reached into his back pocket for his wallet, pushing the tail of the peacoat up to get to it. "Well, no, I mean, I've got my regular wallet, but that's just credit cards and a little American money. My organizer's like my travel wallet. All the stuff I needed for my visit here. American Express Travelers Cheques, that kind of thing. I was just hoping you could take me to an American Express office. I can't even take a cab 'cause I have no British money. I think there's one by Buckingham Palace, right?"

He frowned as though he was thinking hard on the question and actually scratched at the several days' stubble on his chin. With his rustic shirt and his peacoat and how badly he needed a shave, they probably figured him for homeless at first. What he wanted was for them to realize he was just another crazy American.

Oliver grinned and spread his arms, wallet clutched in one hand. "I'm kind of screwed here, boys. Help me out?"

The older cop rolled his eyes and gave a small sneer that spoke volumes on his opinion of Americans. The younger shook his head. He had a stoved-in nose like a prizefighter and wide-set eyes that made him look sad and sleepy. Snowflakes had begun to whiten the shoulders of their uniforms and the tops of their hats.

"Sir, we really need to ask you a few questions," the prizefighter said. "Starting with your name."

He gave them his shallowest American lawyer smile. "Oliver Bascombe, Kitteridge, Maine. U.S.A., obviously."

"Obviously," the older cop said drily.

Oliver gave them a sheepish look. "You can ask me anything you want, guys, but could we do it in the car? I've got a lunch date I'd really rather not miss. Met a girl here in London. Came for a few days and now I don't know when I'll go home. And I really need to get this thing sorted out. There wasn't a lot of cash, but the Travelers Cheques . . . Anyway, can you ask me whatever you've got to ask me on the way? It would be a huge help."

The prizefighter looked at his partner. The older man rolled his eyes again and stepped over to open the rear door of the police car, bowing like a chauffeur.

"By all means, sir. Hop in and we'll have us a chat. We'll help you get sorted."

Oliver smiled broadly, stuffing his wallet back into his pocket. "Really? Thank you so much. Is this a great country or what?"

The whole situation was surreal. Oliver's father had been murdered and mutilated, and his sister was missing. His own life was in peril and back home the police were no doubt wondering what had become of him as well. But on the outside, he was all smiles.

Happy and cooperative, he climbed into the car, brushing snow from his peacoat. The car rolled across the bridge, wipers clearing snow, the world beyond the windows beautifully white now. And the questions began. Oliver remained mystified. He didn't know what the hell those people back at Battersea Park were talking about, he told them. The guy with the feathers in his hair, yeah. He'd seen that guy . . . fellow stole his organizer, after all. He even thought he recalled seeing the Asian woman they described, though he didn't think she'd been bleeding. But a man made of ice?

That was just crazy talk. Weird, the things people imagined. And speaking of weird, wasn't it strange how the weather had changed so suddenly?

Sort of nice, though, at Christmastime.

CHAPTER 17

The snowstorm in South London that morning had not been predicted by a single meteorologist, but it was over too quickly for any of them to have to apologize for the oversight. By ten minutes till noon, at which time Oliver was exiting Charing Cross tube station and emerging into Trafalgar Square, the day had turned a typical London gray and the temperature was falling. The wind across the square had a December bite that made pedestrians turn up their collars and vanquished any thoughts of lunch in the square or a pleasant stroll. The only people in Trafalgar Square that noontime were determined tourists and Londoners on their way from one place to another.

It had been a long time since Oliver had been to

London, but Trafalgar Square appeared largely unchanged. The roads around the square seemed somehow narrower than he remembered, but that might have been a fault of his memory. Once upon a time it had been the King's Mews, but in the mid-nineteenth century it was transformed into a broad city square of marble and granite to commemorate the Battle of Trafalgar, perhaps the most significant British naval triumph during the Napoleonic Wars. Oliver had a great fondness for the place because it was the tangible memorial to a part of history that fascinated him. There were other statues, other monuments in Trafalgar Square, but Nelson's Column was always the most impressive. It towered imposingly over the rest of the square, and the statue of Lord Admiral Horatio Nelson looked out over the city from its peak. Nelson had led a fascinating life with a single-mindedness of purpose that Oliver had always found both intimidating and inspiring.

It was the first place that had come to mind when he had been forced to come up with a rendezvous under pressure. Given time to think, he might not have chosen it. Midday at the base of Nelson's Column could not have been considered an inconspicuous meeting place. And yet he was pleased just the same.

Now he strode across the square toward a pair of older women wielding cameras who were bustling about the base of the column. No sign of his companions. Oliver let his gaze drift, surveying the whole square, almost faltering when he craned his neck round to see the National Gallery and the church of St. Martin-in-the-Fields. His favorite view was to the west, where Canada House stood proudly. Though it was hardly the grandest structure in London, there was something stolid and official about it that he had always admired.

Oliver had no watch, but the clock down in the tube station had been ticking toward noon. He hoped that the others would arrive momentarily, because otherwise he would have to entertain the idea that something had detained them, and the thought was deeply troubling.

When he reached Nelson's Column he craned his neck to gaze up at the great admiral outlined against the sky, and he remained that way until the old women moved on to photograph some other monument. He leaned against the column and crossed his arms as though waiting for a train. There was little else he could do at the moment but watch cars going by at the outskirts of the square and the anonymous people passing through. There were beautiful fountains arranged around Nelson's Column—perhaps a dozen feet from the base—but with the temperature they were not functioning, the statuary not spouting water today. The two he could see from his post by the column were filled with ice.

It was from there that the whisper came.

"*Oliver.*"

He looked up, eyes drawn immediately to the frozen fountain to his right. A smile came unbidden to his lips and a small, relieved chuckle followed after. During the tension at Battersea Park, Frost's departure had been rushed, and though the winter man was likely the one amongst them most able to extricate himself from harm, still Oliver had worried for him.

A pair of dapperly dressed English businessmen strode by, both smoking cigarettes, trailing furling smoke trails behind them in the breeze. One muttered something to the other, eliciting a derisive grunt, but they did not so much as glance at Oliver. He glanced around and saw that the only other people nearby were a small cluster of young tourists, perhaps American exchange students, and a star-tlingly obese man who might have been their teacher or guide. But they were headed for the National Gallery.

There was still no sign of the others, but Oliver crossed to the fountain. The ice that was frozen there was sculpted into familiar jagged ridges that formed the face of the winter man.

"You've done well," Frost said, with the snap of cracking ice. His blue-white eyes gazed up from the fountain.

Oliver grinned. "You were watching me?"

The fountain's ice popped and shifted as Frost frowned. "I hadn't anywhere else to go. When I am on this side of the Veil, I travel alone. It is difficult to be bound by the limits of flesh and bone."

"Well, sorry to hold you up. I wouldn't mind having the wind just carry me away when trouble starts."

The winter man's eyes grew dark. "You do not wish to trade lives with me. Despite the chaos you are experiencing now, there is still a place that you call home. I have never had a home."

Oliver felt the urge to snap at him, to tell Frost that his father had been murdered and his sister stolen away, that his home had been torn apart by violence and grief that would never have intruded upon his life had he never met the winter man. But he knew that Frost was also in mourning, for the death of Yuki-Onna, and so he kept his bitterness to himself and the two of them shared a reflective moment in silence.

The bird passed just above his head, flying low, wings aflutter. He would not have given it a second look save for the uniquely brilliant blue of its feathers, but even so it took a moment to register with Oliver that Blue Jay had arrived. By the time he turned back toward the column, the shape-shifter was there. He had managed somehow to acquire clothing more appropriate for this world, and now wore black denim and thick-soled boots and a long canvas duster of the sort worn by Australian cowboys.

"Midday," Blue Jay said. "As agreed."

Oliver nodded. He didn't ask where Blue Jay had gotten his clothes, mostly because he did not want to know. He himself had been too busy to find something else to wear, but he had grown fond of the gray peacoat Larch had given him and thought he might have kept it regardless.

"Where are the others?" Oliver asked.

Blue Jay raised his eyebrows. "I left Kitsune with you." Then he grinned. "But the dragon has been here for hours."

The trickster pointed toward Canada House. Oliver narrowed his eyes and stared at the regal structure, trying to figure out what Blue Jay was talking about, when he sensed something not quite right about the façade of the building. Something out of balance. It took him a moment to realize that a piece of statuary was missing from the roof of Canada House. There were often lions and eagles and that sort of thing built in to the architecture of such buildings. A quartet of carved lions had been placed around Nelson's Column, in fact. But there was always a balance to such things. On Canada House, the eagle or sphinx or whatever it was that had been placed on one end of the building had no counterbalance.

Oliver blinked.

It was neither eagle nor sphinx, of course, but a dragon perched like a gargoyle on the edge of the roof of Canada House. No architectural flourish was missing. Rather, one had been added, and it was the Black Dragon of Storms.

"He's been sitting up there all morning and no one has noticed?"

Blue Jay tapped a finger just below his left eye. "People see what they wish to see."

Gong Gong remained where he was.

"He's all right?" Oliver asked, wondering why he cared.

"Healing," Blue Jay replied. "Like the rest of us."

As he spoke his gaze shifted and Oliver turned to see Kitsune crossing the square toward them. Something shook inside him, not in fear but elation, like the ringing of a tiny bell. Though she had sworn that she would recover quickly from her wounds, and he had seen her do it with his own eyes, still he wondered how badly injured she had been.

"We're all here now, Frost," Oliver said, voice low, his gaze still on the approaching Kitsune.

"Excellent," said the winter man from the ice of the fountain. He did not elaborate, did not mention the time passing beyond the Veil and the danger to his kin there, but he did not have to.

Several people passed by, pausing to take pictures but without coming very near the column. By the time they moved on Kitsune had joined Oliver and Blue Jay. He felt the urge to embrace her but fought it. A friendship had grown between them, but still Oliver saw her as the kind of woman you didn't simply throw your arms around, any more than you would a queen. And there was another reason as well. Part of the urge to touch her did not spring from relief that she was all right. Oliver had to deny that part of what he felt.

He hoped to go home someday soon. There was no family there for him, but Julianna was there, waiting.

"You look much improved," Oliver said.

Kitsune smiled. "I ache. But it will fade."

He fumbled in trying to find a response to that.

Blue Jay knitted his brow in consternation at the odd moment that passed amongst them. "All right, we're here. But we can't stay here very long before we draw attention to ourselves. I hope one of you has an idea what to do next."

A weight settled on Oliver's heart. "What else can we do but move on? I have to find Collette, but I can't do that with Hunters on my trail. We've come this far. I've got to at least talk to Koenig, find out how to get the price taken off my head."

They were all looking at him curiously.

"What of Collette?" Frost asked.

Grief and dread and a sense of his own foolishness roiled in his heart. Of course he had not told them of his phone call with Julianna. Chaos had erupted outside the phone booth and then it had been all he could do to extricate them from that situation, to get them all moving toward the time when they could get out of London.

"She's missing," he said, his own voice sounding small and distant to his ears. "My dad—" *No, stop that. You never thought of him as Dad when he was alive. There's too much warmth in that.* "My father's dead. Murdered."

Haltingly, he told them the rest, about the removal of Max Bascombe's eyes and the disappearance of his sister and the investigation into his own vanishing.

"They probably think you killed him," Blue Jay said lightly. "Or both of them. Or that you and your sister conspired together."

Oliver stared at him.

Kitsune nodded sadly. "They may, Oliver. How could they come to the truth, these ordinary policemen? How could it even occur to them that the Sandman is loose upon the world?"

"The Sandman?" He stared at her stupidly.

Frost and Kitsune glanced at each other and the winter man blinked once, slowly, in assent, still only his face jutting from the ice in the fountain. "I agree. The coincidence is too great. The Sandman is freed, and soon after, Oliver's father is murdered in that fashion? Someone must have set the monster to the task."

Oliver scowled. "But who? And why?"

Blue Jay grunted with interest, studying Oliver as though seeing him for the first time. "Good questions," he said, the blue feathers tied into his hair swinging in the wind.

"It is all connected," Frost said, his voice a whisper like the wind. His eyes seemed unfocused. "Why should the Sandman be interested in Oliver, unless he has had instruction? Whoever is behind the hunting of the Borderkind, they do not want Oliver to aid us."

"That's ridiculous," Oliver snapped. Realizing how loud he'd spoken, he glanced around, but none of the scattering of people passing by paid any attention to them. "My part in this was pure accident. I'm just a lawyer from Maine. What threat could I possibly pose to anyone?"

Kitsune's jade eyes seemed to glow as she tilted her head and regarded him carefully. "Perhaps it was not an accident at all. Certainly, someone believes you are far more important than any of us knew. Important enough to kill your father to hurt you and to spirit your sister away to lay a trap for you."

"That's crazy!"

Blue Jay snorted. "Truly? Do you have another explanation? Anything at all?"

But he did not. "So, it's the Sandman, then, who has my sister?"

"So it would seem," Kitsune replied.

Oliver nodded. "Fine. As soon as I find out what I need to know from Koenig, I'm going after her."

None of them said a word at first. What could they say? If they were correct and it was a trap, then he and Collette would both die. But she was his sister and he loved her for all that she had always been to him, for the bond they shared. What choice did he have?

The ice shifted in the fountain, cracks running all through it like a splintered mirror. "You know that we cannot go with you?" Frost asked.

Oliver hesitated. "I know I said I would help you find out who sent the Hunters after you—"

"And you will," Kitsune interrupted. "Once you have found Collette."

"Your sister must come first," Frost said, and there was such sorrow in his voice. Yuki-Onna had not been his sister in the same way that Collette was Oliver's, but his grief was no less real.

"For now, though, we stay together," Kitsune affirmed.

Blue Jay nodded. "For now. That would be best."

The ice ridges that made up Frost's face jutted up from the frozen surface. "We must travel north to Scotland as swiftly as possible, but on this side of the Veil."

Kitsune nodded. "Our destination is nearer on this side, and we have to assume there are Hunters waiting for us there."

"We've been here hours," Blue Jay said darkly. "It will have taken them a bit of time to find a border crossing, but they'll be in the city by now, scouring the place for us."

Throwing back her hood, silken hair dancing in the December wind, Kitsune glanced up at Canada House and the rigid figure of the dragon on the roof. She nodded slowly and returned her attention to her companions, but only then did Oliver realize that Gong Gong was up there for a reason. He was standing sentinel, watching over them, in case the Hunters should come.

He had been so driven by adrenaline and grief and so pleased with what he had accomplished this morning that he had thought little of the Hunters. The danger of discovery by ordinary Londoners or the police had been far more on his mind.

"All right. Okay. We'll go right now. But I still don't understand. How did they find you in the first place? The Mazikeen had hidden that place with glamours and spells."

Once again ice crackled and this time when the winter breeze blew it was colder than before. Frost opened his mouth, jagged features thrust out from the frozen fountain, and mist steamed off his eyes.

"Treachery," he said. "Larch was there. He had betrayed us to the Kirata."

"They must have followed our scent to his home and his fear did the rest," Kitsune added. "He surrendered his honor, and our destination, and they forced him to come along to make certain he was not lying. That is my theory, at least."

Blue Jay spit on the ground.

Oliver took a long breath and then shook his head. He had trusted Larch and the betrayal saddened him.

"All right," he said. "Let's get going."

Kitsune glanced around, surveying Trafalgar Square for any sign of threat. "How do you propose we do that?"

"There are drawbacks to being a child of privilege, but the benefits are enormous. People are more than happy to bend over backward to help you. I went to the American Express Travel Office and told them my passport and Travelers Cheques were stolen.

"I now have plenty of cash, a mobile phone, Travelers Cheques, and an international driver's license for ID while I wait for my new passport. I'm supposed to go apply for a new one, but since I'm not traveling home through any normal route, there's really no point."

American Express Travel had helped him get the international driver's license, providing documentation supporting his assertion that he was indeed Oliver Bascombe, and helped him arrange for a car. The rental-car lot was only a few tube stops away. All that remained was for him to pick it up.

If the police were indeed searching for him, he might as well have sent up a flare to let them know where to look.

The law firm of Bascombe & Cox had offices in Augusta, Portland, and Boston. From what Ted Halliwell had learned, the future of the firm was in those offices. The junior partners, the young sharks who were bringing in high-stakes new clients, were in the places where they were most likely to find fresh meat. The original office in Kitteridge was still there, however, and that was where the senior partners still worked, controlling their growing power from afar, brokering politics in the state capital of Augusta from two counties away.

This morning the sheriff had ducked his head into Detective Halliwell's office and rapped softly on the door frame, an odd expression on his face. Halliwell had the feeling that he would know a great deal more about his current situation if he had only been able to read Jackson Norris's face.

Andrew Cox, most senior partner in the firm now that Max Bascombe was dead, had apparently called the sheriff to report that the firm had learned vital information about the whereabouts of Bascombe's son. The news sent a ripple of unease through Halliwell that he didn't quite understand. He wanted to find both of the dead man's children, but thus far his pursuit of Oliver Bascombe had only led to more questions and to a disturbing pattern of child murders that twisted his stomach and fogged his mind.

It was all connected, of that he felt sure. The only possible explanation he could come up with was that there was some sort of new cult operating worldwide that had so far gone undiscovered. The detectives he'd spoken to in Paris and San Francisco shared this theory. The arrival of the Internet had begun to breed such groups. There had always been perverts and freaks and lunatics, but he imagined that a lot of them never acted on their most debased impulses. On the Net, they could search in secrecy for the depravities that fascinated them, and in doing so, come into contact with others who shared their particular bent. Halliwell had no idea what kind of madness could lead to the savage murder of children, what thoughts of sacrifice or malice, but he felt certain that links would be found.

His dreams were haunted by young girls and boys with ragged holes where their eyes ought to be. They all looked like Alice St. John, except the one who looked very much like his own daughter at the age of eight or nine. The truth was, Ted Halliwell didn't want to think about the dead kids or the Bascombe family ever again. But he had no choice. Even had it not been his job, his investigation, there was no erasing the horror from his mind. From his nightmares.

All children, save Max Bascombe. So what was the link? Could Oliver have been part of that cult? Or his sister? Both of them? If he proceeded on any of those assumptions, how then to explain the still-lingering mystery of how brother and sister left the house without anyone noticing, how Oliver departed in the middle of a blizzard with no transportation? And what of Oliver's strange appearance up in Cottingsley, the Asian woman seen with him, and the murder of Alice St. John?

Halliwell had let those questions stew for far too long, but there was little else he could do without more information.

And here it was.

"What's their news?" he had asked the sheriff.

Jackson Norris had frowned deeply at him, as though the question itself offended his sensibilities. "Mr. Cox wants to see you. In fact, the firm's partners want to meet with you this morning. The sooner the better. Whatever they know, you'll find out when you get there. And whatever it is they want you to do with that information, that's what you'll do."

Halliwell had stared at the sheriff. "You're holding out on me, Jackson."

"It's your case, Ted. You want me to send someone else?"

It was an idle threat, Halliwell knew. This had been political for Sheriff Norris from the start. Bascombe & Cox had helped him get elected sheriff in the first place, and if he was to prove their money well spent, he had to make Max Bascombe's murder his number-one priorty. Halliwell knew he was the best detective in the sheriff's department. Maybe one of the best in the state, if he allowed himself that hubris. Whatever the firm wanted, Norris was going to do his best to see they got it.

But it had been gnawing at Halliwell, and regardless of his boss's motivations, there was no way he was letting this case get away.

"No. I'll follow up. Let's see what they've got. It's gotta be more than what we have. If there's a lead that'll help me find Oliver Bascombe, I want it. I don't know if a conversation with the guy is going to solve my case, but it's sure going to fill in some of the blanks. Maybe the firm can help."

The conversation was still fresh in his mind three quarters of an hour later as he pulled his car into a spot outside a handsome brick building that had been a schoolhouse in the nineteenth century. A white sign had been affixed beside the massive doors, engraved with black letters that read BASCOMBE & COX, ATTORNEYS AT LAW.

Halliwell could practically smell the money.

The receptionist was an attractive fortyish woman who looked more than a little like she ought to have been handing out fines at the library. Her hair was tied back tightly and her glasses were so old-fashioned Halliwell was sure they must be back in style by now. When he gave his name she nodded gravely.

"Yes, Detective. Sheriff Norris phoned ahead. They're in the conference room, expecting you."

He waited for her to summon a secretary or paralegal to come and lead him into the back. Instead, the receptionist glanced at the door, hesitated a moment, and then rose to escort him herself. Halliwell followed her past the partition with the firm's name in large block letters, and down a corridor that ran between cubicles and well-appointed offices. Some were empty, while others revealed lawyers staring at computer screens or piles of documents.

They went up a curving staircase and emerged in a second-floor foyer, surrounded by thriving potted plants and elegant woodwork. The maple floor was polished to a high sheen. On the opposite side of the foyer was a glass wall, and beyond the glass a large conference room. The table was not round, but seemed large enough for a gathering of Arthurian knights. Instead, it was surrounded by lawyers. With the traditionalist, Old World attitudes of Bascombe & Cox, Halliwell was surprised to see that several of the partners were women.

The receptionist strode to the door of the conference room, and as Halliwell followed her, every head turned to watch him approach.

"Ah, Angela, this is Detective Halliwell, I presume?" asked the man at the far end of the table. He had the whitest hair and the most expensive suit, so Halliwell pegged him as the boss.

"Yes, Mr. Cox."

Cox smiled. "Thank you, Angela."

The receptionist turned and strode away without a backward glance, returning to her post. Not one of the attorneys watched her go, all of them focused on Halliwell. Only then did the detective notice that to Cox's right was a familiar face. Julianna Whitney nodded in recognition but did not smile. She was pale and there were tired circles under her eyes.

"Detective Halliwell, thank you for coming," Cox said. "I'm Andrew Cox."

The lawyer did not bother to get up. There would be no formal greeting, no shaking of hands. He introduced a couple of the others, obviously the most senior of the partners, but left most of them anonymous. Halliwell nodded and gave each a perfunctory hello. After a moment's hesitation, Cox gestured to his right.

"And you know Attorney Whitney, of course."

"I do. I knew that she worked for the firm, but wasn't aware that she was a lawyer."

Cox smiled. "Oh, yes. Quite an excellent attorney, our Julianna. Though she chooses to use her law degree in other pursuits." He indicated the chair at the very end of the table, nearest the door. "Now then, if you'd like to have a seat?"

Halliwell frowned. He didn't have a clue what the hell the old man was talking about. Also, he didn't like the way the meeting was so entirely one-sided. To people as wealthy as Andrew Cox, officers of the law were always going to seem like errand boys, and men like Jackson Norris only made matters worse by confirming their presumptions. He decided to shift control of things somewhat.

"Mr. Cox, I don't really know what I'm doing here. The sheriff was vague about the purpose of this visit. If you've got information that's pertinent to my case, particularly the location of Oliver Bascombe, there isn't any reason you couldn't have simply passed that along to the sheriff and he to me."

The old man's cheeks reddened slightly and a bit of pique flickered across his face, but then he smiled. "You misunderstand, Detective. Sheriff Norris was fully apprised of the information we've recently acquired. If he did not share it with you, I'd say that's a topic of further discussion between you and your employer. What I wished to discuss with you, what the firm of Bascombe and Cox wished to present to you, was on a related matter."

Halliwell considered that a moment. He wanted to remain standing but it would only insult Cox and his partners. As frustrated as he was, not to mention curious, rudeness would only come back to haunt him later. He slid into the chair and kept his back straight, lacing his hands upon his lap.

"All right. But would you mind, first, telling me whatever it was that the sheriff couldn't be bothered to mention?"

Cox nodded and a shroud of sincerity came over his features. He nodded toward a handsome, slick-looking man who sat only a couple of seats away from Halliwell.

"Steven. Would you be so kind?"

The lawyer reached down into the open briefcase beside his chair and withdrew a manila folder. He slid it across the table to Halliwell.

"We've located Oliver Bascombe."

Halliwell blinked and glanced around the dozen or so faces, but they were expressionless, only watching him expectantly. With a shrug he opened the folder and began to examine the papers it contained. There were records of a sizable cash advance from Oliver's American Express account as well as a car rental receipt and a copy of a brand-new international driver's license. There were photographs of a rather rough-looking Oliver taken from a security camera. He had a scruffy growth of beard but it was unmistakably him.

His frown deepened, and then he glanced up at Julianna before turning his attention to Cox. "London? How the hell did he get to London?"

The old man shifted his gaze to Julianna and for the first time Halliwell thought there might be some heart to Andrew Cox, something beyond the arrogance of entitlement. He hesitated before answering.

"We don't really know. Oliver phoned Miss Whitney

from a public booth in the north of London. He charged it to his credit card. According to that conversation, he claims to have had no knowledge of his father's murder or of his sister's disappearance. He did, however, tell Julianna that he could not return home at the moment. That there was something he had to accomplish first."

Halliwell had stopped listening to Cox. His focus now was on Julianna. "What something?"

She tucked a lock of hair behind her ear, eyes averted for a moment. Then she lifted her chin and gazed directly at him. "He wouldn't say. All I can tell you is that I know him better than anyone except maybe Collette, and his surprise sounded completely genuine to me. I wanted to get him to tell me more, or at least when to expect him back in the States, but something happened wherever he was. Someone was calling to him and he said a quick good-bye and hung up. It sounded . . . well, from his voice, it sounded like whatever interrupted him, it wasn't good."

With a nod, Halliwell went back to perusing the documents in front of him. "You've contacted the police in London, I assume? Have they been able to find him?"

The room was silent. The lawyers stared at him intently, Julianna included. Cox cleared his throat.

"Actually, Detective," Steven began, smoothing his stylish tie, "we haven't involved the London police as yet. If our information is correct, it would be useless to bring them into it. The manager at the American Express office was cooperative when talking to Mr. Cox. It seems in addition to cash and a rental car, they also provided maps, driving directions, and arranged a private ferry passage from mainland Scotland to a place called Canna Island, which is in the . . ."

He frowned, trying to remember. Steven glanced at the

folder in front of Halliwell, obviously wishing he could have it back to double-check his information.

"The Hebridean Sea," Julianna finished for him.

Halliwell turned his attention on her and Cox again. "All right. So we know where he's headed. As you're both well aware, the sheriff's department would like to speak with Mr. Bascombe to see if he can shed light on his father's murder, his sister's whereabouts, and at least one other killing."

Julianna flinched. "What do you mean? What other killings are you talking about?"

He studiously ignored the question and looked only at Cox now. "It would be helpful, I'd think, to ask the Scottish authorities to detain him. Even to question him. But other than that, without some evidence to link him to one of these crimes, it isn't like he can be extradited if he doesn't want to come home."

Cox nodded. "True. Which is where you come in, Detective Halliwell. You're aware that the firm has attempted throughout this process to keep the more sensational details of the case out of the media, and to monitor the progress of the investigation."

Halliwell wanted to laugh. Bascombe & Cox had brought the sheriff's department into a case that was fundamentally not their jurisdiction, exerting whatever power they had to keep it in the sheriff's hands—in Halliwell's own hands—instead of leaving it to the Kitteridge P.D. That hadn't worked out as well as they had planned. The murder had made news, all right. But so far, the mutilation of Max Bascombe had been kept from the public.

"So what am I supposed to do?" he asked. "Go to Scotland and get him? It's a bit outside my jurisdiction, Mr. Cox."

Cox gave him the enigmatic smile of a man who never had to bluff at poker because the other players would sooner fold than dare to beat him.

"We aren't talking about jurisdiction, Detective. Bascombe and Cox has a small office in London. We do business in the United Kingdom. You would locate Oliver and let him know that he is the executor of his father's estate and that he needs to return home to see to his duties to his family and to this firm. We have worked hard to keep the press from portraying him as a suspect in his father's murder. If that were to change, it would create a spectacle that would reflect very poorly on the firm. So we would like you to go to Scotland and tell him all that I've said. That ought to give you ample opportunity to ask him whatever questions you like about his behavior and the whereabouts of his sister."

Halliwell cocked his head and looked around the room, unable to believe the utter arrogance of the man. Of all of them. Julianna raised an eyebrow and one side of her mouth lifted in amusement, but without malice.

"If you have offices there," Halliwell said, focused on Cox rather than any of his silent partners, "I'm sure there are people you could send to retrieve him. He works for you, after all. Though if you have an office there and he didn't go there when he needed cash and a shave, I'd guess he didn't feel like checking in with the firm. In any case, I have a job, Mr. Cox. It isn't as if I can run off to—"

Andrew Cox waved a hand in dismissal. "Sheriff Norris has already agreed to give you a paid leave of absence. On top of that, this firm will pay you quite well for your trouble, as well as covering all expenses. Jackson Norris has made it clear that he holds you in high regard, Detective Halliwell. We need a man we can trust, a man with your skills, and whose credentials will earn him cooperation from U.K. law enforcement if that becomes necessary."

Halliwell took a breath and sat back in his chair. There was a reason for Cox's arrogance. The man was shrewd. He had thought of everything. Looking into his eyes, Halliwell realized that the outcome of this meeting had never been in doubt. Much as he despised the man's presumption and swagger, he was deeply troubled by this case and the firm was handing him the means to pursue the investigation far beyond the parameters he would have otherwise been shackled with. Halliwell would have been frustrated as hell knowing Oliver Bascombe was out of his reach. Now he had a chance to confront the vanishing lawyer, and thanks to Cox, he was even more frustrated.

But he couldn't walk away from the opportunity. Cox had been counting on that. He nodded, but slowly, and he used his eyes to let Cox know he was a prick. Not that the old man would care what Ted Halliwell thought.

"All right, Mr. Cox. When do I leave?"

"You will depart from Bangor International this evening, accompanied by our firm's investigator."

Halliwell raised his eyebrows. They were hiring him to go find Bascombe and fetch him back to Maine. That made him the investigator. Why did they need to send someone from the firm along for the ride? To monitor his expenditures?

Then Cox glanced at Julianna. "I'm sure Miss Whitney will be of great assistance to you."

And Halliwell put it all together. Julianna Whitney had gone to law school, but she wasn't employed by the firm as a lawyer. She was their investigator, doing background checks on clients and opponents alike, digging up dirt, tracing shell corporations, and finding out which way Augusta politicians were going to vote.

She was Oliver Bascombe's fiancée and she wanted to go find him. Cox wanted him found as well, for all the reasons he'd already said. Julianna was likely more than capable of finding Oliver on her own. But Halliwell was insurance. If love wouldn't make the errant Bascombe come home, they were hoping intimidation would.

Halliwell was being manipulated. He was surprised to find that he did not care. What he wanted was answers, and he thought perhaps that having Julianna Whitney along would help him get them. The law firm might be using him, but Halliwell figured two could play at that game.

He stood up from the chair and smiled thinly at Andrew Cox. "I'll pack."

CHAPTER 18

The Isle of Canna was off the western coast of Scotland, part of the chain called the Inner Hebrides. Oliver had driven all through the afternoon and into the evening. Gong Gong had not ridden in the car, choosing instead to pace them from high above in the gray clouds and on into the darkness of night. It had been a relief and a surprise to discover that Blue Jay was capable of driving an automobile. By his own admission he had not done so for years, but Oliver had the distinct impression that the trickster knew the world of men quite well. Though he chose to do most of the driving himself—he was, after all, the only one with a license and the sole driver on the rental agreement—Oliver allowed Blue Jay to spell him twice, for an hour the first time and nearly three the second.

It had been the longest drive he had ever undertaken.

With the clock creeping toward midnight, they had at last arrived in Mallaig, a small coastal town with an inn where he and Kitsune had secured a room. Blue Jay, Frost, and Gong Gong made themselves scarce during the check-in and even afterward the male Borderkind had all chosen to keep watch over the inn rather than try to take any rest.

Oliver could feel their impatience bristling within them, crackling in the air. It raised the small hairs on his arms, so tangible was their need to be moving on. The nights and days might be longer on the other side of the Veil, but none of them wanted to wait another night before making their way to the island where they hoped to find Professor Koenig at long last. But they had made the best time that was possible, stopping only for gas and food and for Oliver to use the toilet. Even without those stops they would have arrived hours after dark and the boat that he had chartered through the travel office back in London would not run them out to Canna during the night.

The night had seemed eternal. Whatever frisson of possibility had made his previous close-quarters experiences with Kitsune so tense had been shattered by his grief and his anticipation. His father was dead. Julianna was frightened and confused and he had abandoned her. Over the course of the long drive, this had begun to sink in to Oliver in a way that it had not before, and by the time they had arrived in Mallaig he was hollow and numb. He had been relieved to learn that the inn had rooms with separate beds. The clerk at the desk had offered to give them separate rooms for no additional cost, the place being nearly deserted this time of year, but Kitsune had quickly declined. And rightly so. If the Hunters managed to track them, they would be better off together.

All through the trip and the night that followed the Borderkind were quiet and grim from the need to resolve their obligation to him, to see this through, and he felt the same compulsion. Blue Jay would flutter on nearly silent wings to land upon their window ledge every couple of hours and Oliver had slept so lightly that night that the scritch-scratch of the bird's feet upon the ledge would rouse him.

But there was nothing they could do to make the night fly more swiftly.

In the small hours of the morning it began to snow, so that when dawn arrived there was a dusting of white outside the window. The snow continued, the sort of gentle winter fall that cast a hush upon the land. This was not difficult to do in a village on the coast of Scotland so late in the year. It took Oliver twenty minutes and the promise of an additional hundred pounds to convince Barclay Moncreiffe, the captain of the chartered boat, to set out for Canna Island in spite of the storm.

Now the grizzled Scotsman stood in the wheelhouse of the boat, peering out at the snow and the tumultuous sea, a firm grip on the wheel. Once upon a time it had been a fishing vessel but had been converted some years past to carry tourists from island to island and to deliver supplies to the smaller islands, where the ferry stopped every week or two. This morning the nameless ship carried three passengers, and for the trip Moncreiffe was likely taking in more money than he normally made all winter long.

Blue Jay stood on the prow with the snow falling all

around him. The swell of the sea threatened at any moment to dash him to the deck or into the water, yet he seemed remarkably at ease. Kitsune was below in the small cabin, nursing a cup of strong coffee the aging, bearded captain had offered from the thermos he had brought on board. The angry seas made her nervous.

Oliver did not blame her. With the snow falling and the sea churning he had at first kept to the cabin himself, but then his stomach began to roil and bile had risen in the back of his throat. Nausea had driven him up onto the deck. Moncreiffe had recommended coffee and some gingersnaps from a box he had below, but the idea of ingesting anything only made his gut lurch. He hung his arms over the railing and waited to be sick.

"Watch the horizon," Blue Jay said, appearing beside him. "Focus on the distance and your belly will settle."

With no better suggestion, Oliver took this advice and within minutes his nausea began to abate. Snow accumulated on his coat and hair and he blinked it away from his eyelashes as he searched for the island ahead.

"Gong Gong is out there somewhere?"

"Somewhere," Blue Jay said. "He's far more clever than he appears. He'll join us when we find your professor."

"And Frost?" Oliver narrowed his eyes and tried to see between the snowflakes, searching for any sign that the winter man was with them.

Blue Jay gazed upward, snow whipping into his face. "Distracted. A storm like this, the snowfall is intoxicating to him, or it might just as well be. He revels in it. He'll be tempted to lose himself in it, but that was how the Falconer nearly killed him the last time."

Oliver felt a tightening in his gut that had nothing to do with seasickness. "I never realized." He frowned, troubled, but said nothing more. If all went as he hoped, Frost should be free to drift with the storm for a while before they all traveled through the Veil again. And if not . . . well, Oliver didn't think he had to worry about Frost losing track of the danger they were in, not with his grief for Yuki-Onna still fresh.

When the captain brought the boat up to the dock at Canna Island, Blue Jay helped tie them up to the moorings. The dock was located within a natural inlet, so the surf was calmer there, but still they knocked against the rubber bumpers hanging from the pier. Oliver was sure he saw a familiar figure in the falling snow, just for a moment. The winter man had been watching them. But when he stepped off onto the dock and glanced around, he saw no sign of Frost. Blue Jay and Kitsune followed and the fox-woman linked her arm with his as though to steady herself. Her features were drawn but her eyes were alight with relief now that they were off the boat.

Captain Moncreiffe followed them onto the dock, hat pulled down tight on his head and coat buttoned up around his throat. He stuffed his hands into his pockets and peered at them through the falling snow.

Beyond him, Gong Gong sat on top of the wheelhouse. The snow seemed to move aside as though it did not dare to fall upon the Black Dragon of Storms. Oliver did his best to ignore the little creature, forcing himself to look at Moncreiffe's face.

"Mr. Bascombe, you've got three hours. Weather report says the storm's meant to subside a bit toward noon, but afterward she's going to get much worse. I'll want to be back to the mainland by then."

Oliver nodded. "Absolutely. We'll be back."

"Captain Moncreiffe," Kitsune said, jade eyes peering

out from beneath her hood with a light of their own, "you're certain you cannot direct us to Professor Koenig's home?"

The Scotsman had a twinkle in his eyes when he looked at her, but then he offered an apologetic shrug. "I'm sorry, miss. I wouldn't know where he lives. Anyone on the island ought to be able to tell you, though. Why, it's tiny, after all. Can't be more than twenty people living out here, all told. Stop at the first cottage with a light burning inside and you'll have your answers. Best hurry along, though."

He glanced warily skyward. For a moment he frowned and his eyes seemed to track something odd he might have seen in the snow above. Then he shook his head, his expression bemused. When Oliver glanced at the wheelhouse, Gong Gong was gone, and he could only imagine what Captain Moncreiffe thought he had seen in the storm.

"I have an old friend on the island. Perhaps *acquaintance* is more apt. But we're acquainted enough that he'll spare me a cup of tea and a scone and a warm place to sit while I wait on you."

Blue Jay started down the dock ahead of them. Kitsune and Oliver turned together and started toward the small village that lay ahead, church steeples stark against the storming gray sky. Several inches of fresh powder lay on the ground and Oliver was grateful for his boots. Blue Jay and Kitsune seemed hardly to notice at all.

As they drew nearer, trekking through the snow, the cottages became more than shapes in the gentle whiteness of the storm. Oliver's heels crunched on the powder but otherwise the village seemed entirely silent. So quiet, in fact, that he could hear the snow fall.

"I don't understand," Oliver said.

Blue Jay slowed to fall into step with them. "What's that?"

"The churches." He counted at least three steeples jutting up into the whitewashed sky. "Why are there only a handful of people here? Why are so many cottages empty? And if there's at best a couple of dozen people, what do they need so many churches for?"

The island was quite small. According to the woman who had arranged for the boat charter to begin with, it measured five miles long and two miles wide. But that was enough for a much larger population, and from the look of the village, once upon a time things had been different on the Isle of Canna. The first few cottages they came to were dark and appeared deserted. One had its windows boarded. The roof of the other had collapsed at some point and never been repaired, and the winter had claimed it.

"Perhaps the ones who live here now are Newcomers. Either that, or they were left behind." Kitsune nudged a bit closer to Oliver, still walking arm in arm with him.

"You can feel it?" Blue Jay asked.

Kitsune nodded. "It is empty here. As though thriving life has been erased. Or vanished."

Oliver paused, breaking away from them, turning to face them. "Hold on. What are you saying? You mean nobody's here?"

"You misunderstand," Kitsune told him, her face nearly lost in the shadow of her hood. "There are people who live here, just as Captain Moncreiffe said. But once this was a real village. Now it is nearly a ghost town. You yourself asked about the churches. Where did those people go? There is a feeling about the place, a hollowness, that suggests it might not have been attrition. They might have been Lost. Slipped through the Veil."

Oliver shoved his hands into the pockets of his wool coat, shivering. "Like Roanoke."

"Something like that," Blue Jay replied, but his attention was not on them. He scanned the snowy sky, presumably for sign of Gong Gong or Frost.

Oliver did the same. He knew there was every reason why the two Borderkind who could not disguise themselves as human had to remain out of sight, but it troubled him just the same.

They continued into the village, passing a sort of park on the left that a sign identified as a Viking burial ground, but under the blanket of new-fallen snow they could see little evidence of the ancient graves. The island was thickly wooded and there were trees even in the midst of the village. Near a stand of towering oak and rowan, all of them stripped to bare branches by winter, a massive Celtic cross jutted from the ground like a cemetery headstone. There were chips out of the crossbar and the cross was ancient and weathered. Nothing around it indicated that it was a grave marker, or supplied any other origin, for that matter. It was simply old, a memory of another age standing in the midst of this diminishing settlement.

"Oliver," Kitsune said.

He looked up to see her pointing toward the cottage beyond that cross. The was light in several of the windows, he suspected from a generator. Even as he began to walk toward the cottage with Kitsune and Blue Jay, aware of what an odd trio the three of them would present to whoever lived there, he saw the dark figure of Gong Gong sweeping down out of the storm to alight on the snowy ledge of the cottage's chimney. It set him somewhat at ease.

"Frost," he whispered to the falling snow around him. "Are you here?"

The only response was the crunch of snow under his boots.

"He's here," Blue Jay assured him. "I told you, he's just distracted. Let's just find your professor. The boat isn't going to wait forever."

Oliver nodded and took one last glance up at Gong Gong before striding up to the cottage and rapping heavily on the door. As he waited with his companions he brushed snow from his hair and shook it from his coat.

He didn't have to knock a second time. With a rattling of the handle, the door was hauled open by a sixtyish woman who might once have been beautiful. There was a hardness about her features now, but Oliver thought that had not always been the case. When she smiled at the sight of them, he was startled. He'd been prepared to quickly explain their presence, but she did not seem alarmed by the arrival of three strangers upon her doorstep in the middle of a December storm, despite the remoteness of the island.

"Not the best weather to be out on the water, I'd say."

Oliver could not help being charmed by her. "You'd be right, ma'am. And our time is short because the storm's supposed to get worse. Captain Moncreiffe wants to get back to the mainland by lunch, and—"

"Ach, well, that'd be Barclay, all right. Though I'd guess he's more worried about missing lunch than he is about any storm," the woman said. "Right. Well, what can I do for ya, then? Didn't come all this way to look at Viking graves or for some monastic retreat like the fellas were out here in September."

Kitsune drew back her hood. The old woman blinked and stared closely at her, perhaps drawn by those jade eyes. Or perhaps there was something else she recognized in the face of the fox-woman, for she studied Blue Jay more closely and a grim intelligence lit her expression.

"We're looking for a man named David Koenig. A professor. We're told he lives on the island. I wonder if you could point us in the right direction?" Oliver asked.

The woman nodded thoughtfully, turning her gaze back to Blue Jay. "Mischief in your eyes, son."

"And in yours, mother."

Most women would have been taken aback at the reply, unless they were somehow aware that in some Native American cultures it was a sign of respect to call older women *mother*. Yet this odd, formidable woman only nodded as though his response was confirmation of some profound suspicion.

"Just beyond the Presbyterian church, along that way, behind the bigger building with the fancy porch—used to be a market once, long time ago—there's a rock wall runs along a path. Won't be able to see the path in this weather, of course, but if you follow the wall it'll take you to a pretty little gate. In warmer weather, the professor keeps a fine garden. 'Tis his gate, you see. The cottage on t'other side belongs to him."

Oliver didn't ask if they might find the professor home. Where else would the man go? They thanked her and started off, and Oliver noticed that she kept watching them until they lost sight of the cottage in the storm. He wondered if she kept on gazing after them even after the snow had obscured her view.

They wouldn't have been able to tell the difference between the Presbyterian church and the other two—whatever denominations they had once been home to—except that the former market with the "fancy porch" was unmistakable. Other than the churches and what had clearly once been a pub or inn of some sort but was now as hollow as so many of the island's structures, it was the only building of any size. The rock wall was the sort that had been built to mark land boundaries in another age. Snow had built up on top, but it was not nearly deep enough to hide masonry. They followed along beside it on what they presumed was the path the old woman had mentioned, and at the end they did indeed find the gate, a delicate white-picket thing that seemed absurdly out of place in such inhospitable terrain.

Oliver suspected that in the summer, with the flowers in his garden in full bloom, Professor Koenig's gate and the fence that ran along the perimeter of his property would have seemed far more appropriate, even quaint.

He paused in front of the gate.

"What are you waiting for?" Blue Jay asked, and when Oliver looked at him the trickster's laughing eyes were dark with uncharacteristic impatience.

Kitsune seemed to understand his reluctance, however. She pushed the gate open and turned toward him. "At least you will have an answer. Even if it is not the answer you hope for."

He nodded and followed her, the three of them passing through the gate. At the door, both of the Borderkind looked at him expectantly. There came a hissing from the air above him and Oliver looked up to see Gong Gong gliding to the ground, body slipping serpentine upon the winds. The dragon seemed thinner as it flew, but upon landing it appeared quite the same as when he had first seen it. The snow was not avoiding him as it had earlier, but the lightning sparks in Gong Gong's eyes gave off enough heat that as the flakes touched his face, they melted.

"Aren't you going to knock?" the dragon asked.

Oliver stared at him. "Where's Frost?"

The dragon spread his wings and shook them before curling them against his body once more. His tufts of hair and beard were wild from the storm and his expression pulled back now into a kind of snarl.

"Look around, you fool. He's everywhere."

Oliver took a long breath and knocked on the door. It had been Frost who had drawn him into this. Much as he admired and respected Kitsune, Oliver had seen that Frost carried a greater weight of authority when speaking to other Borderkind. Not that Koenig was one of them. He was just a man. But even Kitsune deferred to Frost, and it would have been better to have him there.

The knock was muffled by the falling snow. Seconds went by without any response from within, though there was the dim glow of a lamp in the window farthest to the right. Despite that it was still morning—no later than ten o'clock—the day was so dark with storm that a light inside was no surprise.

"Oliver," Kitsune urged.

He nodded and knocked again, but lightly.

"Fuck this," Gong Gong snorted, and he stepped forward and began to kick at the bottom of the door so fiercely that it shook in its frame.

Blue Jay had to step in front of him and nudge him away with one shoe. "Enough of that. You'll terrify the man. He'll never open his—"

The door swung open.

But it was not Professor David Koenig who stood there, holding the door wide to admit them. It was Jenny Greenteeth.

"Hello there!" Jenny said happily. "Don't just stand

there in the snow. Come in. There's cocoa on, and whiskey for those that will have it despite the hour. If you behave, there are some ladyfingers in the cupboard as well."

Beyond her was a tall man with a lanky frame, his pants too high on his waist, wisps of white hair on his head and bifocals propped on the end of his nose that made it seem as though he was scrutinizing everything. And perhaps he was.

Kitsune laughed. It seemed the most beautiful sound Oliver had ever heard. "Jenny," she said happily, and she stepped over the threshold and into the arms of the girl with the matted, filthy, river-bottom hair and the pale green flesh.

"Come here, Kit. Glad to see you in one piece," Jenny said.

They all went through the door. Oliver was last, allowing the Borderkind to savor their reunion.

"Her?" Gong Gong snapped. "What about you? I saw the Kirata take you down with my own eyes. You were dead, pond scum."

When he poked Jenny with a sharp talon, it was obvious he was taller than before, at least half again as high, and there were coils in his body like those of a snake. Oliver was unnerved by this change, and by the way the tip of his tail seemed to track in the air like the stinger on a scorpion, as though it might strike.

Jenny laughed at him. "You give me the sweetest nicknames, love."

Kitsune broke their embrace. "Truly, my friend. We thought you dead."

"How did you manage—" Blue Jay began.

"Better than them have tried," Jenny Greenteeth said. And there was something insidious about the cast of her face then, and the set of her jaw. "You keep hearing premature reports of me cashing it in, but it's wishful thinking. I've a pretty face, don't I? It makes them forget how dangerous my sort can be. Took me hours to wash the blood of those soddin' arrogant kittens off."

They went on like that for a while, but Oliver was no longer listening. He was pleased Jenny was safe and that she'd made her way to Canna Island. The Mazikeen had discovered the professor's location before the Hunters had attacked, so there was no mystery as to how she'd beaten them here. She'd known where to look, and didn't have to worry about bringing a human along for the trip.

But now the journey was over. Oliver had reached his destination.

"You're Professor Koenig?" he asked, moving around the gathered Borderkind and into the cottage, where a fire burned in the hearth and the man stood with an unlit pipe clutched in the fingers of his left hand. "David Koenig?"

The professor nodded. "I am. Which would make you Mr. Bascombe. Jenny's told me of your odyssey, sir. I am sorry to hear of it."

Oliver's heart thundered in his chest. Until this very moment some part of him had not believed that Professor Koenig had ever existed, or that if he did they would find him still alive.

"Then . . . it's true?" he said with a slow nod. "The story about you is true?"

The old man smiled and turned to set his pipe on a rack above the fireplace. "If you mean the tale of my journey through the Veil, it is indeed. I confess I don't believe I am the only trespasser to escape execution. Merely the only one in recent memory . . . and certainly the only one still alive today."

Gong Gong was warming himself by the fire, snout nearly close enough to the flames that at any moment his beard might alight. Blue Jay and Kitsune were talking quietly but grimly with Jenny Greenteeth. Oliver was aware of all of them, and yet for a moment the rest of the world seemed to slip away and it was just Professor Koenig and himself.

He stepped nearer to the man, melting snow dripping from his coat and hair. "With so many Borderkind, I knew there had to have been others who've brought people across with them. But I don't understand. Why is it that every one of them has been executed except for you?"

"You must understand, Mr. Bascombe," the professor said. "It is a rarity for any of the Borderkind to break the law like this, and so ever more rare for the Intruder to be allowed to live. I believe before my good fortune it had been over a century since the last trespasser was spared. It's quite a story, really. I was a folklorist, you see, and working on a study of Eastern European legend."

As the old man rambled, Oliver cast his mind back to that night in the midst of the blizzard when Frost had slid through the window of his mother's parlor, wounded and hunted. The memory of that moment when they had careened off the bluff overlooking the ocean with the Falconer in pursuit was seared into his mind. The moment he had pierced the Veil for the first time. He thought of his father, murdered and defiled, of the Sandman, of Julianna, and especially of Collette, out there somewhere beyond Canna Island, beyond the Veil.

"I'm sorry, Professor," he said, sadly. "Really. I'd give anything to be able to sit and have tea and hear the whole story. If I'm as fortunate as you've been, I swear I'll come back one day soon and we'll hear each other's stories, the good and the bad. But I'm in danger. We're all, all of us—" and he spread his arms to indicate the Borderkind "—in danger. My companions have shared the road with me, helped keep me alive, but they have other troubles to tend to. I owe it to them not to waste a moment."

A sad smile touched the old man's features. "I understand. It's only that it has been so very long since there was anyone I could speak with about all of this. It isn't easy to have your wildest dreams come true, and not be able to share that truth with anyone."

Oliver glanced at the others, who had interrupted their conversation to listen to the two men converse. Kitsune smiled at him, but Blue Jay seemed troubled, a dangerous glint in his eye. Oliver forced himself to ignore it. He was going as fast as he could, after all. What more did the trickster want?

"Trust me. I can imagine," he said, ignoring Blue Jay. "I always believed in magic, but I always wanted . . . I don't know what."

"Proof," Gong Gong growled. "It's what they all want, humans. Proof."

Kitsune stepped nearer the professor and the old man's eyes lit up as he regarded her, though whether it was due to her beauty or the almost tangible feeling of magic that surrounded her, he could not be certain.

"Professor . . . David," she said, "we really cannot stay. Death pursues us all. An execution order has been sworn out on Oliver. Please, sir, you must tell him how it is that you were granted clemency, and the order for your own execution lifted."

The cottage had grown warm with the cluster of bodies inside and the blaze in the hearth, the fire crackling and dancing. Blue Jay moved beside Gong Gong and Jenny between Kitsune and the professor, so that they formed a kind of circle. The center of attention, David Koenig smiled sheepishly.

"I wish there was a better story, or some trick to it. But truly, I wasn't that clever. I simply asked."

Oliver gaped at him. "I don't understand."

The professor shrugged, almost apologetic. "Oh, to be sure, it was no mean feat staying alive long enough to make my appeal to the kings. But I managed. I put myself at their mercy and pleaded for one year to prove myself worthy of their confidence. They granted me that year, and I made the best of it, working with the advisors to both kingdoms, letting them get to know me."

He gestured to a sword that had been mounted above the fireplace. At first glance it had looked decorative, but now Oliver saw that the grip was worn and the scabbard scraped and dented.

"Hunyadi, King of Euphrasia, gave me the very sword he had used as a young commander, as a gesture of good faith, you understand."

Oliver stared at the sword and then at Professor Koenig, and all of the hope that had been flickering in his heart was nearly extinguished. Koenig was spared because of who he was, and what he had proven to be. But what was Oliver? A lawyer, a young man who had not only not fulfilled the dreams he'd had as a boy, but never truly reached for them. How could he expect to convince the men who sat on the thrones of the Two Kingdoms to spare his life?

"Oliver?" Kitsune said, studying him with obvious concern.

He smiled softly and thanked the old man.

"We have a boat waiting to take us back to the mainland, Professor," Blue Jay said. "We ought to start back."

"Of course, of course," Koenig said, but the melancholy in his eyes was haunting. He looked down at Gong Gong. "I would have liked to have heard more about the troubles you are all facing. If I could be of any help, you would only have to tell me. The Borderkind have been my only contact through the Veil for decades."

"Maybe we'll come back, old man," the dragon said, eyes narrowing to slits, sparks jumping from them in the shadows cast by the fire.

The professor looked at Kitsune and Blue Jay and then at Jenny. There was kindness and gratitude in his eyes as he began to speak.

The door blew open, the power of the storm tearing the dead bolt from the wood. It crashed against the wall and the snow howled in, a tumult of icy wind and blinding whiteness that seemed to suck much of the light from within the cottage, dimming the gas lamp and withering the flames in the hearth.

Frost came through the doorway as though riding the wind, fingers elongated into twelve-inch knives of ice, features lengthened and thinned as though parts of him had been carved away. Trailers of mist plumed from his eyes. He stopped, crouched as though he meant to lunge, and then thrust out one hand, twisting the storm winds so that they tugged on the door and then blew it shut, cracking the wooden frame.

"What in the name of God?" the professor cried.

The winter man spun, madness in his eyes. "The Hunters have come! How they tracked us I do not know, but they are here!"

Dark shapes moved past the windows out in the storm.

Jenny Greenteeth laughed softly. "Well, no need for the bait anymore."

She thrust out a hand, wrapped long fingers around Professor Koenig's throat, and twisted. The crack of bone echoed off the stones of the hearth and Jenny let the old man crumple to the wood floor, a scarecrow off his post. His arms sprawled out across the dusting of powder Frost's arrival had spread over the floor, a grotesque snow angel.

CHAPTER 19

Oliver shouted, refusing to accept what he'd seen. He started for Jenny, but a powerful hand clamped on his shoulder and he smelled sulfur. Spinning, he let out another shout. The Black Dragon of Storms had grown, his lithe body now at least eight feet in height, massive snout drooping, long wisps of gray beard draping his chest. The lightning that sparked in his eyes brought thunder from somewhere deep inside of him.

In that moment, Oliver thought he was dead, that Gong Gong had also betrayed them.

"Unarmed, foolish friend," the dragon snarled.

"Jen?" Kitsune said, her voice raw with pain. Her jade eyes seemed impossibly pale. "You are with them? The Hunters?"

"With them? I'm one of them, Kit. Bloody hell, listen to you! You were always a romantic. Life full of drama, right, love? Did you honestly think I'd been hunted so many times . . . that the soddin' Manticore came after me . . . and I survived? You stupid twat. No one's that lucky."

Oliver saw the way her words cut Kitsune, and he winced.

Blue Jay did more than wince. He twisted round with such speed that he was nearly impossible to follow. There was a ripple in the room as though he swung something at Jenny that sliced the air, a blue-tinted wing that whipped toward her. It might have been real and physical. He was a shape-shifter. But Oliver thought perhaps it was a spell. Magic. The power of the trickster. Blue Jay spun and whatever that blue wing was, it knocked Jenny to the floor, splitting the green flesh on her arm where she'd been struck and snapping bones.

Kitsune was there beside her before Jenny Greenteeth could blink or cry out in pain. The fox-woman was only fox now, but in some animal growl she spoke, and Oliver thought he could make out a single word.

"Bitch."

The fox tore out Jenny's throat, and algae-green blood pumped onto the floor.

As the fox began to whine with sorrow, glass shattered and a Kirata came crashing through a window. Two more followed, and chaos erupted. The tiger-men had eyes that glowed bright orange and thick stringers of drool ran from their black lips as they opened their jaws wide in a roar. One dropped to all fours and leaped at Gong Gong. Blue Jay transformed into a bird and darted at its face, even as Frost stepped into the path of the second Kirata.

The third Hunter was a blur of orange and black, fur

rippling with muscle as it careened across the cottage at Oliver. From the pool of blood around Jenny Greenteeth's corpse, Kitsune lunged, but only caught it with one paw, barely scratching the beast.

Oliver's hands were empty and there was no time to find a weapon. He was paralyzed by the numbing certainty of his own impending death, could practically feel its claws in him, tearing at his chest and abdomen, digging in for tender organs.

Frost shouted his name.

The Kirata bounded at him and instinct took over. Oliver took one step backward, throwing up his hands, fists closing on the tiger-man's wrists, fingers digging into fur and flesh. The Hunter's momentum drove him down and Oliver went with it, the damp stink of its breath a miasma in his face. He shot one boot up into its midsection and then used every bit of his strength to propel the Kirata over his head, toward the fireplace.

The tiger-man's head struck the stone hearth and for a moment—as he twisted round and scrambled to his feet—Oliver was sure he had messed up his one chance at survival. In the instant that he'd gotten a grip on the Hunter, he'd been aware of the fire as his target, as his one hope. But the trajectory had been off. The Kirata's head had struck the hearth a foot to the left of the fireplace.

Close was enough, however. It collapsed to the ground, back turned toward the blaze, and its fur caught. The Kirata's eyes went wide and it roared in agony as the fire raced over the surface of its body, fur burning quickly, blackening to char. Aflame, the tiger-man staggered toward Oliver, but then its panicked gaze darted toward the window and the snow outside and it stumbled in that direction. As it passed a love seat, the fabric of the furniture caught fire. The Kirata reached out to steady itself and clutched a heavy floral drape, which went up in flames even faster than the Hunter's fur. It fell to the ground, twitching and mewling. Dying.

The cottage began to burn.

"Frost!" Oliver shouted, thinking the winter man would bring ice to extinguish the blaze.

But when he turned he saw that more Kirata were coming in. Blue Jay, Frost, and Kitsune were fighting them. The trickster was a man again, or something nearly like a man, for he danced with such speed that he was once more a blur, a fan of blue wings battering one of the Hunters.

Oliver needed to help them—or at least to defend himself—and he remembered the sword above the fireplace. The sword of Euphrasia's king. He ran to the hearth and reached up, snatching blade and scabbard down from their mountings.

Thunder shook the floor and rattled the walls. Oliver looked over to see that Gong Gong had continued to grow. The Black Dragon of Storms was enormous now, at least a dozen feet long and curled in upon himself. He had one taloned hand upon a Kirata, pinning the creature to the floor, and lightning struck from his eyes, incinerating the Hunter. At the same moment, a second tiger-man leaped upon his back, claws raking the dragon's hide.

"Enough!" Gong Gong cried. "We need space! Air!"

The massive serpentine beast raced at the door, the Kirata trying to hold on, claws tearing dragon flesh. Gong Gong did not stop at the door but barged through it, shattering wood. As he passed through he swung his torso to the left and scraped the Kirata off his back. The Hunter fell to the floor, broken and bleeding but still alive, still ferocious. Snow blew in and swirled around its head.

The Black Dragon of Storms disappeared out into the storm. Oliver was about to attack the fallen Kirata, to follow Gong Gong outside, when a figure appeared, framed in the silhouette of the broken door. A massive broadshouldered being with the head and wings of a bird, wielding a sword no man could have lifted.

The Falconer.

A shudder of fear went through Oliver. The Kirata terrified him, but this was different. The sight of the Falconer filled him with primal dread, born of the simple fact that the Hunter had nearly slain Frost once before. It had snowed that night as well.

"Frossst!" the Falconer cried.

Oliver thought that the winter man feared the Falconer. He had seen it in Frost's eyes. But he had also been wounded then, and it had been before the conspiracy had begun to be revealed and before Yuki-Onna's murder. When Frost heard his name he turned from the Kirata he and Blue Jay had been facing, and he saw who it was that had called to him.

There was no fear in the winter man's eyes this time. Only hatred.

Frost raced for the door.

The Falconer let out a piercing bird's cry and stepped back outside, making room for the battle that was about to begin.

Oliver raised the king's sword in his right hand, clutched the scabbard in his left, and ran to help Blue Jay and Kitsune against the Kirata that remained in the house, even as the fire spread.

"This place is burning down!" he shouted. "We've got to get outside!"

Kitsune responded not at all. She was the fox now,

quicker than the Kirata, slashing at their most vulnerable places, throats and groins and the tendons in their legs.

Blue Jay smiled at Oliver with his mad, dancing eyes. "Working on it."

The winter man could feel the storm. Not the way he could when he had created it. No, this was nature, the churning weather of an entire world, the brutality of the skies. As Jack Frost, the harbinger of winter's first snow, he could trigger a storm, could even create one, but nothing lasting. Nothing of the weight of the storm that brewed above Canna Island. He could not drive away a blizzard, but he could ride it, could command its power in limited fashion.

The Falconer had caught him by surprise the last time. Not today.

Outside in the snow, along the path between the empty church and the abandoned market, Kirata surrounded the house, nearly a dozen of them in addition to those that had already made their way inside. A black shadow moved through the storm, sweeping from the sky, and talons dropped down to tear one of the tiger-men in two, head, shoulders, and arms separated from the lower torso, blood spraying the snow, steaming a crimson stain into the white. Gong Gong was in the midst of the storm and he was home. Lightning lashed down from above, melting snow and blackening the ground beneath. One of the Kirata raced into the cover of the market's porch.

The tigers would wait. Frost had other prey in mind. He glanced around, searching the sky, and when he saw a shadow moving through the snow he thought at first it was Gong Gong again. But this was smaller than the dragon, and he knew it was his Hunter, his would-be killer.

The Falconer's sword erupted with fire, a beacon in the snow-obscured sky. One of the Kirata growled and raced toward Frost even as the Falconer swept down toward him, crying in that ear-shredding bird voice. The Kirata lunged, claws slashing the air.

Frost slipped into the storm, his body falling away to nothing, to snow, whipping along on the wind. But now he focused, and he felt the storm all around him, and he did what he was created to do . . . he commanded the storm. Images of Yuki-Onna filled his mind, times they had danced in just this way, merging themselves together in the heart of a blizzard.

Hatred burned in his frozen heart.

The Falconer was riding the wind. Frost stole it away from him, used it against him. With the snow and ice and wind that was all a part of him, he clutched the Falconer in his grip, the grip of the storm, and spun him around. His icy wind stole the Hunter's breath, suffocating him. Hail stabbed the Falconer's eyes and the storm beat at him so that his wings would not hold him aloft. He could not wait to pierce the Hunter's thick hide with his fingers and freeze the very blood in his veins.

But first there would be pain.

Frost was all around him, encompassing him, and as the Falconer struggled, the winter man summoned all of the power of the storm and pushed the Hunter toward the ground.

The Falconer shrieked as he struck the frozen earth, impact only slightly lessened by the accumulated snow. Where he lay, his flaming sword made the snow hiss and pop and little rivulets of ice water streamed away from it.

The Falconer began to rise.

With the innate ease that was his, Frost collected himself,

drawing together the moisture in the air to sculpt his body once again out of ice and snow. As the Falconer stood, he staggered slightly, and one of his wings looked bent, perhaps broken.

The winter man smiled. "You are stealthy, Hunter. You wounded me before. But that triumph has made you arrogant. You will not catch me off my guard again. Not when I can remember that ensorcelled blade cutting in to the essence of me."

The Falconer only screamed in that shrill voice and spread his wings, but he did not take flight. He stalked across the snow, raising that burning blade. A pair of Kirata came up behind the Falconer, fanning out to either side, all three of them stalking Frost.

Lightning seared the ground, blew apart the rock wall that lined the path to Koenig's cottage, and one of the Kirata fell dead. The other searched the sky warily and backed away. The Falconer cried again, sword aloft and crackling with falling snowflakes, then ran at Frost.

The winter man fell to his knees, thrust his fingers into the snow, and raised his hate-filled gaze to stare at his enemy. He shuddered with exertion, with the flow of winter and nature that coursed through him, and then he *pushed.* Icicle spikes thrust upward from the ground, razor-tipped and hard as rock, impaling the Falconer through the right leg, the left side, the chest, and both wings.

With one final cry, the Falconer went limp, sword falling into the snow, its flame winking out, ice freezing over it. Blood began to stream down the icy stalagmites that had pierced his flesh, lifting him off the ground. But he still twitched; his beak still opened and closed, attempting to wail out his pain. His eyes were still alight with malevolence.

Frost glanced round once to see that there were no Kirata nearby. The house was burning entirely now and his companions were emerging, in the midst of battle with the tiger-men. For the moment it was just the winter man and the Falconer.

"I was careful not to do very much damage to your vital organs," Frost said, tilting his head to study the twitches of the dying Hunter. "It will take you hours to expire this way. With your constitution, even blood loss will not kill you for some time. And it will be agony. Now that I've pierced your flesh, I can save you that agony, just freeze your blood and kill you instantly. But you must tell me who it is that sent you. Who has set the Hunters after the Borderkind?"

All that issued from the Falconer's beak was a weak cry.

The winter man elongated the ice daggers that were the fingers of his left hand and he tore at one of the Hunter's wings. The fury in the Falconer's eyes was soul-deep, but it was meaningless. He was beaten. Dying.

"I know you can speak if you wish to. Speak now. A name. And I will take the ice away."

The hatred in the Hunter's eyes only deepened, its chest rising and falling in hitching gasps, fresh blood streaming down the ice spikes with each breath. But there was more than hate in the Falconer's eyes. They glistened with agony.

"Ty'Lis," it hissed.

Frost frowned so deeply that the ice of his face cracked. "The Atlantean? Impossible."

The Falconer uttered another sound that was almost laughter.

With a sneer, the winter man touched the bloody point of one of the ice spikes, his influence traveling down into the snow below, and another stalagmite thrust upward from the ground, the thinnest and sharpest of all. An enormous needle of ice, it punched through the Falconer's abdomen and pushed all the way up through his heart, at last emerging with a crack of bone through the back of his head.

Ice formed over the Falconer's eyes and even the blood the Hunter had already shed froze solid.

The laughter ended.

But Frost still heard its echo.

Oliver coughed, eyes watering, his skin tight across his face from the searing heat of the burning cottage. He followed Kitsune out the ruined door, Blue Jay close behind, leaving the corpse of David Koenig to burn. The screams of a dying Kirata came from the conflagration that had been the old professor's living room, but two others were following Blue Jay's exodus, and still more were gathered outside the cottage as they emerged.

The fox darted ahead and leaped at the nearest of the tigers, but Kitsune had also breathed in that smoke and she was slowed by it. The Kirata caught her and threw her to the ground. Oliver held his breath an instant until he saw her roll and spring to her feet, and then Kitsune was not just rising, she was changing. In an eyeblink the fox grew into a woman, her fur becoming a copper-red cloak blowing in the snowstorm, billowing behind her. Her jade eyes flashed and she curled her fingers into claws as she leaped at the Kirata's back, digging furrows in its fur, drawing blood.

Snow whipped into Oliver's eyes but he saw the tiger-man raise a massive hand to snatch at Kitsune, to tear her off its back.

Both hands on the grip, Oliver swung the king's blade and it struck flesh like a hatchet into wood, cleaving muscle and bone. The Kirata roared and staggered away, tripping over its own severed arm, blood fountaining from the stump. The hot blood sprayed through the falling snow.

Kitsune dropped to the ground, fur spattered with blood Oliver hoped was not hers.

"Are you all right?" he asked.

Her head hung, hidden beneath her hood, and her body shook as she caught her breath. When she glanced up at him, the ferocity in her eyes chilled him.

A cry of pain tore through the storm from the direction of the burning cottage. Kitsune's eyes narrowed.

"Blue Jay," she said.

Oliver spun, sword in hand, the copper tang of blood in the air, and saw the trickster under assault by the Kirata. Blue Jay swung his right arm, attempting to begin that strange dance that would create the blurry, ephemeral wings that he used in combat. Claws raked his back and he cried out again, staggered. Blood ran and blue feathers appeared as though from nowhere and drifted to the snow as the Kirata moved in.

They had him. Tiger-men grappled with him from either side, each taking an arm, and a third took up a fistful of his black hair. It opened its jaws with a satisfied snarl, fangs glistening, black lips curling back, and drew his head forward, about to snap its jaws down and bite the top of Blue Jay's head off.

Kitsune dropped to the ground, fur cloak rustling and diminishing, and then she was racing through the storm. Oliver ran toward the Kirata, blade raised high, but ice had formed inside him that made him feel as though he himself was the winter man. There was no way to reach Blue Jay in time.

A great shadow passed overhead and a gust of wind buffeted the burning cottage, fanning the flames higher. The blaze roared, joined by the hollow slap of wings upon the air. Thunder rumbled and lightning lanced from the sky, incinerating the Kirata whose jaws were about to close upon Blue Jay. It fell to the ground, body charred and crisp.

The Black Dragon of Storms snaked down from the gray heart of the squall and alighted upon the snow. Gong Gong had reached a height of twenty feet or more, oil-black body weaving and ready to strike. With one hand he grabbed a Kirata and thrust it alive into the flaming ruin of Professor Koenig's cottage. Then, wings pinned back, his upper body shot forward like a striking snake, and his jaws closed on the head of a tiger, tearing off the Kirata's head, the same fate his kin had planned for Blue Jay.

One final Kirata remained. The fear in its expression was almost pitiable and then it turned to flee. Gong Gong slapped a massive hand down and pinned it to the ground.

Oliver lowered his sword and came to a halt, staring at the dragon, an atavistic terror running through him. Gong Gong's body whip-cracked the air and thunder rolled and he found himself more terrified of the dragon than any of his enemies. So consumed was he with the sight of the Borderkind revealed in his true, monstrous form that he barely noticed Kitsune going to Blue Jay's aid.

Gong Gong toyed with the last of the Kirata like a cat with a trapped rodent. Fascinated and horrified, Oliver could only stare.

Then, out of the corner of his eye, something moved. How long the figure had been standing there—so very still—just beside the burning cottage, he had no idea. The heat from the conflagration must have been searing, the smoke stinging the eyes, sparks flying, but the figure had clearly been there for a time, very still. Somehow, this Hunter had the ability to remain unseen if he wished.

But Oliver saw him now, and knew him at once, for he had seen the ram-headed creature once before in the streets of the village outside Perinthia. Marra wore a robe the color of stone. His horns were as black as Gong Gong's flesh.

He held a longbow, an arrow already nocked, and as he stepped forward he drew back the string. The point of the arrow glistened wetly and seemed to glow with a sickly green luminescence.

"I have been waiting for you to hold still a moment," Marra said.

And loosed the arrow.

At the sound of Marra's voice, the Black Dragon of Storms turned to look and the arrow plunged into his right eye. A spray of blood and yellow fluid came from the socket. Gong Gong reared back, wings fluttering, long body twisting, and then he collapsed, without a single sound, into the snow. There was no thunder. No lightning. The Black Dragon of Storms did not so much as twitch. Gong Gong had proven himself not only loyal but perhaps the strongest amongst them. And now he was dead.

He began to shrink, slowly at first but then more quickly, until he was little more than the dead husk of a thing no larger than a dog.

Blue Jay was up, racing toward Marra. "Bastard!" he screamed, arms out to either side in spite of his wounds, preparing to attack. Red fur glowed in the light of the fire as Kitsune dashed along beside him, the fox on the hunt.

Marra raised the bow and an arrow simply appeared, pointed at Blue Jay's heart.

Oliver raised the sword again and started to run. Perhaps thirty feet separated him from Marra. The Hunter paid no attention to him at all, did not even seem to notice him, and Oliver changed his course, curving out to his right in hopes that he could take the demonic creature by surprise.

Blue Jay began to spin, those almost ghostly wings appearing only as he sped up. Marra released the arrow and it whistled through the air. One of those barely visible wings blurred reality for a moment and the arrow snapped in half. But Marra was ready with another and loosed it so quickly that Blue Jay could not stop it. The arrow punched through the blurred air where one of those ephemeral spirit-wings was outlined, and Blue Jay roared in pain and spun away, the almost spectral wings disappearing as he went to his knees in the snow.

"The dragon poison on these might not kill you, *Myth*—but then, I won't need poison for the likes of you," Marra sneered.

Oliver trembled with fury and disgust. He knew the denigration that word signified on the other side of the Veil. He raised the sword as he ran, but his footsteps in the snow were audible even over the roar of the fire.

Marra turned, brought the bow around to sight his next arrow at Oliver. His body was humanoid, but the horns and face of the ram gave him the appearance of some sort of devil. And his eyes were filled with joyful malice.

"A human?" Marra asked. And then he chuckled. "So fragile."

His fingers tensed on the bowstring.

The fox leaped up from the snow, transforming in midair. Kitsune grabbed Marra by the horns and twisted. The Hunter cried out and the arrow flew wild.

Oliver plunged the sword into Marra's chest, felt it grind against bone, and as the ram-headed Hunter spasmed and struggled to bring his head around to stare in astonishment and pain, Oliver put all of his weight behind it and drove the blade in farther, then clutched the grip tightly in both hands and pulled upward, tearing flesh and cutting viscera.

Kitsune stared at him in surprise as Marra's corpse slid off the sword. Oliver looked up, shaken, and then he backed away from the dead thing. The fire popped and blazed a dozen feet away. Gong Gong's tiny corpse lay in the snow in the midst of a large depression in the shape of a magnificent creature: the Black Dragon of Storms.

Blue Jay struggled to his feet. He clutched his side, face etched with pain. The Kirata had clawed him and he bled, but the wound causing him the most pain was invisible. Whatever damage Marra's arrow had done had been spiritual, yet it had hurt Blue Jay more deeply than the claws of the tigers.

"Are you all right?" Oliver asked him, gaze still shifting around, searching for undiscovered enemies.

Blue Jay took a long breath through his nose, but then he nodded. "I will be." He glanced at the fox-woman. "Kitsune?"

Blood was matted on her fur cloak and speckled her hands and face, but she seemed unharmed. "Tired," she said. "And I feel . . ." Her expression twisted with sorrow. "I feel like something is broken in me. So many of us are dead. And to know that Jenny betrayed us . . . is difficult to bear."

Oliver ignored the blood. He dropped the sword and scabbard into the snow and took Kitsune in his arms, felt her trembling beneath the fur cloak. He held her against him and she lay her head on his shoulder, clinging there, snowflakes drifting down around them both.

Blue Jay met Oliver's gaze and nodded once, as though acknowledging him as a comrade for the first time.

"What now?" the trickster asked.

A gust of wind far colder than the storm whipped around them, and then the voice of the winter man whispered nearby.

"Now?" Frost said.

They all turned to see him kneeling by the charred remains of the dragon. Icicle hair swung as he tilted his head to regard them. Cold mist rose from those blue-white eyes. His sharp features were carved with hate.

"Oliver must find his sister. And he must beg a reprieve from the monarchs of the Two Kingdoms. We will see that he does not embark on his journey unprepared." The winter man stared at Oliver a moment, then looked at the other Borderkind. "But we have other duties now. I cannot be certain he is the one who conspires against us or if he serves some greater master, but I know now the name of the filth who set the Hunters after us.

"Whatever answers there are for any of us, whatever futures we may have, we can only find on the other side of the Veil. Until we have those answers, those resolutions, we are through with this world."

The others were silent.

Oliver held Kitsune in his arms and stared at the winter man, feeling the truth in his words. Whatever the future held for him, and for his sister, and for the woman he hoped to return to someday, he could only find it beyond the Veil.

He looked at Frost and nodded once, slowly. The winter man did the same, then turned and began walking away from the village, searching for a patch of land not owned by anyone, a public space where they might walk between the worlds, searching for vengeance and destiny.

Since the moment of his birth, Oliver Bascombe had been trying to prove himself worthy. Now, in a handful of days, his life had been irrevocably altered and it was not his father's regard or his self-esteem that hung in the balance, but his life.

He would be worthy, or he would die.

Julianna and Halliwell had flown to Edinburgh and
driven straight through to Mallaig. Only the cooperation of local law enforcement and her access to discre-
tionary funds from Bascombe & Cox enabled them to get a
boat out in the Hebridean Sea during the snowstorm. The
price was ridiculous—two thousand British pounds to get
a scruffy, dough-faced bartender to set aside his apron for
the day and venture out into a storm when his girlfriend
thought he was insane to even consider running the boat
out to Canna Island in the snow.

But two thousand pounds silenced the girlfriend and
the part-time bartender/part-time fisherman's nerves.

Now Julianna sat inside the cabin, exhausted, her tem-
perament as brittle as ice. She had not slept well since Oliver's

disappearance and his father's murder. Her thoughts were nearly always of her fiancé and of Collette, who had always been a friend. Sometimes they had been thoughts of rage, other times of sorrow, self-pity, or fear. Sleep had been difficult to come by. And the past twenty-four hours had allowed her only a few brief naps on an uncomfortable plane ride. She had tried to nod off in the car, but had kept bobbing her head, sleep evasive, feeling sick to her stomach she was so tired.

Halliwell had taken time to warm up to her. Julianna could not blame him. The feeling was mutual. In truth, they were awkward companions, not at all comfortable with each other. They did, however, talk quite a bit about the murders and disappearances and Halliwell had clearly been surprised to discover that she was not the society girl he had first taken her for. Julianna was glad, not because she felt she had something to prove—fuck that, she had earned her degree and her reputation as an investigator for the firm—but because it made the job easier if Halliwell respected her.

His drawing of connections between the child murders scattered around the world and the killing of Max Bascombe disturbed her deeply. So much so that she did not want to discuss it with him after their initial conversation. What was the point? Until they learned something new, it was a puzzle they could not complete.

But she had begun to understand Halliwell's obsession with Oliver and the unknown associates he had been seen with in Cottingsley and in London . . . and back in Mallaig.

Buried in a thick winter jacket, she felt nevertheless as though she might freeze to death. Exhaustion and the cold of the storm and the ocean were wearing her down. But soon they would have reached their goal, and the thought warmed her. They were coming up on Canna Island now, so Halliwell had left the cabin of the fishing boat and gone out on the deck, trying to see through the snow. It was shortly after noon, local time, but the sun was nowhere in sight. The sky was nothing but gray storm clouds, an eternal winter twilight.

"Now, you promised we wouldn't be out here for long, miss. I won't forget that promise. Every minute I'm away, my Moira will worry."

Julianna smiled wearily. "You're fortunate to have someone to worry for you."

When he smiled, the otherwise plain, unkempt-looking man was almost handsome. Julianna hoped that he used the extra money to make his life with Moira just a little better.

Halliwell came back to the cabin, snow covering his shoulders and hair. His lips were drawn back and his teeth chattered with the cold. "I see the boat up ahead. But it's pulling away from the dock."

Julianna got up from the bench where she'd been sitting. She peered out through the windshield of the cabin but could barely make anything out through the snow. She shot a panicked look at Halliwell.

"We've got to beat them back there," she said.

The detective ran a hand over the gray stubble on his chin, bracing himself against the door of the cabin. He pointed to the radio. "Mr. Strachan, could you radio Mr. Moncreiffe, please?"

The bartender/fisherman, Strachan, nodded and picked up the handset. Before they'd set out, he had contacted Moncreiffe by radio and through the static caused by the storm had confirmed that the charter boat had carried Oliver and two companions out to Canna Island and that

Moncreiffe was awaiting their return. They'd asked the man to delay, to hold off on returning to the mainland until they reached the island.

"Barc, it's Keith Strachan again, do you read me?"

There was static on the radio and for a long moment Julianna held her breath, wondering what was happening out there in the storm, what had brought Oliver to this island. Then there was a break in the static.

"Hullo, Keith, I'm heading home," the captain of the other boat replied.

"What of your passengers, Barc?"

More static. A hiss, as though the storm itself were talking through the radio. Then Moncreiffe replied. "Told them I wanted to be back by noon. Stayed much longer than I agreed to and the storm is getting worse by the minute. They can spend the night with one of the island folks and I'll run out to get them in the morning."

Strachan gave Halliwell an expectant look, and the detective nodded.

"Thank you, Barc. Safe journey."

"And you, Keith. I'll save you a spot at the pub, shall I?"

Strachan replied but all they heard afterward was static. The other boat passed them near enough to make out in the snow and then disappeared behind them.

Minutes later they were idling next to the dock, Halliwell and Strachan working together to tie the boat up. Julianna pulled her scarf tighter around her neck and tucked it into her jacket, then pulled her wool hat down over her ears as far as she could. Detective Halliwell seemed almost to have forgotten she was there, his eyes gazing into the snow toward the village that was supposed to be there.

"Do you smell smoke?" he asked.

Julianna nodded. She had noticed it a moment earlier. There was a fire in the village.

Halliwell looked down at her. His attitude toward her had gone from doubt to tacit acceptance, even respect. Now, for the first time, she saw concern in his eyes.

"If you're thinking of asking me to stay on the boat, forget it."

He grinned tiredly and nodded. "All right. We'll forget it." Then Halliwell stepped off onto the dock and reached back to help her across. Julianna didn't need the help, but appreciated the gallantry, and so she let him.

They turned toward Strachan.

"Two thousand pounds is a lot of money," Julianna told the scruffy man.

"I won't be leaving you here like Barclay Moncreiffe. You've my word."

Julianna thanked him and started up the dock with Halliwell. The wind blew, carrying the smell of smoke, which was stronger as they stepped onto the Isle of Canna. Through the snow they could make out the steeples of churches a short distance away and they began to trek toward the village in what Julianna guessed was half a foot or more of new-fallen snow.

They had gone less than a hundred yards when Halliwell took her arm and halted her. Julianna had ducked her head down to keep the snow from her eyes, but now she looked up.

Four figures moved toward them through the storm. One of them was a woman in a long fur cloak. Beside her was a man with feathers in his hair. Oliver was with them. And there was a man made entirely of ice. She would have thought him a statue if not for the fact that he was walking toward her, moving through the storm, leading the others. Leading Oliver.

Here he was, at last. Her love. But Julianna found herself afraid to call his name.

Then the man made of ice lifted a hand and the air beside him shimmered. The four of them walked into that shimmering air, and they disappeared.

Oliver had vanished again.

"No," Julianna heard herself say. "What just . . . where did they go?" Slowly she turned to Halliwell and she saw cold anger in his eyes.

"I don't know. But wherever it is, we're going to find a way to follow."

ABOUT THE AUTHOR

CHRISTOPHER GOLDEN is the award-winning, *Los Angeles Times* bestselling author of such novels as *Of Saints and Shadows, The Ferryman, Strangewood, The Gathering Dark,* and the Body of Evidence series of teen thrillers. Working with actress/writer/director Amber Benson, he cocreated and cowrote *Ghosts of Albion,* an animated supernatural drama for BBC online.

Golden has also written or cowritten several books and comic books related to the TV series *Buffy the Vampire Slayer* and *Angel,* as well as the scripts for two *Buffy the Vampire Slayer* video games. His recent comic book work includes the creator-owned *The Sisterhood* and DC Comics' *Doctor Fate: The Curse.*

As a pop-culture journalist, he was the editor of the Bram Stoker Award–winning book of criticism *CUT!: Horror Writers on Horror Film,* and coauthor of *The Stephen King Universe.*

Golden was born and raised in Massachusetts, where he still lives with his family. He graduated from Tufts University. There are more than eight million copies of his books in print. Please visit him at www.christophergolden .com.

And be sure not to miss
the further adventures of
Oliver and his friends in

THE BORDERKIND

**BOOK TWO OF
THE VEIL**

by

CHRISTOPHER GOLDEN

On sale spring 2007

Here's a special excerpt:

"Everything [Golden] writes glows with imagination." —Peter Straub

THE BORDERKIND

BRAM STOKER
AWARD WINNER
AND BESTSELLING
AUTHOR OF
THE MYTH HUNTERS

CHRISTOPHER GOLDEN

THE BORDERKIND

On sale spring 2007

CHAPTER 1

Fire engulfed the church, radiating such heat that the snow falling around it was vaporized instantly. Julianna Whitney stood a moment and stared at the structure, at the flames eating their way through the roof and licking fiery tongues from the shattered remnants of stained glass windows. Four inches of fresh snow had fallen since the storm began, but this close to the fire it was melting away. The dusting of flakes on her hair turned to beads of moisture as she turned to glance around the little island village.

The church was not the only building on fire. There was another large structure that might once have been an office or shop whose elegantly detailed front porch had now been burned black, embers glowing in the wood. A couple of small cottages were also ablaze.

A handful of people—no more than a dozen—had gathered in the center of the village to watch the conflagration. They hung back as though afraid the fire would engulf them. None of them so much as looked at Julianna, but she frowned as she studied them. She had seen dozens of small houses and cottages. Admittedly, some of them had looked abandoned, but could there really be so few people living on this island?

The gray sky hung low and heavy, and with the blanket of snow muffling all sounds, the whole island had a claustrophobic air. When the sound of cracking wood split the sky, Julianna jumped as though it had been a gunshot.

The roof of the church was buckling. Red embers sprayed into the sky.

A strong hand grabbed her arm and pulled her backward. She let herself be dragged a few steps away from the blazing edifice, then turned to glare at the man who'd taken hold of her. It was Halliwell, his sad eyes dark with confusion.

Julianna shook herself free. "Don't do that, okay?"

Halliwell gave her a look as cold as the storm. "You were too close."

Before she could respond there came another crack of wood and then a splintering noise, accompanied by the hiss of the fire. Julianna spun to see the church roof buckle and the steeple fall. It snapped in two, part of it crashing down inside the blazing ruin. The top of the steeple struck the ground only a few feet from where she had been standing, the fire sending up tendrils of steam as it hit the snow.

For a moment she could only stare at the ground, then she let out a shuddering breath and glanced at Halliwell. "Thank you."

The detective replied with an almost imperceptible shrug, then turned to survey the village, as though he were back in Maine and this was just another case for the sheriff's department. Halliwell was thus far doing an excellent job of pretending he was undisturbed by what they had seen as they arrived at Canna Island. They'd come halfway around the world in search of Oliver Bascombe. Upon their arrival, they had been rewarded with a brief glimpse of Oliver as he strode toward them—toward the dock—with the fires beginning to burn in the village behind him. But Oliver had not been alone. He had been accompanied by a man with blue feathers in his hair, an Asian woman wearing a copper-red fur cloak, and a man made entirely of ice.

She and Halliwell had not discussed that particular topic, but she was not prone to hallucination. She knew precisely what she had seen, and that man had not been a mirage.

Then the ice man had stretched out a hand and drawn a kind of oval; the air there had begun to shimmer, and Oliver and his companions had simply stepped out of this world, disappearing one after the other.

Halliwell spoke her name. The man was a curmudgeon by nature, gruff and distant. But somehow the events of the previous few minutes had created a connection between them that had not existed before. When he spoke to her now, Halliwell seemed almost gentle.

"Focus," he said.

Julianna did. "What happened here?"

The detective glanced at the islanders who had gathered. "No idea." He turned to face them. "My name is Ted Halliwell. I'm a police detective from the U.S. Anyone have any idea how these fires began?"

Blank faces stared back at him. Several people began to whisper to one another. Others started to walk away, eyes averted, as though the last thing they wanted was for Halliwell to talk to them.

Halliwell shook his head as he turned back to her. "Had a feeling that was going to be useless. I know from back home that islanders are xenophobic as hell. But this is different. I think they saw something, all right, but it isn't just that they don't want to talk to outsiders about it. They don't want to talk about it at all."

"Maybe they just want to forget." Julianna glanced at the people. Some of them were no more than gray shapes in the storm. More had begun to drift away, going back to their lives. She wondered if any of them had had their homes destroyed, and what they would do about it. No one was coming from the mainland in this storm.

Embers floated and danced with the falling snow.

"Let's keep looking," Halliwell said. He stared at Julianna, waiting for her reply. When she nodded, the detective started around the church, moving toward the large building whose beautifully carved porch was little more than charred kindling now.

"Wait!" a voice called.

A lone woman strode toward them even as the other islanders retreated into the storm. Her grim features were cast into even sharper angles by the firelight.

"Do you know what happened here?" Halliwell asked her.

The woman ignored him, focusing on Julianna. "You'd be looking for them what came before you. The young man and his friends—the fox girl and the others."

Julianna shivered and hugged herself, the thick coat suddenly not enough to protect her from the cold. Or perhaps this chill came from within.

"That's right," she said.

"Ma'am, could you tell us what you saw?" Halliwell urged. "It's not a difficult question."

But the woman only narrowed her eyes and gazed at Julianna. "They've gone. Came to see the professor, and this is what comes of it. Maybe that's the end, though. No more strangers on the island. Better for everyone if you just let us clean up the mess. Turn round and go back to the mainland. Those you seek have gone."

Halliwell sighed and gestured to indicate that since the woman was ignoring him, Julianna should ask the questions.

She narrowed her eyes and gazed at the woman. "What professor? Where is he?"

The woman scowled and pointed. "Continue on the way you're going if you must, but you won't like what you find."

Then she turned and strode away without a single backward glance. Julianna watched until she had left the main square, then turned to find Halliwell watching her expectantly. She took a breath and let it out slowly.

"Let's go," she said.

Halliwell nodded and together they continued on toward the building whose porch was now crumbling in flames. Bits of the ornate woodwork had burned away completely. Railings had fallen, withering in the fire. The flames glowed within the gutted structure, burning inside the windows like the eyes of some gigantic jack o' lantern.

The burning church was behind them, now, along with the two other houses of worship and a number of cottages. Julianna felt the chill of the storm, the snow whipping around her face as the wind picked up, but as they neared this other fire, its heat made her feel as though the skin on her face was stretched too tight.

"What is that?" Halliwell said, his voice barely audible over the hungry roar of the blaze.

Julianna picked up her pace. Her boots slid in the slushy melting snow. To the left of the burning building was an old rock wall that ran out of the village square, the stones piled up decades—perhaps centuries—earlier as some sort of boundary. It lined a path. In the firelight they could clearly see a cottage at the end of the path. The little house had been destroyed recently enough that there was only a dusting of snowfall on the shattered interior now exposed to the elements.

Fire had not been the culprit here. At first glance she thought an explosion had taken place, but then realized that much of the debris had caved inward rather than blowing outward.

Yet she spared only a moment's thought for the cottage.

It was the carnage that drew her attention. In the diffuse daylight that filtered through the storm and the bright glare of the fire, they could easily make out motionless figures scattered on the ground, shrouded in a thin layer of fresh snowfall. Dark stains spread out from the corpses, and already frost was beginning to form on the puddles of blood. There was something odd about the corpses, but Julianna could not focus on them long enough to determine what it was that unsettled her.

Because there was another corpse in their midst that made her breath catch in her throat. She could only stare at the creature—for she could not think of it as a man—impaled upon jagged stalagmites of ice that jutted from the ground. Thin, frozen blades punctured the creature's leg and side, shot up through its chest and belly and skull . . . and its wings.

Julianna could only stare. Though it had the shape of a man, its upper body and head were that of some giant bird of prey, and its wings were enormous, dark-feathered things.

"My God," Halliwell rasped beside her. "This can't be real. None of it."

He started forward and knelt by the nearest corpse, brushed away the snow to find orange and black fur beneath, and a snout full of deadly fangs. The dead man was not a man at all, but some kind of tiger that walked like a man.

"You mean like the ice man we saw with Oliver? And the way he and the others just disappeared, like they were stepping right out of the world?" Julianna asked, staring at him. After a moment she glanced at the tiger-man again, and then at the bird-thing impaled on the ice. "You said we'd follow wherever they went, Ted. You've got a whole lot of mysteries on your hands, not just Max Bascombe's murder and the little girl in Cottingsley, but the other children you think are connected to this killer who's removing their eyes. I'm having just as hard a time with this as you are, but you can't turn back now."

Halliwell's expression darkened. "Who said anything about turning back? I'm not going anywhere. I just . . . the world isn't supposed to be like this."

Julianna swallowed. Her throat was dry and tight and she didn't think it was from the fire's heat.

"Let's go inside," she said.

The detective nodded and they started for the ruined cottage. As she passed the dead things scattered around her she tried not to look too closely, but could not help herself. Some were missing limbs, at least one figure beneath that thin blanket of snow had no head, and one of the things on the ground had horns. There was even a creature that was no larger than a dog, with wings folded against its back.

Julianna hurried on.

She reached the front of the cottage. Where the door had been there was a hole, with no sign remaining of even the frame. For a long moment she studied the wreckage, trying to determine how she might safely enter. In the midst of the ruined home she saw snow-dusted legs poking out from beneath a portion of collapsed roof. Jagged, broken beams jutted out of the ruin, and Julianna thought that perhaps they had come as far as possible. Whatever they could learn about what happened to that cottage, they would have to determine from outside.

"Julianna," Halliwell said.

She turned to see him crouched a short way back along the path and off to the left. The snow there had been disturbed and as she walked over to join him, she saw that in addition to a small pool of frosted blood on the ground, there was a spattering that seemed more recent, even fresh.

Halliwell touched the spots of blood and lifted his fingers to show that they were smeared with red.

Since they had arrived on Canna Island she had been nearly numb. Wonder and confusion and horror had swirled in her mind, but this was the first time she had been afraid.

"One of those things . . ."

Halliwell nodded. He gestured to the ground and she saw that the path of broken snow—where one of those things had crawled or dragged itself on the ground—went around the side of the ruined cottage, past one of the walls that was still standing. Halliwell started to follow the trail.

"Wait. Ted, please. I don't think we should—"

He shot her a dark look. "What did you just tell me about finding answers?"

Julianna moistened her lips. Her pulse was pounding in her temples as she nodded. "All right."

Halliwell went around the corner of the house. Julianna followed warily, peering into the ruin of the house and looking carefully at the stone boundary wall to make certain there was nowhere for anyone to hide. But the trail continued, the broken snow sprinkled and streaked with fresh blood.

The wall went on perhaps fifty yards past the house, where it intersected with another at a tiny structure built of the same stone, with a roof of cracked and faded tiles. The little building might once have been an outhouse or some kind of storage— perhaps even a workshop—but its two small windows were cracked and covered with grime.

The heavy wooden door hung open. The trail ended there.

"Ted," Julianna whispered.

Halliwell did not even hesitate. He went to the door, tensed as though he might jump aside if an attack was forthcoming, and flung it open. The hinges creaked loudly. Inside there was nothing but dust and shadows.

"What the hell?" Halliwell muttered, and he stepped inside, glancing around to be sure there was nowhere for the wounded creature to hide.

Julianna watched him for a moment and then followed. As

she stepped into the little building, she peered into each corner and then up at the ceiling. There was a third window at the back, opposite the door, and Halliwell went over to it and examined the frame and the lock.

"Whatever came in here, it didn't get out this way," the detective said.

"But it didn't go out the door," Julianna said. "So where is it?"

Halliwell looked at her, frowning. Then he inclined his head and pointed past her, to the deep shadows hidden behind the open door. Julianna held her breath. If something was back there, she had been only inches from it a moment ago.

The detective came up beside her. The two of them stood a moment and just listened. If something was in here with them, wounded and enraged, surely they would hear it breathing. But there was no sound at all.

Halliwell swung the door closed. The latch clicked shut. If the storm had turned the afternoon dark and gray, inside that little stone house, behind those grime-smeared windows, it was like midnight. It was a mistake on Halliwell's part. If something had been in the corner, it could have killed them both in the seconds it took their eyes to adjust.

But the corner was empty.

Julianna breathed a sigh of relief. "Let's get out of here."

"Agreed."

She went to the door. It seemed to stick a moment, and then the latch gave and Julianna hauled it open, hinges creaking again.

Outside the door, the world had changed.

The storm was gone, and so was Canna Island. A blast of warm air rushed in to greet them. A light summer rain fell from a sky striped with low clouds, torn through with clear spaces where the blue sky showed behind that curtain.

Julianna could not breathe.

Shaking, she stepped out of the little stone hut. It stood now at the top of a long, sloping hill of rock, striated with colors like thousands of years of volcanic eruption. At the base of the hill, far below, a river rolled gently past. Some small brush and greenery grew on the banks of the river, but on the other side, once again, there was nothing but rock. She turned in a complete circle. Around her there were only mountains, though far to what ought to have been the south she saw the tops of trees in the river valley.

A short way along the rocky slope was the still, lifeless form of the tiger-man, who had escaped the carnage of Canna Island only to die here, alone on the craggy hillside.

"This . . . can't be," Halliwell rasped.

Julianna studied his face. Tentatively, she reached out a hand to touch him. The moment her fingers confirmed that he was real and solid, she felt foolish. Of course he was real. But in that moment, she had been uncertain of everything.

"Go back," she said. "Go back through."

Halliwell looked stricken, but he nodded and quickly reentered the stone hut. She followed him in. Even the warmth of the day and the gentle rain made her skin crawl, simply because they were wrong. Unnatural.

They exchanged a silent look. Trembling, Julianna reached out and closed the door, casting them once more in the grim gray darkness within those stone walls, behind those filthy windows. She expected to feel cold almost immediately, but the warmth remained.

A terrible weight settled upon her and Julianna bit her lip as she opened the door. Beyond it, nothing had changed. There was the barren hillside and the river below, the summer rain pattering the rocks. Whatever sort of door they had just traveled through, it only swung in one direction.

After a moment's hesitation, she stepped back out into the impossible world. Her heavy jacket was too warm and she unzipped it, then slid it off and dropped it on the ground beside the open door.

She wouldn't be needing it here.

Julianna turned and glanced at Halliwell. She was surprised to find not fear or confusion but determination etched upon his face.

He stepped out after her, treading heavily upon the rocky terrain.

"All right, then," Halliwell said. "Let's go."

"Go?" She knew they had no choice, but had no idea how to begin, which direction to take. "Where are we going?"

"The job hasn't changed. We're going to find Oliver. And we're going to find some goddamned answers."

Grim silence embraced Oliver and his companions as they made their way along the bank of the Sorrowful River. When they had crossed through the Veil from Canna Island they had emerged on a rocky slope not far from the water. Blue Jay had transformed himself into a bird and taken to the air to survey their surroundings, and had returned with the news that not only did the river valley become fertile and wooded to the south, but that he knew the area and believed they were not far from a place called Twillig's Gorge.

Kitsune had balked at this. She believed Twillig's Gorge was only a story, a legend amongst legends, but Blue Jay insisted it was real.

So they had set out, following the river as it ran through the valley and then into a forest of whispering leaves and cool shade.

The longer Oliver spent in the forest, the more troubled he became. It was peaceful here, even pleasant, and it simply felt wrong to him. It was jarringly discordant, moving from the carnage of the battle they'd fought in his world to the gentle respite provided here, beyond the Veil. He knew that it could not last, that there would be fear and blood to spare in the days to come. But to experience the calm beauty of this wood and the rushing river was unsettling.

They all felt it. He knew that they did. But none of them would speak of it. Blue Jay led the way, the wind making the feathers tied in his hair dance, and he rarely paused to look back and see that they were following. Oliver and Kitsune were side by side, though as close as she was, still she seemed far away from him. Frost trailed them all, sometimes falling back so that he was nearly out of sight. The winter man's face was a frozen mask. Icy mist trailed from his eyes and from his mouth, but he said nothing.

Soon enough, they would reach Twillig's Gorge and they would rest. And after that, their paths would diverge, and Oliver would be forced to make his way alone.

The Sword of Hunyadi hung heavily at his side, and though

he had acquitted himself well with it back on Canna Island, he felt foolish carrying the thing. He was no warrior. No hero. He was just a smartass New England lawyer who wished he was an actor, trying to survive.

He wanted to scream, just to break the silence of his companions . . . the friends who would soon abandon him. But how could he blame them? They were in just as much danger as he was; they and all their kind.

There was nothing for Oliver to do but keep walking, and enjoy their company until their paths diverged.

Oliver had tied his jacket around his waist. Even with the cool breeze and the shade of the trees, he felt warm, but he would not leave the jacket behind. Experience had taught him that the world beyond the Veil was impossible to predict. He ran a hand over the stubble on his cheeks and rubbed at the corners of his eyes. It had been long enough that he could no longer recall what it felt like to get a decent night's sleep. He would have given almost anything to be able to lie down there on the riverbank, use his coat as a pillow, and sleep with the gentle shushing of the wind in the branches as his lullaby. But there was to be no respite for him. Not yet. Perhaps not ever.

His boots pressed into the damp soil on the bank of the river. He dropped his gaze and watched the water while he walked, wondering again at its name. The river washed over rocks, the current picking up as it ran almost imperceptibly downward, with only the occasional small dropoff or waterfall.

When Kitsune touched his hand, he flinched away.

The sting of his reaction was in her eyes.

"Sorry, you startled me."

Kitsune gave a melancholy smile. "You were very far away."

"I've been far away for a long time. Feels like I'll be far away forever."

She nodded. Her red fur cloak swayed around her as she walked. The hood lay against her back, draped in her silken black hair. Her green eyes were like smooth jade. Kitsune reached out to him again and this time Oliver did not flinch away. As they walked, she took his hand, and they continued like that along the riverbank for several minutes. He took comfort in the contact, but did not fool himself into thinking that all would be well.

Kitsune wanted to soothe him, but she had other allegiances, and he understood that.

After a while he began to enjoy her touch and remembered the way she sometimes looked at him, recalled the sight of her at the inn in Perinthia, when he had seen her coming out of the shower.

Oliver broke the contact. Kitsune did not look up, only kept walking close beside him. She was perhaps the most desirable woman he had ever met—though woman was not entirely accurate—but he was engaged to be married, and instead of shaking his love for Julianna, the wildness and terror of recent days had only crystallized those feelings.

He wanted to say something to Kitsune, to express those thoughts, no matter how foolish she might think him. But even as he opened his mouth, he saw that Blue Jay had paused on the riverbank just ahead.

The Native American shapeshifter turned toward them with a satisfied grin. The mischief had disappeared briefly from his eyes, but it was back now.

"Twillig's Gorge," he said.

Oliver and Kitsune caught up to him and the three of them stood, awaiting Frost. The river turned slightly eastward ahead, and the quiet forest ended in the shadow of a sheer mountain cliff hundreds of feet high.

The river flowed right into the cliff face. Somehow it had carved a cave into the rock, or else the river went underground here.

"I don't get it," Oliver said.

"The gorge is further along. Gods and legends, Borderkind and Lost Ones, all sorts of people live there. Creatures who want to hide away from the rest of the world, who don't want to have anything to do with the Two Kingdoms," Blue Jay explained. "There are a few places I can think of that would be safer havens for us right now, but nothing else within easy distance. It's as good a place as any."

Oliver stared at the cave where the river entered the mountainside. Frost could have gotten over the top easily enough, and Blue Jay could fly, but he would never be able to climb that sheer cliff.

There was only one way to get to Twillig's Gorge for an ordinary man.

As he contemplated this, Frost joined them. Oliver glanced at the winter man, at the blue-white ice of his eyes, but Frost was not looking at him at all. With a toss of his head that made the jagged ice strands of his hair jangle together, he turned to Kitsune.

"You're aware that we're being followed?" he whispered.

Kitsune nodded gravely. "A Jaculus. It has paced us since the moment we made the border crossing."

Oliver began to glance around, looking first across the river and then up toward the branches above them. "What the hell's a—"

But Frost ignored him, focusing only on Kitsune.

"Kill it," said the winter man.

Coiled around the branch of a massive oak tree, Lucan could not hear the whispered words of the Borderkind below. But he saw the Intruder—the Bascombe—go rigid and begin to look around, and he knew that his quarry were aware of his presence.

His instinct was to attack. His eyes were excellent and he could see the way the veins pulsed in the throat of the Bascombe. He could smell the femaleness of the fox, Kitsune. What Lucan desired more than anything was to launch himself from the tree and plunge straight down on one of them, fangs bared. He could use his serpentine body to crack their bones, to crush them even as he drew their life out of their veins.

But Lucan had his orders.

The moment the fox raced toward the tree in which he was hiding, he loosed his grip upon the branch. As she leaped for the lower branches, he spread his wings and sprang upward, bursting up through rustling leaves of the oak and taking to the sky.

There were shouts from below, threats hurled skyward, but the Jaculus did not slow down. If the trickster shifted into bird-shape and followed, Lucan could kill him easily. And the winter man was weakened now, and too slow. In moments, the winged serpent was over the top of the mountain and soaring toward the southern horizon.

The Strigae were excellent spies, but Ty'Lis and Hinque had asked Lucan to come himself to be sure that there were no mistakes, that someone was there to report the outcome of the Myth Hunters' attack. Now they and the others would be waiting for word. The Bascombe was supposed to be dead many days ago, and the Borderkind who had allied themselves with him as well. These were simple measures, precautions to be taken before the rest of the plan could be put into action.

But it was too late now. The whispers had begun, the violence would follow shortly, and then there would be war. And in the midst of that, to nearly all involved, the Bascombes and the Borderkind would be little more than an afterthought.

Yet Lucan knew that to Ty'Lis, nothing would be as important as the death of these most dangerous enemies. The rest of the Borderkind had to be exterminated, no matter how many Hunters had to die with them, or how many others conscripted to the effort. And Oliver Bascombe along with the filthy *myths* he had befriended.

The Veil itself depended upon their deaths.

And an empire would be forged upon their graves.